Get Waffle Jones

Daniel Skinner

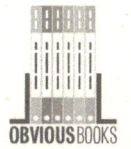

Copyright © 2025 Daniel Skinner

All rights reserved.

This is a work of fiction. Names, characters, businesses, organisations, places, events and incidents are either the products of the author's imagination or used in a fictitious manner. Any resemblance to actual persons, living or dead, or actual events is purely coincidental.

No part of this publication may be reproduced, stored in a retrieval system, or transmitted in any form or by any means, electronic, mechanical, photocopying, recording or otherwise, without the prior written permission of the publisher.

First published in Great Britain in 2025 by Obvious Books, Bury St Edmunds

ISBN: 978-1-9164317-4-4

A CIP catalogue record for this book is available from the British Library.

Cover design by Steve Edwards

Chapter 1

The five young men ran until their hearts were bursting out of their chests. They approached a sharp corner in the pavement which the weeks of dry city heat had left dusty, and cartooned around it with feet hopping and arms windmilling for balance. Pushing forward a little further to clear the knot of mildly alarmed smokers outside the pub, the one carrying the bag finally brought the gang to a panting stop with a wave of his hand and a breathless 'Hold up, 'old up!'

With a quick scan of the road behind to check they hadn't been followed successfully, he peeled off the main path between a pair of anti-traffic concrete bollards, and they limped breathlessly into a cul-de-sac of new-build houses, down another path with high wooden fencing along each side, and into a small children's playground.

Four of the five collapsed wherever they could to catch their breath – two perching on the edge of a low roundabout, one settling on a nearby swing, and one awkwardly straddling a spring-loaded wooden caterpillar, which sagged slowly sideways like a time-lapse video of a wilting dandelion, until he came to rest on one knee at 45 degrees.

The man with the bag muttered something silently with a sneer and a quick shake of his head, then dropped the load onto the ground.

He had to admit to himself that it'd all gone a lot more smoothly than he was expecting. Given they were just five lads, unarmed except for some cutlery pilfered from the greasy spoon they'd had breakfast in, it was pretty incredible that they'd got away so easily. And now, hopefully, they had something to really set them up, enough to make a proper go of things.

He did a full 360 sweep of the area, then filled his lungs deeply, closing his eyes as he exhaled loudly through his mouth. When he opened his eyes again, the sharp glance he gave the other four in turn was enough to have them all pull themselves upright to shuffle over to him, the man on the caterpillar merely letting go of the hand and foot pegs, so that the spring twanged upright with a squeak as he got to his feet and dusted himself down.

Nobody said anything as they circled around the bag on the ground, heads craning forward until almost touching. He took hold of the zip and pulled it back slowly and deliberately.

Five pairs of eyes widened in unison, and they stared unblinkingly for what seemed like minutes. Someone let out a long, low whistle; another merely whimpered softly.

'Oh... my... God...'

Chapter 2

'Evening, Mr K, how goes it?'

Mr Kottarakkara looked up from his paper and allowed his eyes to follow the familiar figure as he strode into the shop and headed straight for the chiller cabinet at the back, the smell of chicken bhuna following the slap of flip-flops on the tiled floor. He listened, as usual, to the sound of the fridge door being pulled open, drinks cans clanking metallically, and then the door sucking itself closed again to the soundtrack of a jaunty but unidentifiable whistled tune.

He watched dispassionately as the flip-flops flopped and flipped in his direction, feeling, as always, something akin to sadness that a grown man would feel comfortable dressed like that in public. It was as if the most regrettable fashion trends of the last five or six decades had been mashed together, against their will, into one unholy ensemble of sartorial conflict. Given that this getup had barely changed over the past several months, Mr Kottarakkara was forced to assume that the clothes were assembled both intentionally and, more disturbingly, with plenty of available light.

A series of items were plunked heavily onto the counter; a six-pack of lager, two tins of cat food, a 1-litre bottle of milk, a packet of Haribo Tangfastics, and the brown paper bag of takeaway curry, fragrant steam rising gently from the opening and a small grease stain slowly growing near the bottom where something had leaked.

'All good with you, Mr K?'

Mr Kottarakkara eyed the bag with disdain, then re-focused past this and onto the Germanic text and graphic, bloodied skull that adorned the black t-shirt of its owner, who was waiting with a smile.

'No thank you, Darren, I've already eaten,' he said flatly.

'Hoo-hoo! You're a funny guy, Mr K, a funny guy!' the man said, grinning widely and wagging his finger theatrically in admonishment as he reached for his wallet. 'But seriously, Mr K, you need to stop calling me "Darren". I feel like I'm in school. Or court. Even me own mum doesn't call me that.'

'You told me your mother was dead, I recall it clearly,' Mr Kottarakkara said, his eyes narrowing.

'Well, yeah. This is true. She has been pretty quiet for a while, but even so. Even when she was up and about.'

'Darren, you're a grown man.' He looked him up and down. 'Sort of. I'm not going to start calling you "Whiffy" or "Wobble" or whatever silly nickname your so-called friends call you.'

'It's *Waffle*, man, Waffle. Like, you know, *waffles*, or *waffling on*. Both of which I'm a fan of as it goes. I'm waffly versatile!'

Mr Kottarakkara looked at him levelly for a second or two without expression. 'Of course, Darren.'

Waffle sighed. 'So. What's the damage?'

Mr Kottarakkara peered slowly into the bag and took a sharp sniff. 'Too much garam masala and not enough time frying the onions properly.'

Waffle laughed again. 'Yeah, well, you're always telling me about your legendary cooking, but I don't recall any invitations cast in my direction. Sad to say, you force me once again into the welcoming arms of the *Taj Mahal* and the delights of Nabil's fine cuisine.'

Mr Kottarakkara wrinkled his nose and exhaled with a sneer. 'Achha, fine cuisine indeed! You know it all comes out of the same pot, don't you? It's takeaway nonsense for the hard of tasting. You might as well eat from a jar.'

Waffle nodded thoughtfully and looked around the shop. 'Like those ones you sell?' he said with a sly grin, indicating down the aisle with a sideways flick of his head.

'Pfft! I sell it to people like you to make a living, I don't have to eat it.'

Waffle started rubbing his hands together and bobbing up and down a little with impatience. 'Yeah, yeah, just tell me what I owe you. I need to get this bad boy upstairs and in me gob! Hoo-hoo!' He licked his lips and patted his stomach, eyes wide.

Mr Kottarakkara stabbed at the keys on the till and made a show of lifting his glasses and squinting down at the total. 'Err, eight hundred and sixty-seven pounds, twenty-four pence please.'

'Woah! Inflation's a bitch, man!' Waffle said, jumping back with his palms up in surrender. 'Maybe I should only get four lagers after all…'

'Perhaps you should; you drink too much.'

'Aww, Mr K! I never knew you cared!'

'I don't. I'd just rather you spent the money on my rent.'

Waffle's smile dropped for the first time since he'd arrived, and he looked genuinely aggrieved.

'Ah, come on, man! I paid you, like two weeks ago!'

'Yes,' said Mr Kottarakkara, 'you did. And that was for April. I was rather hoping for May's payment any day now, seeing as IT'S JULY!'

Waffle looked down at the floor and automatically began patting his pockets. 'I'll sort it, you know I will. I always pay up…' He gave a hopeful wink, '… in the end.'

'That doesn't even make any sense! Yes, you've paid for every month you've paid for, *in the end*. Apart from, oh I don't know, the ones you haven't paid for. I have bills to pay as well, you know, I don't ask you this for my own amusement.'

Mr Kottarakkara let out a deep sigh, and nothing was said for a moment.

'Seventeen pounds, twenty-four pence,' he said eventually, glancing meaningfully at the card machine.

Waffle nodded solemnly and put his card into the machine. 'I'll sort it, Mr K, trust me. I've just had a bit of a rough — '

Mr Kottarakkara's raised finger silenced him. 'Just soon, yes?'

Waffle nodded and picked up his things. 'Adios, Mr K! Au revoir, buona notte and indeed, shubh raatri!'

Mr Kottarakkara watched him leave as the door buzzed, the slap of flip-flops and the sight of the strange, green hat bobbing away into the night, and he shook his head slowly as he turned the page of his newspaper.

* * *

WAFFLE DROPPED his bags onto the work surface in the kitchenette, shrugged off his battered but beloved biker jacket and threw it onto the sofa, then took the hat and frisbeed it onto the jacket without turning round.

He emptied the contents of the various containers onto a plate, mentally chastising himself as usual for forgetting to ask Nabil why some dishes were supplied in aluminium containers and some in plastic. He licked his lips and sat down to join his cans of lager that were waiting impatiently for him at the coffee table.

Holding the plate to his chest, he pushed the food around with his fork to mix things up a bit before spearing a small collection of different items and bringing them to his mouth, closing his eyes and letting out a small sigh of pleasure as he did so. Once he'd stabbed a few more mixed forks and got a suitably good chew on, he sat the plate beside him and reached forward with both long arms, one reaching for the first can of lager and the other for the remote control, beautifully co-ordinating the actions of powering on the TV and pulling open the ring pull in one smooth action, the synchronisation belying his many years of experience in such matters.

The *kschuhh!* sound of the lager actually brought a smile to his face — how could such an innocent and tiny little sound evoke so much promise in its one-tenth-of-a-second moment of glory? Refreshment, coldness, fizziness, wetness, frothiness, sharpness, alcohol. The slaking of thirst, the clearing of the palate, that beautiful marriage of beer with curry spice, the tiny hint of a mild narcotic effect that promised much for the ensuing five cans. *Ah, lager! You beautiful old devil, you!*

'Up and at 'em!' he said, toasting himself with the raised can. He glugged half of it in one, swilled the last mouthful around so that he could sensuously start his curry again, gave an extravagant but disappointing burp, and made the long 'aaaaaah!' sound that was virtually required by law after one's first sup at the end of a hot summer's day.

He clamped the can between his knees, picked up the plate again and let himself fall back into the sofa to enjoy the television that wasn't there.

'Oh, man!' He rapped at his forehead lightly, as if to awaken his brain and its memories, then scratched irritatedly at one of his lambchop sideburns.

He'd loved that TV, it showed all kinds of good things. How could she be so cruel? And why take the TV and leave the remote? He wondered whether it was pure spite; a message to him that she didn't even want the TV, didn't need it and had no plans to ever use it, but felt it important to remind him that she'd paid for it. No. For all her faults and even after what she'd done to him, he didn't really believe that she had any spite in her. Perhaps instead she'd been so upset when she'd left, so riven with doubt and so blinded by tears that in her maelstrom of conflicting emotions, she'd grabbed the TV in between heaving sobs and run forth, completely overlooking its fundamental accessory. No. That wasn't it either. She'd just forgotten to take the remote, that was all.

He sighed a deep sigh and chewed his bhuna with significantly less enthusiasm as his eyes slowly swept the room. Fundamentally, it was much as it had been three years ago, before she'd moved in. Devoid of unnecessary soft furnishings, fairy lights and framed photos of wintry Nordic scenery, she'd carefully peeled off that veneer of femininity like a layer of clingfilm on a re-heated curry, leaving it almost exactly as it had always been before. She hadn't taken anything that wasn't hers and certainly hadn't been petty enough to even disturb, let alone damage his sacred possessions. The record deck, amp and speakers were where they'd always been, the records were left in deep rows stacked against the wall on the floor under the shelf. She'd even restored the misshapen cactus that Harj had brought back from a holiday in Ibiza one year to its pride of place next to the missing TV. 'What a prick!' it declared, in a hilariously comedic font on the pot.

That cactus had been the cause of their first, wholly insignificant argument soon after she'd first moved in, as they re-configured the meagre space in his flat to accommodate her self, her possessions and, to some degree, her tastes. She'd begun to tidy the shelves to make way for a framed photo of a snowy Swedish forest, and was probing a small collection of bottles that Waffle generously referred to as 'the bar'. In reality, it was populated solely by the things neither Waffle nor his friends ever drank, hence their survival (of the bottles that is but also, perhaps, his friends) and comprised ancient and sticky dregs of Cointreau, blue Curaçao, and something milky-looking with an elephant on the label. The only drink of any real use was a bottle of tequila that had a plastic sombrero for a cap, but on closer inspection, Natalie found that it was empty, so she picked it up to throw away. As she did so, she noticed the comedy cactus next to the TV.

'That's seriously not staying!' she'd said through one of those staccato laughs that are designed not to be joined in with.

'Oh come on, man!' he said, defensively, 'It's great! It was a present!'

She arched her eyebrow, allowing him to continue with his case, feeding him rope.

'It's a bit stupid, yeah… but it's funny. Not everything has to be serious in life, y'know. It's just a bit… kitsch.'

'Kitsch?'

'Yeah man,' he said with a laugh, 'it's kitsch.'

Her eyes fluttered with annoyance. 'It's not kitsch, Waffle. Kitsch is ironic… sort of flagrantly tacky but with an underlying style. Maybe even outdated, but with some cool.'

He shrugged. 'Yeah?'

'Kitsch is… I don't know… a lava lamp, an old-fashioned but garishly funky chair, an ostentatious light fitting.'

'Yeah, OK?' He looked deliberately confused.

'Not a cheap and unwell cactus in a tacky pot with a pre-pubescent joke etched onto it.'

She'd worked herself up a little now, the initial playful smirk was gone and her brow was slightly furrowed.

Waffle too was annoyed and was matching her stare with his head nodding quickly but shallowly, filling the space with his silence. 'Yeah,' he said finally, pointing to the cactus with a stab. 'It's kitsch!'

She handed him the empty tequila bottle and walked briskly towards the offending succulent.

'It's not kitsch, Waffle, it's just shit,' she said as she scooped it up, 'and it's not staying.'

'Woah! Course it's staying! That's my cactus!'

They stood facing each other in a Mexican-themed stand-off, neither speaking nor moving for a full five seconds.

'Fine!' she said at last, exhaling, 'It's fine. Of course you can keep it. But it goes somewhere else. Somewhere less conspicuous.'

Waffle bit his lip and looked around. 'Right, cool. How about that shelf?'

'How about that bin?'

Again they locked eyes, but this time they both smiled after failing to keep up the anger. The cactus was duly moved to the spot on the window ledge behind the curtain, where it languished with very little care for three years. And now it was back in its original spot, looking oddly healthier than ever.

Yep, the flat was essentially as he'd last seen it before the big day of her arrival. And he'd loved it then. But it wasn't the same now. It looked empty and forlorn, like the day after the Christmas decorations are taken down, sucking the life out of a house that had been fine without them just three weeks previously. It was worse than that, even. It was black and white now, it was greyscale. The colour had seeped away, leached from the walls and furniture by some giant colour-sucking vacuum cleaner. It was Kansas after Oz. It was a dead planet.

He raised his eyes to the spot on the wall above where the missing TV was, to look at the clock that also wasn't there any more. He could see exactly where it ought to have been by the brightness of the circle it left and the brown outline in the wallpaper. He'd bought her that clock on her 23rd birthday, and this one really was kitsch. It had no minute hand and no other markings other than the numbers for each hour, which were labelled 'Oneish', 'Twoish,' and so on. She'd always moaned about his appalling time-keeping and the fact that he was late for everything they ever did together, so he'd bought it for her as a kind of comedic compromise, a private joke. And she'd laughed, and shaken her head, and rolled her eyes. And they'd hung it on the wall and then made love before going out for a meal. On time for once.

It'd been nearly three days now since she'd gone, but he still managed to be surprised each time he sat down in front of the missing television, and each time he went to tell the time. She'd left the bills though, stacked neatly next to the phone that had been cut off for nearly a month. She was thoughtful like that.

He didn't even know where she was, not specifically. He was fairly certain that she'd gone back to her parents as that was where she'd been threatening to go increasingly often over the last few months, but as he'd never visited or even met them, he had no clue where that was, aside from being somewhere in Yorkshire, which he knew was quite large. Certainly big enough to hide a single, shortish girl in with no real difficulty.

She hadn't left any kind of note at all, which had pissed him off more than he wanted to admit to himself. Didn't they always say "You owe me an explanation at least" in the movies? Some kind, parting words on top of that would've been appreciated too, perhaps some hint that she might come back. Technically he could argue that he didn't even know why she'd gone, but he knew that he'd have a hard time making anyone believe that. She'd made it abundantly clear on numerous occasions now, with and without company in the flat, what she found difficult to live with. He drank too much beer, smoked too much weed, and didn't work enough to pay for even those things reliably, let alone boring luxuries like rent and food. Except maybe he could've afforded more food if he hadn't relied on Nabil's takeaways so often.

She still loved him, though. Possibly. Hopefully. The arguments were just about practical considerations, the day-to-day minutiae that have to be dealt with sufficiently well in order to keep love buoyant. But otherwise, she'd been happy. Possibly. Hopefully.

Either way, it was all his fault and he knew it. She'd done nothing wrong at all and he'd continued to do the things that he knew were slowly fraying their relationship, like someone unable to stop picking at the loose threads in a jumper. He said he'd work more, smoke less, eat better. He'd even meant it. But he didn't — to be completely literal about these things — do any of them. And now she was gone, TV, clock and all. He picked up his can and drained it before putting it down unnecessarily hard on the table. He looked up at the cactus and sneered at it. 'What a prick,' he said out loud.

Chapter 3

Phil Collins pulled up and switched the engine off. He looked to the clock on the stereo just as the little green digits flashed from 11:59 to 00:00. Satisfying. The evening had finally cooled, and he was perfectly comfortable sitting in the car with the windows wound down, but he wasn't familiar with the area and didn't want any nasty surprises. He was by nature a cautious and thorough man, and he'd long been of the opinion that it was these seemingly prosaic qualities that had kept him away from both serious trouble and harm over the years, more so than any of the other more ruthless skills he'd developed along the way.

He shut the car door and took in the building that stood in front of him. It wasn't lit, but the moon was high and full, and a surprising amount of silvery-blue light poured through the rows of broken windows and empty frames in the high roof, marking out a rectangular strip down the centre of the old and cracked concrete that made up what remained of the building's floor. The wide archway that opened into it was devoid of any doors on its huge rusted hinges, and Phil could hear but not see the occasional drop of that evening's sudden rain shower falling from somewhere in the roof to the concrete fifty feet below, the sound of the impact echoing rhythmically around the bare brick walls.

Although he knew it was there, he pressed his hand to the spot below his heart, just to reassure himself one last time with the feel of that familiar, solid shape under his jacket. He was more than confident that he wouldn't have to use it, and frankly, if things got that bad then there'd be a lot of awkward questions, but he just liked to know it was there. Cautious. Thorough.

He pulled a pack of menthol cigarettes from his trouser pocket and bent his head to the lighter, drawing deeply enough to see the reddish glow reflected in a piece of broken glass nearby. He looked at his watch and began a gentle stroll around the open space, just for his own peace of mind before they arrived. He'd had to use bolt cutters on the chain holding the gates shut at the bottom of the lane, and he could tell from the condition that they hadn't been opened in a fair while, but it was clear that the building still saw the occasional guests arrive on foot from the number of fresh-looking cans and empty bottles that were strewn around. He couldn't see much detail on the ground, but there were bound to be needles and other less savoury items lying about too, as well as plenty of broken glass from both bottles and the old windows that had fallen in, so he was careful to step only where he could see.

Much of the building's exterior was overgrown with nettles and bushes, and the only other accessible door he found was firmly nailed shut, so once content that there were no other entrances that were still passable, he walked back to the centre of the interior space and faced out towards the large, open archway, smoking the last of his cigarette. He went to check his watch again but stopped when he saw the glare of headlights swing into view, lighting up the perimeter fencing in its concrete bases and casting stretching, contorting shadows on the bushes beyond. The car approached slowly, its engine idling at a subdued purr and the tyres crunching over the loose stones as it pulled up behind his own with the merest hint of a squeak from the brakes.

He sucked one last time and then dropped the butt onto the ground, grinding it briefly under his heel as the engine was killed and two doors opened and then closed again with the muffled thud of expensive engineering.

* * *

DINNER PLATE DROPPED into the sink for later, or tomorrow, or whenever, Waffle opened his fourth can and moved to the record deck. He peered through the perspex lid to see what he'd left on there; Slipknot, his initial she's-left-me-and-I'm-really-pissed-off-about-it choice when he'd first come home and realised what had happened. It wasn't a Slipknot kind of moment now, so he opened the lid and lifted the vinyl out with practised skill, dropping it back into its sleeve with a satisfying whooshing sound.

He had to kneel down to get into his browsing position and began the ancient art of dancing his fingertips through the albums, pausing occasionally to appraise an option before carrying on. He had hundreds of records, amassed over the years, and of dizzying range. People always assumed that he was some kind of heavy metal freak, and he'd occasionally take mild offence in conversation at a party to demand what it was that had led the other person to leap so unfairly to such a conclusion. Was it his leather jacket, or his longish hair? Maybe his pierced ear or the ostentatious rings and other jewellery? Usually, the person would redden slightly in embarrassment and nod down to his t-shirt, which was regularly an old Iron Maiden or Anthrax one.

'Oh yeah! Hoo-hoo!' He'd laugh while slapping them on the back, feeling bad that he'd taken evident offence. What could he say? He didn't actually listen to an awful lot of heavy metal bands, but he had to admit that they made the best t-shirts. And good break-up music.

Fatboy Slim, Fats Domino, Fela Kuti x2, Flaming Lips, The Flirtations, Fleetwood Mac x4 (strictly Peter Green-era only), Flying Burrito Brothers (both), Foo Fighters, Free (all, natch), Fugazi, Funkadelic. Hmm... maybe Funkadelic? Good Sunday night music? He kept going. He got as far as H and settled on Herbie Hancock's Headhunters album. A solid choice.

Back on the sofa, he leant forward to the tray, which sat on the shelf under the coffee table. He was tense and unhappy and there was only one cure for that — weed. Lager was good, lager was delicious, but it didn't smooth the edges in the same way that a good spliff would. If anything, drinking made him more energetic, more alert, and if he was out somewhere where he couldn't smoke then he'd be wide awake at whatever time he staggered home, eagerly looking forward to at least one goodnight spliff before he could finally relax fully.

On days when he had nothing much to do, he was perfectly capable of smoking from morning to late at night, prided himself on his capacity, in fact. Where friends of his might struggle with a particularly potent smoke and require a little time out for recovery, he would merely smile kindly through the haze and take good care of their joint for them until they were ready to take custody again.

He took the packet of cigarette papers and pulled three out, licking the first to stick to the second — kingsize papers were for amateurs. As he began carefully constructing the perfect arrangement, he caught the missing TV in the corner of his eye and froze. He looked up to where the clock had been and then back down to his fingers holding the proto-spliff between them guiltily.

He stayed like that for several moments before throwing the papers down onto the tray.

'Fuck it.'

He stared hard at them and then once again looked up to the wall, studying the perfect circle left by the clock that had protected the wallpaper from three years of smoke.

What if he stopped now, what if everything changed in this one second? No more smoking, no more drinking, no more takeaways and a diligent attempt to find and hold down a decent job? And not just a string of temping jobs that usually lasted a day, but an actual proper, full-time job? Would that bring her back? How would she even find out if she was miles away? Well, maybe not a complete stop to drinking and curries, but just a normal amount, strictly weekends only. But back to the question: what difference would it make? Probably none; it was exceedingly likely that he'd never see her again whatever he did.

But what if? What if she came back? She hadn't taken the washing machine, it occurred to him, and she'd taken everything else she'd bought. It was a decentish one too, though not exactly top-of-the-range. Now that he thought about it, perhaps the washing machine was at the heart of the whole break-up. When she'd first moved in, he was just using the one that had been left in the flat by the previous occupant. It had functioned adequately, according to the basic definition of a washing machine as being a drum that goes round and round. However, it was otherwise lacking in a few key areas.

Firstly, it made the most godawful noises. Not just a bit of low-grade squeaking as it sped up, but something more akin to an industrial jackhammer trying to drill through an antique diving helmet you happened to be wearing. It didn't help that the kitchen opened directly into the living area, so there weren't even any doors to shut. It would build in pitch and volume until all other activity in the flat would be forced to cease, and it quickly became an unspoken rule that washing could only be put on as they were leaving the house for a minimum period of the 1 hour 14 minutes of the 'economy' cycle.

Secondly, it was a wanderer: one of those inquisitive washing machines that apparently felt constrained by its allotted location and failed to resist an existential need to go forth and explore new territories. Luckily its power cable was only so long, but even then it would often be found in the middle of the linoleum on their return, jiggling excitedly like a guilty baby that's managed to escape a playpen.

Thirdly, it was shit at washing clothes.

After a period of positivity following a new temping job that had been going well, Waffle had promised Nat he'd save for a new one. She'd been delighted at this news and had picked out the model she wanted on a special trip to Currys. It was very sleek, had a great energy rating, a large capacity and a digital screen for choosing your programmes on. It even played from a range of tunes when it was finished. Waffle had set no specific date for this special purchase, but as time passed, it became clear to both of them that there was never going to be a point when he'd have that much cash saved up. As quickly as it built up, it got spent again. Conversations about the arrival of the new machine became increasingly fractious until Nat just gave up and bought one herself. It wasn't as flash as the one she'd been promised, but it stayed where it was told and washed acceptably well in relative quiet. Nothing more was spoken of the matter after that, and Waffle spent the money he'd saved on a microwave instead. A relationship defined by the ownership of white goods.

Maybe she'd be back for it? Or maybe she'd eventually reply to his texts when it had all blown over and she'd realised what she'd thrown away? He could easily drop it into a message that he'd changed, once a decent amount of time had passed to make the point. How long was that? He wasn't sure, but it was probably more than a weekend. But not too long that she might forget him or find love elsewhere. About three weeks sounded right.

That was it then, that was a plan. He had a mission. *A Mission*, even, in italics. He'd change, he'd become a better, healthier, happier man. And if she hadn't come back for either love or the washing machine within three weeks, he'd text her and show her how much he'd improved himself. For her. For them.

He sank back and allowed a smile to creep across his face. This was it. This was going to be his redemption. And if movies had taught him anything, it was that she'd definitely have to come back now. Fate couldn't just leave a man to better himself and turn his life around without anyone noticing; that would be too cruel.

He looked down at the tray in his lap and at the stuck-together smoking papers. Maybe one last spliff would do no harm, though? After all, he'd already started making it, and he was pretty sure he barely had any weed left, anyway. It would seem silly, not to mention wasteful, to leave a small amount unsmoked, surely? Plus, he could hardly claim to have cut right back on drinking when he was already four cans down on a school night. Again, why not just finish off the last two and then start in earnest tomorrow? New week, new start, that kind of thing?

He grinned again. Yeah, why not? He'd allow himself this one last evening and then *The Mission* would start in earnest in the morning. *That* was a plan.

He opened up the weed grinder to see how much was left, and his grin fell away sharply when he saw that it was empty. Properly empty too, not just casually empty. The kind of empty that meant he'd already given it a good shaking upside down and picked out all the last little pieces. He closed his eyes and let himself fall back again, screwing his face up as he remembered the night before. He'd got himself pretty drunk after finding an old half-bottle of cheap brandy behind some soup tins that they'd bought one Christmas to make brandy butter, and he'd drunk most of it after his usual allocation of beers. He didn't specifically recall going to bed, or finishing the weed, but assumed he must've had a good last sweep of his grinder and then forgotten all about calling Learner Joe for a resupply. Damn it!

This was truly unfair. If movies had taught him another thing, it was that a man was entitled to a last blow-out before starting anew and attaining salvation.

Fate clearly wasn't on his side at all, and destiny appeared keen to force him to give up now, without simply waiting for him to wait until morning to give up. Damn you, impatient destiny! How was he supposed to sleep now, anxious and uptight and suddenly nervous about his impending abstention?

It wasn't too late to call Joe, was it? He'd still be awake and eager to sell to his favourite customer. Waffle looked up to where the clock used to be, but it was no help. Still, he estimated it couldn't be much later than midnight. He fished out his mobile and went to his favourite numbers. His thumb hovered over Joe's name, quivering ever so slightly. He looked down at the empty grinder and then up, once more, to the white circle on the wall.

'Damn it,' he said, and threw the phone to his side. So this was how it was going to be. Salvation had been brought forward and tomorrow's new day would be starting from now. He nodded slowly to himself, content that he'd been the bigger man, starting out on his new journey ahead of schedule. This time in three weeks, he thought, she'll be back in my arms where she belongs. He'd even put the cactus back behind the curtain.

Chapter 4

'Alright, Phil, long time no see, hope you're well,' the man said as he stepped down from the passenger seat of the Range Rover, and Phil winced involuntarily at the familiar voice: that combination of gruffness and forced enunciation that made him shiver a little inside. He watched as the man and his companion walked in through the archway, partially silhouetted by the car's headlights that had been left on behind them. The sight, though familiar from the various meetings over the years, was still vaguely comic, but he knew better than to let his amusement show. The two men stood side-by-side, both wearing suits of a similar sombre grey and matching blank expressions. The difference between them, though, was one of scale. One man was huge, in all dimensions; a great mound of meat and muscle squeezed into a suit that must've taken an age to tie, button and zip around him, especially given the indelicate slabs of hands that presumably had to fumble with the ties, buttons and zips. Phil idly wondered what size neck he must have, and what the biggest shirt size was before you had to go custom-made. He was pretty sure he wore a 15½" himself but wasn't convinced that they ever went higher than 19. Surely this fleshy Weeble was bigger than 19?

Next to him stood a man who was far from slim himself, but who stood a solid 18 inches shorter, and looked as though he could be thrown a considerable distance by the giant next to him, possibly one-handed, despite his excess pounds.

Phil cast all thoughts of shirt sizes and velcro walls out of his head. 'Bob,' he said with an acknowledging nod, and 'Big' Bob walked past him and towards the centre of the open expanse while his huge minder followed.

'This is all very... clichéd for you, isn't it? I thought you'd modernised,' said Phil, waving his arm to indicate the surroundings.

Big Bob grunted with a humourless smile. 'It certainly is, Phil, but needs must, I'm afraid. We're between offices, you might say.' He looked up and into the rafters of the old building with a look of slight distaste. 'Our new premises should be ready in a month, but the lease ran out just over a week ago on the old place and it seemed silly to extend for just that short amount of time, you know what I mean?'

Phil said nothing as Bob was still making a show of examining the roof of the decrepit building.

'I like a nice place, Phil, I like a nice office, but I'm not a wasteful man. They'd only take six months minimum and I just couldn't bring myself to do it. But still, leasing's a mug's game, isn't it? All that interest and whatnot. No, I'm gonna buy outright this time, found a lovely location. Ploughing the company profits into *capex* rather than *opex*, the accountants are over the moon! A decent investment for the medium to long term, what with property prices on their current trajectory. And all that asset appreciation is completely honest, all above board!'

Phil smiled wearily.

'Of course, I've got to bribe the estate agents. They'd already sold it to some wanky design agency that provide *solutions* rather than doing any real work. Something about liking the quality of sunlight coming in from the north or some bollocks. Fifty grand that's gonna cost me! Just to have 'em kicked out. Still, it's a lovely office, Phil, you'd like it. The designers aren't very happy, but fuck 'em, eh? Bunch of pony-tailed ponces.'

'Anyway, point is, most of my team are away currently, for one reason or another, so I thought I could probably slum it for a few days in the meantime, you know? Work from the car, set up in Costa, and meet in dodgy ruins like this. Bit like old times, in a way.'

He kicked at a loose stone that scuttled off into the shadows. 'Shame about this place, really. I hear they're converting it into flats. Would've made a lovely little office, as it goes. Some nice wooden flooring. A glass office. Put in a mezzanine. Cost a bomb to do though, it's a right old state.' He tutted while shaking his head.

'Still, it's nice to see you again in... casual surroundings.' He dropped his gaze from the ceiling and locked onto Phil's eyes. 'No jacket required.' He grinned and looked up at the man-mountain standing next to him, who gazed back blankly. 'Eh? Phil Collins?' he said, pointing to Phil. '*No jacket required?*'

Phil waited until Big Bob had stopped chuckling gently to himself before speaking. 'So. You wanted to see me about something?'

Bob's smile fell, and he spoke more quietly. 'Indeed I do, Phil, indeed I do. I have a little job for you, as it goes. Something a little... delicate, shall we say, but right up your alley, nonetheless. Should be a trifle for a man of your talents.'

Phil didn't much like the sound of this, but it came as no great surprise either. He only heard from Bob every few years, and it was only ever for a delicate job that was right up his alley. He took another cigarette out of his pocket and lit it.

'Go on.'

Big Bob watched as Phil took in the first lungful and blew it out from the side of his mouth, the gentle breeze pulling it along and upwards so that it flashed across a beam of moonlight from a broken window, snaking and dancing for a moment. In response, he took out a single cigar from his own pocket, and proceeded to unwrap it and then light it.

'Well, it's like this,' he said, making a few fishlike puffs to get the cigar fully lit. 'I have a certain quantity of goods that I'm rather attached to that have very recently been... uh... liberated from a van by some other boys. Some very naughty boys.'

Phil was genuinely taken aback. 'From you? Someone stole from you?'

Big Bob furrowed his brow in consternation but appeared pleased that Phil should look suitably surprised. 'Indeed, Phil, rather cheeky it was. Their timing was incredibly fortuitous for them as it goes, what with my current office move taking up a lot of my attention and the low staffing levels.'

'And you want to... get these goods back, I suppose?' Phil blew out another long plume of smoke.

Bob wagged a finger and gave a small bow of his head, as if mightily impressed with Phil's powers of deduction.

'I do, Phil, I do! Very keen to actually. Very...' he glanced around while clicking his fingers, as if looking for the perfect word. '...keen,' he said again with a flash of disappointment and a quick twitch of one eye.

'So why do you need my help? Don't you have enough goons to do it for you?'

Bob recoiled slightly, as if suddenly smelling a particularly potent fart that had been widely discussed but had hitherto evaded him. 'Goons, Phil? *Goons*?' He looked up at his companion, who shook his head sadly but then continued to look straight ahead blankly.

'I'm not sure where you're going with that, Phil, I really don't. I don't employ any... goons.'

Phil caught himself about to roll his eyes but nipped it in the bud, instead taking a drag of his cigarette to mask the reaction.

'I have staff that encompass a wide range of skills and sectors, but no... goons, I don't think.' He made a show of searching his memory, jogging his head gently from side to side as if making a mental audit of his employees, one by one.

'I've got several Senior Negotiators, as well as Persuasion Executives at both mid-level and senior, plus all the usual Procurement, Manufacturing, Logistics, and Distribution staff you'd expect, but no goons that I can recall. Unless you're thinking of Walters, my CFO? He can get a little tetchy after a few G&Ts.' He raised an eyebrow in Phil's direction.

'Well, whatever. The point is, why you don't get your... Senior Negotiators to negotiate it back then? Why do you need me?'

Bob looked a little awkward and looked down at the floor for a moment. 'Well, as I say, I've got a few staffing issues, as it goes. Most of my boys are away on a team-building exercise in Scotland; raft-building and so on. I wanted to leave it until after the school holidays but HR were insistent it was overdue and it made sense to get it in before the end of the quarter, anyway. For VAT purposes.'

Phil nodded slowly, squinting slightly. 'Team building?'

Bob straightened to his full, unimpressive height and began to redden. 'Yes, Phil, team building. I'm not a fucking amateur, y'know.' He exhaled slowly and rolled his shoulders to relax himself.

'And, in a stroke of terrible bad timing, I had a load of my remaining boys all go sick at once. Went out on a bender and ended up at some seafood restaurant and are currently indisposed, it seems. Dodgy prawns.'

'I see,' said Phil. 'And so that just leaves me then.'

'Yes. And it's a matter of some urgency. I need it back before it gets into their own distribution channel, and that means now.'

'Now?'

'Well, not actually now, no. It's currently in transit, we believe, and not sure where. But we've got intel on this gang and know exactly where it's heading and it'll be there tomorrow morning. So *you* need to be there tomorrow morning too, to retrieve it for me.'

'I see,' said Phil again, rapidly coming to the conclusion that there was no way out of this.

Bob gave a sign to his associate, who walked back to the car, returning a moment later with an A4 box file which he handed to Phil.

'It's all in there. Location, timings, drop off details, et cetera.'

Phil went to pop open the file with the button but was interrupted.

'Not now, Phil, in your own time. We'll meet again tomorrow evening when you've got everything for me.'

Phil waited for Bob to say more, but after watching each other in silence for a while, he realised that the meeting was over.

Bob clapped his hands together. 'Well, that's it really. Nice to see you again and all that, but I'm a busy man. We should catch up more often, though. Maybe get some tapas.'

'Right,' said Phil, hoisting the box file under his arm.

'You can see yourself out,' said Bob, raising his slug-like eyes to the open archway and, realising he was being dismissed, Phil walked off towards his car. He opened the door and dropped the box onto the passenger seat, then pulled himself in and shut the door behind him. He knew he was obscured by shadow now, so felt comfortable reaching into his jacket pocket for the solid shape that he'd been conscious of pressing against his chest for the duration of the meeting. He took the radio in his hand and placed it behind the box file.

'Oh, and one last thing,' shouted Bob through the darkness. Phil leaned an elbow on the open window sill, and half-turned his head to listen. 'Don't fuck this up, Detective Inspector.'

Chapter 5

'DC Watts?'

Mike Watts rubbed his eyes and instinctively glanced at the time on the alarm clock as he patted his free hand around the bedside table in search of a pen.

'Yes? Who's this?'

'A friend.'

'Okaaay. What do you want? And how did you get this number?'

He looked over at Sarah who was now propped up on her pillow, shielding her eyes from the light of his bedside lamp with her eyebrows raised.

'Never mind that. I've got something for you.'

The voice was strained and raspy and with an ill-defined accent that seemed to be an amalgamation of at least three regions of the UK, depending on the word.

'What do you mean you've got something for me?' He blinked and looked at the time again, 'It's 1:30 am. What are you, a fucking Amazon delivery?'

He turned back to Sarah and mimed a pen writing action to her, but she just rolled her eyes and looked away.

'I've got some information for you. The kind you'll like. The kind that gets results and gets coppers promoted.'

It occurred to him that this could just be a wind-up from one of the lads: Dawson, probably or maybe Gilham. They'd been the worst when

Mike had failed his sergeant's exams and the good-natured ribbing had never fully subsided, especially from Dawson who had passed with flying colours. Even for them, a call like this would be going a bit far though — banter down the nick was one thing, but waking him up before an early shift with a fake informant just seemed a little overboard. A little too imaginative as well, now he thought about it.

He looked at his trousers hanging over the back of the chair and wondered if there was a pen in the pocket. He knew there wasn't.

'OK, I'm listening. Keep it brief, yeah?'

'Oh, it's simple enough. 112b Silver Street, SE11. Consignment of weed arriving first thing to be prepared for sale by some up-and-coming young gang. Very valuable. You might want to be there, let's say 8:30? Should be able to catch them by surprise I would imagine.'

Mike made a mental note, his mind racing.

'Silver Street, 112b?'

'Top-floor flat. Little low-rise block on the corner with Clairmont Avenue.'

'And why are you telling me this? Who are you? How do I know this is genuine?'

There was a pause at the other end.

'What've you got to lose, DC Watts? It's a lead. I'd pick it up if I were you. That's what you do with leads.'

'But what —'

There was a bleep, and he looked down at his mobile screen as the words 'Call ended' flashed up. He checked the call history just to be certain he hadn't missed anything when he'd first woken groggily, but it just said 'No Caller ID - 01:23' as he suspected it would.

He didn't know what to think. It was definitely not a wind-up from Dawson or Gilham, it just sounded too... he wasn't really sure. Too detailed, perhaps? Too convincing, even. But still, this wasn't how things actually worked, surely? There were channels for this kind of thing, specific people to handle grasses. It wasn't his department, either figuratively or literally. People didn't actually just get phone calls out of the blue with good-quality info like this. But, that didn't make it impossible, he supposed. It was just his personal mobile after all, and although he was pretty security-conscious, he wasn't infallible. He made a mental note to check whether he'd locked his Facebook account properly; he could never get the hang of all those settings.

Sarah dropped down onto her pillow and grabbed the duvet, pulling it up to her chin. 'What was that all about?'

Mike was still staring blankly at the phone in his hand. 'A lead. I think. Anonymous call about a drug drop off tomorrow morning.'

'How dramatic,' she said through a yawn. 'An anonymous tip-off in the early hours. So what are you gonna do now, Bergerac? Sit staring at your phone like you've just been dumped by text or turn the fucking light off and go back to sleep?'

Mike opened his mouth to reply but thought better of it and instead put his phone back on the table, reaching down to grab the charging cable that had been pulled out.

'You could be a little more... supportive, Sarah. This could be good for me, if it's genuine. I've not exactly had a glittering first six months and I could do with getting in the new Super's good books.'

'I'm very supportive, my love. But just between the hours of 9:30 and about 7 pm. I get to clock off then and start thinking about dinner. Sometimes even a bath. And it's definitely out of hours when it's past nine.'

He plugged the phone back in and reached for the light, before dropping back next to her.

'And have we seriously not got a single pen in this room? No pencil, nothing?'

He heard a small intake of breath. Nothing major, just a little one.

'You're the detective, you tell me. Would you recognise one if I showed you some photos? Should you conduct a search of the area?'

'Yeah alright, you don't have to be so sarcastic.'

He pulled the duvet up to his own chin with a jerk, and Sarah rolled over to face him in the dark.

'Look. We have pens. There's bound to be a load without tops in the kitchen drawer of doom. I think there's still that biro down the back of the sofa and I *definitely* have one velcroed onto the little shopping list on the fridge because that's where I need one. If you want to start getting exotic leads in the early hours and need to scribble down drop-off locations for ransom payments or the co-ordinates of the next bomb or some other Starsky & Hutch shit then you need to sort your own pen out. A pad of paper too, maybe. Honestly, I used to think you watched too many cop shows — I'm starting to wonder whether you need to start watching more.'

He mouthed his response silently into the dark with a slight head waggle.

Sarah yawned and shuffled into a new position. When she spoke again, she sounded half asleep.

'You must have a stationery cupboard at work full of pens and pads of paper. Grab a load when you're down the nick tomorrow, stick 'em in your bag.'

He snorted. 'Are you suggesting that I, a serving detective constable, steal? And from a police station of all places?'

There was a pause, and he wondered whether she'd actually gone to sleep, but she answered dozily. 'You're a copper, Mike, you're not special. Everyone in the world nicks from the stationery cupboard. That's what it's there for.'

Mike turned over and closed his eyes, running the phone call through his head. He was due in at 7, but he'd need to get there early to get this cleared and sorted with his guv'nor. He'd have to forego his morning gym session and head straight over there first thing. Plus, even if it was genuine, Christ knows what they'd do about it when they were so busy with the Turkish car-theft ring.

'Oh, and while you're there... get us some staples will you, love? Maybe a Sharpie or two. Green if they have any.'

He smiled and shook his head almost imperceptibly. 'Sure. Night, baby.'

'Night, Magnum.'

* * *

'You know you're not even allowed to do that anymore?'

Phil took a long drag while watching DC Watts out of the corner of his eye and then exhaled slowly towards the windscreen.

'Not illegal yet,' he said while studying the lit end of the cigarette for some imaginary imperfection.

Mike paused for a second, unsure if it was worth continuing or just giving up now. He enjoyed working with Phil; he was experienced, methodical, and completely unflappable. But god, he could be a cantankerous old wanker, especially when it came to his smoking. Their weekly arguments on the topic were boring both of them now, but Mike couldn't help bringing up the subject whenever he was close enough to suffer from the effects of it, and Phil couldn't help smoking whenever he was close enough to Mike to draw an argument.

'Well, you know that it is in this case, of course. This is a work vehicle that more than one person uses.'

Phil opened the window a few inches and flicked the glowing butt out of the crack.

'Yeah, well. Maybe you should call the police.'

Mike looked into the rear-view mirror to make sure the paddy wagon was still behind them and then to Phil, who was now gazing out of his door window.

'Anyway, I thought you couldn't buy those menthol ones anymore? Aren't they banned now across the EU?'

'Yeah, it's all a bit of a pain. I have a contact in Switzerland that posts them to me.'

Mike eyed him suspiciously. 'Is that legal?'

'In Switzerland.'

Realising he wasn't going to win that argument, Mike changed tack.

'You know they'll probably kill you? I mean, if you don't mind, then it's OK I guess, your problem and all that, but it's annoying when people are in denial. You do accept they'll probably kill you, right?'

Phil snorted quietly and continued to watch the pedestrians of South London going about their business.

'Unlikely, I'd say. It's all about odds, you see.'

'Exactly! That's what I'm saying! Nothing's for certain, but if you smoke enough cigarettes, then the probability that they'll cause some cancer or other just keeps going up. And you've been smoking for what, 60 years now?'

'I'm not even 60 years old, you cheeky fucker.'

Phil was still looking out of the window, and Mike was still watching the road, but both were smiling to themselves now, settling into the usual roles and rhythms of their conversation.

'Well, there are no guarantees you'll reach 60, not at this rate. What is it now, 40 a day? More?'

A pause. 'It's about 40.'

'Well, I'd be thinking about early retirement then, if I were you. Be a terrible shame to work all your life and then drop down dead from lung cancer when you're halfway through your first jigsaw, or whatever it is you old blokes do when you retire.'

Phil let out a quick chuckle. 'I told you, I'm not planning on getting lung cancer. It's all about the odds.'

'What do you keep going on about odds for? You're not even making sense!'

Phil turned in his seat to face Mike.

'OK, here's a question for you. You're in a room with a single door and on the other side of that door is a 5,000-foot sheer drop off a cliff onto rocks below.'

'Not good.'

'Not really, no. Now, you have to open the door and walk through it — no choice. What are you going to die from?'

Mike thought for a second. 'Is this one of those stupid riddles? Like, you didn't say which side of the door you're on to start with, or you didn't mention there was also a bed with three legs in the room or something?'

Phil continued to look at Mike blankly for a couple of seconds.

'No, Mike. It's not a riddle, it's just a simple question to prove a point. What are you going to die from?'

'Well, a massive overdose of rocks taken orally, I suppose.'

'Exactly. If you absolutely have to walk through the door, then there's a 100 percent certainty of that particular ending.'

He raised a finger. 'But! What if there were two doors? One the same as before, but a second one that led you straight into an electric fence with a million volts running through it? The two doors are identical. Will you definitely still die from the rocks?'

'Well, you know it's actually not the volts that ki—'

'Shut up, Mike. A million amps as well then. Whatever. It's a terminal amount of electricity either way, you can spec it up later.'

'Then no. There's a 50-50 chance.'

'Precisely.' Phil leant back into his seat, victorious.

'So,' Mike began slowly, 'you're not going to die from smoking because you're going to electrocute yourself?'

'Don't be an idiot, Mike. The point is, adding the second door has halved the likelihood of dying on the rocks from a 100 percent certainty to a 50-50 chance. Add a third door and it'll go down to 33 percent, and so on. Odds.'

Mike tilted his head sideways and squinted. 'Okaaaaay. I'm still not sure I follow. So what are you planning to die from then?'

Phil looked upwards in thought, as if weighing up the options for the first time.

'Drinking probably.'

'Drinking?'

'Yeah. I drink far too much as it is, and plan to take that up a notch when I retire. Man's gotta have a hobby.' He took out the pack of menthol cigarettes from his pocket and studied it. 'These would probably get me in the end, you're right, all things being equal. But not if I really go for it with the old booze.' He took out a cigarette and fished around for his lighter.

'So let me get this straight,' Mike said. 'You're planning to drink yourself to death just to avoid getting lung cancer first?'

'No, not at all. I'll drink myself to death for pleasure. I'm just saying that it's more likely I'll die from that than these.' He flicked the lighter and drew a deep breath from the flame. 'That's the beauty of having more than one vice — you're almost guaranteed to get away with one of them scot-free.'

Mike nodded slowly, unsure if Phil was far cleverer than he'd given him credit for, far more stupid, or just winding him up.

'I might take up something else before it's too late, something to bring the odds down even further. Heroin or something. 33 percent seems a bit of a bargain after all these fags and that'd be a nice quick death too, probably take me by surprise one day.'

Mike was shaking his head slowly now. 'OK, we'll take this up again sometime. But we're nearly here. Best put that fag out.'

Mike slowed the car a little and checked the rear-view mirror to ensure the van behind was concentrating — damage to an unmarked Ford Mondeo and a newish Merc Sprinter in one go would not go down well with Sgt Harris at the vehicle pool.

'What number did you say?'

Mike was trying to read the door numbers on his side of the road.

'112b... on the corner of a Clairmont Avenue which should be somewhere arou—'

'WATCH OUT!' Phil shouted as he reached for the dashboard in front of him and slammed his foot down hard on a brake pedal he didn't have.

Mike swung his head back to see what the danger was and saw that a large, one-eared ginger cat with a white face was sitting casually in the middle of the road, watching their car approach with seemingly little interest before beginning to lick at its paw.

'Fuck!' Mike shouted as he stood on the brakes and wrenched the wheel hard to the left. The sound of tortured tyres seemed to fill the car for an age, but in reality it was merely a split second as the Mondeo lurched sickeningly to avoid the cat. Before Mike even had time to correct the steering, he was thrown forward with force as the car came to an immediate stop, wedged into the back corner of a large BMW estate parked at the kerb.

'Fuck!' he shouted again, this time louder and with more vigour. There was a brief pause as Mike and Phil exchanged glances and exhaled slowly, and then they both shouted 'FUCK!' in unison as the Mercedes van ploughed into the back of them.

Chapter 6

Waffle Jones wasn't what you'd describe as a morning person. He was completely aware of mornings as a concept and had experienced thousands of them over the years, but he'd concluded that, on balance, he wasn't a fan.

It wasn't anything specific about the mornings themselves that he had a problem with. It wasn't the crisp air, or the position of the sun, or the birdsong that he disliked. It was really just where the morning traditionally fell in the order of the day. In his view, the first hours after waking didn't lend themselves to industriousness, or enjoyment; it was all a bit of a shock to the system, and becoming fully conscious was a process to be taken gently and with no undue physical or mental strain.

When the morning was positioned at the end of the day, such as after a party or when he had friends round for a late one, then he was generally pretty cool with it. It made a pleasant time to enjoy one last spliff before bed, maybe a beer or a cup of tea, even. A bit of toast and Marmite, perhaps. And then to bed. Afternoon, evening, morning – the correct order, he felt.

And so it wasn't usual for him to be up and about and skipping down the stairwell from his flat relatively vigorously before midday, let alone at 8:20 am, and even less so for the purposes of gainful employment. Over the last five years he'd managed to start 27 jobs, only four of which had lasted more than a full month, and twelve of which had lasted less than a full day. He had no great difficulty finding work, but by his own admission, he wasn't that hot at hanging onto it.

It wasn't that he was actually lazy, though he was acutely aware of his employment record giving that impression. Given a task that was challenging for him, or that he had some vested interest in seeing to completion, he was more than happy to work long and hard, whether mentally, physically, or both. His longest stay in one job had been for nearly two years, though a while ago now, and it had been an entirely unenviable one on the face of it. It had started, as most had, from an application through the Jobcentre, working for the council, clearing ditches from a patch of waste ground on the banks of the Thames, out east. A large plot of land had been sold for housing development, but as part of some government quota, the council were keeping back a small stretch near the river as open land, to encourage the wildlife to stay and to provide the future residents with somewhere to walk, commune with nature and allow their dogs to shit.

When he'd first arrived on the site on a wet February morning, his heart and mood had sunk. The area had been a dumping ground for decades and was home to nesting colonies of shopping trolleys, tin cans, bottles and other general rubbish, filling the ditches and piled high into makeshift bonfires. That first day was long, hard, and depressing, but as time went on, he found it increasingly satisfying. Little by little, the area transformed from looking like a post-apocalyptic battleground to something approaching a nature reserve, and the initial task of clearing rubbish made way for a variety of other jobs, such as fence-building, tree-planting and some general landscaping. He'd even built a little jetty that stretched a walkway out into a marshy pond and had taken a great deal of pride and satisfaction in utilising his growing woodworking skills.

Although the days were long and tiring, he enjoyed the fresh air and the physical exertion, and he found that being partly responsible for such a vivid transformation was hugely fulfilling. When that job was over, he stayed on with the council and was given a variety of other similar tasks, all manual and all jobs that few other people wanted. He only left because an unskilled labouring job on a building site came along that offered significantly more money in the short term, and he desperately needed the cash to pay off some bills and to replace his wandering washing machine.

It was here that he met Harj, a jobbing painter and decorator, who was contracted to do some work on the site. They'd got on immediately, due to a shared love of music, weed, and Haribo Tangfastics, and it turned out that they didn't live too far away from each other, so they'd become good friends over the years.

But when that project came to an end, Waffle again lurched from one part-time job to another, his lack of qualifications ensuring that he stayed firmly at the bottom of the career ladder.

He considered some kind of vocational training for a while, and Harj had suggested he could do an evening course in woodworking or metalwork, something that would fire his imagination and potentially lead to a real career. But he never seemed to get round to it. He always marvelled at how little time there was left free in the day when you had nothing much to do.

Over the last year, his employment had thinned out, and it seemed that he'd spent as much of the time signing on as he had actually working, and this had been the seed of regular arguments with Natalie. She'd worked at the same place the whole time they'd been together, as a PA for an advertising executive, and although she didn't earn a huge amount of money, she did at least bring money home every month.

'My wages may not be much, Waffle, but at least they're reliable and punctual,' she'd said through tears during one of their last arguments, 'two things that can't be said about YOUR income… or you either, for that matter.'

His most recent job had started with vigour on Thursday, and ended with vomit on Friday. He'd been working in the kitchen at a seafood restaurant and had failed to defrost some prawns properly in the microwave, giving a group of six men serious food poisoning. There had been a pretty unpleasant scene the next morning when one of the diners turned up to accuse the restaurant manager of poor hygiene standards. There was a lot of shouting and finger-jabbing from the unhappy customer, as well as some thinly veiled threats about the future of the restaurant and its security, but it ended as suddenly and explosively as it began when the man had to run to the toilets mid-threat and decided to save face by slinking off home afterwards without being seen.

Waffle had been let go as soon as he arrived for his shift an hour later, and his text to Nat giving her the news had remained conspicuously unreplied to. And still was.

His manager at the restaurant had clearly been angry enough to call Mrs Higson, his long-suffering work coach at the Jobcentre, almost immediately, and she rang Waffle suggesting he might "pop in for a chat" on his way home. She apparently had another job lined up already for an immediate start – a cleaning job at the local hospital – so he reluctantly agreed to head over.

As it turned out, he found he wasn't really in a *job* kind of mood any more, and he stopped short of the Jobcentre and instead found himself in the nearest pub, where he remained until closing time. In his heart, he knew Nat would be gone by the time he got home.

The new Waffle of this fine Monday morning was a very different one, however. He'd jumped out of bed before seven, aiming to reach the Jobcentre early enough to beat the queue and speak to Mrs Higson without an appointment about the cleaning job. He'd shaved, fully charged his phone for once, and left plenty of cat food out for the day. He'd even washed his hat especially. He was full of hope, purpose, and determination to see it through. This was the path to salvation and to getting Nat back, and he knew he had to give this mission his all.

The fact that the job was an unglamorous one was almost for the better, and he felt it added a certain element of penance. Sticking with it would provide the perfect redemption he was seeking, and he was sure that Nat would see it the same way. Assuming the job was still available, he'd hopefully be gainfully employed before 9:15.

He passed under the passageway that led out to the front of the row of shops he lived above and whistled the first couple of bars of *Summertime*, which reverberated pleasantly against the brickwork and the wheelie bins. He passed the launderette and the betting shop and then stopped outside Mr Kottarakkara's 'Late Stop Shop' to peer in the window. Mr K was behind the counter but with his back to him, unpacking some cigarettes from a box and loading them up on the shelf behind the roller blind.

Waffle pushed his nose up against the glass and tapped a knuckle a couple of times; Mr Kottarakkara turned quickly with a frown, and Waffle smiled broadly with a wave before walking off and picking up *Summertime* again in his whistle. Mr K stayed looking out of the window for a few seconds, his frown staying until cleared with a shake of his head as he turned back to his work.

Waffle turned into Baker Street, which immediately made him start whistling the saxophone melody from the Gerry Rafferty song as it usually did, even though the road didn't much resemble the more famous one from Sherlock Holmes and sax solo fame. The road was like most others in the area: too narrow for the parked cars that lined each side and had to be parked half on the kerb, but unlike most of the streets nearby it had a fair number of trees regularly spaced along its length. These offered a pleasing change from the otherwise monotonous brick and concrete of the area, albeit at the expense of valued parking spaces, and were the reason Waffle chose this way to walk even though it wasn't the most direct route to the Jopcentre.

From somewhere in the distance he heard two muffled crashes in quick succession that he couldn't quite identify, followed by the more obvious sound of a car alarm squawking away, but these sorts of noises were hardly unusual, and he continued to whistle as he loped along in his unhurried, rangy way.

He'd be at the Jobcentre by 8:50 by his reckoning. The birds were singing, the clouds were sparse and fluffy, and the sun felt warm on his face as he looked up to the sky. Things were definitely going to change, he could feel it in his bones. He was a new man, his life was on the up, and he'd have Nat back with him before the month was out, he was sure of it.

* * *

'WHAT THE FUCK WAS THAT? Soapy, go and have a look, willya?'

Soapy looked around the other faces at the table for some moral support, but nobody offered to do the chore for him, so he gave a loud tut to himself and pushed back on his chair with a screech of protest from the linoleum flooring.

At the window, he cautiously pulled back the edge of the curtain and peered through the grimy glass to the street below. His eyes widened with glee at the scene of minor devastation below.

'Shit, there's a proper car crash! A Mondeo's planted itself into the back of some Beemer and then a Transit or summink's stoved into the back o' that. What a mess, man! There's glass and shit everywhere!'

He turned back to the table in expectation of seeing three rapt faces hanging on to his rich description of the drama, but all were still looking down at what they were doing.

'Yeah?' said Tommo, after a moment, without looking up.

Soapy frowned and stuck his head back behind the curtain to observe the scene in more detail. 'I tell you what though, I think they're Old Bill.'

This time there was an effect. All three stopped what they were doing and looked up at Soapy in one sharp movement.

Tommo put his hands on the edge of the table as if about to haul himself up, but stayed seated for the moment. 'What makes you say that?'

'Well,' said Soapy, his head back behind the curtain, 'for one thing it says 'Police' down the side of that van, and for another, all the blokes getting out of it are wearing uniforms.'

Tommo was up in an instant and reached the window in three strides, pushing Soapy to one side.

He could see what appeared to be a three-way argument in the road between a middle-aged man in a cheap suit, a tall guy in his 30s wearing jeans and a checked shirt, and a uniformed police sergeant in protective clothing. Six similarly clothed policemen had spilled out of the back of the van and were now milling about, apparently unclear as to what to do next.

As he watched, a man in a dressing gown stormed out of one of the houses nearby and joined the argument. Tommo couldn't hear any of the words clearly, but by the wild flapping of the man's arms and the gesticulations in the general direction of the various vehicles, he surmised that he was the owner of the BMW that was now at one end of an automotive spit roast.

After a brief amount of ineffectual placating by the scruffy older guy, the dressing gown man was left alone to continue waving his arms around on the pavement at his leisure.

The two plainclothes men began marching with some purpose in Tommo's direction, the younger of whom had consulted his phone and was now pointing straight at Tommo's first-floor window. The uniformed police all followed behind, doing their best to keep up the brisk pace in their heavy, protective clothing and looking a little like waddling ducklings paddling furiously after a determined mama duck. The last man in the gaggle was struggling the most, as he was the one carrying the large, red battering ram.

'Fuck!' Tommo spat, with a slap on the window ledge, 'Fuck it,' and he walked quickly back to the table.

'What's happ—'

'Search party, loads of 'em. We've got about 30 seconds before they're through both doors and up the stairs. Clear all this shit away, NOW!'

They all leapt up and started to throw everything back into the bag they'd only recently been emptying. Tommo worked fast but kept up a barrage of instruction at the same time.

'Lenny, you get the scales and ziplocks together, Soapy, get that gear back into that holdall. Don't worry about getting all those bags sealed up, just get it all back into the holdall and zipped up tight. Don't spill anything, just make sure it all goes in there. D, get that cloth and wipe the table down.'

Tommo moved fast, heading out of the room and into the bedroom that looked out the front of the flat. The intercom was buzzing and there was shouting coming from the building's front door. He re-joined the others as they were finishing the clean-up job.

'Right, we've gotta get rid of that gear, and fast.'

'There's a little garden out the back,' said Soapy, 'should we chuck it out the window and pick it up later?'

Tommo looked at him with unmasked disdain. 'Yes, Soapy, there's a little garden out the back, but the only window onto it is in the bog and it doesn't open, there's just that little flap at the top to let the smell out. Even if you could get ten huge bags of weed out of that or through the extractor fan in the next fifteen seconds, I suspect that old Morse downstairs will probably think of looking there when he finds us standing here holding our cocks in an empty flat with nothing but scales and baggies.'

Soapy blinked but didn't have anywhere else to look. 'So what are we gonna do with it then? I reckon they might look inside that holdall when they get in.'

They all turned instinctively as the sound of the front door being smashed in with a portable battering ram rose up the stairs to meet them.

'You know what, Soapy, I think you could be right.'

He swung around to Lenny. 'Get Playboy on the phone, now. He's supposed to have been here ages ago, he only lives down the road. Tell him we're gonna have to stick the gear out of the window onto that side street and he's to get here and pick it up, pronto. We cannot lose it, yeah? Get him there now, and I mean NOW.'

Lenny had his phone out of his pocket and was already tapping away as the sudden rise in volume from downstairs suggested that the main front door had been breached and that the police were in the hallway. Hammering soon resumed on the flat door at the bottom of the stairs.

'Right, Soapy, take that bag to the window. Get it ready to drop and make sure you aim right — don't get it in the road or split over the fence or anything stupid. But don't drop it until I say. It's got to be out there for as short a time as possible and I wanna make sure all the feds are happily running up our stairs at that moment, and not loitering around outside or nuffin where they might see it. Yeah?'

Soapy nodded vigorously and hefted the holdall onto the window ledge, holding it in place with one hand as he unlatched the handle and pushed it open a crack.

The battering on the front door was rapidly becoming less boomy and more splintery. The four of them stood in the room, silent apart from Lenny on his mobile.

'Just fucking run, man, yeah? OK, safe.'

He tapped his phone and looked at Tommo. 'He says less than a minute, he's out the door as we speak.'

Tommo looked at Soapy, who was holding the bag with both hands on the edge of the window.

'Anyone out there? Can you see any Old Bill?'

Soapy scanned up and down the road. 'No, nothing.'

'Right. Throw it when I say, then get that window shut and curtains back where they were. You two, sit down. Get your phones out, make like you're chatting an' that, yeah?'

Lenny and D sat down just as the last splintering sounds of the door being destroyed were replaced by the thunder of 14 heavy boots clattering up the stairs.

Tommo looked at Soapy, who was staring back with wide eyes and eyebrows raised.

'POLICE! STAY WHERE YOU ARE!'

Tommo nodded and Soapy lofted the bag out of the window, getting it shut again just as the kitchen door burst open.

Chapter 7

Waffle turned into Clairmont Street and frowned slightly as, for a brief moment, he thought he saw a gaggle of men all dressed in black jog across the end of the road at the junction with Silver Street. He focussed into the distance with a squint but saw no more movement and concluded that it must've just been a dark-coloured car that had looked strangely like a phalanx of men in his peripheral vision. He shook his head to clear the bizarre thought and instead wondered what the new job would be like. Cleaning jobs weren't his favourite kind of work, but there was a certain satisfaction to be had, if he was honest. He found he tended to drift into a kind of dreamlike daze when doing monotonous tasks that didn't require much thinking, and he assumed that cleaning in a hospital might involve the kind of repetitive wiping and mopping that he could use to channel his inner Karate Kid.

The job was only short term, but he'd make it clear to Mrs Higson at the Jobcentre that the Waffle Jones standing before her was a new Waffle Jones, a Waffle Jones Version 2, in fact, and that he wanted to work hard and work regularly. She'd appraise him with her usual expression of open disdain, her thinly plucked eyebrows rising high on her crinkled forehead like two distant seagulls flying low over a choppy sea, but he'd plough on with enthusiasm and charm until he'd managed to get her to agree to look for something permanent for him.

He wasn't afraid of hard work, he'd tell her, or long hours or anything else, in fact.

He'd love to get back into something constructive involving making, building, or fixing things, but he'd take anything going at this point. He'd work outdoors, indoors, overground, underground, wombling free — but he was thinking about the future now, about the long term, and he wanted to provide security for his partner and a stable home environment where a young couple could settle and grow together as people. Maybe even think about bringing a child into the world at some point, he'd say with a smile and a wink; you never know.

A dull thud snapped Waffle back into the moment, and he raised his eyes from where they'd been absent-mindedly watching his own feet traipse along in front of him to see that a large, dark object was blocking his path about twenty feet away. He came to a stop and focused intently on it, taking a moment to try and make sense of its shape and purpose in the context of a South London pavement.

It was a holdall, like a large sports bag — jet black and with two heavy straps that were just about rigid enough to keep themselves upright on a good day, like an Alsatian puppy's ears.

He started walking forward again, a little cautiously and with his eyes not leaving the incongruous object at any point, until he was a couple of feet away, and then stopped. He stood still and silent, looking down at the bag. The bag sat still and silent too, but did nothing more.

Waffle traced a line with his eyes directly upwards until he was staring up at a distant cirrus cloud in the otherwise empty sky. He felt a little silly and predictable, like a cartoon drunk examining his bottle after seeing something odd, but it was an avenue that had to be explored, he felt. A bag falling out of a plane seemed an incredibly unlikely thing to happen, but he supposed that it must still be possible on some level. Maybe not a jetliner, but certainly feasible from a light plane, surely? Even so, the only planes he could see were miles in the distance, visible only from their wispy vapour trails slashing the blue void, and he was pretty sure he'd have noticed a light plane buzzing low over his head.

He brought his gaze down a little lower and scanned the surrounding buildings. Sure enough, the nearest wall belonging to a small, low-rise block of flats nestled on the corner with Silver Street had a window on the first floor almost level with the bag, but the window was shut and the curtains behind it closed. A tall wooden fence ran down the side of the property, presumably along a garden, and extended a further 50 or so feet behind him until the houses on Clairmont Street started. He supposed it could possibly have been thrown over this, and he wondered if the thrower could be standing on the other side of it.

'Hello?' he ventured, a little self-consciously. 'Er... anyone lose a bag?'

There was no response, and he felt a little foolish striking up conversation with a fence, so he fell silent again. He stuck a foot out and prodded the end of the holdall gently with his flip-flop. Nothing happened, so he did it again, with a little more force this time. It didn't feel hard, but it didn't move either — he could already sense from its taut shape that it must be fairly full, and it appeared to be pretty heavy too.

He was curious, but also a little cautious. He was no thief, and the bag wasn't his, plus he didn't need one anyway, so it wasn't like he was desperate to take it. And, presumably, it belonged to someone. Someone must have put it there somehow or other only a few seconds before, whether it was thrown, dropped or whatever else because he heard it land. It must have been in someone's hands, it must've had an owner. But then it was also discarded, in the middle of the pavement in an empty street. There was nobody around that he could see at all, and all he could hear above the distant hum of traffic was a bit of shouting from inside the flats. Nothing unusual there.

He looked all around him, a full 360 degrees taken in two bites from either direction, and then squatted onto his haunches. He prodded the bag once more, this time with his finger, but nothing exploded or started ticking or did anything else out of the ordinary. So, carefully, he took hold of the zip and pulled it steadily along its length towards him until it came to a stop by his knee.

His eyes grew wide, his jaw fell open, and he let out a silent gasp, involuntarily rocking back on the balls of his feet, as though physically pushed by an invisible force.

'Wooooah,' he said, just above a whisper, and took his hat off before wiping his brow with his sleeve.

'Holy… shit…'

He took another quick look from side to side and then pulled the bag open wide with both hands so he could see inside more clearly. Surely he must be mistaken? He couldn't really be seeing what he thought he was seeing? Could he?

He lowered his face to get a closer view, blinked twice, shook his head a little and took in the view with a low whistle. The holdall was stuffed full of large, clear plastic bags, each stretched taut and shiny by their bulging contents and wedged tightly together until they filled the space completely. He assumed that each must contain a kilo of weed, but this was only from having seen photos, not from experience. Each bag was more weed than he'd ever seen in one place, and even at the greediest stages of his life would have been enough to last many, many months, perhaps two or three years, even.

He pushed his hand inside to inspect more closely and did a quick mental estimation that there must be a good 10 or so of these huge bricks. Spread around and over these were also a few smaller bags, the kind filled with a more normal sellable portion, filling in the gaps like loose change around gold bars.

He let out another deep sigh and zipped the holdall up again. This was a lifetime's supply of weed and an enormous amount of money's worth. A fortune. His brain was a little fuzzy now to do any reliable maths, but he knew it must be tens of thousands — 40 grand, 50? More?

In a brief moment, a torrent of conflicting thoughts ran through his mind.

He wasn't a thief, but this appeared to be ownerless. Assuming it had once been owned, it had now been discarded for some reason, left unwanted in the street. If he simply left it where it was, it was sure to be taken by the next person who stumbled upon it. Maybe even a child. Worse still, maybe a policeman. Also, he'd given up smoking but, well, he'd have to talk this over with a couple of people, maybe get a second opinion. Was fate really a thing? Was karma? He looked up at the sky again and scanned the heavens. He didn't believe in God, but he did believe in weed, and there was an awful lot sitting here, ownerless and going begging.

He looked around him one more time, shrugged and stood up, hefting the bag onto his shoulder. It sure was heavy. He thought about the Jobcentre and the hospital job but decided he could always come back tomorrow. There was bound to be some job or other available for him there, it's where they hung out after all. He turned back down Clairmont Avenue and walked back the way he'd come, whistling *Summertime* once again.

A few moments later, a young man came flying out of an alleyway and turned sharply into Clairmont Avenue, his trainers clawing for grip. He headed at full pelt to the end of the road and stopped under the window of Flat 112b, looking around him wildly. There was nothing and nobody here. He flopped forward, grabbing his knees like a marathon runner, exhausted from the half-mile sprint he'd just done and wheezing slightly. He looked up to the window, but it was shut and curtained, and then he looked back down Clairmont Avenue. In the distance, he thought he could see a tall man walking away from him with a bobbing gait, and he shielded his eyes from the sun to get a better look. It was hard to tell, but it certainly looked like he might be carrying a large bag over his shoulder. Also, and this seemed a little odd, but he appeared to be wearing a bright green hat.

He took in a deep lungful of air and was about to launch himself off down the road in pursuit when he heard a loud 'Oi!' behind him. He turned instinctively and was presented with the sight of a pack of policemen in protective gear, four of them holding onto Tommy, Lenny, Soapy and D, who were all restrained at the wrists with cable ties. His eyes widened in fear, and he turned to run, this time managing to get his legs moving, but although he was now pumped full of adrenaline, he was fighting tired muscles and bursting lungs, and he only managed about 20 yards before a tall young man in jeans and a checked shirt brought him down in a flying rugby tackle.

* * *

WAFFLE ARRIVED home and hefted the bag onto his coffee table. He then took off his hat and dropped it next to the bag before falling back onto the sofa, his eyes not leaving the big, heavy holdall the whole time.

He watched it for a second, huge and swollen and almost at eye-level from his reclined position, but it didn't do anything interesting. He pulled himself upright, his face now closer and looking down at the bag from above. For some reason, he felt he wanted to delay opening it, but wasn't sure why. Maybe he'd made a mistake somehow. Maybe in the glare of the morning sun he'd thought he'd seen a large pile of kilo-sized weed bags when in fact it'd just been... what? A gigantic supply of oregano? Dropped, presumably, by an Italian chef on his way to one of those record-breaking world's-biggest-pizza attempts? Waffle weighed this up in his mind, rocking his head from side to side as he thought, but concluded that it seemed unlikely. Quite cool, perhaps, but unlikely.

He got up and did what he always did when he needed to think, which was to kneel at his record collection and look for something to play. He figured that the opening of the bag needed some kind of soundtrack at the very least, and although it made no real sense, he felt the guilty need to mask the moment with sound, as if Mr K in the shop below would hear him opening a zip.

He dropped the needle onto the record and, satisfied that all was well from the familiar warm, scratchy sounds crackling from the speakers, sat back down again just as the bossa nova keyboard opening to The Doors' Break On Through started.

He spent a good ten seconds watching the bag intently, and finally moved his hands into position above it. He waggled his fingers a little, like Indiana Jones about to replace the golden statue with a bag of sand, then took hold of the zip with one hand and pulled along its length as he'd done only ten minutes previously.

This time, it was different. Now indoors, away from the fresh air and breezes of the wide outdoors, the smell filled the room almost before the zip was even fully open. Oregano, this was most definitely not. Once again, the sight of tightly packed, transparent bags greeted him, and with great care, he gripped the topmost bag with both hands and hefted it cautiously out of the holdall.

The smell got stronger; a rich and sweetly aromatic aroma with a touch of citrus, as if someone was cooking honey and orange peel over a hickory wood fire. As he looked at the finely chopped leaves through the plastic, he was surprised to see that the colour was distinctly unusual.

Grass tended to be a flat shade of green, ranging from a dark and rich mossy colour to a paler, almost yellow shade, depending on the particular varietal, but this had a distinctly pink hue to it. He held the bag away from the window to see more clearly and turned it over in his large hands. It was still green in part, the vibrant lime green of some exotic tree frog perhaps, but woven into the tight balls of dried leaves were thin threads of vivid pink.

It was quite unlike anything he'd seen before, and he'd seen plenty. Despite the disappointing lack of variety in Learner Joe's range of wares, he'd been on several trips to Amsterdam with Harj, and they'd made a point each time to try as wide a variety of exotic strains as they could, methodically working through lists they'd prepared like excited kids with an I-Spy book on a long drive. They'd sampled all the classics from across the world, from 9-Pound Hammer to AK-47, from Juicy Fruit to Pineapple Express and from Bubba Kush to Berry White, as well as any up-and-coming varieties that were the latest thing, but this... well, this looked a little odd.

It wasn't just the colour, either. There was something about the way it seemed to catch the light that was unusual: a surreal texture, almost a glassiness that made it sparkle when it caught a sunbeam. Waffle found himself hypnotised for a moment, staring closely at the pink veins that wound around themselves, occasionally glinting. After some time, he lowered the bag onto the table, and feeling along the edge to get a grip on the two halves of the seal, pulled them apart to open the bag fully, edging his face closer at the same time.

The smell, up to that point warm and sweet and gently swirling inside the room, suddenly hit him with an almost physical force. He threw his head back with a loud 'Hoo-hoo!' as he became enveloped in an invisible mist of pungent, heady odour, and he found himself blinking several times as if to clear smoke from his eyes which he could swear were now watering slightly. 'Woooo!'

Jim Morrison's vocals, rising in pitch and fervour in the background, seemed to match Waffle's excitement as he shook his head and placed the bag carefully back down onto the coffee table. This was quite clearly weed of sublime quality and he knew he was in for a rare afternoon. He dragged the holdall a little closer towards him and pulled the opening apart to see exactly how much there was inside. One by one, he carefully took a package out and placed it on the sofa beside him until he'd counted nine full, seemingly unopened bags and one that had a little missing, but joined by another 28 smaller bags of a more familiar, but still generous, quarter-ounce size. Each large bag was about the size of a house brick, though a little longer and flatter, and packed so tightly that they felt almost as solid as one too, belying the leafy makeup of the contents.

Waffle slumped back into the sofa and turned to the pile of glinting bags sitting next to him, shaking his head in wonder. Instinctively, he reached for his mobile, jabbed at it a few times to bring up his chat window with Learner Joe and, fingers shaking ever so slightly, tapped a short message: 'LJ man. You might wanna get over here. Like, pronto.' His thumb hovered over the 'send' button just as he cast another glance to his side, but he remembered that it was only morning still and Joe liked to be in the office until at least after lunch. Waffle glanced up at the clock on the wall but found, once again, that it still wasn't there.

He froze, eyes locked onto the circle of bright wallpaper beneath the absent clock and, once again, mentally kicked himself in the nuts as the spell broke. 'Fuck!' How had he forgotten so quickly what he'd promised himself just the night before? Was he really so easily led by an attractive young holdall with massive bags? He prodded at the phone's 'cancel' button and threw it aside, angry for letting himself get so carried away. He stared again at the mound of weed to his right and thought good and hard about what he'd promised himself, and why.

Did he want Natalie back? He closed his eyes and nodded slowly to himself. He did. He absolutely did. It wasn't just Nat, his girlfriend; it was Nat the anchor in his life, Nat the link with normality and reality, the girl that kept him sane, kept him going and gave him purpose. OK, so he'd fucked up a bit already by bringing this lovely young bag home with him, but nothing had happened. And yes, he was supposed to be at the Jobcentre, but that wasn't anything that couldn't be delayed.

No, he wouldn't do it. He wouldn't throw everything away now, not even for this really rather wonderful-looking weed. OK, the timing was bad. Why now, oh Lord? Why does a bag crammed full with the finest-smelling thing he'd ever had the good fortune to smell fall, almost literally, to his feet at exactly the point in his life when he'd decided to knock it all on the head and change his ways? He looked to the place on the wall where the clock wasn't, but it offered no answer by dint of being both just a clock and entirely non-existent.

Waffle took in a deep lungful, breathing in the last of the thick aroma that he could almost see hanging in the air in front of him, and then exhaled slowly until he was empty. No. He would not give in. He was a man, goddammit; a man of his word and a man on a path to a better life. He would rise above this.

He sealed the bag back up again, placed it back into the holdall with the others, and closed the zip. He watched this luggage for a while, resting on the coffee table taking up most of the space, and then jumped up from the sofa, grabbed the handles and with a determined yank, pulled it up and marched it over to the little storage cupboard at the back of the room where the hoover, spare plastic bags, and assorted random shit lived.

After a quick cupboard clearout, he shoved the hoover more forcefully into the back corner, then balanced the holdall vertically in front, steadying it with one hand while he tossed the other items over the top. He then pushed the door shut and pinned it with his shoulder as he flicked the latch.

Satisfied, he dusted down his hands, nodded contentedly at his handiwork and went to look for his mobile so that he could phone Mrs Higson about booking an appointment.

Chapter 8

'This better be good, Phil.'

Phil took a long drag on his cigarette and flicked the butt into the gloom, its glowing end describing an arc like tracer fire as it fell to the ground and sparked dramatically before quickly fading. If there was one thing worse than having to work for criminals, it was being in their bad books and being expected to grovel. Phil had never been much of a groveller.

'What can I say? We arrived on time, but the flat was clear, apart from a few bits of paraphernalia. There were four males there, and a further one outside that tried to run. They were all placed under arrest and are currently detained in custody.'

Big Bob's eyes narrowed, and he raised himself up to his full, not-considerable height. 'Don't give me that police bollocks, Phil. Don't talk to me like I'm a fucking judge. I don't want your little "police notebook" version of events, I just want to know what the fuck happened.'

Phil didn't quite understand the air quotes that Bob did for 'police notebook' but opted to let it go rather than get into an argument about physical punctuation.

'I heard there was an accident, probably warned the gang you were coming?' Bob said, trying to calm himself down a little.

Phil frowned. 'There was a minor collision, yes. It was about 50 yards from the property, it's possible they heard it and noticed us coming.'

Bob chortled, but his eyes were dark and clouded, and he didn't smile. 'Oh, do you think so? Do you fucking think so? I heard that you lot ploughed into a parked car for some reason, set off the alarm and then had all your uniforms get out of the van one by one and walk around in confused circles like a fucking Benny Hill sketch.'

Phil said nothing, but started reaching into his pocket for his cigarettes.

Bob was animated now, angry and full of energy. 'I can see it now. All running around in fast forward, ogling lollypop ladies and squeezing tits.' He started hopping from foot to foot, mimicking groping actions while doing a saxophone impression of the theme tune. Phil watched without emotion, tapping his cigarette on the packet before placing it in his mouth. Big Bob continued his dance until he'd worn himself out a little, stretched his neck, and appeared to calm down.

'So,' said Bob, 'what you're essentially saying is that of the ten kilos of product I asked you to go and retrieve for me, you've come back with...' He splayed out the fingers from both hands and made a show of trying to count them. '...fuck all.' He looked up at Phil with wide, questioning eyes. 'Yes? Is that what you're telling me?'

Phil was smoking once again, taking in deep lungfuls and then blowing the smoke out of the corner of his mouth into the wide, open space of the derelict building. He looked as impassive as ever. 'I'm afraid so, yes. But we do have the whole gang in custody, it's possible we'll get something out of them.'

Bob exhaled in a quiet splutter. 'I doubt it,' he said under his breath. He took a few steps forward, leaving his minder behind him and coming to a stop only inches from Phil, though having to crane his head upwards to look into his eyes. When he spoke, he spoke quietly and with more composure than before.

'I thought I explained everything last time we were here, Phil. Just last night, wasn't it?' He shook his wrist out of his jacket sleeve and looked at his watch. 'Just... 23 hours ago, in fact. But perhaps I didn't quite emphasise the importance of this particular errand highly enough. You're not in a hurry, are you? Please, take a seat.'

There were no chairs on the bare, broken concrete of the abandoned warehouse floor, but Phil dutifully turned to look anyway and then returned Bob's offer with an even voice. 'I'm alright, thanks, Bob. I'll stand.'

A brief flicker of confusion crossed Bob's face, and for a second or two Phil wasn't entirely sure whether he'd forgotten where they were, but Bob composed himself almost immediately and then smiled as he waved a hand around to indicate their surroundings. 'Another day in paradise, eh Phil?'

They stood watching each other in silence, Phil looking down at Big Bob beneath him until he started talking again.

'Let me ask you a question, Phil. If you don't mind. Put yourself in my shoes for a second, imagine you have my job. What do you think my biggest challenge is? What's the thing that keeps me awake at night with worry?'

Phil resisted the temptation to make a joke about Bob trying to get into his Range Rover, and instead just took a drag on his cigarette. 'No idea.'

'Logistics, Phil, logistics.' Bob waited for a reaction which didn't come, so he ploughed on. 'It's not very sexy, I know. But in reality, it's not the stress of international drug deals or dramatic shootouts or the fear of being double-crossed or anything exciting like that which concerns me. No, it's good old-fashioned logistics. How to get my product from here...' he dug the toe of his foot into a patch of earth to make a small indentation, '...to here,' a second mark a few feet away.

'You see, firstly, import/export is an expensive business. If you want to take a product from one country and import it to another, then there are a lot of overheads: storage, transport, taxes, duties and so on. Now, admittedly, I don't necessarily pay all the taxes and duties, of course, and I don't mind admitting that to you as an officer of the law; we have an understanding. But the other costs are considerable.

'And what I might save in avoiding certain payments, I more than lose out on in other ways. You see, drugs are illegal... you probably covered that in policeman school. And that means there's always someone trying to take them away from people like me, often without paying. So when they're stored somewhere, they're in danger. And when they're being transported from place to place, then they're out in the open, so to speak, and doubly in danger. Maybe triply so. Perhaps even...' he paused for a second, searching the air around him for a word. '...more than that.' He winced slightly, then continued. 'I refer you to the events of a couple of days ago, in fact — this particular shipment was stolen from under my nose in transit, if you recall. You see my problems?'

Phil acknowledged that he did.

'So I incur significant costs, not only for the storage and transportation of a large quantity of product but for the *secure* storage and transportation. It's expensive, Phil, very expensive. A lot of money, a lot of people. My particular target for the next financial year is to work out how to minimise these costs and mitigate the inherent risks while doing so. How do I keep my goods on the down-low and under the radar, beneath the prying eyes of the boys in blue, such as yourself, and the bad boys of other outfits who'd like to take my hard-earned product away from me? You follow me so far?'

Phil smoked and nodded. Big Bob paused for a second and then turned to Phil with a querying expression.

'You like a drink of fruit squash, Phil?'

Phil looked nonplussed. 'Er, no thanks.'

'No, Phil, not now, I wasn't offering. I meant in general. A nice refreshing glass of orange squash, no? Lemon perhaps on a summer's day?'

'Not really, no. Scotch usually goes down better.'

Big Bob turned and walked a few feet away, then turned dramatically with his finger raised. 'Do you cook then? Add stock cubes or tomatoes to casseroles? Or maybe you're green-fingered? Feed your plants to make them grow? Or wash your clothes with detergent, or wash up your dishes? What have they all got in common, do you think?'

Phil shrugged, unsure where Bob was going with this.

'Concentrate, Phil, concentrate!'

Phil felt a little put out. 'I am, I just don't know the answer.'

Big Bob exhaled slowly and cast his eyes downward. 'No, Phil,' he said slowly and with exaggerated patience, '*concentrate*. As in concentrated products. Double-strength, half the size, only a small squirt needed, all that kind of stuff.'

'Ah. Gotcha.'

'And why do they all do it? Hmm?'

'To reduce the cost of storage and transportation,' said Phil with no enthusiasm.

'To reduce the cost of storage and transportation,' repeated Bob, beaming. 'Which got me thinking. Not only does this approach reduce overheads, but it keeps the product smaller, and easier to hide. Easier to move about. What's easier to import — a lorry-load of dodgy goods or a small parcel? It's the small parcel, Phil.'

Phil thought it probably was.

'Now,' continued Big Bob, warming to his schoolteacher role, 'it's much this thinking that has led many an importer of fine herbs and pharmacological products into the arms of the harder stuff. The pills, the powders. Denser, higher value. One big shipment and BANG!' he clapped his hands. 'All the cash! And I can see sense in that, from a business perspective. Silly old me, moving around what's essentially a mown field that's been chopped down a bit and stuck into bags is not the most efficient way of making money. It's large, it's cumbersome. It's the most expensive to transport and store, but the cheapest to sell. Not good business really, Phil, when you think about it, is it? Not efficient at all.'

Phil was by now sensing that he was in for the long haul and about to become exposed to all the dreariest and most obvious aspects of a drug dealer's business, so he rummaged around in his pocket for a breather.

'So what's a boy to do? What's an ambitious, innovative entrepreneur like me going to do if he wants to make more money and streamline his business? Option 1: move into the hard drugs game.'

Bob lowered his head and swept his hand across his hair, patting it down properly over his embryonic bald patch. 'But I don't want to do that. It's not my business, it's too established, too much competition, and the risks are even higher. It's a bad crowd too, Phil, not nice people. No, I like what I sell. What I want to do is to innovate! Extend the boundaries, push the envelope and break new ground, that's more my style. Blaze a trail, do something meaningful that I'll be remembered for!'

Phil felt the urge to snort, but instead coughed a little on his cigarette and regained his composure.

'So, I've been busy, Phil. Working hard. I've poured a lot of money into research for a long time now, employed some very clever people in several countries to work for me to find the answer to my particular problem. And find it we have. We've had a breakthrough, a genuine scientific breakthrough, Phil.'

Big Bob watched Phil closely, failing to conceal the smug feeling of pride that he felt. He was smiling, just about, and his eyes were glittering. Phil was finally interested, for the first time since he'd arrived, and was genuinely curious to know what Bob was alluding to. Bob was happy to milk the moment, his head bobbing slowly in triumph and the small smile growing wider against his will.

'Oh yes, Phil. This is big,' he said, but then said no more for a few moments, trying to build the tension and leave Phil hanging.

'Do you know what's involved in cultivating weed, Phil?' Bob said, suddenly changing the subject. Phil clenched his teeth, aware that Bob wasn't about to give anything away too soon.

'No, Bob. Tell me.'

Big Bob smiled, happy that he got to talk more about his favourite topic. 'I will, Phil, I will. You see, it's a lot more complex than some people will tell you. I mean, sure, you can stick some seeds in a pot of compost or in a field and you might get a serviceable plant at the end of it. It might even be a pleasant smoke. But that's just the beginning. That is not an optimised process.'

He started to walk, marking a figure of eight a few yards across, his head down in concentration and only occasionally looking up at Phil to make a point and check he was still following along.

'To get an exceptional crop, to get international-grade weed, you need to know your onions. Location, soil constituents, nutrient levels, light sources and strength, position on the UVB spectrum, temperature, humidity, air quality, CO_2 levels. All this and more, Phil, has to be assessed, measured and monitored to a high degree of accuracy. And then you can cultivate, breed, cross breed. Keep changing the parameters, one at a time and a generation at a time. Study the results, measure, test, try again. It's a science, Phil, it really is. Some hippy growing a plant in his room at college is just an amateur, he's just trying his luck. But the real professionals, the entrepreneurs in this business...' He stopped walking and held out his palms as if to receive this accolade. 'Well, they employ science. Scientists. Knowledge and know-how.'

He tapped his nose and nodded seriously. 'I'm not an amateur, Phil. It's all about optimisation, about squeezing every last drop out of the ingredients you put in. Getting everything just right through hard work and determination to maximise the efficiency, and maximise your output. Growing time, plants per square metre of growth area, serviceable output in grams per plant, Phil, and strength of the product in both cannabidiols and tetrahydrocannabinols.'

He looked to Phil with a hopeful look, and Phil dutifully set his face to appear impressed.

'But mainly it's the strength, Phil.'

He started walking again, more animated this time, with arms moving around, and Phil sensed that they were reaching some sort of conclusion, hoping desperately that Bob wouldn't continue to bore him with the details.

'I won't bore you with the details,' said Bob, and Phil worked hard to suppress a smile. 'But what we've done is extraordinary. Obviously, I can't give you the ingredients of my secret sauce, as it were, but essentially what I've done is make a strain of weed that's stronger than anything that's ever been grown before.'

He stopped walking again, a foot or so in front of Phil, and watched him closely. 'You've heard of super skunk, yes?'

'Sure.'

Bob sneered and gave a hollow laugh. 'Well, that's yer basic extra strong. It's double-concentrated tomato purée, it's washing up liquid that gets twice the plates done with just one squirt.'

He took a step towards Phil so that their noses were almost touching, and lowered his voice to a whisper.

'No... what I've made is *hyper* skunk. TEN times stronger than that. Scientifically engineered and optimised to pack all that druggy goodness that people seem to like so much into a tiny fraction of the space.'

He laughed and started pacing again triumphantly, and not a little insanely in Phil's view, his eyes sparkling wildly.

'Imagine that! Ten percent of the storage space, ten percent of the transport costs and, most importantly, a tenth of the risk! You can carry a container-load in the back of a hatchback, or a ship-load in a speedboat, a Jumbo-load in a few light planes and a car-load in a small bag!'

He walked at speed back to Phil and grabbed him by both shoulders, standing on tiptoes to reach. 'It's a revolution! And it's beautiful, too!' He let Phil go and began prowling again, talking quickly.

'Strain 237Y, it's called, which gives you some indication of how long it took to develop. But I like to call it Glass Carnation because it's pink! Well, it's got pink in it anyway, and it's almost shiny with crystals. It's a thing of beauty, Phil, it really is. We've tested it on our highly experienced panel of experts, and they all concur — it's the most potent weed the world has ever seen! You only need tiny quantities of it, of course. Just a little rub of the leaf and you're good to go. Put too much in and poof! Your head comes off!' He clapped his hands to illustrate the point, actually making Phil jump, and then started laughing loudly, watching Phil out of the corner of his eye.

After a moment, he became serious, his face fell and his movements slowed as he approached Phil and stopped in front of him once again.

'So you see what I've achieved, Phil. And this isn't just theoretical, either. This isn't just on paper or in tiny lab quantities. Oh no, we'd made up a nice, juicy test shipment. The first batch, imported in secret to distribute amongst some favoured customers. Very important part of the process, you understand, like sea trials — the first time out in the wild, first time smoked in anger, if you see what I mean. Vital feedback to be got from the end-user, customer research, marketing.'

He paused for a moment, his eyes now locked on to Phil's, and he continued in a whisper. 'And valuable too, Phil, as you can imagine. Not just as a one-of-a-kind prototype, but in very real monetary terms. One single holdall, a mere ten kilos of product and a street value of… half a million pounds.'

He was breathing fast now, and a light sheen of perspiration was forming on his forehead.

'Big money, Phil. Real money. And it was taken away from me. Stolen during the night whilst in transit, my beloved Glass Carnation. By some amateurs too, just kids who got lucky.'

He sneered and spat out the words. 'They don't know what they took! They don't know what they've got! They were just in the right place at the right time and got lucky! And they think they nicked a few kilos of normal weed! They probably shit themselves with joy that they'd scored a good 25 grand's worth and have no idea it's worth a fortune!'

A vein in his neck was starting to swell and pulse.

'And so I sent you over to retrieve it for me. Simple job, Phil, simple task for a man of your talents. Just go over there with all your big, strong men and pick up a single bag of product for me. So little, in fact, that it would've hardly been noticed when it went missing again. But it was IMPORTANT, Phil! IT WAS IMPORTANT! And what did you bring me? You brought me fuck all, Phil, FUCK ALL! I'M NOT A FUCKING AMATEUR, PHIL! I'M NOT A FUCKING AMATEUR!'

Big Bob let out a deep breath and spat onto the ground. He was beetroot red and the vein in his neck was now bouncing up and down like a disco worm. He stayed looking at the ground as if he was embarrassed by the force of his outburst and jiggled his arms about like an Olympic sprinter limbering up. Phil watched on impassively and reached for his cigarettes.

'So there we have it,' said Bob with an incredibly forced smile. 'Maybe I should've gone into a bit more detail last time. But I hope you understand now why I need that weed back.'

Phil lit his cigarette and took in a deep lungful.

'So please, Phil. Pretty please. Get me my fucking weed back.'

Chapter 9

Waffle was sitting in his usual place on the sofa, his long, thin legs crossed over each other on the coffee table, one flip-flop hanging loose in the air. Miles Davis' Kind of Blue was spinning lazily on the record deck, the sound of the trumpet swirling as light as air around the room, circling the coffee table and the sofa, and floating off into the space beyond, to the open door of the little storage cupboard and around the hoover and plastic bags that were strewn around it.

On the coffee table was an open plastic bag, spilling its contents of chopped pinkish leaves that twinkled slightly in the sun, and in Waffle's mouth was a fat, ripe spliff, filled to bursting with a generous amount of the windfall weed. With a well-practised flick, the lighter flared into life and the flame danced and grew as he brought it to the tip of the joint, while he breathed in deeply. He puffed at it a couple of times like an old man with a pipe, filling the air with clotted wreaths of smoke that ballooned and fell apart and then swam lazily with the notes from Miles Davis' trumpet. He took in a thick lungful, almost chewing on it as he inhaled deeply and allowed his eyes to close and his body to lean slowly back with an air of deep contentment.

By his own admission, he'd tried hard to resist its siren call but ultimately failed. He'd lasted more than 24 hours, in fact; productive hours, too. He'd booked his appointment with Mrs Higson at the Jobcentre, and had arrived on time without anything unusual falling from the sky. The hospital cleaning job was still available and his for the taking, and he even made Mrs Higson smile a little, which was the first time she'd done that in Waffle's presence. He was a little startled to see that she had surprisingly perfect white teeth; the ones that were still remaining, at least.

But when he'd returned to his flat, for no particular reason his mind had been filled with the image of what lay wedged behind the hoover, and he'd succumbed. He felt guilty. He felt very guilty, in fact, knowing that he'd failed not just another person, but himself. If he couldn't keep a promise he'd made to himself, who could he keep one to? But, as was usually the case, he'd reasoned that one spliff couldn't do much harm, and he'd resolved to do something about getting rid of the whole lot afterwards. One spliff. One small spliff.

Waffle breathed out a long, steady stream of smoke until his lungs were empty. He opened his eyes and looked around with the unnerving feeling that he'd perhaps dozed off while his thoughts had wandered and now felt a vague disconnectedness from the actions of a moment before. He looked up to the clock on the wall but that was clearly no help, so he looked down at the spliff in his hand as his standard way of measuring time passing, but it was still there, still just-lit and fuming gently. The smoke was fascinating, the way it left a small gap above the burning end of the joint before forming an incredibly smooth and sinuous wave of bluish-grey that swayed almost imperceptibly, like the folds of a flamenco dancer's dress in slow motion. He brought his face closer to the smoke strands, then realised it was more efficient to move his hand towards his face instead, and compromised by meeting it halfway. He'd never really studied smoke so closely, and he marvelled at how it was transparent, but only just, allowing the merest glimpse of whatever lay beyond behind a thin, grey veil. It reminded him of looking at glass marbles as a child, the serpentine flash of... whatever it was they put into marbles, that became more and more fascinating the closer you looked.

He allowed his gaze to wander back to the joint, and then to his fingers, which he studied as closely as he had the smoke. He looked at each finger in turn and frowned. Had he always had five fingers? He supposed he must have, five being the norm after all. And yet looking now and counting them back and forth, 1, 2, 3, 4, 5.... 1, 2, 3, 4, 5, he had the same feeling you get when you repeat a word until it loses its meaning, loses all familiarity and eventually sounds entirely foreign. Was it the Simpsons who have four fingers? Or was it the other way round? He stared open-mouthed at his hand. My god, he thought, do I have too many fingers?! Or, possibly worse, am I a Simpson?

He yanked back the sleeve of his shirt to study the colour of his arm and discovered it was purple, sparkly and glowing gently with a pulsating light from under the skin. Thank god, he thought and rolled his sleeve back down with some relief.

He found his gaze searching the room slowly, convinced that there was something he was supposed to be doing, but the memory of it kept slipping from his grasp, like a wet bar of soap. His eyes settled on the record deck, slowly shimmying back and forth along the shelf in perfect 6/8 time, but that wasn't it. He turned in his seat to look behind him, but there was nothing there apart from the hoover, quietly busying itself with cleaning the carpet as it hummed along tunelessly. Out of ideas, he turned back with a shrug and went to reach for the TV remote, startling himself to see the spliff still held between his fingers as he looked down.

'Aha!' he said out loud, and brought the joint towards him, finding his mouth successfully after just two attempts. He listened to the music for a few moments, becoming lost in its smooth and breathy melodies that circled and swam around him. He was enjoying it immensely and found that he seemed to understand it more than he ever had before now. The notes seemed to dance around his head, just out of arm's reach, but in patterns that seemed predictable and logical rather than merely beautiful. Even so, he made his mind up that he'd change the record soon. This one was wonderfully light and tasted mildly of peppermint, but he decided that he'd prefer something with a bit more bite, something with a little resistance to it. Sgt Pepper, perhaps, that might be just the thing. A fruitier taste, but also more chewy and marshmallowy.

He took another long, hungry drag, picked up the TV remote and flopped back into his seat once again, tapping the power button as he did. He felt the smoke sink heavily and slowly down into his trachea, swirling happily as it went, and then divide as its path split into the two bronchi. From here, he was entirely conscious of it creeping along

61

the thousands of passageways in his lungs, half going left and half going right, spreading and dividing into ever smaller pathways like a giant crack in a frozen lake that stretches on towards the horizon.

The smoke was filling his whole respiratory system, making it glow and sparkle as it went, inching ever more slowly into smaller and smaller pathways until it reached the hundreds of millions of alveoli, the mesh of minuscule air sacs at the end of the hair-sized bronchioles. From here, he could feel the smoke diffuse through the fine gauze of cells and into his bloodstream, suddenly speeding to a blur as it was whisked away by the fast-flowing current, each molecule of smoke like a microscopic Frogger that had jumped onto a log.

He stretched his arms out to the side and lifted his feet into the air, vividly aware of the smoke spreading outwards from his lungs to all the extremities of his body at the same time. He turned to his right and watched as the smoke spread along the veins in his arms, glowing and sparkling even through his shirt, edging towards his wrist and into each finger.

He turned to face forward again, arms and legs still outstretched, distracted momentarily by the images on the TV channels flicking from one to another faster than he could keep up with. In the space of two or three seconds — or was it two or three hours? — he watched a thousand images flash onto the screen as the smoke passed down his body towards his legs, and upwards from his chest into his neck.

Mastermind, The News at Ten, Starskey and Hutch, Cagney and Lacey, John Craven's Newsround, Thomas the Tank Engine, some swans taking flight, a volcano erupting, Columbo's just one more thing. The sequences sped up faster and faster until they were one long blur of motion, the last wisps of smoke working their way down his legs and up his neck. The crack in the ice still splitting, spreading, dividing, accelerating.

A tiger mauling an antelope, a car exploding, a flash of lightning, Al Pacino machine-gunning a swarm of drug dealers, the crack spreading further and further, finer and finer, the smoke inching up his neck and into his brain. A Bruce Lee howl, the Grange Hill sausage, a whale breaching, a bullet train exiting a tunnel, the Challenger disaster, a Smurf laughing, Laurel and Hardy bumping heads, the crack spreading, the smoke rising, the images speeding to just milliseconds of a single colour each, a noise, a flash, a punch, a scream, a snap.

The smoke filled the last few millimetres of his body, into the ends of his toes and into his brain.

CRACK.

THE ICE SPLIT APART EXPOSING the infinite murky depths of the water below and Waffle felt his brain split too, like a coconut dropped onto a rock from a great height, its two halves flying off in opposite directions while whatever milky goodness swished around in his head leaked pointlessly away. His arms and legs fell heavily as he slumped back and onto his side. His eyes flickered, briefly showed just white and then closed, the speakers crackling over and over as the needle fell into the last, endless groove on the turntable that played to an otherwise still and silent room.

* * *

CONSCIOUSNESS CAME to Waffle like a wet duvet being dragged through a pub car park — it was slow, there was a lot of resistance, and it kept snagging on things. After a few moments, he managed to open one eye enough to recognise his surroundings, and was relieved to discover that he wasn't actually dead, though he was yet to see evidence that he was sane. For a while he was content to survey the scene in front of him at 90 degrees, the coffee table rising up in front of him like a monolith with his green hat, ashtray and bag of weed seemingly stuck to its side.

The record was still turning lazily, the warm hum punctuated rhythmically every couple of seconds by a crackle as the needle bounced into the groove, and something somewhere was on fire. He tried to open his mouth but found his lips had somehow been glued together and he exerted pressure slowly to part them as if they were the two halves of a flimsy sealed envelope, scared that rushing the manoeuvre would tear something. He thought about burnt-out cars.

He tried to lift his head, but his head wasn't keen, so he agreed to leave it where it was for a bit. Instead, he reached his hand down to his trouser pocket and extricated his mobile, bringing it slowly and carefully to his face so he could see the time: 9:15 am. It wasn't even nighttime, he must have passed out and been unconscious for around an hour. He stretched his arm out unsteadily to put the phone on the table but, with only one eye still open, lacked the necessary depth perception and instead merely dropped it on the floor. He decided to leave it there for a bit. He thought about bonfires.

He closed his good eye and determined to marshal his thoughts and his strength enough to pull himself into an upright position. This he did with more success than he'd expected, though his eyesight seemed to be out of sync with his movements by a couple of seconds, and the room joined him after a sickening delay that made him gag. He pushed his palms into the sofa cushions on either side to steady himself, there being a very real danger of him simply falling back down again, but he recoiled when one hand felt an unexpected object under it. He looked down to see the remains of the spliff lying on the sofa, half of it having burned by itself, leaving a pile of ash and a black strip in the fabric where it had smouldered for a while but not caught fully alight.

'Oh, fuck,' he said, angry with himself, and he picked up the remains with one hand while his other tried to brush the burn mark away, with a stunning lack of success. He deposited what he could into the ashtray and then retrieved his phone from the carpet, unlocked it and tapped his way into the address book. He reached Learner Joe and stabbed at the green button, then waited for nearly thirty seconds for Joe to answer.

'Mr Waffle Jones, I do believe!' came a voice with far too much enthusiasm for Waffle's current mood, 'It's been two weeks, I've been wondering where you'd got to. Would you like re-stocking?'

Waffle licked his lips slowly to lubricate them enough to speak and let his eyes fall closed as he did so.

'Yeah, something like that. Come over, yeah? Got something to show you.'

* * *

THE TWO OF them sat on the sofa, eyeing the holdall carefully.

'Fell out of the sky? Do you mean like "fell off the back of a lorry"? Is "fell out of the sky" some kind of euphemism I've not heard? Have I lived a sheltered life?'

Waffle blinked slowly and continued to watch the bag with heavy eyes.

'No, man. Just as I said. I was walking along, minding me own business, and then blam. It just landed in front of me.'

'On the pavement?'

'On the pavement.'

'I see. Can I have a look at it?'

'Help yourself.'

Joe leaned forward and picked up the plastic bag that was still lying open on the table. He held it up to get the best angle from the light fitting on the ceiling and turned it over a couple of times.

'It's sort of... pink. It looks pink.'

He turned to Waffle with a frown. 'Is it pink?'

'Sort of pink, yeah.'

'Huh. Pink. Well, well.'

Joe brought the bag to his nose and took in a deep sniff.

'Jeeesus wept!' He looked at Waffle with wide eyes and a crooked smile. 'That's got some heft to it, hasn't it? I reckon a few long sniffs of that alone would get you a bit giggly!'

Waffle turned away, distracted by his curtains.

'So how is it?' asked Joe with some enthusiasm. 'How does she smoke? Hmm? Does she deliver on her promise?'

Waffle looked vacantly at Joe for a second as if not hearing him, and then with a small jolt, focused fully again.

'Oh... yeah, yeah. Yeah, it's got some... kick to it.'

'I bet it has!' said Joe excitedly, smelling at the bag once again. 'Mind if I... y'know, roll one up?'

'No, man,' said Waffle distantly.

Joe leaned forward to the cigarette papers on the table and ripped a couple out of the packet, but stopped when Waffle placed a hand on his arm.

'No, man. Sorry... I uh, meant No. Man.'

Joe looked at Waffle with confusion, and then with a little embarrassment.

'Oh. I'm sorry. I didn't mean to be rude, I just thought you'd —'

'No, it's OK. I just don't want any more of that at the moment. I'd just like to clear the air in here a bit. I might open a window, actually.'

Waffle stood up, rocked gently on his feet for a moment and then plodded unsteadily to the window, which he unlatched and pushed wide open. He pulled the curtains, but left a gap of a foot or so between them and sat back down again.

Joe looked at him seriously. 'Are you alright, Mr Jones? You seem a bit... under the weather? How are you feeling?'

Waffle's head turned slowly to face Joe's concerned gaze. 'Yeah. I feel a bit unusual. I might get some water. Do you want anything? Water?'

Waffle walked over to the sink. 'Cup of tea would be nice if you don't mind,' said Joe behind him. 'Milk two sugars, please.'

Waffle didn't reply, but clattered around in the cupboards for a while before returning to the sofa. He handed Joe a glass of water.

'Oh, right. Lovely, thank you.'

They sipped at their drinks in silence for a moment, both again looking towards the holdall on the table.

'So. What are you going to do with it all then?' said Joe, flicking a finger towards it. 'That could last you years! Are you keeping it for yourself? Personal supply, that sort of thing?'

Waffle closed his eyes and tipped the rest of the water down his throat, wiping his mouth with the back of his hand as he placed the glass on the table a little heavily.

'No. I really don't think I will.'

He shuffled in his seat a little so he could face Joe better. 'I was wondering, actually, if you wanted to buy it off me?'

Joe chuckled. 'Seems funny though, you selling to me. I mean, I'm supposed to be the drug dealer and you're one of my best customers. It's the wrong way round!'

Waffle nodded deeply and slowly. 'Yeah. Bit like solar panels, isn't it?'

Joe looked at him sideways. 'Solar panels?'

Waffle was still nodding. 'Yeah. Like, when people get solar panels fitted and they make more electricity than they use. They sell it back to the electricity company, don't they? You know, the excess. They use what they can and then sell the rest back. Same thing.'

Joe weighed up the answer. 'Yes, I suppose it is. Well, I can be Southern Weed and you can sell me some of that lovely sunshine in a bag there!'

He laughed and picked up the bag to study it again.

'Seriously though, I'll buy some from you, but not the whole lot, obviously. I can't afford anything like that much. I can't even afford a whole kilo. How about I buy maybe one pound of it for now and see how it goes? It looks like excellent quality, but I'll have to see how it sells. What do you think? How much do you want for one pound?'

Waffle looked at the bag in Joe's hand and watched it for a while.

'Yeah, cool, OK. Nice one. How much do you usually buy it for?'

'Well, it varies, of course. But good quality skunk's about 1500 if I buy it by the pound.'

'Give us a grand then.'

'Are you sure? I don't want to do myself out of a deal, but that seems almost too good.'

Waffle was gazing vaguely into the distance. 'Yeah, man. I got a few bills to pay, that should sort me out for the time being. I might even go away for a while, clear my head a bit.'

'Well, if you're sure,' said Joe, getting up to leave. 'I can get the cash today if you like, can be back in a few hours?' He sealed the bag and put it back with the others in the holdall. 'What are you going to do with the rest of it, then?'

Waffle took a deep breath and leaned back on the sofa. His eyes were glazing over and he was staring without focus at the clock-shaped circle on the wall. 'I don't know, man,' he said quietly. 'I really don't know.'

Chapter 10

The summer sun rose early and bathed the west side of the wide street in a warm, orange glow. Despite several tower blocks nearby, most of the area was fairly low rise in that typical South London way; streets lined with predominantly Victorian three and four-storey buildings with shops on the ground floor, randomly interspersed with ill-matched and anonymous post-war constructions wedged awkwardly into old bomb sites like cheap dental fillings. Dance music played from an open window somewhere hard to pinpoint, only just audible over the background hum of a city awake, and regularly drowned out entirely by a revving engine, the chuntering of a bus or louder music still that spilled from passing cars.

Between a bookie and a dry cleaner's sat a large and entirely bland building whose only redeeming feature, architecturally speaking, was that it currently had sunlight on it. Its facade was almost entirely flat and of bare sixties brick, its dozens of regularly spaced windows all sealed shut and obscured by either reflective material or closed blinds. Slightly off-centre was its raised entrance, which dropped to street level via a generous choice of concrete stairs or concrete ramp, and at the bottom were three noticeboards behind whose glass were ranged a variety of faded, miniature posters. Half of these warned informatively about the dangers of mobile phone theft, lax vehicle security and alcohol consumption, and the other half warned threateningly about the punishment meted out to mobile phone muggers, car thieves and drink drivers. They had all the bases covered.

The door opened and five young men came blinking into the sun, the spring in their steps at odds with their tired eyes and crumpled clothes. As four of them made for the stairs, the fifth turned to walk down the ramp but was grabbed by the arm and steered back towards the rest of the group. At the bottom, they huddled close together and waited in silence as a woman trundled past, holding a toddler by one hand and a pushchair with the other. She gave them a sideways glance as she passed, and five pairs of eyes followed her closely until she was out of earshot.

'OK, right. So you all stayed cool yeah, nobody said anything stupid?'

'Course, Tommo,' 'Didn't say nuffin,' 'Never said a word,' they replied in unison, except for Soapy, who just mimed his mouth being zipped shut.

'OK, safe. Well, we need to find somewhere to talk now, we've got things to discuss.'

'How about over there?' said Lenny, nodding to Dave's Cafe across the road, whose culinary delights were advertised in the greasy window on star-shaped pieces of day-glo cardboard. Lenny was staring hard while his mouth twitched involuntarily. 'I'm starving. I could murder an all-day breakfast.'

Tommo followed his gaze and paused for a second in thought before giving a quick shake of his head. 'Nah, man. I ain't discussing business in that little place. We need to be able to speak freely. And anyway, it's ten past eight, it's not an all-day breakfast yet. It's still just breakfast.'

Lenny hung his shoulders in visible disappointment and put his hand to his stomach as if to soothe it, while Tommo slipped his wallet from his back pocket and pulled out a twenty. He flicked his chin to a newsagent a couple of doors along from Dave's.

'Soapy, take this and get some chocolate and crisps and shit. See if they have any sandwiches, maybe. But nothing rank like prawns or just cheese on its own. And some Red Bulls, yeah? We'll see you over in that park.'

He passed the note over and Soapy set off at a jog, realising too late that there was no clear path through both lanes of traffic and having to spend a considerable time stranded in the middle of the road, jogging on the spot and waiting for his moment.

Five minutes later, they were all squashed onto a single park bench, two on either side of Tommo, greedily tearing off mouthfuls of food and taking slugs of drink from their cans.

'So,' said Tommo, pocketing his half-eaten Mars Bar and dusting off his hands. 'Talk to me. Tell me what you're thinking, give me some ideas. Where are we in all this?'

The silence was broken by Soapy, who chimed in enthusiastically. 'Brocklington Park, I think... I saw a sign just as...'

'Shut up, Soapy,' said Tommy with a withering stare. 'You can be a stupid prick on your own time, yeah?' He shook his head sadly as Soapy frowned and studied his trainers.

'Lenny. Help me out. Summarise the events so far for us. I wanna hear it out loud, so we can all take it in and let it settle. Let our minds work on it.'

Lenny finished off his Ginster's pie quickly, licked his fingers and cleared his throat.

'OK. So. Well... we nicked a load of weed. Then we went back to yours to get it ready. Then a load of Old Bill turned up and arrested us. Then we got let out and now we're here.'

He looked up at Tommo hopefully, who was rocking his head from side to side as if weighing up the answer.

'Well, yes. Those are most of the key facts. A little... bare maybe, but nothing if not concise. But, more importantly, where did the weed go?'

'Out the window,' said D, with a confident nod.

'That's right. Out of the window. And Playboy was there, what, less than a minute later, yeah?'

'I got there flat out, man,' said Playboy, miming his speed with an outstretched hand and a brief whistle. 'I got the call from Lenny as I was getting my shoes on an' that, just watching Bargain Hunt, but I was almost leaving anyway. I was out the door before he even put the phone down and then I was like, flat out, man.' He made the mime and whistle again.

'OK, safe. And how far is it, would you say? From yours to mine?'

Playboy sucked air through his teeth as he visualised it. 'Not far, man, not far. It's like, what, free or four roads, innit?'

Tommo said nothing, so Playboy ploughed on. 'Come out my flat, take a left on Warrington Road, down there to the end, then another left. Shortcut through Goodrich Gardens, into Dunstan Street and then down that alleyway behind the garages and onto Clairmont and then it's like 50 metres to your place at the end.'

'So how long?'

'90 seconds tops, I reckon, maybe less.'

'Right. And actually, it must've been, what, ten seconds from Lenny hanging up the phone before Soapy even chucked the bag out the window. So there was just over a minute for that weed to land, sit on the pavement, get found and then get out of sight.'

They all nodded thoughtfully, shaking their heads and tutting.

'You reckon it was planned, then?' said Lenny. Then his eyes widened as another thought struck him. 'Or was it the Old Bill? You reckon it was all a scam to get the weed?'

Tommo sat in silent thought for some time.

'I dunno, Lenny, I dunno. S'possible I suppose. Either that or some jammy bastard just turned up at the exact moment, thanked his lucky stars and thought he'd make off with our weed.'

Lenny chuckled and took a swig from his can.

'What's funny?' asked Tommo, looking hard at Lenny and making him splutter slightly on his drink.

'Oh. Nothing really. Not funny as such. Just you saying "our weed". Y'know, when we nicked it ourselves. Only had it less than a day.'

'Yeah, well,' said Tommo, leaning back on the bench, you know what they say — possession is nine-tenths of the law.'

'Yep, and possession of an eighth is against the law,' said Lenny with another chuckle, 'so I guess ten keys is seriously frowned upon!'

'Well, I don't make the rules. I just know that I worked hard for that weed. We all did. We risked a lot going up against those boys, even if we did outnumber them. I dunno who they were, but they looked pretty mean. And we won. And it was all ours to sell on and make an honest profit from. And then we lost the whole lot by throwing it out the window just so some fucker could take it from us.' He spat onto the pathway in front of him. 'It ain't right.'

The five of them sank into a miserable silence, broken once again by Tommo, who pulled himself up straight and turned to Playboy.

'So. What happened when you got to mine, then? How long were you there before we came out? Did you get to search around or anything?'

Playboy shook his head. 'Nah, man. I was literally stopped for about a single second, just catching my breath when that copper come for me. I barely moved before he took me down, it was like a rugby tackle or some shit.'

'Yeah, we saw that bit,' said Tommo, smiling. 'And you didn't see anybody around at all, no one nearby just before you got flattened?'

Playboy paused and frowned, then scratched his cheek slowly, as the other four heads turned slowly towards him.

'Well... there was one guy, yeah. He was sort of in the distance.'

Tommo moved his face closer towards him, his eyes narrowing.

'One guy, in the distance. Yeah... go on. Did he, by any chance, appear to be carrying a bag?'

Playboy screwed his face up and closed his eyes, trying to will the image back into his mind.

'Well, y'know what... it's possible. I couldn't see all that clearly, but... yeah, it's possible.'

'And was he running? Did he get into a car or anything? Was anybody waiting for him?'

Playboy was more sure this time. 'Nah, man. He was just... strolling along. Just... taking it easy.'

Tommo clicked his fingers and leapt up. 'OK, finally! Something to go on. But man, why didn't you say before?'

Playboy looked aggrieved. 'I didn't *not* say, I just haven't had the chance. I mean, I saw him for a split second in the distance, then I got tackled to the floor and handcuffed the next second, and I've been getting interrogated for most of the time since. It's been a long night, man.'

'Yeah, well, don't sweat it. This is good news.' Tommo stopped to think for a second and then sprang into life. 'So.. what have we got? We've got a guy wandering down a residential South London street. No car, no hurry. Where does that road even go to in either direction? Nowhere really, just more houses and a few shops. So this guy's just wandering along at 8:30 on a weekday morning, where's he going? Work, right? A bus stop maybe? There's not even a station for nearly a mile. So he must be local, there's no way he's just randomly miles from home walking down my road.'

Tommo's enthusiasm spread to the others. Playboy and D both sprang up while Lenny started murmuring 'yes, yes, yes' to himself. Soapy stayed sitting and just looked from one face to the next with an empty expression.

'Right, well, that's it then. We're looking for someone local, let's say within a mile of my place, max. We know he walks down Clairmont Avenue at 8:30 am so we'll all be there tomorrow morning and tonight from 5 to 7 too, in case he's coming home from work. If he's not there after that, then we'll spread out. There's what, three pubs in the area? The Anchor, the Wessex and the Gunnery? D, Soapy and Lenny, you take one each, keep your eyes peeled, your phones on and ask around a bit.'

Soapy and D both clenched their fists and were knocking them into their thighs in unison.

Tommo grabbed Soapy by the wrist and glared at him. 'What the fuck are you doing?'

'Um, one potato, two potato,' Soapy said, shuffling his feet and lowering his head. 'To decide who goes to which pub, innit?'

Tommo took a deep breath and bored his gaze into each in turn, running his tongue around his mouth. 'You – Anchor! You - Gunnery!' he said, stabbing each of them in turn with his finger. 'And Lenny, you take the Wessex. I've got the car, so I'll cruise around and take Playboy with me as he knows what he looks like. We're gonna get our fucking weed back, boys!'

Tommo whooped and the others all joined in, shouting for joy and clapping each other on the back.

'Yeah, Playboy,' said Lenny as the gang settled down again. 'what *does* he look like? So far, we've just got a geezer with a bag. It's possible he won't be lugging ten keys of weed to work or the pub when we see him next.'

All four of them turned once again to look at Playboy, who scanned the horizon for inspiration, thinking hard.

'Well,' he said slowly, 'like I say, I couldn't see him that well, and I only saw him from behind. But he was tall, I think white, and pretty skinny.'

They all deflated, realising they'd probably rounded it down to just a few thousand possibilities in one dense area of South London. D sat down heavily on the bench and looked at the ground as he exhaled.

'One thing, though,' said Playboy slowly, scratching his head as if to develop his visual memory 'I think he had a bright green hat on.'

Chapter 11

DC Mike Watts finished work at six on the dot, as he always tried to do on Tuesdays, and drove straight from the nick to the Turlington Green Sports Centre. The weekly *X-a-side* football game had been the highlight of his midweek for over seven years now, though admittedly there had been highs and lows over that time. It had started out, traditionally enough, as a five-a-side game back in the days when it was possible to muster ten of the boys reliably every week, but it rapidly became four-a-side more often than not, and over the years had been anything from one-a-side upwards, including — but not limited to — two-a-side, three-a-side, six-a-side, three-against-four, four-against-two and Tasty Ben against all-comers.

In principle, it was a means to combine exercise with some male bonding — catching up with mates for an honest game of football, followed by some friendly banter over a couple of pints in the Duke of York afterwards. 'Friendly banter' was of course shorthand for telling each other to fuck off as often as possible, and the couple of pints had usually extended to seven or eight in the early days, even twelve on the night of that infamous lock-in that saw seven of them barred, three of them arrested and one of them deported. But work, families and the general slide into their 30s meant that the Wednesday X-a-side was now usually a bit of a kick around with whoever turned up, followed by two pints at most and often just a lemonade for the drivers.

The banter hadn't changed much, though.

'Fuck off, you fat bastard,' shouted Tim a little too loudly, swatting Bobby's hand away from his open pack of Mini Cheddars, 'there's only about seven in a pack as it is.'

Bobby sucked his stomach in and feigned to look hurt. 'Fat? Me? It's not me that's fat, mate, you've just got blubbery eyes. Those glasses are like a hall of mirrors, I'm surprised your eyeballs don't catch fire every time the sun comes out.'

Tim upended the crisp packet into his mouth and then folded it carefully into a tight square before dropping it onto the table where it just opened up again like a flower in a time-lapse video. 'Don't let it get to you, Bobby mate, it's just a friendly observation. You should take it on the chins.'

The others laughed and took draws on their pints.

Mike appeared from the bar nestling three glasses together precariously and holding a couple of bags of snacks between his teeth. 'Eungh, engher,' he said with a flick of his head, and Bobby took the hint and cleared away some space. The glasses were lowered carefully onto the table with not a drop spilt, and at the same time, Mike leant forward and opened his mouth to release two bags of salt and vinegar crisps, like a particularly low-rent, albeit gratifyingly successful, arcade claw machine. He sat down at the empty chair, knocking the table as he did so and causing all three pints to wobble enough to lose a valuable gulp of beer each.

'Fuck's sake,' he said quietly, without any detectable annoyance, and picked up his pint. 'OK, I've got a joke,' he said as the others groaned in unison.

'It's not the one about how many cops it takes to change a light bulb, is it?' asked Bobby, screwing his face up.

Tasty Ben swallowed his mouthful too fast and spoke on the same flow of air as an escaping burp. 'No, no! Is it the one about the midget clairvoyant that escapes from a police station?'

Mike's eyes roved the ceiling, but he was used to this. While neither particularly fat, thin, bald, hairy, tall, short, stupid, ugly or even ginger, his choice of career surpassed any physical or personal trait and ensured that he was always only ever one step away from a ripe piss-taking from his mates. This, of course, was the reason that most of his colleagues socialised exclusively with other coppers, but for at least one day every week, Mike enjoyed getting away from work completely and spending it with his old friends, even if there was an inevitable price to pay.

'No, no, no,' he said wearily, quietening the boys with outstretched hands, 'this isn't a police joke at all.'

Tim raised his eyebrows in exaggerated disbelief and looked around the group. 'Really? I'm assuming you got this from work, and you're honestly telling us there's not a single copper in it?'

'Er, not as such,' said Mike, awkwardly, 'but there might be a police dog in it.'

The boys all laughed and Tasty Ben booed, but they sat back and looked on expectantly, anyway.

'Right,' said Mike, when they'd become quiet enough for him to be heard. 'A bloke's on his way home from work one day when he sees a sign outside a house that says "Talking dog for sale — enquire within"'.

'Heard it!' boomed Bobby, but he made no further comment and instead picked up his pint, so Mike continued.

'The bloke's intrigued, so he pulls up and rings the doorbell. Fella comes to the door. "Yes?" he says. "I was interested in the talking dog", says the bloke, and the guy at the door beckons him inside. "He's out the back in the garden," he says, "go on through"'.

Mike looked around at the faces, who were all suitably attentive and quiet, and so, satisfied, he carried on.

'Bloke goes into the garden and sees a little Cocker Spaniel sat on the lawn, so he walks up to it and, slightly embarrassed, asks "So... er... do you talk then?" There's a pause and then the dog says, "Well yes I do actually, thank you very much!" The guy's absolutely gobsmacked and says, "Wow, that's amazing! Tell me your story, I can't believe what I'm hearing!"'

'"Well," says the Spaniel, "I was a police sniffer dog for years —"'

Mike's audience all groaned again. 'Here we go!' said Bobby, leaning back in his chair with his arms folded, but Mike ignored him and ploughed on.

'"I was a police sniffer dog for years and I was very successful, as it goes. Best nose in the business. Over a hundred people were arrested, thanks to me: drug dealers, terrorists with bombs, the lot. I could sniff out a line of coke from 100 yards away!" The man was impressed and sat down on the grass to listen as the dog carried on with his story. "Oh yes, travelled the world I did. I was the best sniffer dog the country had, so I was sent abroad to cover all the biggest cases. Plus, I could understand what was being said, of course, being a talking dog, so I was sent into big arms deals and the like. Nobody suspects the little dog in the corner, but I was listening out and would report back to my superiors. Oh yes, I brought some big international arms dealers down a few years ago. Avoided a war in the Middle East, they say, all down to me."'

'"Wow, that's incredible," said the guy, "what an amazing life you've had!"'

Tasty Ben threw a peanut at Mike's head for no apparent reason, but Mike ignored it.

'So the bloke walks back inside and speaks to the dog's owner. "He's incredible!" he says, while reaching into his wallet, "I'll buy him! How much do you want?" The man shrugs and says, "Oh, a fiver should do the trick." "A fiver?!" says the bloke, "For a talking dog that's averted a war?!"'

Mike paused for effect, taking a long draught of his lemonade while watching his friends over the rim of his glass as they jeered him for holding up the inevitable punchline.

'"Oh," said the man, "don't believe a word of it. He's a fucking bull-shitter."'

More peanuts came in Mike's direction along with guffaws, and he decided to capitalise on his modest success by standing up to go. Always leave the audience wanting more, he thought contentedly to himself.

'Right lads, quick piss, then I'm off. Crime doesn't solve itself, I'm afraid, some of us have got proper jobs,' he said, nodding meaningfully at Tasty Ben, whose life working from home as a day trader was considered a rung even below Mike's in the piss-taking stakes, though it was mainly borne of jealousy that he was apparently able to earn so much money without ever needing to get dressed.

Mike skipped down the short flight of steps and pushed open the door to the gents, suddenly aware that telling his joke had meant putting off a rather desperate need for the loo. Standing at the far ends of three urinals were two young men, leaving the middle one free between them. They'd been talking as Mike entered, and by the rhythm of their voices they sounded to Mike like friends, but they stopped mid-sentence as he opened the door. They both glanced at Mike in unison, then turned back to continue in silence.

Mike paused near the door, caught in the headlights of a male conundrum, unsure whether to take the forbidden centre urinal or show weakness by skulking into the sole enclosed toilet. His decision was made for him as both men finished at the same time and walked to the sinks, the taller one taking a long look at Mike as he did so. Mike took the far urinal, abiding by the unspoken toilet etiquette, and the two lads carried on talking, apparently continuing their previous conversation, albeit more quietly.

'So yeah, seriously good.'

'Yeah, is it?'

'Yeah, man. Like… proper strong, and I mean proper strong, yeah?'

It was fairly banal, but something about the way they were trying to talk at not much above a whisper piqued Mike's interest, and as much through professional habit as anything else, he strained hard to listen to them while appearing to concentrate fully on the task in hand.

'So TJ said it was, like, pink an' that? Like actually more pink than green?'

'Yeah, bruv! It's well weird. But fuck me, TJ basically passed out, y'know? TJ an' all, too! He's usually a monster!'

Mike finished his business and turned towards the sinks just as the boys were leaving.

'E're, mate,' said Mike, trying his best to sound 23 rather than 33 and a little more street than is usual for a detective constable. The two men stopped at the door and gave Mike a cautious look up and down in silence, but didn't immediately make to leave.

'Yeah, I was jus' wondering, yeah? You don't know where I could get some of that weed from, yeah? It sounds like just the sort of thing I really like. I like it strong, y'know, and there's nuffin decent around these days.'

The two men looked at Mike carefully, then turned to each other in silence as if to compare notes mentally and decide whether he was trustworthy or not.

Back in his car, Mike pulled out his mobile and tapped the screen a few times until he had the right number. It rang only twice before a gruff voice came on. 'Mike?'

'Evening, Guv, sorry to call so late.'

'What is it?' said Phil in a flat voice, conveying neither urgency nor annoyance.

'Well, it's just that drugs bust the other day. You said it was supposed to be some mega skunk or something, and a funny colour, and to keep my ears open? Well, I think I've got a name for you.'

Chapter 12

The Top Gear School of Motoring was open for business as usual, but was not having a particularly busy afternoon. This was also usual. Its sole employee, 'Learner' Joe Maloney, was hunched over his desk with his face close to the desk fan, playing a game on his phone that involved matching pairs of similar items. He stabbed repeatedly at the screen, pairing off objects against the clock, and when he'd successfully cleared the deck with 14 seconds to spare, a fanfare of trumpets and an explosion of confetti announced his new high score before three glowing and desperately bulging treasure chests materialised with a cartoonish popping sound. Joe tapped on each in turn with one fast and fluid movement, and they exploded with a palpable, almost sexual, relief to reveal 1000 bonus points, 3 extra diamonds, and the addition of wellington boots to the panoply of items that he could now be expected to match. With an aural barrage of something that might have been cannon fire, an animated pirate slid onto the screen to announce with barely contained glee that Joe had now completed an unbroken winning streak of 167 games. The pirate's gold tooth and cutlass both glinted as he slid back out of view, and the screen was taken over by an advert for a game that involved making sandwiches in commercial quantities.

Joe pushed the phone away from him with a tut and sat back to survey his premises. It didn't take an awful lot of effort, surveying-wise. His desk ran almost the full width of the room, allowing him just enough of a gap to squeeze his considerable bulk behind it. It was often joked by friends and customers alike that the world's smallest office seemed at odds with an occupant of such an opposing scale. He attributed his size to a variety of factors, depending on the dimension being measured: his height he got from his father, his width he got from the gym, and his girth he got mainly from cake.

Two plastic chairs sat emptily in front of his desk, and behind these was just enough room for the door to open unimpeded, but not much more.

He was grateful at least for the window, which offered a pleasing view of the middle section of a small-leaved lime tree that was planted just outside the fried chicken shop downstairs. His window being quite small and the tree being quite large unfortunately meant that he could see nothing at all except tree for much of the year, though he didn't mind this. He enjoyed watching the branches swaying gently in the breeze, and the birds hopping around, and it was a mild disappointment for him when autumn came each year and stripped away the greenery, leaving him instead with a view of wiry, bare branches and a dismal rooftop of aerials and satellite dishes across the road.

The plus side to the tree losing its leaves was that he could pick up Radio 4 again, and he'd fire up the ancient Roberts device that he moved from his drawer to the windowsill each autumn. Although most people wouldn't guess to look at him, Joe was an ardent devotee of The Archers, and it was a guilty and closely guarded secret of his that he followed the goings-on in Ambridge religiously, albeit only from October to April.

The fact that his window didn't open added a further problem in the summer months, and he tended to roast slowly in his little office, the only fresh air coming from a vent in the wall that was then blown into his face by the tiny portable fan. He kept the door wedged open on days like this when he wasn't out and about.

Despite the office being old and drab, Joe took great care to ensure it was always spotless, particularly the window, so he could look out at the lime tree with an unimpeded view. As soon as there was any kind of noticeable smudge on it, he would take the bottle of supermarket own-brand window cleaner and cloth from his desk drawer and give it a quick going over until it was perfect again.

He stood up and edged around his desk, then rested a large palm on either side of the window and let himself lean forward to watch the pavement below. It was averagely busy for a Wednesday morning, and trade was slowly picking up for the chicken takeaway as the day crept lazily towards lunchtime, but nobody rang on the door to the side of the shop that led to his staircase and the opportunities afforded in the realm of automotive tutelage by the Top Gear School of Motoring.

This neither surprised nor bothered Joe one bit. His office didn't exactly attract much casual footfall and existed more for tax reasons than marketing. He found that almost all of his business came from word-of-mouth, which was to say that both of his current students had come recommended by two of his previous nine students. This meant that he was gainfully employed for two hours a week, which he found left ample time for his hobbies, such as sitting in his office playing on his phone and fulfilling the duties of his primary job, which was selling weed. In fact, although he'd started the driving school as an attempt to get a proper job and run a legitimate business, the outfit only really existed these days as a front for drug selling, and he found that financial matters such as banking and tax were so much simpler when you ran a loss-making business. It even meant he could buy a car through the company which he almost exclusively used to drive to clients in order to sell them weed. It was old and shitty, but as long as it had a large, plastic, Toblerone-shaped roof ornament advertising his business, he was pretty much free to do what he wanted.

Not that he made much effort with his weed business either, mind you. He was pretty uncommitted to that too, but it had slowly blossomed from an occasional way to earn a few bob from friends to a fairly regular concern and, eventually, his main source of income. He'd buy a pound at a time from his usual supplier, bag it all up into nice little portions and then spend the next few weeks dropping them round to his regulars. From time to time, when business was slow, he'd sell to strangers in pubs and clubs, but he generally tried to avoid this and sold almost exclusively to clients he knew pretty well and had dealt with for a long time. This kept the risks to a minimum, he felt, and made the whole thing a little less tacky.

Business had rather been on the up over the last few days though, and the strange, pink weed he'd bought from Waffle was selling like hotcakes. He'd initially sold the usual small bags to two or three of his other regulars, but all of these had got back to him within the day to order more and in larger quantities, and his mobile had been ringing several times a day from people he didn't know directly, but had been recommended to him by his regulars. It was all rather exciting. He was nearly a third of the way through the pound he'd bought already, and would be needing to go back to Waffle to persuade him to sell more within the week, he reckoned. Maybe this could be the start of something. Maybe he could finally make something of his life and become a proper drug dealer.

It seemed particularly odd that this breakthrough had come via Waffle too, one of his genuine friends. A friend, but also a longtime customer, and it seemed a strange reversal indeed that he was now buying supplies from one of his oldest and stoniest of his stoner customers.

Just as he was making a mental note to call Waffle again and discuss another sale, he was aware of a car pulling up outside and disgorging its two occupants. The car was uninteresting enough, a silver Vauxhall Corsa, but the two men who got out didn't seem like typical chicken shop customers. One was older, perhaps in his late fifties, and had a cigarette hanging out of his mouth, while his companion was a good twenty-five years his junior and fairly tall and athletic-looking. Joe watched with interest as they looked around themselves and consulted a phone before turning their gaze directly up to his window. They didn't come to the door though, and Joe relaxed for a moment, though only until he saw them walk up to his be-Tobleroned Nissan Micra and take rather too much interest in his number plate.

* * *

'COME IN,' shouted Joe, in response to the knock on his open door, while he shuffled some papers in front of him and flicked an imaginary piece of dust from his otherwise pristine desk.

The two men entered and looked around the office, though it didn't take long. The younger man walked towards Joe's desk with a polite smile and indicated the chair, while the older man stayed turned away, carefully studying a poster that listed the "Five Steps to Gaining a Driving Licence".

'Alright if I sit down?' asked the younger man, but he was already pulling the chair back as Joe nodded his assent.

'How can I help you, gentlemen?' Joe asked brightly, 'Are you both looking to learn, or is it perhaps a present for your son here?'

The younger man's expression stayed neutral as he watched Joe, but neither of the men said anything immediately.

'Mind if I smoke?' the second man said to the wall he was still facing before a long plume of minty fog appeared to emanate from his head and slowly filled the room.

Joe let his smile drop, and he took on a serious demeanour.

'Well, actually, it's been illegal to smoke in the workplace for well over a decade, not to mention the danger and discomfort it poses to other customers and students of mine who might well arrive at any moment.'

Joe looked at his watch to illustrate the point, and then picked out an empty Coke can from his waste bin, gave it a little shake to dislodge a bit of home-baked ginger cake, and placed it near the front edge of the desk as an offering. The man turned and came to sit in the remaining chair.

'Ah well,' he said sadly, looking longingly at his half-smoked cigarette, but instead of dropping it in the can, he merely placed it back in his mouth and took a long drag.

'Fuck all that though, eh?' he said as his squinting grey eyes stared through the smoke and bored into Joe's. 'I bet you enjoy the odd smoke yourself, don't you?' he asked without averting his gaze or blinking, and Joe's face took on an expression of mild disgust and he recoiled ever so slightly.

'I don't smoke, actually. Disgusting habit, I think.'

The man smiled without humour as he took a last drag to the edge of the filter, plucked the cigarette from his mouth and, without turning his head, casually flicked it towards the window, which it bounced off in a flash of sparks before coming to rest on the carpet.

'Shit, sorry about that. I genuinely thought that window was open,' he said with apparent surprise, and he strained to study the glass with some confusion as his colleague bent to pick up the glowing butt and deposited it with a faint sizzle in the Coke can.

Joe let out an audible sigh as he looked at the ash mark on the windowpane with horror, but said nothing.

'Look, do you want to book a lesson or not?' he said, with growing impatience, taking the Coke can from his desk, giving it a little shake and then dropping it back into his wastebasket.

'I'm DI Collins and this is DC Watts, and we wondered whether you could help us with something.'

Joe wracked his brain, genuinely unsure whether this was likely to be a drug matter, a problem with his driving school or something else entirely. He concentrated on hoping it was the last of these and kept his face neutral without too much effort.

'Well, I'm sure I can try,' he said, aiming to sound helpful. He stroked his moustache and twirled its ends a little, noting that it was finally at the stage where it could rightfully be described as "bushy". It wasn't exactly on-trend currently, but he enjoyed the Victorian strongman vibe it gave him. It wasn't something that the majority of ladies seemed to find attractive, but it was definitely a hit with a small minority he liked to think of as *retrosexual*.

DI Collins watched him closely for a good five seconds before saying anything, and then when he finally spoke, he did so without emotion or emphasis, but merely as if outlining some dull and straightforward facts that were well understood by all.

'You deal weed and you've got hold of a new batch recently. Three days ago at the latest. It's sort of pinkish and very strong, and we need to know where you got it from.' He tapped the fingers of both hands on the chair arms. 'That's it really, all pretty simple.' He sniffed casually and looked around the room, his eyes settling on the window once again with a slight frown. 'Give us a name and we'll be on our way.'

Joe pushed himself back from his desk, his face a picture of moral outrage, and he even found himself wagging a finger angrily in the general direction of the detective inspector.

'Well, that's preposterous! I've never heard anything more ridiculous in my life! This is a driving school, I give lessons!' He shook his reddened face from side to side in barely contained anger, like an old codger who'd just witnessed two women kissing in public.

'Ah yes,' said Phil calmly, as he got to his feet and looked out the window, 'the Top Gear School of Motoring. *Top Gear*, eh? As in quality drugs? Good joke, that, very clever. Like it a lot.'

Joe continued to shake with anger, though he gave an involuntary nod of the head in receipt of the compliment in between shaking.

'So,' said Phil, still gazing out the window, 'a name, please. And sooner rather than later, if you don't mind, we've got other things to be doing.'

Joe's mind was whirring away. How could this copper know so much? He certainly seemed very sure of himself and had all the facts to hand, even so far as knowing exactly when he'd picked up the weed. Probably came from one of his new customers, he thought with some anger; he knew he shouldn't have got greedy and tried to sell to a load of strangers. They have no loyalty. Goddammit!

'I can assure you, officer, I have absolu—'

'A name, please. Chop, chop. Give us the name and we'll get out of your hair. You can continue with your busy day, unmolested.'

Joe thought quickly. Maybe he should just come clean? It certainly seemed as if the police had no particular interest in him, and he was getting the distinct impression that his delaying tactics were starting to piss the old guy off a bit. But even if he wanted to, he couldn't drop Waffle in it, could he? It wasn't like he was just some random small-time drug dealer he didn't mind dropping in the shit. This was his actual good friend. And a lovely bloke too, eccentricities aside, not a bad bone in his body. He'd done nothing other than do Joe a favour, and for a knock-down price to boot.

Joe decided to change tack. He took a deep breath and calmed himself.

'Look... officer. I'd love to help you out here, I really would. But even if, for argument's sake, I knew what you were talking about, and I'd bought this... this stuff, then even so, hypothetically speaking, I wouldn't necessarily know the person's name, would I? I'd probably have bought this alleged bag of drugs, theoretically, from a stranger. In a notional car park, probably. In the dark.'

Phil still hadn't turned away from the window and was now craning his neck to study something down below.

'That red Micra down there. Yours, I assume? The one with Top Gear School of Motoring on it?'

Joe swallowed, and his eyes narrowed slightly. 'Yes, of course. So?'

'The registered owner, I assume?' Phil continued, conversationally.

'Yes, of course. It's in the company's name, actually. All above board.'

Phil nodded slowly, his head now tilted to one side as he continued to look outside.

'Bit odd though, wouldn't you say?'

Joe's eyelid twitched.

'What?'

'Well. Just you without a valid driving licence and everything.'

Phil pushed himself away from the window ledge and fixed Joe with a hard stare.

'You never having had a driving licence, in fact. Provisional issued in, what, two thousand and five?'

He turned to Mike, who spoke for the first time since sitting down.

'Four.'

'2004, my mistake. And even that only lasted a year, of course. So it looks a little like a man with no driving licence, or, we have to assume, a valid licence to teach driving, has a business here at the Top Gear.'

Joe swallowed again, this time more loudly.

'All a bit of a house of cards, really, isn't it? Seems like one word could bring it all crashing down and there'd be some pretty hefty penalties too, wouldn't you agree, Detective Constable?'

Mike grimaced. 'Would be pretty ugly, Guv, a right old mess.'

Phil nodded seriously. 'Custodial do you think?'

Mike looked to the ceiling, weighing it up. 'Distinct possibility, Guv. Would depend on the judge I guess. But I wouldn't be booking any holidays, that's for sure.'

Joe caught DI Collins' gaze with wide eyes and felt his heart beating under his damp shirt. Phil leant forward onto the desk with both hands, his smoky, minty breath in Joe's face and his flat, grey eyes unblinking.

'A name, please.'

'Darren Jones, 9a Jubilee Parade, above the shops on the Fishbourne Road Estate, SE11.'

Phil snorted lightly, and he stood up straight as DC Watts pushed his chair back. 'We'll see our own way out,' Phil said, already at the door, 'maybe you should think about taking your driving test, eh?'

He tapped at the third bullet point on the poster that was entitled "Now book your lessons!" 'You might have to give one of your competitors some business, but it'd probably be worth it in the end.'

He gave a humourless smile and followed his partner out of the office.

Chapter 13

'Oi! Harj!'

Waffle was standing next to the wall, looking up with his hand shading his eyes, and he knocked a couple of times on the aluminium ladder as if checking whether anyone was in. Harj looked down with annoyance etched into his face, but this was quickly transformed into a beaming smile when he recognised his visitor.

'Hey, Waffle! One sec, mate, I'm coming down.'

Waffle waited for Harj to secure his roller brush and descend the impressively long ladder with a rhythmic clanging. When he reached the ground, Harj rubbed both his hands down his overalls, gave Waffle a brief hug and then wiped his brow with his sleeve.

'Man, it's too hot to be working outside. I need to get me one of those computer jobs, with air conditioning and sexy secretaries.'

'Thought I'd find you here still,' said Waffle, looking up at the half-painted wall, 'how much more you got to do?'

Harj looked up and down the wall, weighing up an estimate in his head. 'Another few days maybe. It's been nearly two weeks so far and, to be honest with you, I'm pretty sick of it.'

'Maybe it's time you got an assistant. Or maybe you shouldn't have added "and Co." to your company name?'

Harj smiled. 'It just scanned better. But yeah, maybe I should start coming clean when I get offered contracts.'

'Well,' said Waffle, digging into his jacket pocket, 'I got you something. Got time for a break?' He pulled out a packet of Tangfastics and draped it across his arm as if presenting a diamond necklace.

'Now you're talking!' Harj looked at his watch. 'Come on then, I can spare ten minutes. I've not even had lunch.'

He took a bottle of water from his work bag and lowered himself onto the ground with his back sliding down the wall. Waffle sat next to him, pulled open the bag of sweets, and produced a can of Coke from his jacket.

'So,' said Harj, resting his head against the wall, and closing his eyes as he chewed, 'give me all the news, not seen you for a week, have I? What you been up to?'

'Yeah, good, man. Can't complain, y'know? I mean, it's had its up and downs, of course. Been a strange week as it goes.'

'Oh yeah? How so?'

Waffle looked down at the Haribo for a moment as he smiled to himself, then alternated frowning and smiling as if trying to work out whether to say something or not. He didn't look at Harj as he spoke.

'Well, thing is...' he took his hat off, scratched his head and replaced it. 'Thing is... Nat's left me.'

Harj lifted his head from the wall. 'What? When??'

'Friday.' He took a swig of Coke, still not catching Harj's eye. 'Maybe Thursday, technically, guess it depends how you count it. I mean, she said she was going on Thursday but I didn't think she was serious, and she left early for work, but was gone when I got back later.' He affected a TV newscaster voice and wobbled his head as he continued. 'Police say she disappeared at some point between 2 am and 11 pm and are appealing for witnesses.'

Harj reached into the bag for another chewy sweet. 'Oh fuck, Waffle, that's fucking shit, mate. I'm sorry to hear that. Has she gone for good, d'yer think? Did she leave any stuff of hers or anything?'

'Not really. Washing machine.'

'Ah. Right,' Harj said, grimacing slightly. 'You should've called me, I'd have come round, been a shoulder to cry on. We could've made a proper night of it, y'know, got really wrecked!' He picked up his water bottle and proffered it for Waffle to clink against. 'Fuck 'em, yeah? Can't live with 'em, can't live with 'em.'

Waffle took a deep breath and picked up his can somewhat reluctantly and tapped it against Harj's bottle.

'I just needed a bit of space. Bit of time on me own to chill out and, I dunno, do nothing. Listen to a bit of music, not watch the telly. Y'know.'

'Yeah, of course, of course. You do what you gotta do. Still, it's good to see you, and just shout whenever you like and I'll come over. I got some blinding Moroccan hash on Saturday, I'll bring that round... I think you'll approve!' He leaned back and took a long glug of water.

Waffle raised his eyebrows to himself as he toyed with his can. 'Yeah, well, maybe not exactly that. I've given up smoking, I think.'

Harj didn't specifically choke on his water, but a fair amount came out of his nose as he lurched forward. He slammed the bottle down and wiped his face with the back of his sleeve, unsure whether to swallow the water or just spit the rest of it out in order to breathe properly again.

'Shit! Fuck. You've done what? You've given up... you've done what?' he repeated, uselessly.

Waffle turned to face him for the first time since they'd started talking, and tried to muster up a bit more energy, as he was aware now of sounding a little downtrodden and whiny.

'Yeah, man. It's no big deal. I know it pissed Nat off, and then she actually pissed off in the end. Plus it's for the best. I can't spend the rest of my life getting stoned every night and living off takeaways. I'm gonna sort myself out a bit, straighten up, y'know?'

Harj was watching him as if he'd just started talking in fluent Russian, his eyes somehow managing to widen and squint at the same time. 'Yeah?' was all he managed to say.

'Yeah,' Waffle said with as much positivity as he could muster. 'I'm gonna get her back, man. And when she comes back, she needs to see a better me, or else I'll just blow my last chance. So I'm gonna change. I'm on a mission.'

Harj was nodding slowly, trying to take everything in. 'And you think she will come back then?' he asked, not sounding entirely convinced.

Waffle sat up straight and pushed his chest out a little in defiance. 'Of course. She has to. If nothing else, she has to pick up her–'

'Washing machine?' Harj finished for him, the conviction still missing from his voice.

'Yes,' said Waffle with some force, looking Harj in the eye, 'her washing machine. It's not even a shit one. Stays where it's supposed to be and everything.'

Harj raised his eyebrows as he looked away, but said nothing.

'She'll be back,' continued Waffle, almost to himself, 'she has to.'

They both sipped their drinks in silence for a little while. Waffle started idly reading the blurb on the back of the Haribo packet.

'How long do you think it'll be before she...'

'About three weeks, I reckon. I've worked it out.'

Harj mouthed a kind of 'Ah' sound with a gentle nod and picked through the bag of chewy sweets until he found a crocodile.

'So, what's next then? What are you gonna do for the next... three weeks until she comes back? Do you have, like, a schedule for this mission to transform into Waffle Jones Mark 2?'

Waffle ignored the note of sarcasm in Harj's tone.

'Well, kind of, yeah. First, I'm gonna give up the weed. And, roughly speaking, I've done that bit already, give or take. Then, I'm gonna stop ordering takeaways — I'm gonna start shopping for proper food and I'll cook it myself. Good, nutritious, healthy, home-cooked food.'

Harj was now looking at Waffle sideways and grinning widely.

'Well, home-cooked food anyway. I'm not incapable. I can do a mean chilli and I'm sure I can rise to the challenge of a few stir fries and maybe even the odd salad. I mean, it's just a few specific items on a plate with some peppery green leaves, it's not rocket science.'

Harj was now the picture of incredulity.

'You may mock, young man, but I'm a man of my words and a man of action!'

'Uh huh.'

'And then, a job. I mean, I've got a job already, but I've not been to it much. I really must sort that out, but I'll have to say I've been ill or something. Either way, I'm gonna knuckle down and stick at it, work hard and start getting some regular money in. When Nat comes back, I'm gonna be a breadwinner, contributing to the household in a meaningful way.'

'Buying the salad items?'

'Exactly that!' said Waffle through a mouthful of Coke. 'Exactly that.'

'And this all starts now, does it? You've got a job, you say, and you're back to it in the morning? What is it?'

'Well, it's nothing much, it's nothing major. Just cleaning up at the hospital. But it's something. It pays, and it's regular and it'll do me good. And yes, I'll try and get back to it very soon. I just need to get my head back together a bit, y'know? I sort of need a couple more days. It's been a strange week.'

'So you said. Maybe you should do some exercise? Maybe go for a long bike ride or take up yoga, or some shit like that. Clear your mind.'

'Yoga?' Waffle screwed up his face at the suggestion and Harj looked defensive.

'Well, I dunno. Not necessarily yoga. My sister does it, that's all, says it helps her when she's stressed, it relaxes her. But could be anything. Just maybe something physical and a bit different and maybe a change of scenery, y'know?' He looked around him. 'Get out of this dump for a while.'

'Yeah, maybe.' Waffle took in a deep breath and drained his can. 'I think you're right about a change of scene, though. I've not spent a night away from my flat for about... five years I think. Not deliberately, anyway. I mean, somewhere where you actually plan to take your toothbrush with you.'

Harj too emptied his bottle and threw it into his bag. 'Well, maybe you should give it some thought anyway, might do you good.'

Harj looked at his watch. 'Right, better get back to it, mate. Sorry I haven't got longer to chat, but this wall won't paint itself. Unfortunately.' He pulled him up to a standing position and arched his back in a lengthy and noisy stretch.

Waffle stood up too, and they shook hands. 'No problem, my man, you climb that corporate ladder. Anyway, I've got things to do, I need to get a bit of food in for a start. I can get some basics at Mr K's for now, I'll do a proper shop later.'

He watched as Harj took hold of the ladder with both hands and started his way back up to continue his work. 'You've missed a bit!' he shouted up as Harj was nearing the top, but Harj just gave him the middle finger without turning or stopping.

Chapter 14

The sun had finally dipped lazily below the horizon, and as the reddy-orange light was washed from the sky, it became replaced by the sodium glow of street lamps, the backlit red and white hoardings above the chicken shops and pizza places, and the occasional red and blue animated LED sign advertising kebabs within.

Being a Tuesday, even St James Road was fairly quiet at this time. The buses regularly disgorged workers late home from offices, shops and industrial estates, and the large Pricecutter late-night convenience store was bleeding an eye-scorching white light onto the pavement along its length and making a kind of reality TV show of its patrons inside for anyone so inclined to stop and watch. Assuming, of course, that anyone was interested in watching lone individuals reading the ingredients and prices on the packaged ready meals, selecting packets of cereal, tea or biscuits, or perusing the discounts on six-packs of lager. Nobody much was, apart from Roger and his dog Scamp who were nestled together on a blanket on the opposite pavement, sharing the remains of a cheese sandwich, and even they preferred to watch the traffic or dip into the worn and tatty copy of *Zen and the Art of Motorcycle Maintenance* that they'd been reading together during the evenings.

Crawling past the Pricecutter at this moment was a red 3 Series of indistinct vintage which slowed as it passed and then pulled up at the beeping pedestrian crossing to let a small knot of people past who'd just alighted from the number 461 bus. Sitting a little closer to the ground than the gods of BMW had originally intended, it looked sleek and mildly ominous as it idled its straight-six burble through enlarged twin exhaust pipes, hinting at a turn of speed that, while objectively impressive enough, couldn't match the promise made by the post-purchase addition of 'M3' badges on the front grille and rear boot lid.

Tommo eyed the digital clock on the dashboard and was still watching as it flicked from 8:59 to 9:00.

'OK, ring round again.'

Playboy turned over the mobile that was already in his hand, swiped across the screen and made a series of quick taps before lifting it to his ear.

'Alright, Lenny... anything?' A brief pause, and then Playboy turned to Tommo while covering the phone's mic with his hand. 'He says he's hungry. Says he hasn't had anything since before five and wants a burger.'

Tommo raised his chin and tightened his jaw, but didn't take his eyes off the road in front of him.

'Tell him to get some crisps from the bar. Tell him to get as many packs as he likes. Tell him to enjoy himself.'

Playboy nodded and started to lift the phone back to his ear.

'Oh, and also,' continued Tommo in the same flat tone, 'could you maybe ask him about the reason he's fucking there in the first place, please? Like, what's changed from before... anyone new come in? Any lanky white boys in green hats at all?'

Playboy cleared his throat and spoke into the phone. 'Um, yeah, Tommo says to hold off on the burger and gets some snacks from the bar, yeah? And what's the update? Seen anything?'

He nodded in silence a couple of times as he listened. 'OK. Safe, bruv,' he said and hung up.

Tommo raised his eyebrows in expectation.

'Nah, nuffin. He says it's quiet still. Few old codgers drinking their pints, couple of posh blokes playing pool and an old couple who've been there since he arrived but haven't even looked at each other yet, let alone spoken. He reckons he's standing out a bit on his own, just playing the fruity and eating crisps.'

Tommo considered this for a moment. 'Yeah, well. Will be a

complete change of scene for him tomorrow night, the lucky bastard. He'll be in the Gunnery and Soapy can take the Wessex. Also, and I know this for a fact, the Gunnery do Scampi Fries, so he'll be sorted for dinner.'

Playboy smiled and tapped again at his phone.

'D, it's us. What's the score?... Uh huh... yeah? Is it? No way, seriously?' His voice rose significantly in pitch and Tommo wrenched the car into a space at the side of the road with a jerk of the wheel and came to a stop inches behind a parked Fiesta with a screech of tyres.

'What it is? Tell me now.'

'Hang on D...' Playboy turned to Tommo. 'Nah man, it's nuffin... D was just saying that there was nearly a fight, that's all.'

'Nearly a fight? You serious?'

'Yeah, but it calmed down.'

Tommo looked at him levelly for a moment and then snatched the phone from his hand.

'D, it's Tommo. Now listen. Has there, or has there not been anyone in that might be our man? Yeah, so I heard and I don't give a shit. All I want to know is, were either of them wearing a green hat at the time, or looking tall and skinny, or maybe lugging a large, black holdall of drugs around? No? Then get back to it and ring me if anything important happens.'

He stabbed the phone into silence and passed it back, breathing heavily as he gripped the steering wheel tightly with both hands.

'C'mon, man,' said Playboy, soothingly, 'it's early days. We've only been looking for one day, it might take a bit more time.'

Tommo tapped the palm of his hand steadily against the steering wheel in silent contemplation, then took a deep breath and exhaled slowly.

'Yeah, I know,' he said finally, 'you might be right, but I just wanna act fast and get this thing sorted. It sorta feels like it might be slipping away from us, y'know? Like, the longer we have to wait, the less chance there is of finding it.'

He leant back into his seat and turned the engine off, then began to massage his temples.

'I know, man, and I know you're anxious an' all that, but I don't think we have to worry. It's like you said, the man's probably local and he doesn't know we're onto him. He might just be taking it easy and carrying on like nuffin's happened. So, y'know, we just need to be... patient.'

Tommo continued to rub at his temples, his eyes shut.

'It's like that Attenborough thing, innit?'

Tommo stopped rubbing for a second and then continued as before, his voice calm and level.

'What Attenborough thing, Playboy? What the fuck are you talking about?'

Playboy shuffled in his seat to face him, warming to his subject.

'Well, I watched this thing the other night, yeah? Like a nature thing an' that. They had these tigers out in Africa or some shit, and were following them around with cameras everywhere. It was mad, they had all this aerial stuff, watching them hunt from the sky with drones and shit, it was mental!'

Tommo was shaking his head. 'No, you're wrong.'

'Huh? Not drones? Do they use helicopters then? Aren't they really noisy?'

'No. I mean it's tigers OR Africa, not both. Tigers live in Asia, not Africa. So it was either tigers in India or Russia or somewhere, or it was Africa but with lions, or cheetahs or whatever. Not tigers AND Africa.'

Playboy sat in silence for a moment, brow lightly furrowed in thought. 'Right, yeah. Well India or wherever then. It was definitely tigers. They're the stripy fuckers, yeah?'

'Yes, Playboy. Tigers are indeed the stripy fuckers.'

'Yeah. So, anyway, they're following these tigers and watching them as they hunt... whatever they hunt in India.'

'Probably a deer of some kind, or a wild boar maybe. Maybe even a water buffalo if they're big enough.'

Playboy was caught in between annoyance at being interrupted, and respect for Tommo's natural history knowledge. 'How do you know so much about tigers, anyway?'

'Well, Playboy, as it happens I also own a TV. I don't even watch it much these days, but if it's on then I concentrate a bit. It's not much to ask.'

'Right. Yeah, OK. Anyway, the point is that tigers don't rush it. They see their prey and then they take all the time in the world. They're hidden, see? In the long grass or the forest or wherever.'

'Probably the forest.'

'OK, yeah, it was a forest. And the thing is that whatever they're hunting doesn't know it's there, so it's not worried. Well, not too worried anyway, like, the same as usual, I suppose. I mean, they live in a forest with a fucking tiger. But you know what I mean.'

'I do, Playboy, amazingly.'

'Right. So, the tiger's just chillin' out of sight. He knows if he moves too early, or makes too much noise or starts running from too far away, then he might lose his prey, yeah? But he's chill. He's cool as. He just waits it out, creeping closer and closer. And then, just when the... thing?... it was like a pig I think?'

'Wild boar.'

'Yeah, wild boar is busy eating or drinking water or some shit, then bam! Mr Tiger comes out of nowhere like a fucking Exocet missile and has his teeth around the poor bastard's neck before you can say, "Would you like a can of Whiskas?" It was mental, man. Gotta respect the tiger.'

Tommo contemplated this for a moment. 'There is a big difference here, though, isn't there?'

'We're not tigers?'

'Oh, we're fucking tigers all right. We're the kings of the fucking jungle, Playboy, we're the jungle VIPs. No, the difference is that your Mr Tiger had already found his prey and was just waiting to pounce. Our problem is that we're sat in this car holding our dicks while Lenny, D and Soapy are wandering blindly around the pubs hoping to catch sight of a lesser spotted wild boar in a green hat. And that's a rare sight around here.'

Playboy looked out of his window, eyes following the rear of a young lady in a short skirt as she walked past the car with her ear to her phone.

'Yeah, maybe. But still, the point's the same. The tiger doesn't go running around the place, noisily looking for prey either. He lies still and silent and waits for the prey to come to him.'

Tommo snorted, but said nothing.

'Oh, and the jungle VIP is King Louie, the big monkey, by the way. Not a tiger.'

Tommo raised his eyebrows in silent respect.

'See? I do sometimes listen properly when I watch TV.'

'Yeah. When it's a kid's film. Now, get on the phone and call Soapy. Let's hear what that useless prick has to say for himself.'

Playboy raised his phone, but as he did so it started ringing, and the sound of Drake's *Hotline Bling* filled the cabin of the BMW.

'Huh, it's Soapy. He beat me to it.' *Tap.* 'Yes, Soapy, what's the news?'

Tommo let his gaze drift lazily at the passing traffic, curious as to what Soapy had to say, but highly doubtful it would be anything of value. He'd allocated him to the Anchor, which was the longest shot of the three local pubs as it was the furthest from Clairmont Avenue, the last sighting of the mystery man. Plus, time was getting on, and it seemed a little late to start getting new information on a Tuesday. Plus, it was Soapy, and, well, he was Soapy.

'Woah, slow down, slow down! Say that again....'

Tommo was suddenly alert, swinging round to catch Playboy's wide eyes as he barked into the phone.

'He what? Are you sure? Hundred percent? A green hat, you sure? And he what? A large what?'

Tommo didn't wait to hear any more but had already started the car and flung it several feet in reverse before standing on the brakes, slamming it into first and entering the flow of traffic without even looking, a cacophony of screaming engine, tyre squeal and car horn providing the soundtrack as a black cab swerved out of the way and nearly drove into the front of an oncoming bus. He could hear more conversation from the seat next to him but was too focused now to take it in, his concentration saturated with visualising the quickest route to the pub from his current position. He rammed the car into third and managed to hit nearly 60 just before locking up the wheels in a gut-wrenching and smoky slide towards the back of a line of stationary traffic up ahead, just letting off the brakes in time to negotiate a sharp and violent left turn into a narrow side street.

Playboy didn't voice any concerns, but he failed to stop certain terrified gurgling sounds from escaping his throat, and his face was a picture of wild-eyed fear as he groped manically for something to grab onto.

'So,' said Tommo in a clipped voice as he swerved to avoid a parked car and crashed into the opposite kerb with the slewing rear tyre, 'what did he say?'

Playboy swallowed, hard. 'Er... he said he saw a man with a green hat leaving the boozer and...'

'LEAVING the boozer?! Fuck!' Tommo gunned the engine harder still and hit a speed hump flat out in second, causing both men to leave their seats temporarily as all four wheels left the tarmac in unison. The fleeting smoothness and quietness of the short flight gave a brief respite to the sensory overload, but in no time at all they came crashing back to earth in both a metaphorical and a very physical sense.

'Fuck!' they both wheezed breathlessly as they were forced down hard into their seats, and a half-full Coke can that had been stowed safely in the cup holder bounced free from captivity and set off to seek its fortune somewhere in the rear of the car, splashing Playboy a gentle farewell as it went.

'Yeah, er... he said he was leaving the boozer alone and had a large bag with him...' They lurched around another corner, this time both left-hand wheels striking the outer kerb as Tommo fought for control in the tight residential street. '... but that there was no rush.'

'No rush?! Why not?! Has he knocked him out or something?'

There was a short pause, filled only with a sort of quivering, ghost-like murmur from Playboy.

'Er... no, I don't think so. Actually, I added that bit myself.'

Tommo glanced quickly at Playboy with his face scrunched up in disgust, but said nothing as he straightened the car up and headed towards a set of width-restriction bollards at a significant pace. Playboy balled both hands tightly into fists and brought them to the side of his face as his knees jerked upwards and together subconsciously, trying to make his entire body as narrow as possible. They passed between the bollards with a whoosh and a sharp clanging sound, but no critical damage. Tommo had never been a big believer in wing mirrors, anyway.

There was one more short straight weaving between parked cars and a final screeching corner and then the pub was in sight around 100 yards into the distance. Tommo picked up speed but then suddenly slammed on the brakes as Soapy leapt rather bravely into the road, the headlights reflecting brightly off the stripes on his tracksuit top as he waved his arms wildly in the air. The car slid in a rather graceful, shallow arc, coming to a halt in a cloud of blueish tyre smoke a mere three feet from where Soapy was standing. Keen to get out and give chase, but also reluctant to ruin the rather stylish arrival, Tommo merely pressed the window button and waited patiently for the whirring motor to slide the glass partition down from between his and Soapy's alarmed face.

'Where?' he said, succinctly.

'Over there, bruv!' Soapy gabbled excitedly, gesticulating vaguely into the darkness beyond the streetlights. 'He went past that tree and into that little park. I had my eyes on him until you got here, honest, but he's just out of sight now. There's about 50 yards before the houses on the other side!'

Tommo and Playboy both leapt out of the car, not even bothering to shut the doors, and all three raced off the road, vaulted a low barrier that separated the pavement from the grass and sprinted into the relative blackness. Their eyes adjusted quickly once the lights were behind them, and up ahead they could see a lone figure walking away from them, one hand in a pocket and the other hanging down at the side, clutching a bag. Playboy pulled ahead of the other two, his honed athleticism and more specialised running shoes giving him both speed and traction.

The gap was now closing quickly enough that they all knew they'd be onto their prey in a matter of seconds. The only sound was the drumming of six feet on dried grass, but even this gave them away and the figure ahead slowed as he turned with curiosity, then almost leapt into the air with alarm as he took in the three silhouetted forms bearing down on him with terrifying speed. He let out a gasp as he turned to run, but it was too late. Playboy threw himself into the air and reached the man with arms outstretched, the momentum carrying them both to the ground with a dry thud. Tommo and Soapy arrived as one, and both dived to the writhing bodies on the ground, trying to grab hold of an arm each to pin down, but Playboy's weight was fully upon the man's chest and he had no chance of escape now.

'You bastard!' spat Tommo as he grabbed his phone from his pocket and fumbled with it in one hand, trying in vain to get the torch function to work. 'Fucking *Control Centre*,' he mumbled angrily under his breath, 'sure it was always swipe up before.' Finally, the phone shot out a beam of light directly into the man's eyes, and unable to shield his gaze with his restrained arms, he tried to turn his face away from the light in vain with a muffled cry.

For several seconds nobody spoke, the only sound a sinuous, echoing wail from a far distant siren.

'Soapy. Talk me through this,' said Tommo in a calm, measured voice.

'Well,' said Soapy, with an audible lack of assertiveness, 'he's a bloke with a green hat on. And, and he's got a bag! Look!'

Tommo shone the torch across the ground to where the bag had fallen, and then back to the man's face before standing up and waving the light from head to foot and back again, like he was scanning a giant bar code.

'Well,' said Tommo again, 'I mean, I've never seen the man, so I'm not really in a position to say, am I? Playboy... have a good look. Is this our man?'

Playboy lifted some of his weight from the man's chest to get a better look, though didn't release him fully. The man exhaled sharply as he regained the ability to breathe again.

'No, man,' said Playboy slowly, 'it's not him. Definitely.'

Playboy stood up and Soapy followed, leaving the man still lying on the grass, a look of wounded pride, anger and fear in his eyes.

'That's a nice tie, Grandad. Very smart.'

The man eyed Tommo with suspicion and then spoke in a clear, strong voice. 'Royal Marines, son. Four-Two Commando, if you must know. 1963 to '72. Before you was even born.'

Tommo moved the light past the man's face until it glinted on the badge pinned to the front of his beret. He kissed his teeth and glared at Soapy for several full seconds with eyes burning, then reached down and offered his hand to the old man who hesitated but then accepted. Playboy leapt forward and took his other arm and they carefully brought him upright, like a fallen flagpole. Soapy collected the supermarket carrier bag from the ground and handed it to Tommo with a wince. Tommo took a brief look inside, recognising a couple of cans of Guinness and some dog food amongst a few other sundries, and handed it over.

'You alright, man? Nothing broken or shit?'

The man took in a deep breath and raised himself to his full 5 foot 6 inches, and jutted his chin out as he spoke, never moving his eyes from Tommo's. 'I'm fine, no thanks to you. Now... if I may?' And with this, he held his palm out in the direction of the row of houses that lined the far edge of the patch of field. Tommo awkwardly brushed some grass from the man's sleeve, but it was pulled away as the man turned and began to walk stiffly off into the darkness. 'Pricks!' he shouted over his shoulder. 'Bloody animals!'

The three of them stood watching as he left, and when he was finally out of earshot, Tommo turned to Soapy, his jaw set tight and lips parted slightly, showing a glimpse of teeth. Soapy twitched, unsure whether he should make a run for it himself or stand his ground and take whatever was coming. Lacking the conviction to make any proactive move, he stayed where he was and tried to avoid Tommo's gaze instead.

'Soapy. Soapy, you... you... massive, fucking idiot.' Soapy said nothing and concentrated on a spot of bare, grassless earth near his feet. 'Soapy... I... just get in the back of the car. NOW!'

With this, Soapy jumped and then ran towards the BMW that was still straddling the middle of the road outside the pub, its front doors open and its headlights picking out a fox that was pawing at a black rubbish bag leant against a wheelie bin.

Chapter 15

'Just this, please,' said the man as he dropped a Mars Bar and some coins onto the counter. He turned to his companion. 'Anything for you, Mike? Protein bar? Rehydrating ionised sports water?'

Mike didn't turn from the magazine rack he was browsing. 'No thanks, Guv.'

Phil pocketed the change and then took the chocolate bar, but didn't make any move towards the door. Instead, he tore the top of the packaging open and took a bite, chewing noisily and making the odd gentle moan as he did so, all the while watching the shopkeeper who was, in turn, watching him eat with a barely disguised grimace.

The two stood for some time, eyeing each other in silence while Mike waited patiently and turned a page in a cycling magazine he'd picked up. When Phil had finally finished his mouthful, he swallowed extravagantly with widened eyes and put the rest of the Mars Bar in his pocket.

'Mmm, I do love a Mars Bar, I don't mind saying so. Filthy, I know, but a nice little treat from time to time, you know?'

Mr Kottarakkara continued to watch him in silence and was just wondering why they wouldn't leave.

'Still, a good way to get some nuts inside you, eh Mike? Full of antioxidants and vitamins and all that.'

Mike was engrossed in his magazine and didn't look up. 'No nuts in a Mars Bar. You're thinking of Snickers. Or Topics.'

Phil's face lit up in alarm, and he swung around to face Mike. 'No nuts? I thought that was the point of them? One of your five a day and all that?'

'No. Just fat and sugar. And nuts aren't one of your five a day, anyway.'

Phil let this sink in for a second. 'So what's a Snickers?'

'Marathon. They changed the name.'

Phil turned back to the shopkeeper with a pained expression that was evidently expected to be met with the kind of sympathy one normally affords to a man who'd just found out his family had all been killed, but Mr Kottarakkara was still eyeing him blankly.

'Would you like to buy anything else? We have nuts,' he said, nodding down an aisle, 'or Snickers.'

'No, thank you,' said Phil, clearing his throat. He reached into his jacket pocket to retrieve his notebook and ID. 'I wonder if you can help us, though. We're looking for a 9a Jubilee Parade. One of the flats above these shops, I believe.'

Mr Kottarakkara's eyes widened a little, but he stayed otherwise impassive. 9a? Yes, that's above this shop. I own it.'

'Ah, marvellous. Are you then a Mr…' Phil checked his notebook again, 'Darren Jones?'

'No. I rent the flat out. Darren is my tenant.'

Phil gave a perfunctory nod as he put the things back in his jacket.

'What's he done then?' Mr Kottarakkara asked, with a mixture of surprise, lack of surprise, concern, curiosity, and dread. It was an odd mix, and a complicated one to decipher accurately.

'Oh, could be nothing. Just following some leads,' Phil said with a smile. 'Mind pointing us in the right direction?'

Mr Kottarakkara waited for a moment, then gave them the directions and watched them leave. He surprised himself by realising that his overriding feeling now was just the concern. Darren was a pain in the backside, and trying to get the rent out of him was a relentless job that he neither had the time for nor enjoyed, but much as it pained him to admit it, he was rather fond of the strange young man. Sure, the overfamiliarity irked him, the clothes and nickname were somewhere between childish and just plain odd, and he had to make a show of never rising to Darren's lame jokes or constant waving through the window, but when push came to shove, it was hard to dislike the kid.

After all, he was always in a good mood it seemed, and usually either whistling happily or smiling, and that was something to cherish in this world, Mr Kottarakkara thought with a sneer. Plus, he'd finally paid all his rent up to date, over £800 in one go; certainly the most he'd ever paid at one time, and possibly the first time he'd never been in debt.

It had occurred to him to wonder where the money had come from, but he was more interested in having his accounts settled than prying into another man's business. Darren had often mentioned money he was owed from various people, plus it seemed he was working again, at last, and Mr Kottarakkara had been at least as happy about that as Darren had been.

Still, he seemed an honest sort when it all came down to it. Lazy? Probably. Feckless? Almost certainly. Unreliable? Most definitely. But decent? Seemingly so, yes.

Mr Kottarakkara was a suspicious man by nature, something he was fully aware of but considered a quality rather than a negative. When you've worked in a late-night shop on a South London estate for as long as he had, it was a valuable asset. Casual shoplifting from shops like his was rife, and he'd long since learned that a default position of suspicion trumped any accumulated sixth sense. Sure, gangs of loud and cocky kids that eyed him cautiously and then went quiet when out of sight were easy enough to spot, but polite middle-aged men in suits weren't beyond stuffing the odd cheap bottle of booze under a jacket, especially when the evenings got later and the customers drunker.

His two daughters had dreaded the thought of introducing their father to boyfriends, and he'd delivered in spades when the time had come. It wasn't that he was particularly old-fashioned in his attitudes, and if anything had actively encouraged them to socialise widely and enjoy themselves, but he did insist on potential suitors being invited for dinner at the earliest opportunity where he could meet them and judge them. His standards were set high, and his base assumptions were set low, and dinner with the Kottarakkaras was very much in the good cop/bad cop vein for any young man who had aspirations of spending more time with one of his daughters. While Mrs Kottarakkara would smile kindly and ask earnest questions about hobbies while ladling endless food onto their plate, Mr Kottarakkara's line of enquiry was more focused on any previous criminal form or future expectations of having one.

It was many a young man who left the Kottarakkara's with beads of sweat on their foreheads, and it wasn't from the food.

One thing he did take pride in, though, was being able to adjust his assessment of someone if they were proven to rise above his expectations. Everyone started from zero in his book, but he was man enough to promote anyone that deserved it, and he took genuine pleasure in being wrong about someone. Darren Jones had been one of those people.

Even before Darren had enquired about renting the flat above the shop, Mr Kottarakkara knew his face. He didn't come in often, but there weren't many customers that wafted in wearing flip-flops, especially in winter, let alone combined with the various other rather unique items of clothing. Plus, he wasn't exactly the kind that came and went quietly, so by his second or third visit to the shop he was familiar to Mr Kottarakkara.

On one such occasion, he'd left with a cheery wave over his shoulder, but returned a few seconds later clutching a ten-pound note he said he'd found outside and assumed must belong to a previous customer.

Given Mr Kottarakkara's suspicious nature, his initial assumption was that this must be some kind of scam, and he frowned deeply at both Darren and the note for some time while he tried to work out the angle, but he eventually came to the conclusion that the strange young man's open expression and seeming concern for whoever had lost the money were genuine, if unusual. Darren had left again, whistling something cheerful, and Mr Kottarakkara was forced to concede that his previous assumption that the man was some kind of fruitcake, definitely up to no good and quite possibly dangerous, was seemingly wide of the mark. He even allowed his view of humanity to ratchet up by the tiniest notch.

Quite what was he expected to do with the money, he wasn't sure. He was pretty confident that a notice in the window would be met with scores of claimants reluctantly coming forwards with tales of woe and dropped tenners, so he left it in the till with a note attached for some time, but nobody ever asked for it. He even tried to return it to Darren the next time he saw him, but the gesture was met with some confusion and was waved away.

Mildly irritating though he found him, and potentially unreliable though he suspected him to be, he'd never have let his flat out to someone as strange as Darren Jones if it hadn't been for the incident with the money.

'Me again,' said a voice, snapping him back into the present, 'I'm afraid there's nobody home. Can I ask when you last saw Mr Jones?'

Mr Kottarakkara thought for a second. 'A couple of days ago, I suppose. Definitely not today, and not yesterday either, come to think of it.'

'You wouldn't... um... happen to have a key for the flat, would you?'

'A key? Yes, of course, but what for?'

'Well, sir, we were just wondering if you'd mind letting us in so we could check... that everything's alright.'

Mr Kottarakkara frowned. 'Is that legal? Don't you need a warrant?'

'Well, it's complicated. Normally, yes, but in certain circumstances, it's... y'know, OK.'

Mr Kottarakkara looked to the other policeman, but he was concentrating on the ceiling.

'And what are your reasons, if you don't mind me asking?'

'Well, sir, we'd just like to be sure that Mr Jones is definitely not in. I mean, that's he's definitely OK.'

'And how will you know if he's alright by me letting you into the flat if he's not there?'

DI Collins thought for a moment. 'Well. He probably isn't there. But what if he was and had just fallen over or something? I just think that while we're here we should go in and have a look round. For him.'

Mr Kottarakkara had watched enough episodes of *The Bill* to know that this wasn't the correct procedure, but a small seed of doubt had formed in his mind now. He hadn't seen Darren for two days after all, and this was unusual. And people did fall over, didn't they? Anyone could knock themselves unconscious, especially that useless fool who drank too much beer most nights. There was no harm in letting them have a quick look, Mr Kottarakkara supposed. He'd be there with them after all, he'd make sure everything was above board.

'Well, alright then. I'll go and get the keys. But I'll be watching you. And I'd like to see your ID again please, if you don't mind.'

* * *

Mr Kottarakkara led the two policemen through the passageway between the launderette and the chippy into the parking and bin area, up the open stairwell and onto the covered walkway that led to the flats above the shops. He turned left, unlocked the third door along and took a step back, gesturing inside. Phil went first, pushing the door open gently and walking in without delay but with a surprising lightness of feet that belied his middle-aged suit and middle-aged spread.

The flat was very warm, with summer sunlight streaming through the closed windows, and Mike loosened his tie as he followed his boss in.

Mr Kottarakkara stayed in the doorway, curious to have a look around the flat, but not so much that he was prepared to contravene his landlord's code of conduct. Instead, he watched the two men as they walked in different directions, covering the ground of the small flat quickly and quietly. After a few moments, they reconvened in the centre of the living room. 'Definitely not here, Guv,' said Mike. Phil nodded.

Mr Kottarakkara had stood in the doorway several times over the last couple of years as he discussed his need for the latest rent, usually in vain. But he'd rarely had an uninterrupted view in, as the space was usually filled by Darren's lanky frame, arms of seemingly unrealistic length hanging onto the top lintel as he leant forward to chat and make his excuses. The flat looked tidier than expected; the main living area looked almost clean, and there was no washing up to be seen on the draining board in the kitchen off to the side.

DI Collins put down the cactus he'd been looking at and strolled off towards the back of the room.

'What a prick,' he said to himself under his breath, 'Ha, like it a lot.' He reached the low cupboard door built into the wall and half-turned to Mr Kottarakkara who was still in the doorway.

'What's this?'

Mr Kottarakkara frowned. 'A storage cupboard. A small one. I very much doubt Darren has managed to get himself lost inside there, seeing as it's about two foot square.'

'To a great mind, nothing is little!' said Collins with a flourish. 'That's Sherlock Holmes, y'know.'

'Yes,' replied Mr Kottarakkara, 'and completely out of context. Plus, fictional. *Y'know.*'

DI Collins opened his mouth to respond but decided against it with a quick shake of his head. Instead, he reached out and took the cupboard handle in his hand. 'Always best to make sure.' He glanced over to Mr Kottarakkara 'That's DI Collins,' he said with a wink.

'Guv,' called Mike from the bedroom, 'in here.'

Collins let go of the handle and walked towards the open door, taking a cigarette out of his pocket on his way. He joined Mike, who was in the flat's only bedroom, a squarish room that was big enough to fit the double bed, but only just. The walls were of the kind of orange hue that was probably very on-trend in the 70s, but both its popularity and brightness had faded considerably since. It didn't matter much, as a large percentage of the walls were covered in posters, all related to either music or films. Bob Dylan, Miles Davis, Pink Floyd and The Godfather were the largest, with a few other smaller ones dotted around. Across from the window was a large space with a rectangular area of slightly deeper orange, and inside its four corners were hardened chunks of Blu Tack.

Phil held his cigarette in his mouth as he gently pulled open the old and tatty wardrobe, its mirrored front specked with various stickers around the edges from someone's childhood. Inside, only the left half was full, several shirts and loose woollen jumpers of various striking colours and patterns hanging from the rail, alongside some kind of old, military trench coat. The right side was completely bare aside from four coat hangers, hanging unencumbered and dispiritedly in the empty space.

Phil took a drag on his cigarette and turned to join Mike, who was still waiting for his attention. He nodded down to a laptop that was perched on the bedside table, jostling for position with a couple of empty beer cans, some loose change, three paperbacks in an untidy pile and a roll of toilet paper. There was also both a pencil and a few scraps of paper, Mike noticed for the first time, and he nodded slowly in appreciation.

The laptop was old and dated, but had clearly been low-end even when new. It was thick in a way that laptops tend not to be anymore, and its aged and dirty shell was of a cheap-looking plastic. It was, however, clearly working as it was both plugged in at the wall and glowing from the screen, Mike's fingertips were still holding the corner of its thick bezels to make clear that it was him that had shown the initiative to open the lid.

'Well done, DC Watts,' Phil said with a faint hint of sarcasm, 'did you guess the password too?'

Mike retrieved his hand somewhat awkwardly and let his gaze wander the room.

'Er, no. There wasn't one. It just came on.'

Phil moved closer and bent his knees to lower himself to the screen, peering forward, but straightened with a dissatisfied grunt and dropped his cigarette butt into one of the beer cans. He reached into his jacket and pulled out a brown leather case, from which he retrieved a pair of thick-framed reading glasses, all the while staring at DC Watts in a rather threatening manner, as if daring him to say anything. Phil slowly slid the glasses on, still eyeballing Mike the whole time, until he gave a little shake of the head and looked away, suddenly concentrating intently on the Bob Dylan poster.

Phil gave a little, satisfied nod, and then bent down again to study the screen. Internet Explorer was displaying a website called "Discount Yoga Retreats" that showed a logo of a sitting Buddha above a strapline that claimed "The Yogi Bare Minimum". The page was showing a list of search results for "London", ordered by ascending price. The first result, which took up the rest of the small screen, was for a business called The Yoga Lawn, which was improbably situated in one of East London's least lawn-filled areas. A photo showed a whitewashed room with a handful of people contorted into an awkward position that reminded Phil of a shitting dog, though he assumed from his very limited knowledge that it probably went by a more stirring name.

Underneath a brief description were a set of icons that announced it warranted a modest single pound sign out of a possible five, alongside three stars and a handful of reviews. There were a few other icons that Phil guessed indicated certain facilities, but these were mainly greyed out.

'Can you bring up an email program on this thing?'

'They're called "apps" these days, Phil. But sure.'

Phil moved aside to allow Mike to kneel down by the laptop. He tapped a few buttons and brought up an email inbox. The latest email was titled 'Booking confirmation,' so he clicked and opened the message.

'Booking confirmation for Darren Jones - The Yoga Lawn, Wednesday 12th August to Friday 14th August' ran the title, followed underneath by an address, travel directions and a few other details. Mike grinned and then stood, indicating the laptop to Phil, who pinched his trousers and pulled them up slightly as he crouched down again in front of the screen. He peered closer to read the address in more detail.

'Got a pen, Detective Constable?'

Mike picked up the pencil and paper from next to the laptop with a wry grin. 'Always, Guv. Shoot.'

Chapter 16

Waffle stood up for the last minute of the journey and held on to the pole for support as the tube train squealed loudly and rattled itself into the station. The last death throes of the carriage's motion ended abruptly, and Waffle allowed the momentum of the jolt to form the start of his swing towards the opening door, like an urban chimpanzee, timing the motion perfectly to synchronise with Ray Charles' backing band in the headphones of his ancient but beloved Sony Walkman. The platform was quiet; a few people were shuffling onto the waiting train, a few were shuffling off, and a small group of young men were just shuffling around generally with shouts of delight, loosely following one of their number who was pretending to hide something on his phone that he desperately wanted his friends to see.

The station was above ground, and despite it being early afternoon, the sky was grey and dark with the promise of rain that would soon puncture the chewy August air like a balloon. Waffle skipped up the concrete stairs, the slapping sound of his flip-flops echoing and merging with the distorted voice over the PA whose muffled appeal to report suspicious packages was recognisable only by its familiar rhythms. Once out of the station, he pulled out a sheet of paper from his jacket pocket to check his direction notes, scanning the roads in both directions to get his bearings. Satisfied, he replaced the paper and began a loping walk in time to his music.

The roads were initially lined by a mix of old Victorian terraces and squat, rectangular blocks of 1960s shops, but the streets began to narrow and wind as he moved further from the station and into an area that was clearly once more industrial. Wrought-iron gates still guarded some wide open yards, and tall paned windows shone into two-storey warehouses converted into modern business units, but these had mostly made way for modern, low-rise flats with bicycles and plastic children's toys stored in the narrow balconies.

He passed a large construction site on one side, the area protected by a temporary wooden wall marked with various company logos and health and safety warnings, as well as large computer renders of people relaxing on benches in landscaped public gardens, admiring their new block of flats. "1, 2 and 3-bedroom suites with city and park views," the bold text proudly informed him, "Phase one 80% sold!"

Over the wall and through the spidery scaffolding he could see two old gasholders in the near distance, their great iron pillars holding up giant latticework rings against the sky, like the burnt-out remains of enormous steampunk hamster wheels on their sides. Over his shoulder, he could still see the tight grouping of the Canary Wharf skyscrapers, glinting their glass and steel in the morning sun.

Coming out of a side street, the road opened up for a short stretch before bunching up under the railway. The tunnel walls were heavy with graffiti, both old and new, where amongst the many indecipherable tags and sketches, he learnt that Millwall are wankers, the government are scum and that Michelle's a slag. He moved off the pavement to avoid a patch that was strewn with the remains of several broken bottles – not something you take chances with in flip-flops – and as he emerged again under the heavy sky, he saw what he was looking for at the end of the road and bounded back onto the pavement with a spring in his step.

A last row of terrace houses petered out, to be replaced by overgrown verges and chain-link fences, but running across the end of the road was a small group of various businesses sitting on their own, backing onto open wasteground for several hundred yards behind them. One of these buildings was boarded up, but the others appeared to be operational, if not exactly in their prime, and situated between Ali's Kebabs and the literally named, though oddly formatted, 'second-

Hand furniture Shop' was the Mad Parrot Inn. Waffle stopped outside and pulled the headphones down onto his neck before self-consciously looking around him. He became aware that he was a little nervous, a realisation that surprised him, and for a brief moment, he considered turning back to the station and forgetting the whole thing. Was this a stupid idea? He thought for a second and decided that it probably was, but that it didn't matter. He was on a path to being a better person, and this was a step that could only help. Plus, it'd be nice to have a bit of a break from everything.

He took a deep breath, closed his eyes, and pushed the door open.

Inside the pub was a scene exactly as he'd expected: the landlord, a balding man with a belly that almost defied gravity, was leaning against the back of the bar while reading a newspaper, and three customers — all men in their fifties or sixties — were sitting at tables nursing their drinks in silence. Two of these men were occupying separate, but adjacent, tables where they could presumably converse if necessary, and the third was alone in the corner with a small dog curled at his feet.

All five of them looked up as Waffle entered, but only the landlord kept watching him for more than a second as the others almost immediately went back to staring at their drinks or licking their balls. Waffle walked towards the bar, thinking that perhaps he could get a swift pint in before going any further. He placed both hands on the bar and scanned the beers available on tap as he smacked his lips, but when he looked up at the landlord and opened his mouth to speak, he found the big man still staring down at him with newspaper held open. His expression wasn't what you'd describe as full of contempt; it was much more ambivalent than that, but it was perhaps 45 percent ambivalence and 55 percent contempt. He looked Waffle up and down slowly, a proper full-length appraisal straight out of a cowboy movie, and then flicked his head to the far corner of the room before bending back down to his open newspaper.

Waffle, still standing with mouth half-open in silence, turned in the direction of the nod and saw a sign above a door which contained an arrow and the words 'Yoga Lawn' in a font that was vaguely Eastern in style and contained a lotus flower above the letter 'g'. The sign itself was simply printed onto a sheet of A4 and pinned above the doorway, but it was at least laminated, which always gave signs a significant air of authority in Waffle's mind. Lamination was the official uniform of paper and could turn a merely informative request into a direct order, and in all weathers too.

The landlord was showing no signs of withdrawing from his newspaper and Waffle had no inclination to make an uncomfortable moment out of a merely awkward one, so he put his mouth back to where it was supposed to be and wandered off towards the door, heading on through as the sign dictated and up the stairs beyond.

After a couple of tight turns in the staircase, he came out into a narrow hallway which stretched on for twenty yards or so with a few closed doors on either side. The staircase continued back on itself for another floor, but there was a counter curving around in front of an alcove like a miniature version of the bar downstairs that was apparently the reception, so he leant on this and waited patiently. Behind the counter was a low desk, and this was empty aside from a large, closed book, a pen holder with a few assorted pens and pencils in, and a small tabletop gong, hanging in a red metal frame with a beater.

On the wall behind the desk was a series of small cubby holes, some of which contained post or keys, and above this was a sign made from individual wooden letters that were each mounted to the wall in an arc that read 'Welcome to the Yoga Law'. Dotted around the remaining wall space were various laminated printouts offering counsel that ranged from the profoundly sagacious ("If you don't bend, you break") to the strategically practical ("Fire meeting point is in front of Ali's Kebabs").

The sound of a door grinding slightly on the ground roused Waffle from his advice-based reverie, and a young woman appeared through the doorway behind the desk, frowning a little as the door failed to shut smoothly behind her, but then turning a faint smile towards Waffle. She was wearing leggings and a close-fitting but long t-shirt, her hair pulled into a tight ponytail that combined with her solemn expression to give her a very severe look, despite her youth.

'Good afternoon, young lady!' Waffle boomed, 'Nice place you got here, very nice!'

He stood grinning at her, expecting a reply, but she just looked at him coolly before wrinkling her nose. She pointed to one of the signs behind her, which Waffle dutifully read out loud.

'Silence is not silent. Silence speaks. It speaks most eloquently. Silence is not still.'

Waffle wasn't sure what to say next, given the context, so he just nodded slowly and whispered 'OK'. The woman continued to watch him closely, still not speaking, but with her head turned slightly as if challenging him to say something. Waffle leaned forward on the counter and re-read the notice to himself.

'Well,' he continued in a loud whisper, 'I'm not really sure if I'm supposed to say anything now. I mean, I know this is a yoga place an' that, but presumably I need to book in and give you my name, yeah? Plus…' he moved in closer to her while checking the coast was clear on either side of him, 'that sounds very nice and poetic, but I'm not entirely sure what it means. Like, I get the vibe and everything, but it's a bit… vague, isn't it?'

He watched her closely as her eyes narrowed, and he became convinced that this was going to be the shortest ever stay at a yoga retreat. She held his gaze for several seconds, then broke into a crooked smile with a soft giggle.

'Don't worry, I'm just messing with you,' she said in a gentle Scottish accent, and opened the large book on the desk, scanning down a list of entries with her finger.

'Ah, you got me there, hoo-hoo!' said Waffle with a deep sense of relief. 'I thought this place was gonna be like a monastery or something for a second there, ha ha!'

She looked up at him with a half smile, her head tilted a little. 'Well, it is supposed to be pretty quiet here, but no, it's not silent or anything weird like that. But maybe… y'know… somewhere in between?'

Waffle made a mental note to be less loud generally. 'Gotcha,' he said, tapping his nose and winking.

'Aye, you're right, though, it is sort of bollocks, that.' She looked up at the quote on the wall. 'I've just typed it out on a white sheet too, ideally it ought to be superimposed over a misty mountain scene or a breaching whale or something.'

'Yeah, but at least it's laminated,' said Waffle, with reverence.

'Oh yeah, big time. I bought a laminator recently and went a bit wild. Can you not tell?'

Waffle scanned the wall for a second, and counted twelve shiny A4 notices, not including the one above the door downstairs. 'Um... no. All seems legit. Very... official.'

'I know, right? If it's under a thin layer of plastic then you'd better obey!' She smiled. 'Well, apart from the silence thing. And, well, everything else really. It's all just friendly advice.'

Waffle motioned to the wooden letters arranged in an arc on the wall behind her. 'Still, *Yoga Law*, eh? Maybe that's taking it a bit seriously.'

She smiled and bent down to retrieve something from a low drawer, then reappeared brandishing a wooden letter 'n'.

'Fell off weeks ago... DIY is not my strong point!'

She went back to the guest book and picked up a pen, holding it above the list of names as she looked up at him expectantly. Waffle returned her gaze and smiled awkwardly before tapping his fingers on the edge of the desk as the silence started to lengthen.

'Um, name?' she said, with a hint of exasperation.

Waffle stared blankly for a second before snapping back into focus. 'Oh yeah, right! Er... Jones... Waffle Jones.'

She arched an eyebrow but said nothing, and scanned down the list, but shook her head slightly at the bottom of it and looked up at him again. 'I do have a *Darren* Jones, is that right?'

'Oh yeah, yeah,' said Waffle, reluctantly remembering the name he'd had to book under. 'That's just for banks, bookings and courts!'

She checked the time from her phone on the desk and then wrote it into the book next to his name.

'Right,' she said, snapping the lid back onto the pen with the palm of her hand, 'you're in room 4, which is just down the end of the corridor on your right. You can take your things down there and settle in. Bathroom's upstairs past the other rooms.'

Waffle followed her eyes as she looked down to his hands and then the floor by his feet, and then raised her brow questioningly.

'You don't have anything with you?' she asked with curious politeness. 'You are planning to stay for the full three days, though?'

Waffle looked down, sheepishly. 'Yeah, I like to travel light,' he said, fishing a toothbrush out of one of his trouser pockets and brandishing it with a lopsided grin. 'Plus, I didn't know what I was supposed to bring, y'know, yoga-wise. It's my first time.'

'OK, well, that's no problem,' she said, smiling, 'we have spare mats we can lend out and there's a towel on your bed. I'm sure I can find some soap and shampoo for you.'

'Nice one, cheers!' said Waffle with a grin, 'I'll know for next time!'

Her smile faltered almost imperceptibly for a second, and then she lifted it again, closed the book and tidied a few items on the desk in a businesslike manner, before taking a key from one of the cubbyholes on the wall and placing it on the counter in front of Waffle.

'So! The main room is just here on the left and we'll meet there at 11:30 for the checking in. Lunch is at midday and the main yoga session runs from 2 till 4, then everyone is free for personal meditation or reading until supper at 6. We have a last, brief session of gratitude meditation from 7:30 to 7:40, and then everyone's in their rooms by 8 pm sharp. We wake at 5.'

Waffle took a second to digest all the information. 'Right, yeah. Wow. Yeah.' He blew air into his cheeks and then slowly exhaled. '5... am?'

'5 am, yes. Is that OK?'

Waffle nodded slowly for a second before replying. 'Course, yeah.' He raised his eyebrows and then beamed widely. 'Look forward to it, hoo-hoo!'

He was about to pick up the room key, but paused for a moment. 'And, um, what sort of food is it? Y'know, for lunch and, er, supper?'

She put down the pen she'd just picked up and linked her hands together on the desk in front of her. 'Well,' she said, talking slowly and clearly, 'it's all food cooked freshly on the premises. All healthy and nutritious. Vegetarian, of course.'

'Ah, vegetarian,' he said, sounding slightly unsure, 'lovely!'

'Yes, lunch today will be a falafel and beetroot salad, and supper tonight will be a lentil curry.'

Waffle's eyes lit up. 'Curry, eh? Well, that doesn't sound too bad after all!'

She smiled thinly and then busied herself with some paperwork.

Waffle put his hands in his pockets and looked down the hallway ahead of him.

'11:30 then... first door on the left?'

'Yes, that's right. You've got...' she looked at her watch, 'just under 15 minutes. Why don't you relax in your room for a while and unpack your... thing.'

Waffle patted his toothbrush through his trousers and picked up his key. 'See you soon!' He said cheerily as he turned to head towards his room.

The girl looked up to see him sauntering down the corridor and shook her head ever so slightly as he disappeared from view.

* * *

WAFFLE UNLOCKED the door to room 4 and then closed it softly behind him. The room was small and basically furnished with a single bed and a small chest of drawers that had been painted white at some point in the indeterminate past.

On this were a book and a single candle, though it was unclear whether the candle was intended purely as an ornament or as a practical light source. Its unlit and pristine white wick taunted anyone bold enough to assist in its functional destiny by setting fire to it and watching it die.

The walls were bare, apart from a poster in a clip frame that showed an illustration of a young Buddha sitting cross-legged on a bed of lotus flowers, and on the back of the door were some fire regulations printed on a laminated A4 page.

Waffle took out his toothbrush and placed it on top of the chest of drawers, then walked to the window to take in the view. It looked out onto a small walled yard behind the pub that appeared to be a combination of storage area and outdoor seating, though the latter was represented only by a round, cast-metal garden table with a very large ashtray on it and two rusting camping chairs placed on either side. The remainder of the space was crammed with various items that were presumably pressed into action on occasion or retired from action entirely. The round, kettle barbecue below his window, despite having seen better days and plainly too small to cater for any more than a very small group, was at least covered with a lid and looked potentially serviceable, and the piles of plastic crates were partly filled with empty bottles. Several planks of wood, stacked down one side of the wall with an old tarpaulin had the air of failed promise about them, and Waffle idly wondered if perhaps the landlord had once harboured ambitious plans to build a pergola-style roof over the yard but never got round to it. Whatever their original purpose, the planks were now partly rotted through, and it occurred to Waffle that they might be in better condition had they been stored under the tarpaulin rather than on top of it.

In the far corner, wedged between a gas cylinder and a pile of bricks, and taking up a significant chunk of the overall space, was a 1980 Yamaha XS750 motorcycle, or most of one at least. Various parts were missing, including the front wheel, the seat, and the handlebars. There didn't appear to be any specific pub association with the bike, and Waffle's estimation that the landlord had owned it since it was a viable mode of transport was entirely correct. A new seat wrapped in clear plastic sheeting nestled inside a solitary car tyre attested to another project that had evidently borne little fruit over the years.

With nothing much else to do for a while, Waffle picked up the book from the chest of drawers and lay back on the bed to flick through it. The title was 'Mindfulness in the Modern World – A Step-by-Step Guide to Discovering Inner Peace' and it was worryingly thick. He decided that although discovering inner peace sounded like an admirable aim in life, the number of pages hinted at an awful lot of steps, and he was concerned that he wouldn't have time to get there.

He turned to a random page and began to read.

"It is in this way that it becomes helpful to visualize mindfulness as the act of scaling a ladder—each step, a deliberate advance; each pause, a moment of presence. In the same way that reaching the summit necessitates careful consideration of each individual step, so too does the practice of mindfulness thrive on the cultivation of awareness at every level. Just as you wouldn't leap from the base of a ladder to its top rung, so you also wouldn't rush through mindfulness. Embrace each moment, like each rung, with intention and an open heart. In doing so, you'll find that the ladder of mindfulness becomes a

transformative journey, offering you insights and perspectives that grow richer with each deliberate step you take on it."

WAFFLE FOUND the prose to be rather calming and soporific, though he hadn't been expecting mindfulness to be so centred around ladders. He flicked to the front cover again to make a mental note of the title, thinking that maybe Harj would enjoy a copy for Christmas.

Feeling a little sleepy now, he let the book fall to his side as he leaned further back, and he lazily let his eyes roam the walls and ceiling, noticing that one end of the curtain pole was held in place by a single screw, and even that looked a little loose. He could also see a patch of old wallpaper in one corner where the more recent paint hadn't quite been applied all the way to the ceiling; a striking 1980s red and white zig-zag pattern, faded now but still poking through the sombre magnolia paint with all the brazen shamelessness of a porn mag cover showing through a tear in its anonymous wrapping.

He let his eyes close for a moment, promising himself that he would get up off the bed in a couple of seconds, and ran through his impressions of the yoga retreat so far. He was a little scared of the early mornings, if he was being honest with himself, and perhaps the idea of living off vegetarian food too. But he had to admit that the place had a certain charm, and he felt a long way from home, despite only being half an hour away by tube. On balance, he decided that he liked it a lot more than he was expecting, and was glad he'd come, though he surmised that the word 'Lawn' in the business's name was probably more metaphorical than literal.

Chapter 17

'Ah, Phil, got a second?'

Phil and Mike both turned on their heels to see Superintendent Fletcher standing outside his office, a manila envelope held tight to his body with one elbow while his hand balanced a cup of tea. He pulled the handle and nodded into his office before disappearing inside, leaving the door softly closing behind him.

Phil and Mike exchanged a quick, wordless glance, and then began to walk back down the corridor towards the office.

Phil had always had a lot of time for Supt Ted Fletcher, certainly more so than he did for most of the brass. The new breed were far too stiff for his liking, too constrained by forms and targets, but he suspected it wasn't so much their fault as it was the role itself and the regulation it involved. They were suffocated by paperwork and it had the effect of snubbing out any flair, any imagination. Ted was a similar age to Phil, and he had less stuffiness about him than the younger crowd. He wasn't exactly what you'd call "old school", mind you. There was no Scotch in the filing cabinet and nonces accidentally falling down the stairs, like in the good old days. That generation had all long since retired or been cleared away, but Ted was generally one of the few that was prepared to show Phil some leeway and flexibility. Despite his time on the job and his senior role, he still seemed to care more about putting the bad men away than filling quotas, and Phil appreciated that.

That wasn't to say that Phil actually liked him as such, though. He found him to not only be a pompous prick, but too quick to toe the line of his own superiors, even if it was the wrong decision in the circumstances.

The main reason Phil had a lot of time for him was that he generally had decent biscuits in his drawer.

'Have a seat, gents, won't take too much of your time.' Fletcher set the tea down and was looking seriously at the two of them over steepled fingers. Phil was hoping for Jaffa Cakes.

'So, Phil,' said Fletcher, pulling his tie straight and flattening it down, 'what's new? Any progress on that Turkish car ring then? I hear the next batch is nearly ready to ship, we need to move before it does. Getting a bit of pressure from the sixth floor, need something good for that cross-border seminar he's doing the week after next. I think he's got a couple of *blank slides* still.' Fletcher raised his eyebrows to convey the significance of this and then reached forward to pick up his tea.

'Yeah, it's coming together. We've got enough to pull them in, but we're just waiting to maximise the catch. They've got some nice stuff already, the usual Beemers and Range Rovers, but there's room for more and they've always had at least one of something pretty special in each shipment — Ferraris are their favourite. It's just a matter of timing, really. They've never gone without a full load before, and they're showing no signs of being spooked, so I want to get them with as much stock on their hands as possible. We're only going to get one chance.'

Fletcher was nodding slowly as he listened, and then moved his hand to his desk drawer as he spoke. 'Well, that all makes sense, but you can't eff this up. If we miss the boat, as it were, then it'll all have been for nothing. And that's weeks of surveillance, as well as your informant, if I'm not mistaken?'

Phil watched closely as Fletcher revealed a packet of dark chocolate HobNobs, opening the packet slowly and taking two for himself that he balanced on his saucer. Phil nodded appreciatively and winked discreetly at Mike, but the packet stayed in Fletcher's hands as he waited for a response.

'Ah, yes,' said Phil, dragging his eyes reluctantly back to Fletcher's, 'it's been a few weeks now but I'm confident we're very nearly there, and we'll get our men, don't worry about that.'

Fletcher seemed satisfied and proffered the packet to his guests. Mike mouthed a silent *no thanks* with a quick shake of the head and a smile, while Phil reached forward and plucked two for himself, frowning at Mike while he did. 'You can't tell me oats aren't healthy,' he said quietly, shaking his head. He sat back in his chair and began nibbling.

'And anything else going on besides that?' Fletcher asked, with a slight inclination of his head and a thin smile. He began to dip the biscuit into his tea before arching his neck forward and down to collect the damp portion in his open mouth, all the while watching Phil closely.

'Actually, yes. Drugs case, looking pretty hopeful. We busted a gang who'd taken in a recent shipment, possibly of something very interesting. We're hoping to track that down today, as it goes, got a good lead to work on.'

Fletcher looked sideways at Phil, narrowing his eyes. 'Today? What about the car gang?'

'Oh, all taken care of. I've got DS Turner down there now just across the road, he's on strict instruction to call if anything happens.'

Both Phil and Mike were closely watching the HobNob that Fletcher had been dipping into his tea for over three seconds now; he was playing a dangerous game.

'I see,' Fletcher said, removing the sodden snack from the tea but, after a quick visual appraisal, resigning himself to the sad fact that it would never survive the journey to his mouth. He placed it carefully back onto the saucer to dry out a little and brushed his hands together.

'Isn't it your case though, DI Collins? Shouldn't you be there personally overseeing the operation?'

'Well, I have been much of the time. And I'll be there again very soon, but we just need to follow up this lead, as I say. Turner's got everything in hand and er, well, we're on the phone.' He smiled brightly and waggled his hand to his ear, with thumb and little finger outstretched, but Fletcher didn't smile. He flattened his tie against his chest again and relaxed into his chair.

'So, tell me about this drug shipment then. What exactly is it?'

'Can't be 100 percent sure, as yet, but by all accounts it's some very high-quality weed.'

'Okaaay. How much are we talking?'

'Not exactly sure, but quite a lot possibly. Apparently pretty valuable.'

Fletcher pursed his lips and waited a moment before speaking again. 'But you said you'd made a bust, presumably made some arrests? So how is it you don't know what you have? I'm confused.' He held his palms out and looked at Mike questioningly, as if he should share his confusion.

'Yes,' said Phil, beginning to sound a little strained. 'We made a bust and brought some lads in. But the drugs weren't on the premises, it seemed.'

'And these lads?'

'Well, we had to release them. There was paraphernalia but nothing we could stick on them.'

Fletcher frowned deeply and rubbed his forehead as if trying to work out a particularly nasty crossword clue. 'I'm sorry, Phil, you've lost me. Where did the information come from then?'

'An informant.' Phil glanced at Mike, who looked mildly alarmed that he might get brought into the conversation. 'DC Watts had a tip-off.'

'A tip-off? As in... an *anonymous* tip-off?' Fletcher was now looking as if the only possible answer to the crossword clue was something insulting his mother in very specific terms.

'That's right, sir, yes. But we believe it to be credible and if we can jus–'

Fletcher pulled his chair forward and began waving his hands to interrupt, his eyes closed and head shaking.

'No, no, no. Phil. DI Collins. Let me get this straight. You've received an *anonymous* tip-off that someone has some weed. Not heroin, not even coke or pills, but some *weed*. So you went to wherever this stuff was supposed to be, but there wasn't any present after all. You pulled in the people you found there, but had to release them without charge. Is this right so far?'

Phil cleared his throat, his face beginning to redden and his fists closing on his knees. 'Yes, but it's not...'

'And now you want to endanger a major haul of stolen luxury cars that happens to be considered very important internally,' he bounced his pointed finger towards the ceiling, 'while you go around chasing some mystery load of weed that *may not even exist*? Have I got this right?'

'Oh, I'm sure it exists, we've already...'

'You can't know that, Phil! You've never even seen it! Am I right?'

Phil hadn't heard Fletcher raise his voice for several years and decided it would be better to avoid further confrontation until he'd calmed down. He nodded. Fletcher took a deep breath and sank back into his chair, wiping imaginary crumbs from his trousers, his eyes still dark.

'I'm sorry, Phil. You're a good copper and I trust your instincts, but this isn't acceptable, and you know that. It doesn't even make sense, for Christ's sake. If you've got something that needs following up, then give it to someone else, I don't care who. Ellison perhaps, or Abega. But you're working on an important case and this drugs thing, it's... it's nonsense.' He shook his head, clearly unable to make sense of it. He exhaled slowly and continued more calmly. 'If this Turkish case gets fouled up then there'll be hell to pay. For you as well as me. It just can't happen.'

A silence fell between them, Phil and Fletcher still maintaining eye contact, while Mike's gaze slid down to his shoes. Phil made one last attempt.

'OK, but until DS Turner calls me, what if I just...'

'No, Phil! No.' Fletcher's eyes flared again, and he held up both hands like stop signs. 'No more. If you want to give this to someone else, then that's fine. It's your call. Frankly, it sounds like a complete waste of time and resource if you ask me. But you're to leave it alone, as of now, understand? I don't want you spending any time at all outside of this Turkish case until we've made arrests, and especially not chasing after some pathetic load of weed that nobody's even seen or is sure exists! Do I make myself clear?'

Mike turned to watch Phil, who lifted his chin slightly with the last remnants defiance.

'Yes, sir.'

Chapter 18

Waffle walked through the open door rubbing his eyes and his knee, cursing himself for falling asleep and leaping out of bed so quickly he'd fallen into the chest of drawers. He was following behind two young women of identical height who walked almost as one, the dark-haired girl to the right holding onto the arm of her blonde friend, their heads tilted towards each other in quiet consultation.

'Oh, I love the windows at the back,' whispered the blonde head, 'great natural light!'

'Literally,' whispered the dark head.

There were several people already waiting silently in the room, all sitting cross-legged in an unfinished circle that had begun to form in the centre of the space. At the head of the circle, if indeed a circle can have a head, was the girl from reception, the epitome of perfect poise and posture, looking dead ahead and with an expression of peaceful calm. Next to her was the gong from the reception desk.

The light was catching the side of her face, and Waffle noticed that her skin was china-white with a few freckles. Although she was wearing leggings and a long-sleeved top, he could also tell that she appeared to have not an ounce of fat on her. He put his hand to his own belly and gave it a little wobble; he was naturally skinny and rangy but had to concede that the years of takeaways and lager had provided him with the beginnings of an insulating layer that he hadn't possessed a few years before, and he made a mental note that sorting that out should constitute a phase two of The Mission.

Waffle found an empty spot and sat, looking around him at the others to check that he was following the correct conventions. All were cross-legged in some way or another, with straight backs and heads facing forwards, though with their eyes steadily surveying their new companions, occasionally smiling or nodding. One older lady with cropped grey hair who was almost opposite Waffle had adopted what he considered to be a much more *pro* posture and had her feet folded impressively onto the top of each thigh. Her hands were resting on her knees, facing upwards with thumb and forefinger forming a circle, and her eyes were shut. Clearly, this wasn't her first rodeo.

The only sound now was the muted shuffle of the last bare feet entering the room and the low whisper of the two girls Waffle had followed in who were sitting next to him.

'Loving the vibe. Like, so serene.'

'Literally.'

The gong sounded, its warm and muffled tone rising cautiously to a soft crescendo before fading slowly for five or more seconds until the point at which you couldn't be fully sure whether you could still hear it or not.

'Good morning,' said Reception Girl, softly. She looked around the circle and took in a deep breath, which she let out slowly with her eyes closed. 'Let's all just take a few moments of silence to reset, and then we'll begin.'

Waffle's curious eyes swivelled from side to side, scanning the circle of unfamiliar faces arranged around him. Everyone apart from him was sitting perfectly still with their eyes closed, and he had the distinct feeling he used to get at school assemblies, and later at church weddings, when it was time to pray. Admittedly, most of the other kids at his school weren't the kind to do as they were told either, so being one of the watchers rather than one of the watchees made him far from unique, but here he was alone. There was a strange feeling to be had from being the sole person in a room with your eyes open, he thought. You rarely get the opportunity in life to study other people so closely and for so long without being kissed, punched, or arrested. There's a sense of liberation mixed with an overwhelming feeling of intrusion, as if the light reflected off their skin belongs to them alone, and to take too much of it in one go is to be a thief.

Waffle counted eight guests plus Reception Girl. All were women apart from one other guy who was smiling contentedly to himself, his streaky blonde hair the same colour as his stubbly beard and tied into a man bun. He too was exposing a taut and muscular body, his white vest top showing lightly tanned and sculpted arms.

Waffle wondered whether yoga made people taut and muscular, or whether it just attracted taut and muscular people who liked to hang out in loose clothing.

He'd been led to believe that he was in for some light and gentle stretching for the purposes of relaxation and inner peace, and hadn't particularly been planning on working any muscles unduly over the next couple of days.

He had a sudden flashback to the after-school karate lessons he'd taken up very briefly when he was nine, which had started off in a similarly calm vein with lots of polite bowing and breathing exercises, to be rapidly replaced with high-speed press-ups and having his nuts kicked in by a smirking, older boy called Trevor. He'd been promised fitness, strength and discipline, but all he'd got out of that was an aversion to group activities, and sore nuts.

As Waffle continued to observe discreetly, the muscular guy opened his eyes wide, and Waffle felt caught. He looked away guiltily, and carefully studied the far wall for a second or two with its old brickwork that had been painted over too thinly, in parts looking almost uniformly grubby white and in others clearly showing the pattern of the bricks beneath it. Three of the room's walls were much the same, but the fourth contained a large, arched window that was the sole source of light. In front of this was a large potted plant of a kind Waffle didn't recognise, basking in the sunlight. It was fairly tall and exotic-looking, its thin stem branching into several others as it rose, with rich green leaves surrounding a cluster of vivid orange flowers.

He looked back to the young man, who smiled a crooked smile at Waffle, took a quick sweep of the other faces, and then shut his eyes once more.

The gong sounded again, and the room came alive to the breathy chorus of nine lungs exhaling at once, and all eyes opened and blinked meekly in the light. Reception Girl put the gong hammer back on its hook and smiled widely at the group. She spoke with feeling, but in hushed tones.

'Good morning. Thank you for joining us here at the Yoga Lawn. I'm pleased to welcome you all here for three days of yoga and reflection. It's nice to see a few old friends...' she nodded at the lady next to her with the short, grey hair, who nodded back with a flicker of a smile (*I knew it!* thought Waffle triumphantly)... 'as well as some new faces that I hope will become friends.' She smiled unhurriedly at each person in the circle, twisting only from her neck while her body stayed almost completely still.

Man! thought Waffle, suppressing a whistle of respect, *that's some seriously supple neck movement there; she's like a fucking owl.*

'My name is Fran, and I run the Yoga Lawn,' she said, continuing in the same unruffled manner. 'I'm here to facilitate and to ensure you have a satisfying stay, so please don't be shy and come and say hello or ask me for anything you need.' She blinked slowly, her dark, round eyes shining brightly on either side of her long, thin nose.

A barn owl, thought Waffle.

'OK,' said Fran, breaking Waffle's train of thought, 'we'll go round the room now. Please just say a little about yourself, why you're here today and perhaps something of your intentions.'

She indicated the person to her left, the lady with the short, grey hair with an upturned hand and a silent smile, and gave the gong a gentle strike to underscore the moment. The lady nodded and spoke unselfconsciously, confidently meeting various eyes around the group. 'I'm Vivienne. This is my third visit here, but I've been to many other retreats too, over the years, both here and abroad. I think it's important to take some time out of our lives on a regular basis, to listen to our bodies and let them heal.'

Waffle was listening closely, hoping to get some tips for when it was his turn. He watched as a tendon in Vivienne's neck tensed into view every few seconds as she spoke and also caught a glimpse of a tattoo on the inside of her ankle that he hadn't noticed before. He couldn't quite make it out from where he was sitting, but it appeared to be a penguin, and he found himself desperately trying to work out what the story of someone's life could be that led to a tattoo of a penguin.

'My intention is to listen to my body as usual and to nourish it. Also,' her smile flickered briefly, 'to improve my *Karna Pidasana*, if possible.'

Waffle nodded in supportive agreement, without understanding a great deal of what she'd said, though he did like the sound of her Karna Pidasana and patted his stomach in anticipation.

The gong sounded again, and the man with the vest top smiled a broad, white-toothed smile around the group. 'Hey guys! So yuh, I'm Arlo, and it's great to be here. I've been, how might you say, *dabbling* for a while now in yoga, and really all the Eastern arts.' His expression switched quickly to one of serious contemplation and he tilted his head to one side as if in deep thought. 'I think it's rilly, rilly important to open your mind to all new experiences and be the best version of yourself you can be, you know? You have to grow as a person and learn to love yourself. Because, if you can't love yourself, then you can't love anyone else, right?' He looked around the group and broke into another wide smile. 'And what can I say, I love people! So, my intention is to make new friends along the way, because I believe that friendship is a precious thing.' He seemed pretty pleased and nodded to himself as he continued to smile at everyone in the group. 'Oh yuh, plus, y'know, get better at yoga, natch.'

Waffle was slightly alarmed to see him actually wink at this point, but despite his evident cheesiness, it was hard to dislike the guy's puppy dog enthusiasm.

Arlo turned to the next person, who looked suddenly startled that she was up so soon to introduce herself. She cleared her throat and looked a little wide-eyed at the floor in front of her.

'Um, hi. Yep. Er... Hi, I'm Carol, and er...' she chewed her lip and scrunched up her eyes as if trying to remember something important that she'd just forgotten. 'Yep, I'm here for... well, it's my first time to tell you the truth. I've read a lot about yoga and always fancied trying it but never seemed to find the time to get away, what with... well, y'know, *commitments*. But, well, that doesn't seem to matter now, does it?' She shook her head and started to fiddle with her wedding ring. There was a lengthy pause, and she seemed to drift off into her thoughts, but then became aware that everyone was still watching her and she sat bolt upright with her eyes wide.

'Oh, sorry, I'm rambling. Um, so, yep. Er, Carol.' She smiled weakly and turned to the next person before remembering there was something else she was supposed to say. 'Oh! And yes, er, my intentions. Well, each day's a new day, isn't that what they say? So I'm planning to take each day as it comes. And finally do what *I* want to do, without having to compromise for once.' She made a firm nod of finality and lifted her chin as she blew out her cheeks.

A Spanish student called Isabella was next, though her English wasn't really up to the task, and she was followed by a lady called Misha who Waffle decided was probably too old for her girlish pigtails. She spoke at length in a soft drone that Waffle had to fight hard against to stay awake through, and he became aware that he would be next to introduce himself, so started making a mental note of what to say. He had no problem with speaking in front of strangers generally but did feel a little out of place in the setting, especially as he hadn't thought to buy any special clothing for the occasion. He looked around the group at the clothes they were wearing, and the overall theme appeared to be simple, plain cotton, mainly in light and summery colours. Arlo was the exception, and despite his white vest top, he'd matched this with thin, baggy trousers that were made up of a patchwork of abstract patterns and motifs in rich blues, reds and golds. There appeared to be some Sanskrit text on one patch, and another may possibly have represented an elephant, but it was hard to tell while he was cross-legged.

Waffle looked down at his own clothes and briefly regretted not picking out something more suitable. He'd left his flip-flops at the door and so at least his bare feet fitted in, and his leather biker's jacket was in his room, but he wasn't sure that his old, purple-striped jeans were necessarily going to afford him much freedom of movement, despite the rips at the knees. He was sure he'd spotted Vivienne eyeing them up with a slight look of distaste, though it could've been the *Napalm Death* t-shirt, he supposed, and he momentarily wished he hadn't worn the one that featured all the naked, dead bodies with giant, bloody nails sticking out of them. Still, he remembered with some relief, at least his hat was clean.

Given the relative sombreness of the surroundings, and with Fran's earlier friendly warning about keeping his volume down, he decided that he'd make his intro short and sweet, and most definitely not fall into his usual trap of trying too hard to make light of any situation with a joke that often fell flat. No, he'd be Mr Cool this time, just introduce himself simply and maybe try and borrow something spiritual-sounding from Vivienne's introduction.

The gong sounded, and it was Waffle's turn. He pulled himself up straight and tried to think about his posture. 'I'm Waffle, how's it going?' He waited for a response but didn't get anything apart from a few mildly confused faces. Vivienne was *definitely* looking at his t-shirt this time. He remembered that this wasn't supposed to be a conversation, and so ploughed on. 'So, yeah, this is my first time! I dunno if you'd guessed,' and with this he indicated his clothes with a flourish of his hand down his body and a grin, hoping to diffuse any awkwardness by getting in there first. Everyone was looking at his t-shirt now.

'Don't worry, I know I look a bit dodgy sometimes, but I'm not really, hoo-hoo! I haven't done any long stretches or anything. Geddit? Long stretches?' He scanned the faces around the circle but could only see confusion. 'You know, long stretch... like prison?' Many of the faces were frowning now, and mostly from sideways glances, though he noted that Arlo was still smiling broadly and looked as if he was enjoying a particularly engrossing cartoon.

'Sorry, that was supposed to be a yoga joke. I haven't, like, been to... y'know...' He caught Fran's eye who had the expression of someone who was being lightly strangled in polite company, and he took a big breath, confident that he was on the home stretch.

'So, yeah... my intention is to do some yoga. Thanks.'

He looked again at Fran with raised eyebrows for some affirmation, but she just looked a little shell-shocked.

Chapter 19

'All I'm saying is, it was easier for you back then. Things aren't like that any more.'

'You'd be surprised. Not everything in life changes, you know, it's often the same people, just with different clothes and music. And what do you mean 'back then' anyway? It's not like I grew up in the Victorian era, you cheeky little bastard.'

Mike smirked to himself, but kept his eyes on the road. 'Weeell, it was the seventies, wasn't it? That's long enough ago.'

'Oi! I was fifteen when the eighties started, I'll have you know, I hadn't even left school then! And anyway, seventies or eighties, you seem to be thinking about some fictionalised version of the sixties. I can assure you, the residential suburbs of South Croydon were not teeming with girls in miniskirts and beehives, cruising the empty streets in E-Type Jags, picking up blokes. The best you could hope for was a quick snog outside the Wimpy before the bus home, assuming you'd spoiled her and splashed out the 25p for a knickerbocker glory.'

'Yeah, but it was just simpler, wasn't it? People weren't so offended by everything all the time, or wanting to sue anybody that they think is getting in the way of their life being perfect. And there was none of that bloody Instaface and Tick-Tocking all the time... people just got on with their lives and didn't worry about how they look constantly. And I bet if you did try to snog someone outside the Wimpy, they wouldn't try to cancel you if they weren't up for it.'

'Nope. They'd smack you round the chops, that's what they'd do. And you'd get no sympathy from your mum either when you went home with a black eye; she'd say you deserved it.'

Phil pulled out a cigarette and tapped it on the box a couple of times before placing it between his lips. 'And Jesus, you keep going on about how old *I* am, listen to yourself. You sound like an old codger banging on about the price of flour before the war. What are you, 32, 33? You sound 90. You need to take a chill pill, as you youngsters say, and be grateful for mobile phones and the internet and microwaves, and all that bollocks.'

Mike glanced over to Phil, who was breathing smoke out of the window that was open little more than a crack. 'Do you honestly believe that? Would you rather grow up now rather than the seventies and eighties?'

'Nah. The music's shit now and you can't smoke anywhere. Plus the traffic's worse. But I'd take a big wide-screen TV back with me to replace that shitty little black and white thing we had with no remote.' He took another long drag. 'And anyway, what've you got to worry about? You're happily married. You don't have to brave the murky waters of single life any more, risking social excommunication and finding women by *apps*,' he said, putting "apps" into air quotes.

'Yeah, I know. And thank god I met Sarah when I did. The thought of going through all that swiping rubbish gives me the willies, to be honest. She's for keeps, luckily, I think if we ever split up I'd just stay on my own forever. Maybe buy a cat.'

Phil gave a hollow laugh. 'Yeah, I could see you with a cat. You're a bit of a neurotic old lady in your own way, aren't you?'

Mike gave a sideways sneer as he pulled up at a t-junction behind a queue of cars. 'What about you then? Not planning on finding Mrs Collins number two? Is it two? Or do you have a string of failed marriages behind you? You seem the type, to be honest, all old and bitter.'

Phil gave him a silent stare with raised eyebrows.

'No offence, like. Sir.'

Phil held the button down to lower the window a few more inches and flicked the butt into the road, then took the cigarette pack out of his pocket again, but seemed happy to just read the wording on the back rather than open it.

'There was never a number one, even,' he said after a few moments. Mike waited for embellishment but none came, so he ploughed on.

'Oh, really? I just assumed, I suppose. Hardly unusual for a copper to get divorced, I guess, it's sort of the tradition, isn't it? All the unsociable hours and moaning when you get home, we're supposed to manage about ten years and then get walked out on. I just figured you'd been married before and… well, that was it, I guess.'

'Nope.'

'Right, OK. And err, no plans to then?'

Phil turned and looked at him like he was a child asking for a third portion of ice cream.

'Hardly. That boat has long since sailed, assuming I was ever booked on it in the first place.'

'It's never too late, y'know. I mean, you read all the time about…'

'Not gonna happen, trust me.' He continued concentrating on the fag packet and started tapping his finger on it absent-mindedly. 'You know how people sometimes say, oh, I'm not looking for love, and all that bollocks, and then get hitched to the first person they meet that they get on with? Well, that's not me, it really isn't. And that's absolutely fine by me, seriously. I mean, it's like you say — coppers are pretty shit at being married, and rather than have a wife to leave me after too many years of coming home too late, too bitter and too drunk, I managed all that in advance. Scared them all away, and quite right too. And I'm just not interested any more, I'm honestly not. I've had 54 years of being set in my ways now, there's nobody that would want to deal with that and there's nobody I would want to ask. I'm perfectly happy the way things are, I enjoy my own company, and I don't even need a cat.'

Mike considered this for a moment, concentrating in silence on his wing mirror as he pulled out to pass a parked car. 'Well, in that case, I won't invite you round for dinner so you can meet Sarah's friend from work. Isobel, I think she's called. Late forties at a guess, but very attractive, very classy. Kind of in that Parisian sort of way, you know? Stylish.' He tried to repress a smile as he watched Phil from the corner of his eye.

'Good. Sounds shit. I wouldn't come anyway.'

Phil's phone started ringing; he pulled it out of his jacket and glanced at the screen. There was no name, just a number, but he knew who it was all the same. He pressed the 'Decline' button and slipped it back into his pocket.

'The Super?' Mike asked with a wry smile.

'Worse.'

'Worse than the Super? Well, you don't have a wife, so I'm stumped.' He cleared his throat. 'Seriously, though, I was half joking, but Isobel is actually real and she's re-'

From within Phil's jacket, the phone started up again, and he let out a sigh though made no move to check it.

'Look, pull over here, will you? I've got to take this, won't be a minute.'

'It's a bus stop.'

'So? You're the police. I'll be two minutes, tops. Look, there's a bus up ahead, must've just left, so the next one won't be here till October now.'

Mike eased the replacement Vauxhall Corsa to the kerb and pulled the handbrake, but kept the engine running as a sign of impermanence. Phil yanked the door open and used both hands simultaneously to reach for mobile and cigarettes, kicking the door shut behind him. He ignored the ringing until he'd reached an old, glass phone box about 20 yards away, and decided to take the call inside, more for old times' sake than any need for further privacy.

'Bob,' he said flatly, through an exhalation of smoke.

'Ah, DI Collins. Nice to know you've got time to speak to me.'

'I'm working, Bob. I can't just take calls any time of the night or day at the drop of a hat. We'd arranged to speak tomorrow if I recall correctly.'

'Indeed, Phil, that's as maybe. And far be it from me to inconvenience you at all, or get too ahead of ourselves. You can't hurry love, as they say, isn't that right, Phil?'

'What do you want, Bob?'

'I want information, Phil. I need a progress report. I'm sat here like a fucking lemon, waiting to be squeezed. I need my possessions returned to me, and I'm getting impatient. I don't like silence and I don't like waiting. So, no, forget our meeting tomorrow, I want to know what's happening now. So... where are we?'

Phil took a drag on his cigarette and waited a little longer than he needed before replying.

'I'm making progress. I've got leads and it's coming together. These things don't just happen overnight, it involves work and time, and it's not like I don't have a proper job to do on the side.'

'Yeah? Well, I don't give a shit. That all sounds very much like a you problem, and not a me problem. I've got a business to run here and currently, you are holding things up. I need that merchandise back and I need it back quick fucking smart, you understand? I'm not a fucking amateur, Phil, I run a tight ship and as things stand I've got a very large number in my red column and I don't much like it. I've invested heavily in the future of this enterprise and I'm not about to stand idly by and watch it fall apart around me.'

Phil focussed through the smeared and cracked glass of the phone booth and saw that Mike was on his own mobile. Probably calling his wife, moaning about Phil and complaining about the drugs case. Frankly, he'd far rather be home, too, and started thinking about the weekend. He could see himself reclined in his favourite chair in front of a nice, relaxing film, a good meal inside him and a glass of single malt to hand. Perhaps a comedy. Something not too taxing, not too depressing. Something with Bill Murray in, perhaps, or maybe Steve Martin. He quite liked Steve Martin, though only up to — and just about including — the first Father of the Bride.

'Well, that sounds a bit like a you problem, Bob,' he said, though partially regretted it before he'd finished.

'It's a what? A fucking WHAT?' Bob was now choking on his words, struggling to get them out. Phil could visualise the veins in his neck starting to appear and the flush of blood filling his cheeks.

'Listen to me, Detective Inspector. I have a very simple job that needs doing and I need it to be done now. Do you understand that? I mean immediately. Not later tonight, not tomorrow, not next week. This isn't one of those little jobs that can be put off until after you get back from your holibobs, or after a lovely bank holiday weekend tending to your tomato plants, or whatever the fuck you choose to spend your free time doing. As it is currently, YOU'RE the man on this job and I need

YOU to start showing me some solid fucking progress! Do you understand me, Phil?'

Phil took the last drag on his cigarette and dropped it onto the floor, which, despite being in a phone box, was partly exposed earth. The concrete had cracked and risen in places with the years of disuse, the weeds forcing their way up after being held back for too long.

'Are your own staff not back yet? Where did you say they were? A management training programme? Or were they ill? I forget.'

Phil heard Bob take a deep breath, the sound distilled and compressed by the phone line into a dry crackle.

'They'll be back soon, rest assured,' Bob continued slowly and calmly in a measured, almost sing-song voice, clearly holding his anger at bay with no small effort. 'Won't be long now. But there is no time to delay, I feel I've made this point already. So yes, if you like, you can just step back from this little task and wait for the cavalry to take over. It's your life, Phil, you're a big boy and can make your own decisions. Don't let me tell you what to do, for goodness' sake.' He forced a small laugh.

'But it's only right that you understand what will happen if I'm left to wait too much longer. I mean, we both know what that means, don't we? I'm sure you remember as well as I do the events of your murky past that you'd rather not see get into the public domain, don't you Phil Collins? Or should I say Phil Duggan?'

Phil said nothing, but allowed his eyes to close for a second as he became aware of the thickness of the stale air inside the phone box.

'What's the going pension for a DI in good standing these days, anyway? I don't know if it's one of those urban myths or not, but I'd heard they were surprisingly generous, like you always hear about Tube drivers. Perk of the job and all that, payback for the endless years of dealing with all the scum on the streets, all the filth in society, all the pressure. You're not far away now, are you Phil? I imagine you've got plans. Gardening, wasn't it, that your thing? Or was it sailing boats? Either way, a proper little copper cliché aren't you? Retire to the coast, buy a little cottage with a garden and a sailing boat and spend the rest of your days floating around, wandering gloomy beaches, and writing shit poetry? Well, that's all very lovely, but it wouldn't be such a happy ending with a sacking in disgrace, no pension, no future, nasty articles about you in the paper and maybe even a conviction, now would it?'

Bob gasped theatrically in mock horror. 'Goodness, what if you got sent down? Dear, oh dear, that would be terrible! Now if there's one place even more depressing than an English seaside, it's most definitely an English prison, isn't it? And who's every old lag's favourite kind of cell-mate? Why, it's a fallen copper, isn't it?'

Phil let his weight lean forward until his forehead was resting against the dirty glass pane of the phone box. He squeezed his eyes closed before blinking them open, and stared down at his shoes, noticing for the first time that there was a section of leaf stuck to the bottom of one, probably with chewing gum.

'You still with me, DI Collins?'

Phil cleared his throat. 'I've told you, Bob, I'll find it. I've got somewhere to check out tomorrow and I'm confident it'll all be cleared up either then or maybe Friday.'

'Oh yes? Well, I'd seriously suggest you make sure that happens, and I'd most definitely favour tomorrow over Friday. I'll be checking in again before then and if it's looking even remotely like my possessions are still out of my... er, possession, then the cavalry will indeed be called in with me at the helm. And if that happens, then I suggest you start making plans for a very early, but very unhappy retirement indeed.'

Chapter 20

'Great work today, everyone,' Fran said earnestly, with a quick clap as everyone stood up and went to find their shoes at the side of the room. 'I'll see you all here at 5 am, I hope you get a good night's sleep; you've earned it.'

Waffle looked up at the clock on the wall. It was 7:43. He looked through the tall window to see the orange glow of the evening sun light up the whitewashed walls of the kebab shop next door, and a clear blue sky beyond that. He frowned as he looked again at the clock and shook his head. He couldn't remember the last time he'd been told to go to bed before 8 pm, but it was almost certainly as a punishment for something, and definitely at some point before puberty. His brain started fizzing as various thought processes short-circuited. What was he supposed to do now? Was he seriously supposed to just read the mindfulness book in his room, as had been suggested to the group in one of Fran's sessions? For how long? Until bedtime which, he calculated, should by rights be at least five hours away?

He suspected the book wouldn't be interesting enough to hold his attention until sunset, let alone midnight, and that he'd be left staring at the ceiling by 9 pm, waiting for sleep to come early. But even if he found something more engrossing to do, then the risk was that he'd still be at it until it was near enough time to be up again at the crack of dawn. He'd never understood the interest in seeing the dawn. Very overrated stage of the day, in his opinion.

The rest of the group were saying their goodnights and heading out into the corridor with a bit of general, good-natured milling about and the odd hug or shaken hands. Arlo appeared to be the most enthusiastic and was beaming at pretty much everyone in turn and hugging with abandon. Waffle caught his eye for a moment and received a cheerful grin, along with what almost seemed like a rolling of the eyes. Arlo then looked at his watch and made a kind of theatrical grimace at Waffle, followed by an exaggerated stretch of the arms and a yawn.

'Waffle, wasn't it?' he said as the two fell into step together. 'Great name, by the way. Love it!' He broke into another wide smile as he gestured for Waffle to leave the room before him with a wave of his arm.

'Thanks, man,' said Waffle, responding to both the compliment and politeness as a 2-for-1.

'It's surprisingly tiring, isn't it? All that stretching and stuff? Pretty exhausting actually. I mean, sure, it's mainly sitting down, but yuh, if the old bod's not used to it, then it definitely takes it out of you!'

Waffle agreed, with a polite smile, and admitted to himself that he was aching in many places, though he wasn't convinced that Arlo's youthful and gym-honed 'old bod' had likely suffered too much, and was certainly showing no signs of fatigue or lack of energy.

'Right then, I suppose I'll be toddling off. I didn't bring anything to read, unfortunately, but there's a rather wonderful-looking book provided in my room all about the philosophy of yoga in the context of the rise of Hinduism, so I'm looking forward to getting stuck into that bad boy! I might allow myself 30 minutes of literary decadence before I attempt sleep.'

'Yeah, I've got one about ladders in my room,' said Waffle absent-mindedly, to a bemused Arlo.

Waffle looked around at the other guests dispersing down the corridor towards their rooms or up the stairs up to the second floor and he lowered his voice. 'Fancy a quick pint first?' He made the motion of sipping from an invisible glass, but Arlo knocked it away with a scandalised glare as he looked over his shoulder at Fran, who was tidying away some things at the reception desk. He turned back to Waffle with wide eyes.

'My god, are you serious? Fran would kill us!' he whispered, but with eyes glittering. 'You know the rules!'

Waffled glanced over Arlo's shoulder towards the reception desk. 'Well, I didn't see any laminated posters about it.'

Arlo snorted with a suppressed laugh. 'Perhaps not, but there aren't any about murdering the other guests, either. Some things are kind of implied, and go beyond lamination.' He cocked his head to the side and looked down at the floor. With nobody now left in the corridor apart from the two of them and Fran at the far end, it was just possible to make out some sounds from the pub below. It clearly wasn't exactly kicking, and there was no music or wild clinking of glassware, but there was the occasional muffled voice that could just about be heard. He looked back at Waffle with eyebrows raised.

'You're not seriously suggesting we go down there and drink under the very noses of our host?'

Waffle thought for a second. 'Nah, man, that wouldn't be too bright. There's gotta be another boozer around here though, can't be hard to find a drink.'

Arlo smiled. 'Indeed there is, and I know where. I've not been inside but I passed it on the way here. It didn't look particularly... savoury though.'

Waffle laughed quietly and noticed Fran look up with a frown.

'I don't really care whether it's savoury, sweet or bitter,' he said quietly, 'long as they have lager.' He lowered his voice further, conscious that they were still being watched. 'Look, we should probably move along now. I assume Fran will be off to bed herself any minute, though. I'll meet you out the front in fifteen minutes, yeah?'

* * *

'Hi,' Arlo beamed. 'How did you, er, get out then?'

Waffle lowered his headphones to his neck, pushed himself away from the lamppost, and lifted his chin in greeting. 'Alright? Yeah, I just shimmied down from my window onto a barbecue. The gate out the back only locks from the inside, so all good. You?'

Arlo looked impressed. He flicked his head back to remove the now-untied blond hair from his eyes and nodded his respect. 'Good work! I just… well, I waited for Fran to go to bed, actually, and then left down the stairs and through the pub. The door locked behind me, but I figured I could address that particular issue later. I mean, if push comes to shove, I can just go home, I suppose — she's not the boss of me!'

Waffle smiled broadly. 'Yeeess, my man! Hoo-hoo! Now. Let's get us some beer, I could murder a pint.'

Arlo pointed up the road, and they headed off in the opposite direction to Waffle's arrival earlier that day. The sun was now low in the sky and most of the street was in shade, but the evening was warm and still as they sauntered along, the sound of a siren in the distance the only accompaniment to the slapping of Waffle's flip-flops. He'd thrown his leather biker jacket on over the clothes he'd been wearing all day, which was pretty much the closest he ever got to dressing up for an evening out. He was, however, mildly relieved to see that Arlo had taken the opportunity to change completely, and had swapped his baggy yoga gear for some presumably expensive skinny jeans and a crisp, white shirt that was undone just enough to hint at his pectorals, topped by a thin woollen jumper tossed casually about his shoulders. Waffle thought he looked worryingly like an escaped catalogue model and that perhaps this wasn't the best look for a backstreet East End pub, but decided to be grateful that he wasn't wearing a bandana or a pair of entirely unnecessary thick-rimmed glasses to smoulder through.

They made polite chit-chat as they ambled along, and after a few minutes approached a row of shops and businesses built into an anonymous 1960s flat-roofed block. The last of these proclaimed itself to be the Earl of Wessex – purveyor of fine ales, wines, spirits and big-screen Sky Sports.

'Oh God, it looks even worse out of the sunshine,' said Arlo with a sniff.

Waffle looked up at the worn sign hanging unevenly by its rusty hinges. 'Same name as my local! Looks very similar too. I like it already.'

He pushed open the door and let the warm scents of spilt beer, prawn cocktail crisps and stale cigarette breath envelop him. He closed his eyes and let out a satisfied sigh.

'I spy with my little eye,' said Arlo through a ventriloquist's mouth, 'something beginning with… shithole.'

'Come on, man,' said Waffle brightly, 'we're free! And I'm buying.'

The pub was half full, and considerably more lively than the Mad Parrot, though admittedly Waffle had only seen that during the late morning. They found a space at the bar and Waffle placed his hands onto its sticky surface as he took a quick visual sweep of the wares it offered, his lower lip curled over his top in earnest appreciation of the selection. Perched atop stools next to him were two men who'd been in conversation, but who were now both silent and looking Arlo up and down with ill-disguised disdain. They turned back to each other with a smirk and a shake of the head, then continued to watch the new arrivals in brazen silence rather than continue their conversation.

'Alright, gents?' Waffle sang loudly, 'Lovely evening for it, innit?' He rubbed his hands with glee, and the two locals raised their eyebrows and went back to a low conversation.

'So! Pint of your finest cold lager please, Landlord, and for my friend...'

Waffle turned to Arlo, who had retrieved a pair of thick-rimmed glasses from a case and was just putting them on. 'Oh... um, could I please have a Malibu and—'

'Two pints it is, please,' said Waffle with a clap of his hands, and he turned to lean on the bar as the drinks were being poured. 'So... not your usual kind of night out then?' he asked with a mischievous grin.

Arlo flicked the hair from his eyes and looked around the bar. 'To be perfectly honest, no. But life's for living, isn't it? We shouldn't all be stuck in our little worlds forever, it's important we get out into the big, bad world and really experience life, you know?'

Waffle wasn't entirely sure whether he was being sarcastic or not, but gave him the benefit of the doubt. 'So what about the yoga place, then? It seems a little... low-end for you. I mean, it's not exactly a luxury yoga retreat in Mayfair, is it?'

'Oh, I don't mind slumming it a bit, it's good to get away from the usual clubs on the scene and it's got a kind of authenticity about it, you know? I've been a couple of times, actually. But Fran's great, there are usually plenty of other lovely ladies that are easy on the eye, and I'm a little low on funds currently, anyway.'

Waffle raised his eyebrows and then turned at the sound of the pints being placed down. He paid, thanked the barman and gestured to a free table.

'Up and at 'em!' he said, raising his pint, and Arlo matched his movements, followed by a tentative first sip. 'Actually, I thought you were...'

'Rich?'

Waffle swallowed a glug of beer. 'Eh? Er no, I was gonna say gay.'

'Oh, I see. I get that a lot, to be fair.' Arlo seemed unfazed and looked with curiosity around the bar.

'Are you then?'

'What, gay?'

'No, rich.'

'Ah! Well, I'm not but Dad is, I suppose. He's *big in "maritime insurance"*.' Arlo said with the aid of air quotes, 'He's always saying I should dress down a bit though, or else people will always assume I am.'

'Rich?'

Arlo looked confused. 'No. Gay.'

They both took long draughts of their lager in silence, Arlo looking slightly confused when a burp appeared to come from nowhere, as if to try and make him jump, and sat his glass down at a safe distance.

'I'm not though, since you ask. Gay, that is.'

Waffle too allowed a small burp to escape, though his was more contrived, less surprising and more clearly enjoyed. He let out a satisfied 'aaaaah' as he rested his glass.

'Oh yeah? Well, doesn't make no odds to me. I just thought with the clothes and the muscles and the yoga and things. No offence and all that.'

'None taken. People are often saying I'm a bit camp but I don't mind at all. If anything, it helps with the ladies. I'm not exactly very threatening, if you see what I mean?'

Waffle wasn't sure he did, but was intrigued nonetheless, and allowed a smile to creep across his face.

'What... you mean you act it up to pull the birds?'

Arlo considered this for a second before answering.

'Well, I wouldn't say I act it up as such. But I certainly don't dampen it down. Does me no harm at all,' he said with a sly grin.

'You old fox!' Waffle took a long slug of beer and wiped the foam from his mouth as a thought came to him. 'Hang on. Is that why you do the yoga?'

Arlo laughed. 'God, what must you think of me!' He paused a moment, his eyes gleaming. 'Of course it is! You're the first man I've seen in the last three retreats I've been to. It's wall-to-wall totty!'

Waffle shook his head with a chuckle.

'I mean, seriously, why else would I go? I bloody hate it! All that vegetarian bollocks and bloody whale music. I'd far rather have a juicy steak and go to a club, or even just go to the gym. But where else can you go and spend hours at a time in the company of trim young ladies, usually without any male competition in sight?'

'I dunno. Karaoke?'

'Voice like a tortured seal, I'm afraid.'

'Bingo?'

'Way too old.'

'Spa day?'

'I don't mind them wondering if I'm gay, but not being convinced.'

'Salsa classes?'

'Two left feet.'

'Book club?'

Arlo paused. 'Actually, that's not bad.'

'Gin tasting?'

'Ooh, also good!' He had his phone out now and was thumbing the screen.

'Zumba?'

'Hang on a sec. What was the first one?'

Arlo tapped away while Waffle drained his pint, gently shaking his head. He dropped the empty glass down on the table with a flourish and sat back in his chair. 'Same again?'

Arlo finished with his phone and put it back into his jeans, then picked up his half-drunk beer and appraised it. 'Sure, but I'll get these. Just give me a moment.'

Waffle watched him as he took a few stabs at the lager, taking in a small mouthful each time and trying to swallow it hurriedly.

'Sorry, man, I shouldn't have ordered for you. Just thought, y'know, was maybe better to blend in a bit.'

Arlo watched him through the foamy glass as he took a few more swigs, stopping eventually for a little gas to escape. 'That's OK. I'm not much of a drinker anyway, to be honest. I mean, I enjoy a nice G&T before dinner and don't mind a couple of short drinks if I'm out, but it's not really my thing.'

Waffle was half listening, looking towards the bar. 'Oh yeah?'

'Mmm. Tell you the truth, I'm a bit more into the old er...' He swivelled his eyes quickly around them and lowered his voice to a whisper. '...*wacky backy.*'

He watched Waffle closely as if to gauge his reaction, and Waffle turned to meet his gaze.

'Is it? Do you?' He nodded appreciatively, his interest clearly piqued, but he said no more.

'Yup, big fan actually. I find so many people get aggressive when they drink, but the old weed? Just chills people right out, doesn't it?'

Waffle nodded. 'Yeah, I guess so.'

Arlo was still watching him closely and spoke tentatively. 'So er... do you like a smoke then, or not your thing? I must admit, you strike me as the kind of guy that's probably tried most things.'

Waffle considered this, unsure whether to take it as a compliment or an insult. 'Yeah, matter of fact I do. Or did, anyway. Used to smoke a lot, as it goes, but I've given up as of this week.'

Arlo looked disappointed. 'Ah, really? Shame.' He looked around him before shuffling his chair forward and continuing more quietly. 'You see, I was wondering if maybe you knew anybody. My usual guy has become a bit unreliable and I'm running low. I've been on the lookout for a new source, actually.'

Waffle considered him carefully and narrowed his eyes slightly. 'Oh yeah? What sort of thing were you after, and how much of it? Just out of interest.'

Arlo brightened, sensing he was maybe on the right track after all. 'Well. I like weed, not hash. And the stronger the better, to be honest. I like a good, solid kick, you know? Don't mind if I need to have a nice snooze after, I quite like it if it knocks me out a little.'

Waffle was nodding slowly.

'And, well, I'm looking to buy a fair bit, I suppose. I generally buy about once a month and my place tends to be where my friends hang out, so I like having a good stock in to be a good host. Like I say, my usual guy's left me a bit high and dry. Well, dry and not high!'

He laughed heartily at his own joke and waited for Waffle to respond, which he did after a little time.

'I thought you said you were low on funds at the moment?'

'Well, yes, I am currently. But it's just a cash flow thing. I get my allowance from Dad monthly, so I'll be topped up again in a few days.'

'Right. Well, it's a possibility, I suppose. I mean, I'm sort of keen to knock the whole thing on the head really, in both directions, but I might be able to sort you out, I'm not sure.' He picked up his empty glass and drained it thoroughly to get the last few drops out. 'Let me think about it, yeah?'

'Sure. Of course. Thank you. Much appreciated.' Arlo stood up and checked his jeans pocket for his wallet. 'Right then, bar it is. Just this one though, if you don't mind, before I head back — it's an early start after all.'

Waffle nodded in agreement. 'Yeah, I'm with you, brother. Don't want a late one, but bed before 8 pm is a little too early for me. Just thought a swift one or two would be nice and might help me get off to sleep. I wouldn't wanna get on the wrong side of Fran, either!'

Arlo smiled. 'Oh, Fran's great, honestly. I adore her. But yes, she does take it fairly seriously and doesn't exactly approve of alcohol on a yoga night, as it were. Oh, and um... not that you would, I know... but the last conversation... that's definitely not for Fran's ears. Drugs of any kind are most certainly not on her approved list. They'd require a laminated poster a lot bigger than her printer goes up to.'

Waffle tapped the side of his nose and winked. 'Understood!'

Arlo headed off to the bar while Waffle settled back into his chair. It occurred to him that the topic of weed had caught him by surprise and that he'd not thought about it all day. This in itself was rare and quite an achievement at that. Normally by this time of the evening he'd be well into a second or third spliff, and if he'd been out somewhere where he couldn't smoke, then he'd either be thinking about heading home or else getting a little twitchy. Maybe he was making progress, after all. Maybe the yoga had been a good idea and had taken him away from his usual surroundings and all that he associated with it, as well as giving him other things to think about. Maybe the exercise had even been good for him, God forbid.

He remembered the book about mindfulness that was waiting for him next to his bed. Perhaps he'd have a little read of that after all. It couldn't do any harm, could it? If nothing else, it would send him to sleep. But there was still the issue of the weed – the enormous bag of windfall weed stashed guiltily behind the hoover back in his flat. He still hadn't decided what to do about it, and although giving up smoking was his primary aim, becoming a drug dealer in its place didn't exactly sound like it would be anyone's idea of redemption – most certainly not Nat's. He pictured her unlocking their front door and walking into an exquisitely clean and tidy flat, with not a lager can, bag of dope, or dirty curry plate in sight. 'Guess what?' he'd declare, proudly standing in the centre of the pristine living room, sporting ironed clothes, a close shave and a new haircut. 'I've changed! I've knocked it all on the head and I'm a new man! I don't smoke, I've cut down on the drinking and there's a homemade shepherd's pie in the oven! And I've even got a job!'

'Oh, that's wonderful, darling' Daydream Nat says as she rushes into his open arms, 'I'm so proud of you! Forget the shepherd's pie, let's go out to celebrate!'

'Ah. Can't tonight, Nat. I've gotta head out in a bit, I've got 20 customers waiting for their weed deliveries down the estate.'

No. That wouldn't work well. But on the other hand, he needed money and had a big bag of something very sellable in his possession. What if he just got rid of it all as quickly as possible and used the cash for good? Paid off all his debts, paid the rent for a year in advance, and booked a holiday for them both for when she returned? Was it possible to sell something bad for a good reason? Didn't even the Bible say it was OK to steal bread to feed yourself if you're hungry? What about selling bread you'd found in the street that probably belonged to someone else? And what if you hadn't found bread on this occasion, but a load of drugs?

His train of thought was broken by raised voices at the bar. He looked up to see the two men he'd spoken to earlier, now both standing, red-faced and with fists curled. Arlo was placing two pints back on the bar, one of which was almost half empty and dripping foam down its side.

'Shit, I'm so sorry, guys. I just tripped. Here, let me help you.' He picked up the bar towel and moved as if to wipe the t-shirt of the nearer man, which was stained dark with fresh liquid over its shoulder and down one side.

The man took a step back as his face set into a snarl. The idea of being mopped dry didn't appear to be an attractive one to him. 'You come anywhere closer with that, you little ponce, and I'll knock your FUCKING head off,' he spat, smoothing his lank and thinning hair back across his head as he stabbed an outstretched finger towards Arlo's chest. The second man, shorter but thicker set and with dense, black stubble, stepped past his companion to face Arlo. He was rolling up the sleeves of his jumper to reveal forearms that spoke of spending a lot of time working in the sun. They were rough and weather-beaten to a deep, ruddy hue, but taut and solid. The multiple tattoos down their lengths added to the overall impression of a well-graffitied wall. Waffle leapt up and bounded across the room in a few, long strides, and was quickly alongside Arlo, taking the bar towel from his hands and gently pushing him to one side so that there was a clear space for himself to stand between the two parties.

'Woooah, don't think that's gonna help, is it, hoo-hoo!' He tossed the towel back onto the bar and faced the two men with a wide grin, as if seeing old friends for the first time in years. 'Now, what you drinking, gents? Pints, is it?' He looked past them to their abandoned drinks to confirm this was the case. 'Two more of those, please Landlord, and um… maybe a couple of whisky chasers, yeah?'

He turned back to the men with raised eyebrows. 'Yeah? Whisky alright for you, is it?'

Neither moved nor spoke, but the first, taller man nodded ever so slightly, his brow still deeply furrowed and a vein in his temple raised and throbbing. Waffle opened his wallet, drew out a twenty and pushed it across to the barman who wordlessly busied himself with the pints. Waffle then stuck out an elbow and relaxed onto the bar, still smiling and nodding along to himself. He looked down at the shorter man's exposed arms and then grinned even more widely, as if seeing something he'd been looking for. 'You see the match on Sunday? Absolute disgrace!'

There was another short silence before the man spoke, quietly and a little unsurely. 'How so?'

'That free kick, man! Hoo-hoo! Ref must've been fucking blind, no way was Bowen offside! And frankly, that second yellow was dodgy an' all. I didn't see any contact, did you?'

The man twitched slightly, and his top lip quivered. He had the look of a man who had to decide between having his arms cut off or having his legs cut off, with the decision causing him much inner turmoil. His companion turned to face him as he stared unblinkingly at Waffle for what seemed like an age.

'No,' he said finally, just as the two pints and two whiskies were placed in front of them by the barman. 'I didn't.'

Chapter 21

'Thank you, gents. And take it easy on the way home, yeah?'

The pub door shut behind them, swiftly followed by the sound of the bolts being slid into place, and a moment or two later the frosted glass panels in the door dimmed to a soft glow.

Waffle took in a deep lungful of cool, fresh air and let it escape slowly over his lips so that they vibrated with a horse-like flutter. Arlo stretched his arms with a yawn, but lost his balance when he closed his eyes and he fell back heavily onto the pub door with a hollow thud. He then bounced back off the door, pinball-style, and pitched forward, his speed building with a series of short, squirrelly steps in a doomed fight against momentum until he reached the kerb and took a brief but dramatic flight that ended with him face down and spreadeagled in the empty road.

Waffle looked on blurrily, and surveyed the scene for several moments before showing any sign of acknowledgement.

'Y'alright? he slurred eventually, followed by a long burp.

A surprising amount of time passed before Arlo moved, it being possible that he fell asleep briefly, but then he slowly got himself onto all fours and spat out a little gravel. 'Carncomplain.'

'Shouldproblygetback,' Waffle said, seemingly to himself, and he waved his wrist wildly in front of his face as he tried to follow it with a squinted eye to get the time. After a few unsuccessful passes, he managed to maintain focus for long enough to get a clear view, remembered he didn't own a watch, and nodded his satisfaction anyway. He figured it was probably about 11. Arlo meanwhile was shakily getting to his feet, and on finally attaining the vertical once more he beamed proudly to the street in general as he unsteadily joined Waffle on the pavement.

'Have a good night then, lads, nice to meetcha. Should do it again sometime.' The heavyset man with the tattoos shook both their hands, and then he and his mate staggered off into the darkness with their arms around each other's shoulders, singing 'Show Me the Way to Go Home' fairly loudly and very badly.

'Thought they'd already gone,' said Arlo, watching the two men disappear into the dark with a look of confusion.

Waffle frowned. 'Me too.'

They both swung their heads up and down the street to get their bearings, and then set off together in the direction of the Yoga Lawn, zigzagging along the pavement and occasionally bumping into each other, but not conversing much other than the occasional hiccup, each concentrating hard on co-ordinating which leg needed to be repositioned in which order to maintain motion.

After significantly more time than it should reasonably take to walk, the pair arrived at the Mad Parrot, which was quiet and dark. It looked rather foreboding in the gloom, the nearest lamppost ten or so yards off to the side casting harsh shadows across its black-painted facade.

'What's the plan, then?' said Arlo, now regretting his original strategy of just seeing how things panned out when he arrived back later – a strategy which, throughout history, has seemed stronger when setting out from somewhere than when arriving back later.

Waffled smiled. 'No problem, brother. I left the back gate unlocked and my window open for this very evench… evenchoo… moment!' He motioned for Arlo to follow and then headed off across the rough patch of unlit concrete next to the pub that passed for its car park and around to the back. The gate was indeed still unlocked, and Waffle pressed his thumb down on the latch and pushed it cautiously open, with Arlo close behind and holding onto his arm for security in the blackness. There was a loud creaking sound from the unoiled hinges that Waffle hadn't noticed on his way out, and it seemed to pierce the still night air in a way that could surely be heard by the whole borough. The slower he pushed, the more tortured it became, so he took a deep breath and employed the 'plaster removal' technique, pushing as quickly as he could in one smooth motion. The plan worked perfectly, and the gate swung open with the briefest of almost inaudible sounds that was more like a low swoosh than a squeak, and they were safely in.

The only downside was that Waffle had overbalanced himself by pushing forward so forcefully, and he continued to barrel through the open doorway, taking Arlo with him for the ride, and they both skittered through the darkness before falling in a heap onto the unseen pile of wood and tarpaulin. Fully protected by the virtual safety clothing provided by sufficient alcohol, neither was hurt, or had indeed felt anything at all, but convinced that the ruckus must surely have disturbed someone, they both stayed where they fell in silence for a few moments, deciding to wait until the coast was confirmed clear before moving.

When nothing continued to happen after an adequate amount of time, Arlo started giggling softly.

'Ssssh!' hissed Waffle, stabbing him in the stomach with a finger.

'Ow!'

'SSSSHHH!'

'You shsshh!'

'Be quiet.'

'Ssshhhh.'

'Ssssshhhhh.'

'Sshhhh.'

They both began giggling now in between shushing and got to their feet with difficulty, though Arlo fell once again as his foot got twisted up in some loose tarpaulin. Finally, they were both upright and tried to focus their eyes on their destination. Above the line of the yard's surrounding high brick wall, there was enough light cast onto the back of the pub from the distant street lamps and the general glow of the city beyond, but beneath this was a pool of gloom, and as their eyes continued to adjust, they could only make out vague shapes from the various heaps of junk stored there. A dim light from the bar inside leaked around the edges of the pub's back door, and this was enough for Waffle to identify the little barbecue that he'd lowered himself onto earlier. About six feet above this was the window in his room, clearly visible on the white wall and hanging invitingly open.

The two of them took tentative steps forward into what they determined was clear space and Waffle started thinking about how they were going to manage this reverse escape from the Yoga Lawn. Lowering himself from his window ledge hadn't been that difficult, but he'd had the advantages of being alone, sober, in daylight and not having to worry too much about noise near an open pub. Arlo was a good three or four inches shorter than him, plus a good deal drunker. And there was no getting away from the fact that gravity is most definitely a force that is easier to work with than against, especially so as the night wears on.

Waffle's other thought at this point was that he was particularly unimpressed with the building's lax security. He had no doubt that the door of the pub itself would be thoroughly locked and bolted, as well as probably alarmed, but nobody had checked to lock the yard gate since he'd left in the early evening, and his window was open to all. Admittedly, these were both things he'd deliberately done himself, so he had to concede partial responsibility, plus he was very grateful, but even so, he couldn't avoid feeling a kind of misplaced disappointment.

He wasn't sure if there was a great deal to steal from a yoga retreat, though, its main possessions of worth being peace, silence and mindfulness, none of which could realistically be stuffed into a swag bag even if they'd had any value on the open market. Still, there was a gong, he supposed. And a laminator somewhere.

At this precise moment, he heard a soft electrical clicking sound and was met with a wall of blinding light that seemed to bore its way through the backs of his eyeballs and directly into whatever part of his brain handled vision, overpowering it completely. Both men instinctively threw up their arms to shield their scrunched up eyes from the burning whiteness as Arlo let out a low whimper, and Waffle was sure he could even feel the heat emanating from the floodlight that had clearly been over-specced, and would've been perfectly sufficient to illuminate a good-sized car park.

'Shit!' Arlo whispered, 'Someone's bound to see us.'

Waffle was quick to reply, but didn't turn. 'Just don't move, stay still.' They both froze like the statues of two mortals facing God's wrath, hands across eyes and faces turned slightly away in fear. 'It'll go off in a sec, it's just a motion sensor.'

'But it's brighter than the sun! Someone will be down any moment, surely?'

'Just... stay still,' Waffle whispered through clenched teeth, 'it'll turn off.'

'But... but what if someone's seen the light? They'll know something's triggered it.'

Waffle exhaled with a little impatience. 'I dunno. They might think it's a... cat or something.'

They waited in silence, both listening out for any signs of life emanating from the pub. At first, there was nothing, but after a short time came the unmistakable clattering of a window latch being released somewhere. Waffle and Arlo froze with renewed attention to detail.

'Shit,' said Arlo, so quietly that even Waffle barely heard.

The clattering noise from above was replaced with a dull thud as the window frame was palmed loose with some force, and this was immediately followed by a sharp squeak as it began to swing open.

Neither of the men moved, and being blinded by the floodlight and with eyes shielded, could only visualise where the opening window was in their minds.

Suddenly, as quickly as it had come on, the light clicked off and the glow through their eyelids faded quickly from white to orange to black, albeit with a few stars pinging around their vision. The shout from above that they were both expecting didn't come, but neither did the sound of the window being closed, and they continued to stand in darkened, frozen silence waiting for something to happen.

'Meeeoooow!' Arlo sang out loudly, and Waffle's heart sank. He wanted to elbow Arlo in the ribs rather badly, but knew the game would be up if he did, and so did nothing but shake his head sadly in the gloom. Time seemed to stretch for an eternity, but then to Waffle's incredulity, the next sound that came was that of the window being swung closed and latched again. Peeking out from behind his hands, he could see that the room it belonged to had a light on behind net curtains, but after another second, this flicked out and they were left alone in the courtyard.

He turned slowly to Arlo.

'Meow?' he hissed slowly. 'Meow? Are you fucking mental?'

He could hear the smile in Arlo's voice. 'It worked, didn't it?'

Waffle took a deep breath and tried to suppress a grin. 'Yeah. Maybe. Look, we need to move out of the way of that sensor. Back away slowly and keep nearer the wall.'

'This is all quite exciting, isn't it? I mean, that was pretty close! One more second and we'd have been done for!'

'"Done for?"' Waffle was grinning widely now. 'C'mon, man, this place ain't the Bank of England. We're just trying to get back into a rundown yoga retreat above an East End boozer that we've both paid for in advance. I think the rozzers would go easy on us, you know?'

'I was thinking more about Fran, to be honest.'

Waffle pictured Fran – hair tied back tautly, eyes narrowed and her arms folded tightly across her chest, and he shuddered involuntarily.

'Yeah, fair point.'

'Right, what's next, then? We've got to get up into that window…'

Waffle sniffed. 'To be honest, I might just head home. If I can get the last tube then I can easily–'

'Wooah there!' Arlo turned to Waffle and grabbed both his arms through the leather jacket. 'You made me come out for a drink with you. The least you can do is get me back in again. I've paid good money and there's untapped totty in there. I'm not leaving in disgrace, I'll never be allowed back!'

Waffle sighed.

'Yeah, man. OK. Let's get this done then.'

They made their way to the barbecue and Arlo checked it for stability, quietly rocking it from side to side to see how much give there was. There was quite a lot. He pushed it gently back the last inch so that it was at least tight up against the pub wall, and readjusted the lid so that the handle left enough room for a foot to stand on either side.

'Is this safe?' he asked hopefully.

Waffle shrugged. 'Probably safer than eating anything cooked on it. And it took my weight on the way down, I'm sure it'll be fine.'

Waffle climbed up onto the garden table via one of the camping chairs until he was standing upright, feet apart and wobbling only slightly. From here it was about a yard to the barbecue, so he stuck one wiry leg out and stepped across the divide, leaning forward to allow his momentum to carry him across until his other leg followed and his nose was pressed up against the wall, a flat palm either side to balance him. The barbecue rattled quietly below him as it shook a little under his weight, but with the wall to lean into, he felt fairly stable.

He looked down at Arlo to indicate the route required so far, and could just about make out enough in the darkness to see a nod of understanding. From here, he reached upwards with both hands and was able to get a pretty firm grip on the open window ledge. He took three shallow practice bends with his knees, and on the fourth he jumped upwards with some force and an audible groan, managing to convert his hanging position to one where he was above the ledge and pushing down onto it in one fairly smooth motion. With elbows locked, he held this position for a moment and looked down to Arlo with a wide grin, before dipping his head in through the window and projecting himself into it, his feet last to disappear from view.

Arlo was mightily impressed with the apparent effortlessness of his technique and wondered for a moment whether perhaps Waffle had more experience in climbing into properties via their windows than he'd let on. He continued watching until Waffle reappeared, arms resting on the window ledge and his eyes searching for Arlo's in the darkness below.

'OK,' he said in a stage whisper, 'up you come. Just get onto the barbie and I'll help you up!'

Arlo took a deep breath and did as he was told, recreating the steps Waffle had taken to get in striking range of the window. Sobriety was still a little further out of reach for him than it was for Waffle, and although he managed to get onto the barbecue with no real drama, there had been a lot more wobbling along the way. Once in position beneath the window, he reached up as Waffle had done, but he was nowhere near being able to grip the ledge itself.

'Come on, man,' whispered Waffle helpfully, just stretch up and grab.'

'What do you think I am doing, Inspector Fucking Gadget? My arms don't get any longer!'

Waffle reached down and grabbed Arlo firmly by the wrists.

'OK... I'll count to three and then help pull you up, yeah? Do a little bounce on each count and then jump up on three and try to grab onto something.'

Arlo let out a deep sigh of frustration, but nodded his head. 'Yup, OK.'

'Nice one. Ready?'

Arlo nodded again.

'Right then. Three...'

'Hang on, I'm not ready! You said count to three!'

Waffle frowned. 'Yeah? Gimme a chance!'

'You need to start at one if you're counting to three, obviously. Or else start from three if you're counting down to one.'

'What did I do, then?'

'Started at three.'

'Did I?'

'Yes.'

Waffle took a moment to ponder this.

'Does it matter?'

'Of course it does!'

'Whatever,' said Waffle with a shake of the head. 'Which do you want?'

'I really don't care. I just need to know which word to jump on.'

Waffle thought for a second. 'OK,' he said, 'new plan. I'll say "X, Y, Z, jump", OK? No room for error there. You just jump on "jump", yeah?'

'Yes, thank you, Waffle. I worked that out.'

'OK, cool. Here we go... X, Y, Z...'

Arlo bounced a little on each count, the barbecue wobbling slightly under his feet and punctuating the countdown with a rattle.

'JUMP!'

Arlo pushed upwards with all his strength, kicking down hard with his feet as he tried to aim his hands towards the window ledge or beyond. With Waffle pulling strongly on his wrists, it felt like he had thrust himself skywards with enormous power, and the window came to meet him with seeming ease. He also felt his right foot catch on something as he lifted off, and although it pulled free easily enough, his toe momentarily snagging on the barbecue's lid handle was enough to unbalance it and yank it loose.

With a moan from Waffle, and some scrabbling of shoes up the pub wall, the two of them managed to get Arlo high enough up that he was able to get one hand and one elbow onto the window ledge, at which point Waffle – still grabbing on to Arlo's wrists with some force – allowed his weight to fall backwards into the room so that Arlo was dragged successfully, if unceremoniously, inside.

As soon as Arlo's knees were on the ledge, Waffle let go and fell to the floor with a heavy thump, and although Arlo was now free, he continued to fall forward and landed on Waffle's stomach with enough force to elicit a loud 'Oooof!' At that exact moment, the barbecue lid which had been flung loose from its base and had flown in a graceful arc through the air for a few moments, collided with the speedometer of a 1980 Yamaha XS750 with the crash of a loud cymbal that reverberated around the enclosed yard, before clanking to the bare concrete where it took several seconds to quieten as it settled itself like a spinning coin that refuses to come to a rest.

Arlo lifted himself from Waffle's stomach and got to his feet unsteadily as Waffle took a few deep breaths to ease the pain of being winded.

'A success of sorts,' said Arlo with a grin, 'home and safe at last!'

Waffle rolled onto his side clutching himself and then he too pulled himself into a standing position.

'Yeah, man,' he said with a wry smile, 'told you it'd be easy.'

He pulled the curtains shut and switched on the lamp by the side of the bed, illuminating Buddha with an eerie glow from below. He then walked to the door and pulled back the latch.

'I don't wish to be rude, but I think it's time for me to get some kip. Need to get a good night's sleep and all that so I'm ready to start in, what, about four hours?'

Arlo pulled back his sleeve and looked at his watch with a squint. 'Yep! Breakfast in four hours and twenty… something minutes. Can't do the maths.'

'Well,' said Waffle, 'it's been a good night. I'll give some thought to what you asked and I'll see you bright and early.'

Waffle turned the handle quietly and pulled the door open,

revealing a woman with arms crossed, hair pulled back extremely tightly into a ponytail and a look of murder etched with considerable detail across her face.

Waffle froze for a moment, then managed to force a broad smile.

'Ah, Fran! Good evening! Did you want to borrow the mindfulness book to get to sleep?'

Chapter 22

K *nock knock*

'Come in.'

'Hi Fran, er, it's me.'

'Yes, Waffle, I can see that. Come in, please.'

Waffle shut the door behind him, which took a fair amount of strength as it dragged a little across the floorboards and needed freeing at the halfway point. Fran's eyes followed the source of the noise with a frown and a shake of her head, and Waffle could just about make out her mutter 'bloody door' under her breath.

He stood awkwardly in front of Fran's desk, holding his hands together in front of him. He was reminded of the regular bollockings he used to receive from the headmaster at St Mary's Comprehensive, and felt oddly ill at ease, despite merely standing in front of a young woman who can't have been out of her twenties, and whose customer he was.

'Um... you asked to see me, Miss.' He couldn't resist the hint of a smile, but at the same time, he felt a vague prickle on the back of his neck.

'Sit down, Waffle,' she said, perfunctorily, and put down the pen she'd been writing with.

The room was not that dissimilar to Waffle's, in that it contained little more than a single bed, chest of drawers and a window, but it was a little larger and managed to squeeze in a wardrobe and a small desk on one side. The furniture was no newer or less tatty than in his own room, either, and looked like it had probably been sourced from a second-hand furniture shop. Possibly the 'secondHand furniture Shop' next door, it occurred to Waffle.

Fran watched him for a moment with a look that was hard to decipher but appeared to contain a mixture of annoyance, frustration and, possibly, a reluctance to want to start giving her guests a dressing down. Waffle decided his best strategy was to get in first.

'Look, Fran, about last night. I'm really sorry about the noise and everything and, well, the whole escaping and stuff.'

Fran looked at him levelly but without expression. 'It was more the coming in through a window, drunk off your face that I was concerned with.'

'Oh, well that too, of course. Goes without saying.'

'And dragging Arlo out with you? I know he's a grown man, but he's also an impressionable kid in a way. And a delicate one, too – he's been retching his guts out all morning.'

Waffle had noticed Arlo's absence from the morning session, but had suspected that he'd merely overslept. 'Ah...' he said, with a grimace, 'sorry about that too, then.'

They eyed each other for a moment in silence, Waffle adopting what he pitched as a slightly hopeful expression, while Fran chewed her lip and took deep breaths.

'Are you gonna kick me out?' asked Waffle, eager to break the tension.

Fran took another breath and rolled her eyes in annoyance. 'Look Waffle, this is a yoga retreat. It's not school, or a gang, or even a shop or a... I don't know, a library. We don't "kick people out", I've never kicked anyone out, and you know why?' She didn't wait for Waffle to respond. 'Because I've never had to! Why should I? People come here voluntarily, they pay their money and they practise yoga. Peacefully and silently. Because they want to.'

Waffle opened his mouth to respond but was cut off before he had the chance to speak.

'I've had this business now for nearly three years, and so far do you know how many times in total I've called someone into my room to have a talk like this?'

Waffle thought for a moment. 'Maybe one or two, tops?'

Fran looked exasperated. 'None, Waffle! I can even count the number of times there have been raised voices on one hand. Look!' She raised her hand and closed it to a fist. 'None too! Cos it's a fucking yoga retreat, Waffle! People don't sneak out in the middle of the night and... what did you call it? Escape! People don't *escape* in the night and go and get rat-arsed, and it's not because they're *not allowed*.' She said the last words in a childish cry as if mimicking an angry five-year-old that's been told they can't have sweets before their dinner. 'It's because they don't want to.

'I'm not the yoga police, Waffle. That's not part of my job description, y'know? I didn't think to myself, "Ooh, what business shall I build that'll give me the opportunity to monitor and reprimand drunks coming in and out through the night... a nightclub maybe or, I dunno, a rehabilitation centre? No, a yoga retreat, of course!"'

Her eyes were now wide and imploring, but Waffle decided that silence was perhaps the best response to this, and only partly because he couldn't think of anything to say. She took another extremely deep breath and let it out very slowly and with her eyes closed, then clicked her teeth together absent-mindedly a couple of times as if thinking something through internally. When she spoke again, it was more calmly.

'The thing is, Waffle, I've not had anybody here before who didn't seem to want to be here. Everyone that comes here just wants to do some yoga, and eat some healthy food and, I don't know, chill out. I don't *force* anyone to go to bed early or think about mindfulness or any of the other stuff. It's what people come here for. Do you understand?'

Waffle nodded.

'And you...' she looked him up and down. 'Well, you don't seem to be interested in any of that. You've come here wearing jeans, a hat and... that t-shirt, all of which you've been wearing for two days, I might add, and you don't seem to have any interest in doing the things that we offer.'

Waffle started to protest, but she cut him off with a wave of her hand.

'I mean, you're just not taking it seriously. Look at Arlo, for example. He loves it here and he's passionate about the same things I am. All he wants to do is improve his yoga.'

Waffle could feel the threat of a smile on his lips and worked quickly to snuff it out. He nodded solemnly instead.

'Whereas you, Waffle... well, to be honest, I just don't know why you're here.' She looked at him seriously for a moment. 'Why are you here?'

Waffle had understood his role in the conversation till now had very much been of the 'shut the fuck up and take the bollocking' kind, and he was acutely aware of the change of flow. He opened his mouth to speak but then realised he wasn't entirely sure why he was here either, and he sat like a goldfish for several moments while he tried to arrange his thoughts.

'Why am I here?' he repeated, pointlessly. He began to nod, as if ruminating on a serious and poignant question that he was about to respond to with the wisdom of the Dalai Lama. He resisted the temptation to steeple his fingers on his lips and close his eyes, but instead took a few more seconds to ponder a response.

'Why am I here?' he said again, making his first answer seem almost useful in retrospect. 'Look, Fran. I know what it must look like. I know what *I* must look like. I mean, I come here, I'm wearing all the wrong gear and everything.' He looked down at his t-shirt of the nailed, screaming bodies and pulled it taut at the seam to analyse the image from above. 'And yeah, I'm sorry about the t-shirt, it's completely inappropriate. I see that. And these jeans, you're right. They just don't afford me the flexibility I need at all.'

She looked at him slightly sideways, unsure if he was being serious or just taking the piss.

'I'm not taking the piss, by the way,' he said quickly, correctly reading her expression, 'I can just be a bit of an idiot sometimes, that's all.'

Fran's expression softened, though her eyes narrowed as Waffle looked down at the floor to find the words he was looking for.

'The thing is, I *am* here for the right reasons, honest. I didn't come properly prepared, that's true, and I didn't really know what to expect, I suppose. You probably didn't guess, but I'm actually new to this.' He tried a quick smile and Fran shook her head but smiled too, despite herself.

'What I'm trying to say is that I'm not here to just mess around. I'm sorry about last night, that was stupid. I was stupid. I just can't help myself sometimes, and I'm pretty good at messing things up. But I'm definitely here for the right reasons. I guess I've had a lot to think about recently... personal stuff and all that, and I needed a break. Needed to get away from my flat and my friends and clear my head a bit. And I thought yoga might be the answer. Admittedly, I didn't think about it for very long – maybe not long enough – but I think I did actually make the right decision.'

Fran pursed her lips and raised her eyebrows, just a little, but the hard edge to her eyes was easing.

'I like it here, I really do. And I've enjoyed the yoga. It's good for me, and although I might still be capable of being a twat from time to time, it's helping me with my mission.'

Fran looked at him quizzically. 'Your mission?'

'To be a better person,' Waffle said earnestly, his palms outstretched.

Fran snorted through her nose and then guffawed loudly, but checked herself when she saw Waffle's pained expression and reddening cheeks.

'Oh,' she said quietly, looking at the floor, 'you were serious. I'm sorry.'

Waffle shook his head. 'Nah, you're alright. It's no big deal. I'm just trying to work through a couple of things, that's all, and want to do better in life, you know? Improve myself a bit.'

'Well, that's... um, great, really. I'm sorry I laughed, that was very rude. I just thought you were taking the piss again.'

'No, I'm sorry. For everything. And I'll go now, it's for the best I think.'

'That's not what I'm saying, Waffle, I'm saying you can stay if–'

'No, really,' Waffle interrupted. 'It's all good. I need some better gear, anyway. But I'd like to come back sometime, if you'll let me. I'll still be crap at yoga, but I am trying, honestly I am. I was knackered after that first session yesterday! You can really feel it in your hamstrings, can't you? And I solemnly promise to try and be less of a twat next time and definitely, definitely won't try to escape again.'

Fran laughed as she raised her finger in admonishment. 'We don't use the 'E' word here, Waffle. You make it sound like a mental facility.'

Waffle swivelled his eyes theatrically from side to side. 'I'm saying nothing. Nurse.'

'OK, fine. Maybe you should go. And yes, you're welcome to come back, of course. But no more alcohol next time, and no leading any of my other guests astray, alright? And maybe a different t-shirt?'

Waffle raised two fingers to his temple. 'Scout's honour.'

'Good. Glad to hear it. I've got a business to run here, this is my livelihood, you know.'

Waffle nodded, happy that things seemed to be OK between them again.

Fran opened the desk drawer and retrieved a business card from a little plastic box, then scribbled something briefly on the back.

'My contact details are on there and I've put the dates on the back for our next few 3-day retreats,' she said, handing it to him. 'The website you booked through is fine but it's easier to just email or call, to be honest. It's a bit quicker now I have your details in the system and, well, I don't pay their fee that way.'

Waffle smiled and put the card in his wallet. He looked around the room and then scanned the items arranged on the desk. There was a row of very small, brown dropper bottles with rubber pipette lids, each with a different-coloured pastel label, and next to these was a framed document that appeared to be some kind of contract, and a flower in a vase.

'So how long have you been here, then? Three years, did you say?'

'Well, two years and ten months now, yes. You know what they say: it's not much, but it's mine! Well, it's rented, but you know what I mean. The business is mine.'

'How come yoga then? How does someone become the owner of a yoga retreat above a pub in East London?'

'Looking to start one of your own, are you?' she asked with mock suspicion. 'Gonna give me some competition?'

Waffle laughed and stretched his t-shirt out again. 'I should probably own proper yoga gear before that. And manage some of those poses without breaking into a sweat!'

'Oh, I thought your *shavashna* was perfectly decent.'

'Shavashna?' said Waffle with a frown, his eyes searching the ceiling for a memory. 'Isn't that the *corpse pose*? That's just a fancy word for having a lie down!'

'Everyone has to start somewhere. Your lying down was strong. Very... um, symmetrical.' The corner of her lips curved slightly and her eyes twinkled.

Waffle narrowed his eyes through a smile and waited for her to continue.

'Seriously though, I've wanted my own yoga place forever. I got into the whole thing in a big way when I was pretty young, really. I suffered badly from stress, and my GCSEs were a nightmare. Then when it got to preparing for my A-Levels, I couldn't handle it at all and I had a complete meltdown. My mum sent me to an 'alternative counsellor' who recommended I give it a go. Just as something to try first, before they started getting more serious and prescribing me anything, which my mum was dead against. She was a bit of a hippy, you see.'

'Was? But she got over it?' asked Waffle with a grin.

Fran fixed him with a flat stare. 'No, Waffle. As in, she died of cancer.'

'Right. Yep. Shit, I'm sorry.' Waffle swallowed and flushed.

Fran took a breath. 'Anyway, I just fell in love, I guess. Absolutely loved it. And it really helped my stress too, I soon stopped the counselling sessions.' She broke into a smile. 'Messed up my A-Levels anyway, mind you, but that was more down to Jack Haverhill and his deep brown eyes!

'Anyway, after I left school, I did all the qualifications and then did night school to learn business. I was just working in a restaurant at that point. But all I wanted was my own yoga place, it's the only plan I've ever had, I think. Fast forward a couple of years to when my mum died, and she left me a bit of money. I used that for the first year's rent and then got a loan for the next year. It's pretty difficult in London to find this kind of space, but a friend of a friend told me about it and it was perfect.' She pulled a face and wrinkled her nose. 'Well, not *perfect*, of course. It's not had that much TLC in a few hundred years, everything's falling apart and it's not exactly in the Cotswolds, but it had two stories for rent, a nice big room for the studio itself and it's in spitting distance of the Tube station. And round here,' she said with a sideways grin, 'that's a valid unit of distance.'

'Nice, nice. What did it used to be, then? Up here, I mean.'

'Well, I think it was a hotel bar from the late 1800s if you can believe the idea of this being a destination. Then it apparently had a brief phase in the 80s as a dance studio, back when everyone was wearing leg warmers and watching 'Fame' on TV. I think it was pretty much unused for years after that, not counting the occasional local wedding reception or dodgy poker game. Don't think Dave the owner could believe his luck when I said I wanted to pay a year's rent up front for both floors!'

'Yeah? That's all pretty cool. Must be nice to find what you want to do in life and then actually achieve it.'

Fran thought for a moment. 'Oh, it's been amazing. It won't last much longer though, Dave won't renew my lease after next spring. I think the building's going to be sold off with the others and the whole row flattened. New flats is what I hear, it's no great surprise really, it's half falling down as it is.'

'What will you do then?' asked Waffle, his face clouded with concern.

'Not sure yet, to be honest. I mean, I've been looking around for somewhere else, of course, but I've not found anywhere yet that I can afford. But I'm trying not to think too much about that, I'm trying to focus on growing the business here still. A few more customers would be helpful, and if I can make some cuts and save hard enough, then maybe I'll have a few more options. Or maybe I'll finally win the lottery and be able to afford somewhere with an actual lawn too!'

'Yeah, I was gonna ask about that,' said Waffle, looking out the window to where he could just make out the top of the yard wall and the side of the kebab shop next door. 'It does seem a little... *light* on the lawn side of things.'

'You're joking, aren't you?' Fran said with an air of extreme offence.

'Out the front door, take a left, next right, down another 200 yards, and there's a playground opposite the new flats. Gotta be a good ten square metres of grass if you add all the little patches together. Bit dog-shitty, mind you, but it's all present and accounted for.'

'Living the dream,' said Waffle, nodding appreciatively.

'It's what Buddha would've wanted.'

Waffle's eye again settled on the little glass bottles on the desk, and he reached forward to pick up the nearest one. He brought it close to his face to examine the tiny label. 'De-clouder,' he read out loud. 'Juniper, sandalwood and ginger,' he added slowly, squinting hard at the text. 'What's that for, then?'

Fran pursed her lips but replied after a few moments. 'It's to help you focus,' she said, cautiously.

'Is it?' Waffle said, nodding his head impressively, 'You'd need some to read the label.'

Fran went to reach for the bottle, but Waffle had already picked up the next one and was eyeing it from a distance, turning it around in his fingers as if poring over a jewel with an expert eye. 'And what does this one do?'

Fran took a breath. 'It's to help you find your path.'

'Oh yeah?' said Waffle, holding it up to the light to examine the liquid through the glass. 'What is it then, weedkiller?'

Fran frowned and snatched both bottles from him, carefully placing them back in position with the others. She felt her cheeks redden with mild embarrassment, but when she looked back at Waffle he was smiling, and his eyes were twinkling with mischief.

'Hmm,' she said, noncommittally, picked up her pen and began to roll it around in her fingers. Waffle took this as his cue and stood to leave. Fran turned back to her paperwork with a 'Thanks Waffle. Maybe I'll see you another time, then,' but as Waffle turned towards the door, she spoke again.

'Oh, Waffle, one more thing.'

He raised his eyebrows questioningly.

'Last night, when you two were clattering around in the courtyard and shushing each other deafeningly…'

'Er… yep?'

She tilted her head to one side. 'Seriously? Miaow?'

Chapter 23

'Lenny, Soapy, come in. S'up? What's so important you couldn't tell me by text?'

Lenny walked through into the lounge but stayed standing, a nervous energy in him clearly evident from the way he kept shifting his weight from one foot to the other. It appeared that Soapy had already learned whatever news Lenny had and was just looking quickly between the other men, the effort of staying quiet putting visible stress on him.

'I've just had a phone call, I think you're gonna like it.'

'Come on then,' said Tommo, circling the air with a finger, 'let me have it, Lenny, don't keep me in suspenders.'

Lenny nodded quickly. 'Well, there's this geezer I sell to regularly. Posh bloke I met in some fancy club up West a couple of years ago, and been my customer ever since. Don't think you've met him but you drove me to his place once and waited outside; swanky apartment just off Sloane Square?'

Tommo shrugged. 'OK, yeah. Rings a bell maybe. What about him?'

'Well! He's a decent enough bloke, always has the cash, no messing about or anything, but he's a bit of a drip and he's a talker, y'know? My main problem with him is just getting out of his place, it's like he wants to be your friend or something. I just wanna give him his stuff and get my dough, yeah, but he'll start telling you about his day or some shit like he's your best mate.'

Tommo said nothing but circled his finger again impatiently while looking to the ceiling.

'Right, yeah. Well, he'd called me a couple of days ago to tell me he needed some weed, right, and I said we had a temporary supply issue and I didn't have anything to sell for a few days. Told him I'd get back to him in a week maybe when it's all sorted.'

'OK.'

'Well, he's just rang back and he says not to worry, he might've found someone else to buy from. Like I say, he's a talker, I think he was actually just phoning to apologise to me, like I give a shit.'

Lenny paused for effect and allowed a smile to creep across his face. 'He tells me he's met some bloke who reckons he might have some, y'see. Some lanky bloke with a green hat.'

Tommo's eyes widened, but then he frowned. 'He gave you a physical description of his new dealer?'

Lenny laughed. 'What can I tell you? He's a talker! He was going on about how he went for a pint with this bloke and how it turned out he might have a supply, and then he just mentioned that he was a bit of a crazy guy and always wore a hat. I asked him about it and he was happy to tell me whatever I wanted, so I just started making conversation. Coaxed some details out of him.'

'Nice one.'

'Yeah. I reckon we have our man!'

'Well, let's not get ahead of ourselves just yet. There's more than one green hat in London.'

'Yeah, but someone who's just got a load of weed in? Seems like a bit too much of a coincidence to me. I reckon it's him.'

'Alright, alright. Let's check it out now. What's his address?'

'No idea.'

Tommo stared unblinking into Lenny's eyes. 'Come again?'

Lenny looked pained. 'I don't know, that's the only problem.'

'Yes, Lenny, that's a bit of a problem. Didn't you ask your posh bloke?'

'Yeah, course, I got it in really subtly and everything, but he didn't know either. He said he's not even at home himself, he's out East somewhere doing yoga.'

'Yoga?'

'Yeah, that's what he said. He's staying at some yoga place for a few days.'

Tommo shook his head sadly. 'Fuck's sake,' he spat with incredulous disdain. 'Posh people.'

'I know, right?'

'But you got a name, yeah? Tell me you got his name?'

Lenny smiled broadly. 'Of course I did! You'll like this... apparently his name's Waffle.'

'Waffle? That's a ridiculous name.'

Soapy giggled. 'I think it's his nickname.'

'Oh, do you think?' Tommo started to move around the room, rubbing his chin in thought. 'Well, it's something I suppose. We still don't know where the fuck this guy lives, but we've got a nickname and we still think he might be local. The name's unusual too, which is good. There might be more than one guy out there with a green hat, but I don't think there can be many blokes called Waffle with green hats and bags of our weed.'

'Well, there's one more thing, actually. You know I said he was banging on about going for a pint with this guy, telling me all about it?'

'Uh huh.'

'Well, he told me the name of the pub they went to.'

Tommo screwed his face up.

'So what? You said it was out East? How does that help us? He's not still in the pub is he?'

'Nah, it's not that. It's just that this Waffle geezer apparently said that the pub had the same name as his local.'

Tommo pursed his lips and angled his head slightly to the side. 'Did he now? And what's this pub called then? Please don't tell me it's the Red Lion or King's Head, or some common shit like that.'

A wide smile cracked across Lenny's face. 'That's the best bit. It was the Earl of Wessex.'

'The Earl of Wessex! Shit! I thought ours was the only one.'

'I know, me too.'

'D'yer reckon it's named after our pub, then?' asked Soapy, looking up to Tommo hopefully.

Tommo narrowed his eyes. 'No, Soapy, I expect they're both named after Queen Victoria.'

Soapy began to nod, but it fizzled out with a frown.

'So, what's the plan then, Tommo? Head over there?'

'Well. We have a pub, we have a name and we have a description. There's gotta be someone there that'll know him. But let's not go all guns blazing, yeah? We don't wanna look too suss. I reckon we head over at about 12, get a couple of pints in over lunch and then make some casual chitchat, you know? We just need to find out where he lives. If he's a regular there, then someone's bound to know. And then, my friends, we shall pay this Mr Waffle a visit.'

Lenny was nodding seriously and Soapy began to rub his hands. Tommo checked his watch.

'OK, it's 10:35. Call Playboy and D and tell them to come over. We'll head off from here in an hour.'

* * *

'Good afternoon, Miss. Would I possibly be able to speak to the manager?'

'Oh, no no no, not here you don't!'

Phil looked nonplussed. 'I can't speak to the manager here?' He looked around himself. 'Where can I, then?'

'No, I meant you can't smoke in here. Please put those away.'

Phil looked down to his hands and seemed a little surprised to find a menthol cigarette in one and a lighter in the other, as if they'd been plotting a secret liaison without his knowledge.

'I do apologise, force of habit I'm afraid.' He dropped the lighter into his pocket and fished out the packet to return the cigarette, then clapped his hands together and smiled, as if to start the meeting again. 'Now, where were we?'

'You wanted to speak to the manager.'

'I do, yes. Would that be possible?'

'Aye,' she said, 'you already are. I'm the owner and manager. How can I help you?'

'Ah, are you? Marvellous. I'm DI Collins and this is DC Watts, we just have a couple of questions for you, if you don't mind, Miss…?'

'MacRae. Fran MacRae. Sure, go ahead.'

Phil paused for a moment, then did a quick nod and continued.

'Well, Miss MacRae, we're looking for someone we'd like to have a chat with. We understand he's staying here at the moment, a Mr Jones. Mister...' he turned to Mike for assistance.

'Darren.'

'Darren Jones, that's it. Is he here at all?' Phil was looking down the corridor, his years of experience meaning it was impossible for him to avoid looking for any movement or escape routes.

'I'm afraid you've just missed him,' Fran said, spinning the guest book round so that they could read it. 'He was due to stay until tomorrow but left this morning – a couple of hours or so ago, actually.' She tapped her pen on the time she'd entered into the book. '8:27, to be exact.'

Phil peered closer to the book to confirm the entry and let out a long breath through his nose.

'Ah. Well, that's disappointing.' He turned to Mike, who flicked his eyebrows up in agreement but said nothing. He'd felt that Superintendent Fletcher probably had a point when they'd been called into his office yesterday, and nothing had changed his mind in the meantime. This was starting to feel a lot like a wild goose chase and they had a very real and very important case they needed to be working on. Maybe now that they'd missed their man again, Phil would just let it go, or give it to someone else to deal with, as Fletcher had suggested.

'Did he say where he was going at all? Home perhaps?'

'I wouldn't know. I assume home though, aye.'

Phil held her gaze for a moment, then tapped his fingernails in succession on the edge of the desk in a particularly arhythmic way and stared down, deep in thought.

'Is there anything else I can help you with?'

Phil made a final rap on the desk with all his fingers at once and looked up with a smile.

'No. Thank you, you've been very helpful. Though, perhaps you'd be so kind as to call us if you hear anything from Mr Jones?' he nodded to Mike, who had taken a pen from the holder on the desk and was now scribbling on the pad of paper Fran proffered him.

'If you like.'

Phil nodded. 'Thank you.'

Mike rolled the pen in his fingers, examining it quickly. It was just a cheap, disposable biro. 'Mind if I...?' he asked with meaningful eyebrows, his hand frozen halfway to putting the pen in his pocket.

Fran exhaled loudly. 'If you must.'

'Thanks again,' said Phil as he was heading towards the staircase, but as he reached for the bannister, he stopped and turned back.

'You said he was booked to stay until tomorrow?'

Fran looked up from where she'd been busying herself with the guest book. 'Yes, that's right.'

'So how come he left early then?'

The hint of a smile curled at Fran's lips. 'Well, let's just say he left by mutual agreement.'

Phil frowned as he turned his head to the side. 'Oh really? For what reason?'

Fran thought for a moment. 'Hmm. How to put this?' She twisted her mouth in thought and then wrinkled her nose. 'He was just a bit of a dick.'

* * *

WAFFLE PUSHED OPEN THE DOOR, which buzzed as he did so, and cast his eyes around. There was nobody at the counter, but he could see the back of a figure towards the rear of the shop stacking tins of soup, so he let the door fall shut behind him and wandered over.

'Good afternoon, Mr K, how goes it?' he boomed, his face cracked with a broad grin.

Mr Kottarakkara turned his head about two degrees to the side for a moment but continued his task without pausing.

'Hello Darren,' he said flatly, 'you're still alive then?'

'Couldn't be more so, Mr K! Did you miss me?'

There was a short pause, punctuated only by the clacking of tins being stacked carefully.

'No. Why on earth would I miss you?'

'Oh, I dunno. My friendly demeanour, our little chats. Maybe even just my regular custom.'

Mr Kottarakkara flicked his eyes towards the beer section of the fridges. 'Actually, yes. I did notice lager sales were down a little.'

'Well there we go! If nothing else then I contribute to your income and well-being.'

There was a quiet snort of derision, and then silence fell between the two of them, with Waffle continuing to stand behind his landlord, watching him work in silence. Mr Kottarakkara let out an exasperated breath.

'Go on, then. Where have you been? You clearly want me to ask, not that I particularly care.'

Waffle clapped his hands together and smiled. 'Well, since you ask, I have been on a long and difficult journey of inner reflection, including much physical endurance and exertion.'

Mr Kottarakkara put his last tin in place and looked Waffle up and down dispassionately. 'If you just mean that you got the bus to a more distant pub than usual and also had to walk for a bit, then I'm not impressed.'

'Hoo-hoo! You're a funny guy, Mr K!' Waffle said, grinning widely and wagging his finger at him. 'But, no. This wasn't a pub, and this wasn't about drinking. Well, technically it was above a pub, I suppose, and there was a little drinking, but that would definitely be missing the point. No, Mr K, I have been practising the ancient art...' He closed his eyes and moved his hands together as if in prayer, '...of yoga.'

'Ha!' roared Mr Kottarakkara, his face crumpled in amused contempt. 'And which yogi master did you learn under, then? Did some guru fly in specially from India to give you emergency lessons?'

'Um, no. Her name was Fran. I think she was Scottish.'

Mr Kottarakkara snorted again. 'Of course she was.'

'Well, she seemed to know what she was talking about,' said Waffle defensively, 'she even had a gong.'

Mr Kottarakkara looked at Waffle sadly. 'Honestly, Darren, you're a tourist in your own country, aren't you? You eat Nabil's awful take-away curries, you drink exotic foreign beer brewed in the West Midlands, and now you're learning the ancient art of yoga from a fellow Briton. Look, if you want to go to India, get on a plane at Heathrow. But otherwise, just go upstairs, have a Pot Noodle and watch Only Fools and Horses.'

'What can I say, Mr K? I enjoy all the meats of our cultural stew.'

Mr Kottarakkara appraised him with narrowed eyes. 'Oh, and where did you appropriate that quote from?'

'Homer, actually,' said Waffle, jutting his chin proudly.

'Really? The ancient Greek poet?'

Waffle wrinkled his nose. 'Nah. The modern American cartoon character. But he's wiser than he looks.'

'Achha, you're an idiot sometimes.'

Waffle grinned. 'Anyway, Mr K, I must be getting on. Toodle pip an' all that. I just popped in to say hello and to have one of our nice chats.' He dug his hands into his pockets and started for the door, his flip-flops slapping as usual on the tiled floor.

'Yes, yes,' said Mr Kottarakkara, heading out to the storeroom for more tins. 'Oh, and Darren, you made me forget…'

Waffle stopped and turned. 'Yes?'

'You have company upstairs.'

'Company? Someone's waiting for me?' Waffle looked confused. 'Who?'

'Oh, they said not to say. A surprise, if you like.'

Waffle scanned his memory for any plans he'd made to meet anyone, but he only regularly saw Harj and Learner Joe so it didn't take very long to scan. 'Hmm! OK then, I like surprises! Adios, Mr K!'

Chapter 24

Waffle whistled as he passed under the passageway between the shops, and then bounded up the stairwell, his long legs taking two at a time as usual. He rounded the corner and began to fetch the door key from his pocket, but as he did so he noticed that the front door was ajar. He stopped whistling and pushed gently on the door so that it swung slowly open as his wide eyes peered around it.

He stayed outside until the door had stopped moving, and he could see the whole of the living room. His eyes widened further as he took in the scene.

'Hello, Waffle.'

'I wasn't expecting you,' he said without thinking, for once at a loss for words.

'Surprise!' Nat said, faking enthusiasm without conviction. She was on the sofa, her phone, handbag and the remains of a cup of tea on the coffee table.

Waffle stood awkwardly in front of her, unsure where he should go. There was only the one sofa and it didn't seem appropriate in the circumstances to sit down next to her, so he remained standing, one hand rubbing the other arm nervously. Despite him feeling her absence so keenly over the last few days, it seemed odd seeing her back in the flat again, even though she was doing nothing more novel than sitting on the sofa where she'd always sat. It was as if the context was all wrong, like when a work colleague comes to a party at your house, or you spot an old teacher in the pub.

She looked a little different too, but he couldn't put his finger on anything specific. The clothes seemed familiar, he thought, maybe she'd just done her make-up differently, or had a subtle haircut. There was definitely an unusual minty smell in the air, perhaps she was wearing a new perfume.

'How long have you been here? If I'd have known, I'd...' His voice trailed away.

'Half an hour maybe. I saw Mr K first, and he said he'd not seen you for a day or two. Didn't know where you were. I decided to come and wait with a cup of tea, and if you didn't turn up by the end of it then I'd leave a note and head off.'

They both looked down at the nearly empty cup. 'Top up?' said Waffle.

'Go on then.'

Waffle shuffled into the kitchen area and picked up the kettle to shake it. It was virtually empty, so he filled it at the tap, put it back and flicked the switch. Nat was looking at something on her phone, so he decided to put a record on to fill the silence and to give him somewhere to sit, even if it was just knelt on the floor. He flicked through the records as usual, one by one, but was conscious that he wasn't just trying to pick something pleasant to listen to, but something appropriate for the occasion. He didn't want to scare Nat off with anything he knew she didn't like, or anything they couldn't talk over easily, but then he was also conscious that anything overtly flirty or sensual might give the wrong message and come across as presumptuous. This was also his first opportunity to show her how much he'd changed for the better already, so he was keen to play something sensitive, something mature. But nothing pretentious.

After he'd flicked through the first stack of albums with no success, he realised that his list of requirements was a little prohibitive and that the Venn diagram of acceptable choices had a vanishingly small overlapping area. It was like trying to find an appropriate gift for a teenage member of the Spanish royal family who'd just suffered a terrible bereavement on their birthday.

Led Zeppelin? Too loud. King Crimson? Too weird. Al Green? Too sexy. Velvet Underground? Too druggy. Jeff Buckley? Too deathy. INXS? Too sexy, druggy and deathy. He took a deep breath and searched out Ella Fitzgerald. It was a bit of an obvious choice as it was one of her favourites, but it seemed like the safest ground he could find in the circumstances, and he couldn't just sit there with his back to her forever. He put the record on and finished making the tea.

'So,' she said, once he was sitting back on the floor on the other side of the coffee table. 'Where have you been then? Out on a bender? Or, maybe... um... with a girl?' She arched an eyebrow over her teacup and forced a small smile, trying to look as if either answer was perfectly acceptable.

Waffle spluttered on his first mouthful of tea. 'What? No, no, neither!' He put the cup down and wiped his mouth. 'God, no, nothing like that.'

She held her smile but continued to watch him, trying to look relaxed and comfortable, but still apparently waiting for an answer.

'No, I've just been away for a couple of days, that's all. I've been trying to... y'know...'

She shook her head. 'No?'

The words swimming around Waffle's head that were trying to escape were 'self-improvement', 'mission', and 'yoga', but although he was desperately keen to get the point across, he was acutely aware that the words alone, if not used with care, could just make him look like a massive wanker. Although he'd been wishing desperately to have this conversation since she'd left, he realised now that maybe he should've spent a little bit of time planning how it might go when the moment came.

'I've been... trying to fix things,' he said cautiously.

Nat looked confused. 'Fix what?'

'Well. Me, I suppose.' He looked down at the floor, struggling with confidence in what he was saying for the first time he could remember in years. 'I just want to be a better person.'

She held her hand to her mouth to stifle a laugh, and it occurred to him that straddling the line between honest self-confession and wankerdom was going to be an even more difficult balancing act than he'd thought. He decided to stick with simple statements.

'I've given up smoking,' he said hopefully. 'And I've got a job.'

Nat looked genuinely taken aback, though her eyes immediately darkened with suspicion. She leant back a little so she could peer under the coffee table to the shelf that usually held his smoking gear, and noted that it was empty.

'Really? Since when? And what job?'

'A few days now. Packed it all in. Not had a takeaway either. Not even had meat, come to think of it, but that wasn't deliberate. And the job's just cleaning in a hospital, but it's five days a week, regular money, and something to get started with.'

Nat was nodding slowly. She seemed impressed.

'And the job's going OK, is it?'

Waffle paused and chewed his lip. 'Well. The days I've been, yeah.'

She rolled her eyes and let out a disappointed sigh. It was a reaction he was fairly familiar with. He decided to correct course a little.

'No, I mean... well, I did the training and then it starts properly soon, that's all. Next Monday.'

'Right. I see. OK.'

It seemed to have worked. They both sipped their tea in silence, her eyes slowly scanning the room. She nodded towards the lack of TV. 'I thought you'd have replaced that by now. Didn't think you'd cope without it.'

He tried to ignore the accusation in her tone and scratched the back of his neck. 'Was going to wait till I'd saved up some money from the job. I've been paying off my debts and from now on I'll just save everything I earn and will only buy what I need when I've got enough saved.'

'I see.'

'Plus, I've not been here anyway,' he added, realising almost immediately that this undid all the good work he'd just done.

'Ah yes. Where did you say you'd been again?'

'Umm, well...'

There was no getting away from it now. He only had two paths available to him: lies and obfuscation, or the truth and possible ridicule. But then what did he have to be embarrassed about, really? The whole point of the yoga was to try and improve himself, it was an essential part of The Mission. This was the moment when he had to lay bare the effort he was making for her. She'd see that it was all real, that he meant what he'd been trying to say, and that he was genuinely changing. Plus, she was a good person, she'd value his honesty as well as his efforts.

'I went to a yoga retreat.'

There. He'd said it.

'Yoga?'

'Yep.'

'Are you serious?'

'Yes. Of course I am.'

This time, her hand didn't even reach her mouth in time to cover the laugh, and it wouldn't have been enough, anyway. She guffawed loudly, a proper belly laugh that burst out of her with the force of a water balloon being dropped onto concrete. Waffle studied the curtains and ran his tongue along his teeth, the embarrassment beginning to curdle into irritation.

'You?' she managed through heaving sobs.

'Yes, Nat, me. I went to yoga. What's the problem?'

Nat took a couple of breaths and fanned her face, then used the edge of her finger to wipe a tear away, a move that Waffle considered entirely unnecessary and dramatic, especially as she wasn't even wearing makeup. She composed herself with a final, deep breath with eyes closed, and then opened them again to appraise Waffle. Her expression was very hard to read, and Waffle was desperate to see affection in there, but if it was there, then it was definitely mixed in with a few other things. After a moment she frowned, something evidently on her mind.

'Have you just got back then? You've come straight from there?'

'Yeah. Why?'

'So what did you wear?' Her eyes fell from his face to look at his clothes. 'Don't tell me you...'

Waffle looked away and felt his cheeks begin to redden.

'NO! Really?'

She looked back to his t-shirt and began to laugh again, this time clutching her belly as she rocked back and forth. She was clearly aiming to cover all the bases when it came to the clichés of showing amusement.

'Waffle, seriously! I mean... God!'

Waffle chewed his lip and found himself fighting to contain the annoyance that was bubbling up from within him. It simply hadn't occurred to him that his recent efforts would be met with derision when he opened up to her, and he felt a mixture of extreme embarrassment and resentment. He knew deep down that he needed to do everything in his power to win Nat back, but his overriding feeling at this precise moment was one of being pissed off. He decided to try another course of conversation entirely.

'So. What did you come back for?'

Nat brought her laughter to a close, but the jut of her chin and quizzical expression made Waffle realise that his question had probably sounded a lot more combative out loud than it had in his head.

'I mean... did you forget... um, can I do something... er, have you....'

He couldn't think of a way to finish the sentence appropriately, and he realised that he wasn't entirely sure why she *was* here, after all. It appeared that his original hope that she'd come running back to beg his forgiveness and leap into his arms probably wasn't it, though deep down he'd always known it was pretty unlikely. It was still possible that she was open to some kind of discussion, though, some open and honest conversation where he could apologise for his behaviour and promise to make amends. However, if this was her reason for coming back, then she was doing a pretty good job of hiding it so far, and he'd have to show her how he'd changed for the better without going into any specifics that might amuse her.

The third likely reason was that she was here to pick up the washing machine, the thing he'd suspected all along that she might make the trip for. His heart sank as he acknowledged to himself that, deep down, he'd already accepted this as fact.

'Well,' she said, taking a quick sip of tea, 'I had a few things to sort out. I've taken some holiday off at work but had to go in to pick up a couple of things. Plus, I'm only off for ten days, I can't work from my parents' place forever, I need to find a flat.'

Of course. Waffle had forgotten that she'd need to go to work, stupid though that suddenly seemed to him. The commute into central London was a bit of a pain from the flat, but he suspected it would be significantly worse from Yorkshire. He felt like an idiot to even consider that she was back for any kind of reconciliation when it was abundantly obvious she had to find somewhere else to live in order to go to work. He decided not to mention that he'd forgotten about her job, as he didn't think it would go down too well in the circumstances.

'Right, yeah. Course.' He picked up his mug and buried his face into it, letting the hot steam warm his nose and cheeks and then dampen them with condensation.

'I came to see you too, though,' she said. 'It seemed silly to come all this way back and not pop in to say hello. I mean, I needed to check you weren't comatose on the sofa, the first person ever to OD on lager and chicken bhuna.'

He extracted his face from the mug and saw that she was watching him with a curl of a smile before her eyes flicked downwards to her own tea. Perhaps it was the right moment to try again at opening up a little, Waffle thought, to allow her a quick peek at his vulnerable side. Nothing as extreme as admitting his urge to experiment with stretching and breathing exercises, but just something to show that he was human after all.

'Thanks, Nat,' he said with solemnity. 'It's been hard, to be honest, and I've had a few low moments these past few days, I'm not gonna lie. But you've got to get on, haven't you? Can't just sit and sulk in front of daytime TV, even when you have one. You've got to try and think through what went wrong and find ways to make yourself better and stronger so it won't happen again.'

She was looking at him with an open expression of sympathy. Head tilted to one side, hands clasped tightly around her mug, eyebrows knitted above wide-open eyes. Could that even be a tear forming? Her eyes looked pretty shiny, he thought, and she blinked rapidly a couple of times as if to clear them.

'Ooh!' she said, suddenly sitting up straight and putting the mug back onto the table. 'That reminds me!'

She reached behind her, stuffing both hands into the sofa and under the cushions, feeling about while she looked up to the ceiling, biting her lip in exaggerated concentration.

'Aha!' she exclaimed with relish, her face lighting up. She brought her hands round to her front and brandished her discovery to Waffle with a wide grin. 'TV remote! Bloody thing... can barely change the TV volume without it! I knew there was something I had to remember.'

Waffle sagged and breathed out very slowly as he let his head fall. Of course. There had to be a good reason for her visiting and it was the ability to control their old TV without having to physically move.

'I thought it might be the washing machine,' he said despondently and almost to himself.

'Hmm?' She was standing up and collecting her things together, only half listening to him. 'Oh, that? It's just a cheap one, I'm going to get something decent when I sort a new place.'

Waffle nodded. 'So that's it then, is it? After all we've been through together, you just needed the TV remote?'

She looked at him with genuine curiosity, her head tilted to one side. 'We haven't been through anything together, Waffle. You were just nearby for a while.'

Chapter 25

The silver Vauxhall Corsa was driving at speed down the bus lane of the A13 towards Limehouse station, with both occupants wishing they still had the Mondeo with its siren and hidden blue lights.

'So you're not going to let it go, then?'

'No,' said Phil, simply. 'We need to get hold of this guy and it seems very likely he'll be back at his flat.'

Mike grimaced and then bit his lip. 'But you heard what Fletcher said. He wants this dropped, wants us to get back to the car ring.' He paused for a second. 'And I have to admit, I think I'm with him. I mean, we can't risk that for anything and all we seem to be doing is running around town chasing after some guy with a bag of weed when we could be nailing some proper scumbags.'

He turned to look at Phil, who was looking resolutely ahead of him in silence. 'Guv?'

Phil said nothing and just looked down at the cigarette packet he was holding in both hands. Mike reached the turnoff for the Rotherhithe tunnel, but both lanes were on a red light and he was forced to slow in the queue.

'Go round,' said Phil, quietly enough to be almost inaudible but accompanied by a light flick of his hand, and Mike pulled out into the oncoming traffic and around the wrong side of the pedestrian island, carefully threading through the cars screeching to a halt in his path before wrenching the Vauxhall round to the left and into the narrow lane that led down to the tunnel.

He took another quick couple of glances at Phil in between steadying adjustments of the steering wheel, but Phil continued to stay silent and unmoved.

'Are you telling me everything?' asked Mike warily. He'd never pushed Phil before, aside from the odd bit of teasing banter, but there was something that didn't feel right and it was starting to make him uncomfortable.

Phil finally turned to face him, but his grey eyes had hardened to flint. 'What do you mean?'

Mike shuffled in his seat and concentrated on threading the car at speed down the narrow, twisting lane that led into the dark tunnel ahead.

'It just seems like... I dunno, that maybe I'm missing something. I don't get it. You've been saying for weeks that we can't mess up this job and yet just as we're reaching the end, you seemed to have stopped caring about it. You've barely mentioned it for the last two days and all we've done is chase after this Jones character. I'm not sure I understand why.'

'I told you. We can do both. It's not a problem. We just need to nick Jones, find out what he's got, and then we can get back to the car ring. They're not going anywhere just yet and Turner's got it all under control. You need to relax.'

Mike cast a last glance at Phil in the open daylight as they entered the tunnel and saw a face less relaxed than he'd even seen it before. The jaw was tight, the brow furrowed, and the eyes fixed into the distance ahead of them.

Mike's grip tightened on the wheel. 'OK. Well, you're the boss–'

'That's right, Constable!' shouted Phil, suddenly animated and swinging around in his seat to glare at the side of Mike's face. 'Just do me a favour, will you, and do what you're told? You're here to learn, not dictate orders, so just let me get on with it and offer me whatever support I need. Got it?'

Mike stared fixedly ahead, concentrating on driving. 'Yep,' he said in a small voice.

The drive through the tunnel was slow going. There was traffic in both directions and no feasible way to pass, so once he'd closed the gap to the car in front, Mike throttled back and slowed to a more reasonable speed. An uncomfortable silence settled between the two men. Mike stared fixedly ahead, concentrating on driving through the narrow tunnel, while Phil fiddled irritably with his cigarette packet, flicking the lid repeatedly open and shut again.

As the archway of light began to grow and brighten, Mike anticipated the opportunity to overtake by changing down and flashing his headlights wildly. As soon as the road burst into the bright sunshine, the car in front slowed, and Mike pulled past with the rough roar of paltry diesel acceleration. He looked across at Phil from the corner of his eye and noticed the fidgeting had slowed, but not stopped altogether.

They headed straight on at the roundabout, and with the traffic being relatively light in the middle of the day, Mike found that he was able to make pretty good progress. Sometimes when they were driving together, Phil would navigate, providing brief directions as they approached junctions, his years of experience often proving better than the sat nav at searching out useful shortcuts and back roads. His instructions were usually offered at the very last moment, which infuriated Mike, but not so much that he'd ever pointed it out. Today Mike had felt that Phil would either not bother with the help or else it would lead to an argument, so he'd taken the opportunity in the slow-moving tunnel to tap in the address on the sat nav, enabling the two of them to sit in relative silence, aside from the occasional chirpy guidance of Default Female Voice 1.

'Look,' said Mike tentatively, keeping his eyes firmly facing forward, 'I'm sorry, OK?'

Phil said nothing, though Mike thought that maybe he'd heard a small grunt.

'It's just that, well... I think we should be working togeth... SHIT!'

Mike swung the car violently to the right to avoid someone pulling out of a side road between some shops. He swerved briefly towards the oncoming traffic but managed to bring the car back under control and on the correct side of the road with no incident.

'Jesus!' Mike shouted, with some relief and a shake of his head. 'Fucking idiots! Honestly, you'd think me beeping and flashing my lights would be enough for anybody, even for those that can't be arsed to look before pulling out onto a busy road!'

He turned to Phil to get some kind of acknowledgement, hoping perhaps that the shared moment of drama would help to defuse the tension between them, but Phil was looking away from him, seemingly distracted and watching the car behind them in the wing mirror.

'You know, I was talking to a mate of mine the other day who's a paramedic on the ambulances. He reckons that at least ten percent of callouts are held up by... what the fuck?'

Mike frowned and swung around in his seat, then turned back again and focused on his rearview mirror. The car that had pulled out was not just still behind them, but driving only a few feet from his bumper and flashing its headlights repeatedly as it tracked the movement of Mike's speeding Corsa.

Phil's gaze hadn't moved, and he was still staring intently at the side mirror. 'Pull over,' he said, as calmly and quietly as it was possible to be heard over the strained complaints of the little engine.

'What? Oh right, yeah. You gonna nick 'em? I think you're right. We've got time, and that driving is absolu–'

'Just pull over, Mike. Now, please.'

Mike shot him a wordless glance, and then let off the throttle, easing the car into an empty bus stop and switching off the engine. The car on their tail, a black Range Rover, followed them into the space and came to a jerky halt behind them with a short skid on a patch of loose gravel. Phil had the door open before they'd even come to a full stop and was out of the car with a surprisingly youthful spring, but he peered back through the open window just as Mike was reaching for his door handle. 'Stay here.'

Slightly stung by the order, Mike let go of the lever and slumped back hard into his seat, watching the rearview mirror intently. Nobody had got out of the car behind, and Phil walked unhurriedly to the passenger window, which had presumably slid down out of Mike's sight because he could see Phil apparently in conversation before nodding curtly. He looked over towards Mike with a flick of his chin and spoke briefly, then began walking back to the Corsa.

'Look, I'll meet you at the Queen's Head in an hour. Just kill some time until then, OK?'

'What?' Mike's mind was racing and he couldn't make the events he was seeing slot together into any kind of meaningful pattern. 'What's going on, Phil? Who is that? Are you nicking them or what?'

Phil held his gaze for a moment, but there was nothing Mike could hope to read from the flat, grey eyes.

'Queen's Head. One hour.'

Phil walked back to the Range Rover, opened the rear door, and stepped inside. The car was moving before he'd even shut the door, lurching forward in a smooth burst of acceleration, rocking slightly on its soft suspension as it swerved around Mike's parked Corsa and into the road.

As the car passed briskly alongside him with a cultured growl, Mike turned to watch it go, his features knitted into an utterly confused frown. The side windows were lightly tinted, but with the summer sun pouring in through the windscreen, Mike could clearly make out Phil's face, staring resolutely forward from the back seat.

With a bolt of shock and a dropped jaw, he also recognised the man sitting in front of Phil. He only got a split second's glance, but there was no doubting the profile of a man who had featured in many a presentation back at the nick. For some unfathomable reason, DI Phil Collins, Mike's partner and ranking officer, had just driven off with the infamous drug lord Robert 'Big Bob' Cole.

Chapter 26

Mike sat at the bar, staring without focus into the pint of lager that was still held tightly in his grip. He'd been in this position without movement for five minutes now, his brain so engrossed in thought that it left no room for motor function of any kind.

As a rule, he never drank while at work. To be fair, it was an actual rule, not just a personal principle, and one that would result in instant dismissal from the force. But it was a personal principle too. It wasn't one shared by Phil, and in their first weeks together there'd been several 'quick halves' in the Queen's Head over lunch, but Mike's initial polite refusals (which were ignored and overruled by Phil) quickly became more strenuous, and Phil soon stopped suggesting the lunchtime pints completely. It'd been over a month since they'd even been to the Queen's Head, and that last occasion had been for lunch with lemonades only.

It was therefore extremely unusual for Mike to be in the pub on a Thursday afternoon nursing a pint, but the large Scotch he'd downed first was completely without precedent.

His mind was racing.

He'd watched Phil get into the back of a car which also contained Bob Cole, infamous drug importer and dealer with a supplier network across South London. He hadn't been bundled in with force, or taken at gunpoint, he'd simply had what appeared to be a short chat with Cole before coming back to see Mike briefly and then leaving. It seemed that he'd had a free choice in the matter, that he'd gone willingly. It made no sense.

Did this mean that Phil was a bent copper? Was he on the take and working with Cole? Mike shook his head slowly as he continued to stare into space. Surely not. Phil could certainly be unconventional and would wind up the brass down at the station, but that was just him playing the whole ageing rebel cliché to amuse himself. Everyone said he was a good cop, and he had a reputation for being a man of principle when it came to nicking villains, even if he didn't give much of a shit about adhering to smoking policies, or lunchtime drinking.

A shadow falling across Mike's pint glass caused him to focus and look up, and he watched as Phil walked slowly up to where he was sitting. Mike turned away from him and instead nodded to the clock behind the bar.

'You're late,' he said flatly, then took a sip from his pint.

'Sorry.'

'How did you get here, then?'

'Taxi.'

Phil pulled the next stool nearer to him and began to slide himself onto it, but stopped halfway and winced sharply, his hand moving to his right flank reflexively. Mike looked at him with a frown but wasn't in the mood to overdo the concern.

'You alright?'

Phil paused his attempt to get onto the stool and gave a half-hearted smile to nobody in particular.

'Absolutely fabulous.'

He took a deep breath and managed the last hop onto the stool, clearly attempting to hide the discomfort that made him redden with the effort.

Mike was keen to hurry up and be angry with him, but couldn't completely ignore what was happening.

'Does it hurt?'

Phil let out a soft, but sardonic, chuckle.

'Only when I laugh.'

'Look,' said Mike with rising anger, 'you've made me doubt you in a pretty fundamental way, I've got some serious questions for you and all you can do is waltz in here with some kind of injury, looking for sympathy and listing old sitcoms!'

Phil turned to him with a look of genuine confusion but was interrupted by the barman, who'd just spotted him and had wandered over, raising his eyebrows questioningly with a flick of his chin.

'Are you being served?'

'Fuck's sake,' spat Mike under his breath as he picked up his drink and moved to an empty table in the corner.

Phil joined him after a couple of minutes, placing a pint of bitter down carefully on a beer mat before sitting. Mike chose to look away and ignore the stifled intake of breath, instead opting to take another sip.

'So,' Mike said after a lengthy pause. He'd run through this moment over and over for the last hour and a half, trying to come up with a way of dominating the questioning in the way they were taught to deal with suspects. He'd always had a deep respect for Phil, and although they chatted like mates a lot of the time when alone in the car, this was definitely not a moment for friendly banter. He put his pint down meaningfully and cleared his throat. This was a moment that called for all the seriousness and professionalism that his police training had given him.

'So. you and Bob Cole are "best friends" now, are you?'

He even did the air quotes. He swore to himself inwardly and looked away to scrunch up his face.

'Yeah, well,' said Phil slowly, picking up his glass. 'Things aren't always what they seem, are they?'

'Oh really? It seemed to me very much like you got into a car with a known drug kingpin and drove off. Did you not, then?'

'Well. OK, that bit was what it seemed, but it wasn't... well, y'know.'

'No, Phil, I don't. I really, really don't. What are you gonna tell me then, that you're working deep undercover and that Bob Cole thinks you're one of his blokes when secretly you're gathering evidence to build a case? Is that it?'

He looked around the bar, aware that his voice has risen significantly in anger, but none of the other drinkers appeared to take any interest, assuming they'd even noticed above the lunchtime hubbub.

'No, not exactly.'

'Not exactly? Not exactly, or not at all?'

'Well, not so far, but it's a possibility for the future, I suppose.'

Mike shook his head. 'This is ridiculous.' He turned to his pint as if noticing it for the first time and picked it up to take a long slug of it.

Phil pushed his own glass away from him and straightened in his chair. 'Look. Mike. We need to talk.'

'Ha!' Mike nearly spat out the last of his mouthful. 'Do you think?'

Phil eyed him levelly, tapping his fingers in turn on the edge of the table.

'Yes, I do. But not like this. This is getting us nowhere. Could you just…'

Mike spread his palms wide and raised his eyebrows in question. Phil took a deep breath.

'Could you just… let me explain a few things. Give me a few minutes to talk without us bickering.'

'We're not *bickering*, Phil. That's normally a two-way thing. No, I'm pissed off at you and I'm trying to get some sense out of you and you're just sat there being vague.'

'OK, fine. Well, can you just… stop doing that for a few minutes then?'

Mike took in a deep breath and clasped his hands together in front of him. 'Fine.'

There was silence between them as Phil picked his words carefully.

'I know what you must be thinking. It looks bad, I know that, and you're probably assuming I'm bent, or that I'm on the take somehow.'

Mike made a show of not speaking, pursing his lips and looking up at the ceiling rather camply.

'But I promise you, that's not what's happening. It's not that at all.'

They looked at each other for a moment, each seemingly daring the other to start speaking first. Mike didn't want to be seen as interrupting, but he felt that Phil was now waiting for him to ask.

'OK,' he said, finally. 'So what is it? Tell me.'

Phil said nothing for a while, but lowered his gaze to the table. He seemed to crumple slightly as if he was an inflatable toy that someone had opened the valve on for a moment, and as his brow began to knit and his shoulders slump, Mike felt that he was ageing in front of him.

He realised now that Phil wasn't so much waiting for him to speak before, but just putting off doing the deed himself.

'I made a mistake. A big one.' Phil continued to look directly ahead at the table, seemingly unwilling or unable to hold the weight of his head higher. 'Years ago, many years ago.'

Mike was watching him closely now, but he'd stopped deflating and had instead simply frozen. His eyes were open but locked into the middle distance somewhere, remembering. Suddenly he became animated again as if switched on at the plug and turned urgently to Mike.

'I've never told anybody this, Mike. Seriously, nobody ever. And I'd planned to never have to, but I suppose I can't escape it forever. And it might as well be you, Mike. You're a good copper, and I trust you.'

Mike felt himself go cold and could sense the hairs on his arm start to prickle, despite the claggy summer air of the busy pub. He didn't know what to expect from Phil, but he'd never heard this tone in his voice before, and never seen such distant sadness in his eyes. He dismissed all hope of trying to interrogate him and realised instead that his job was now to sit and listen in silence, perhaps to play the priest to Phil's confessor. He said nothing, but just held Phil's stare until he began talking again.

'Have you heard of the SDS? The Special Demonstration Squad?'

Mike's eyes widened a little. This wasn't a direction he was expecting. 'Er, yeah, loosely. Some secretive unit set up to spy on protest groups? It was shut down ages ago, though, wasn't it?'

Phil nodded. 'Yep. Lasted a while under various names and commands, but essentially the work it did was much the same throughout. And yes, the idea was to infiltrate direct action groups in an attempt to avert any violent protests and sabotage, that kind of thing. To fight extremism at its source, basically, using undercover techniques borrowed from the intelligence services.'

'OK,' said Mike, simply, his mind now racing again.

'Well, long story short, I was recruited in 1990 and went undercover.'

Mike reeled. 'What? But... I mean, you're old, but you're not that old. In 1990, you must've been, what...'

'Twenty-two.'

'Right.'

'And thanks,' Phil said, archly.

Mike grimaced awkwardly.

'They wanted us young, it was deliberate. We were less suspicious, less police-like. They thought we'd be more full of righteous principles, not jaded and cynical, but also less likely to slip into police lingo or procedure. It wasn't our habit yet. Plus, we just didn't look like coppers being so young. Six months of growing our hair long and we could slot straight in, get right in amongst them and then nab a load of extremists just as they were planning some kind of violent protest to tear the fabric of decent society apart, or something along those lines. No families either, of course, that was another factor. We could work away from home for months without anyone needing to know where we were.'

'And did you?'

Phil's brow furrowed. 'Did I what?'

'Nab a load of extremists?'

Phil smiled out of the side of his mouth and shook his head slowly.

'Course not. Was all a load of bollocks.'

'What was? How do you mean?'

'They were all harmless. Or mostly. Just a load of young people with ideals and dreams and principles, trying to make the world a better place. Same as us really, just playing for a different team.'

Mike nodded, trying to take it all in. He was attempting to picture what a young, smiling, 22-year-old Phil with long hair would've looked like. It wasn't an easy mental image to muster.

'So there was nothing, then? Just a waste of time?'

'Depends how you look at it, I suppose. I mean, yeah, there were all kinds of arrests across the unit as a whole, over the years, and there was definitely the odd plan that was scuppered in time, some quite big, even. There was a plan to torch an animal vivisectionists once that they managed to avert. Worthwhile stuff, sure, but in the scheme of things? Of all the crime in London? Three blokes, that one took, each working undercover for between nine months and three years! Think of all the work they could've done, just as bobbies on the beat!'

He puffed his cheeks out and tapped his fingers on the table for a moment, then stopped as he became aware of the noise.

'Nah, it was a waste, in the main. I was with them for nearly two years, working with a group called the Campaign for Peace & Solidarity. For two years I was Phil Duggan. Deep undercover the whole time, lived my entire life with them apart from weekly debrief sessions in various safe houses. A *deep swimmer*, they called it. Down so deep, we rarely came up for air. Barely knew who I was by the end of it.'

'So no big arrests, then? No sabotage averted?'

Phil shook his head. 'No arrests at all. Nothing. I mean, I drove them around in my van to all the marches, we made placards, we chanted, we sang. We sat around all night, putting the world to rights and planning our next march or leaflet campaign or strongly worded letter to the Prime Minister and all that. We were young, we were principled. We wanted to end war and promote peace.'

'We?'

Phil looked up at Mike, not understanding. 'Huh?'

'We. You said 'WE sat around, and WE were principled. Not *they*.'

Phil chuckled silently to himself. 'Well, that's the thing, isn't it? You go in that far, the lines begin to blur. And make no mistake, you have to believe it. I mean, sure, my group weren't exactly the IRA, but they wouldn't have looked particularly kindly on a copper lying and cheating his way in to spy on them. Undercover work is a serious business, whoever it's with, and you have to have total conviction at all times.'

He paused and screwed his face up at some distant memory.

'A few of the SDS lads were found out, over the years. It wasn't pretty in some of those cases, I can tell you. Not a situation you want to be in, ever. And the groups were on the lookout, all of them, all the time. There were always rumours of cops everywhere, a lot of suspicion. A lot of accusations, even. A lot of paranoia, though quite rightly so as it turns out.'

'So were you found out, then? Is that what happened?'

'Me? Nah. I mean, there's always someone that mistrusts you to start off with, but you just had to show them you were honest – that you were one of them. A slow process, but then we had time to burn, so we used it. Bit by bit, gaining trust slowly until you're beyond suspicion. After nine or ten months, I was one of them. I looked like them, talked like them, did all the things they did. I was accepted totally. I was one of their friends, and they were mine. I barely knew anything else by then, I spent virtually every day with them for a longer period than I'd even been a police officer beforehand. Like I say, the lines blur.'

Mike thought for a while, trying to decide if this was the big secret, but failing to make a connection with Big Bob.

'And you've not told anybody any of this before?'

Phil watched him for a second, his head titled slightly at an angle like an inquisitive dog, but seeming to understand the meaning.

'Well, yes and no. I mean, various senior officers knew, of course, but I didn't speak of it to anyone else after I came out, no. But that's not the problem.'

'I'm confused. So what's the problem?'

'The problem, young Michael, is one that's been a problem for man since the Garden of Eden.'

'Er… poisoned apples?'

Phil laughed. 'No, you idiot. The problem was that I fell in love.'

Chapter 27

Tommo stopped outside the entrance to the Earl of Wessex and looked up at the pub sign that was rocking gently in the breeze with the slightest hint of an unoiled squeak. Lenny, Playboy, Soapy and D took his cue and waited behind him, following his gaze to the sign.

Tommo sniffed at the air. 'I think we're getting close, boys, I think we could be homing in on our man. I can feel it in me bones.'

He turned to the eager faces behind him. 'Just remember, yeah? Let's take it cool, take it easy. We're going in there for a lunchtime pint, just like we're taking a break from our normal jobs. We're going to drink our pints quietly and then maybe put out some feelers. They've got a pool table here, right D?'

'Yep.'

'Sweet. I think I've got a plan. Let's head inside. Cool?'

The four faces nodded vigorously at him, their eyes bulging with excitement. Soapy grinned and gave a thumbs-up.

Tommo looked down at the floor with a quick shake of his head, then brought his eyes back level with them as he stroked his chin. 'Maybe it's best if you leave the talking to me, actually.'

They filed in, and Tommo and Playboy took seats at a largish table at the furthest end of the room which gave them a good view of the entrance and most of the main bar area. D and Soapy positioned themselves opposite, while Lenny went to the bar to order drinks. One end of the table butted up against the edge of an archway that led through to a smaller room with a pool table and a couple of fruit machines. In the corner above their table was a TV mounted high on the wall that was showing a squash match on some obscure sports channel with the sound down, and Soapy was immediately transfixed by this.

'Remember,' said Tommo, 'just nice and easy. We'll get our drinks and then take it from there, yeah? D, turn back to face this way, man. You look suspicious already, scanning the place like that. I can see everything I need to from here. Just chill, all of you.'

Lenny arrived balancing a tray with their drinks on, as well as a couple of packs of crisps. He lowered the tray carefully to the table, then passed each pint along to its new owner before taking his own seat.

Tommo took his pint and nodded to the crisps. 'I expected you to be more hungry, Lenny. That's pretty restrained for you.'

'Oh, those are for you lot,' said Lenny, fishing into both pockets of his joggers, and then dropping a chocolate bar, two packets of peanuts and a scotch egg onto the table in front of him. 'We will be getting some lunch soon though, yeah?'

Tommo decided to ignore the question and instead took a steady sip from his beer. He then held up both of his palms to gather the group's attention, and looked meaningfully at each in turn before speaking quietly but assertively.

'Right. Lads. Let's talk strategy. It's been several days now without that weed in our possession, and we need to be absolutely sure that we get it back, asap. We've got customers waiting and I don't wanna let them down any longer, yeah?'

The others nodded.

'So here's the plan. When I've finished speaking, we're gonna take our drinks and head on through to that pool table, right? A couple of us will have a game and then it's winner stays on. We'll sit back a bit, try and get some of the geezers in here to play us. It's starting to get a little busier, so I'm sure there'll be some takers. And we keep it nice and friendly, get some banter in and get them talking, yeah? You all keep to the friendly chit-chat, I'll do the important stuff. I'll make a casual enquiry about our lanky, green-hatted friend, maybe say that I played him at pool recently and was hoping for a re-match. Just drop it in, see if we get a bite. If it looks like they know him, then I'll reel them in, try and get some deets off them. Hopefully an address – maybe I'll say that I owe him a tenner from a bet we made on our game, something like that. I'll play it well cool though, so it don't look suspicious, got it?'

They all nodded again, Lenny slowly feeding peanuts into his mouth as he did so.

'If we don't have any luck, then we need to move on to some more people. Playboy, you're obviously the best at pool so you're on cue detail. If we're getting somewhere, then you need to lose the game so that they hang around, and then D, you can play the man. But if they're no use, then you need to try and win so that they piss off and we can try and get some new customers. Make sense?'

'Got it,' said Playboy, and the others murmured their assent.

'Soon as we get an address, we'll head round there and stake it out for a bit in my car. We don't wanna go busting in there and find he's got ten big mates with him, we need to get him alone. And then, when we're sure, me and Playboy will knock on the door with the rest of you out of sight, and when he opens we'll bundle in, catch him by surprise. Once we're in, we gently subdue him with a couple of hard punches to the face, locate our goods and head off into the sunset, ready to make a good, honest living selling those drugs we nicked. Any questions?'

'Nope,' 'all good Tommo,' the group responded, though Soapy's attention had already moved back to the squash game on the TV.

'Oi, Soapy!' Tommo barked. 'Keep with me, yeah?', his two splayed fingers pointing to his own eyes.

'Sorry Tommo, I was listening, honest.'

Tommo picked up his pint and stood, and the others followed suit as he started to make his way towards the archway. 'Yeah? Good, there'll be a test later.' He looked up at the TV as he passed it. 'Who's winning, anyway?'

Soapy followed his gaze and shook his head. 'Oh, no one,' he said dismissively. 'They're just practising against the wall. Maybe it's raining outside.'

Once at the pool table, Playboy and Tommo selected cues while the others found seats.

'Rack 'em up, man,' said Tommo as he flicked a pound coin into the air towards Playboy, who plucked it out of the air with the deftness of a frog catching a fly with its tongue.

About halfway into the game, the two men were standing side by side, leaning on their cues like bored medieval guards holding their pikes, examining a particularly awkward positioning of the cue ball behind the black.

Tommo nudged his partner with his elbow and discreetly flicked his eyes towards the bar. 'Hold up, I think we might have some company.'

Together, they watched as a pair of men picked up their pints and started threading their way past the tables towards them.

The men, despite having 20 or so years between them, were both clothed in matching oil-stained blue overalls, unclipped at the shoulder with the unoccupied arms tied around their waists exposing green, branded t-shirts.

The elder of the two had a round, rosy face, the faded remnants of a thick, bright orange thatch of hair, and remarkably bushy eyebrows that resembled two urban foxes squaring up to each other. His open overalls offered a tantalising glimpse of a splendid beer gut, which was clearly a project that significant money and lager had been sunk into. His younger companion, whippet-thin and clean-shaven, was sporting a curly mullet that served as a tangible testament to the axiom that those who cannot remember the past are condemned to repeat it.

Tommo nodded a silent welcome as they approached and moved aside to let them squeeze past the table. 'Alright, lads,' said the older man with a rustle of his brows, 'you up for a game then?'

'Definitely,' Tommo replied, 'winner stays on, yeah? We'll just finish up and you can play whoever.'

The man acknowledged with a nod, then fished around in his overalls for a pound coin, which he placed on the table edge. As he went to join his partner leant against a radiator to watch the game, Tommo eyed up the balls studiously, lowered himself into position, and took careful aim with a practised and steady stroke. He then fired off a powerful but appalling shot that struck the black first, then ricocheted violently into the corner pocket with a loud thunk.

Tommo clicked his tongue with apparent disappointment as the two guests both winced audibly. 'Bad luck,' said the older man with an obvious lack of sympathy.

'Not my day, it seems,' replied Tommo, as he moved closer to the two men to pick up the chalk. He rubbed the end of his cue thoroughly before giving it a single sharp blow. 'I'm not usually so bad. Having a bit of gyp with my hand today, though,' he said, turning his right palm around at the wrist to examine both sides carefully.

'Yeah,' said the man with no conviction whatsoever. 'Maybe we should stick a fiver in the pot, eh? Make the game a little more interesting!' He gave a chuckle as he winked knowingly to his partner. His sentence was punctuated by the harsh cracking sound of Playboy's number 11 ball, though it was unclear whether the noise emanated from it slamming against the back of the pocket, or from it having broken the sound barrier en route. By the time all eyes had swung to watch, he was already in position for the next ball, which almost immediately suffered the same fate. The man's smile fell away quickly, and he gave his eyebrows a twitch. 'Or maybe not, eh?' he said, more to himself than anyone else.

Tommo suppressed a smile as he leant back against the wall with folded arms. 'Freak of nature, that boy,' he said, tutting. 'No job, no prospects, but put a cue in his hand, or a ball at his feet and watch him shine! He can run the 100 metres in under 11 seconds too, y'know. Though admittedly usually away from jealous boyfriends.'

'That so?' said the man, appraising Playboy as he continued to slam balls in. 'I was a pretty tasty player myself, as it goes. Right wing.'

'Oh yeah? Nice one.'

'Yep. The Deptford Destroyer, they used to call me,' he said, pulling himself up to his full height and puffing out his chest somewhat. The exertion from this made him catch his breath, which led to a splutter, and this in turn led to a brief bout of a hacking smoker's cough that made him red-faced and breathless.

'Couple of years ago, now', he wheezed quietly as he wiped a bead of sweat from his forehead.

A final whump from the pool table indicated the conclusion of the game, and Playboy picked up the pound coin to feed into the slot.

'You're up,' said Tommo with a nod, and the man cleared his throat, smoothed down his t-shirt and chalked his cue in preparation.

'So, are you a regular here, then?' asked Tommo casually, as Playboy began racking up the balls.

'You could say that. I pop in for an occasional pint or two, outside of my other hobbies and activities, of course.'

Tommo nodded. 'Nice, nice. Yeah, I'm fairly new to the area myself, I've just come in a few times. Good to meet new people and that, innit? Plus get in a bit of a pool, of course, and get a few tips from this feller.'

Playboy smiled in acknowledgement as he flicked a coin onto the back of his hand.

'Heads!'

The man smiled on seeing he was correct, and then spent an extended period of time at the head of the table, looking down the length of his cue with one eye closed and carefully appraising the position of the balls, which were in exactly the same places as in every game. Eventually, he took his shot, and the pack split in all directions but with nothing being sunk. For a moment he looked crestfallen, but he recovered quickly to give a knowing nod and a subtle smile, as if he'd laid the perfect trap.

'I was just wondering, actually,' said Tommo cautiously, to the soundtrack of two balls being potted in quick succession behind him. 'You must know a lot of the other regulars in here, then?'

'Everyone worth knowing.'

Playboy looked up with a grin, but Tommo caught his eye and gave a very quick and subtle shake of his head. Playboy frowned, before settling back into position and making a very safe shot to play the cue ball back up the table. The man's eyebrows rippled with a little Mexican Wave as he moved to the table, his eyes trying to avoid staring at the easy ball near the centre pocket that it seemed only he had noticed.

'Well, I was thinking. I played a geezer in here last week and was hoping to bump into him again. I owe him a few quid from a game, y'see, didn't get the chance to give it to him at the time. Maybe you know him?'

The man lowered his gut onto the edge of the table as he lined up his cue, playing a clean shot that dropped the yellow ball gently into the pocket with a satisfying *ker-dunk*.

'Oh yeah?' he said with a restrained smile, before standing slowly and licking his lips. 'Did you get a name?'

'I did, as it goes. It was Waffle. Nice bloke, gave me a good thrashing.'

'Waffle,' said the man, frowning in thought and scratching his stomach. 'Tall feller, green hat?'

Five pairs of eyes swung round to look at the man, all set within faces that were trying to hide any outward reaction. Tommo took in a breath as subtly as possible and forced himself to wait an extra two seconds before answering casually. 'That's him. Do you know him then?'

'Only vaguely,' the man said, without much interest, then pointed his cue towards the bar. 'But he's just walked in.'

* * *

'Up and at 'em!' said Waffle, as he put the glass to his mouth and didn't remove it until half the beer was missing in action.

Harj took his own sip but raised his eyebrows at Waffle's enthusiasm. 'So, how's the mission going then?' he asked cautiously.

Waffle was already back to his glass, and merely shook his head as he downed the remainder of his pint. 'On hold,' he said, when he'd come up for air. He waggled his empty glass in front of Harj as he gave a small burp. 'Another?'

Harj looked down at his remaining 96 percent of a pint. 'I'm good for now, thanks.'

When Waffle returned from the bar he was carrying two pints, but he positioned them both in front of himself as he sat down, and proceeded to take another big gulp from the first.

Harj looked at his watch with a concerned frown. 'So. Um. How was your morning?'

Waffle nodded with enthusiasm for quite a while. 'Oh yeah, great. I got thrown out of a yoga retreat first thing for being drunk and disorderly, then traipsed my sorry arse across town to find Nat was back when I got home.'

Harj put his drink down and widened his eyes in surprise. 'Nat's back?'

'Nope. I said she *was* back. She's now left again.'

'Ah.'

'Yep.'

'She's not moving back, then?'

'All signs point to the negative, my friend.'

'Oh dear.'

'Oh dear indeed.'

Harj thought for a moment. 'What did she come back for?'

Waffle gave a hollow chuckle. 'The TV remote!'

'Ouch,' said Harj with a wince. 'So the new Waffle Jones Mark 2 didn't have an effect on her then?'

'Oh, he had an effect on her alright,' said Waffle as he swallowed a mouthful of beer. 'He had the effect of making her laugh out loud.'

Harj settled back in his chair and sipped thoughtfully at his pint. 'I'm really sorry to hear that, Woff. That does sound like a bit of a shit day.' Waffle didn't reply, but Harj could see him raise his eyebrows in acknowledgement through the bottom of his pint, his eyes made bulbous and wobbly through the magnifying effect of the glass and the beer. 'What about that yoga place then, how was it? You said you got kicked out?'

Waffle wiped some foam from his mouth with the back of his hand. 'Yeah, a little bit. What's that phrase they use when someone gets kicked out of a job? *Mutual consent*, that's it. I left by mutual consent.'

'What happened then?'

'I went out late and got a bit pissed.'

Harj looked down at Waffle's collection of pint glasses. 'Not like you.'

'I was a victim of circumstance. Someone made me go to the pub.'

'Ah, I see. The effects of the mission hadn't kicked in by then?'

'It was a lapse. I've had a very strange week.'

'Yes, you said last time. You mean with Nat leaving?'

'Well, yeah, there's that. But there was something else I didn't tell you about.'

'Oh?' said Harj, his eyes shining in anticipation. 'And what was that?'

Waffle looked around him to check that nobody was in earshot and scratched his cheek nervously. 'Well. Odd thing happened. You know those big holdalls you can get? Like a big, black sports bag type of thing with handles?'

'Yeah?'

'Well... imagine one packed full of really, really strong weed. Like, ten kilos of the finest and strongest weed you've ever seen.'

Harj closed his eyes, then opened them quickly again and nodded. 'OK, I'm there.'

'Right. Well, one just like that fell to the ground in front of me on Clairmont Avenue on Monday morning.'

Harj narrowed his eyes and looked sideways at Waffle. 'Oh really? How come?'

Waffle shrugged. 'Gravity I guess.'

'Yes, but where did it come from?'

'Couldn't tell you. I didn't see it actually falling as such. I just know that it fell to my feet, pretty much.'

Harj was nodding slowly, but his brow was furrowed into a deep frown.

'And this bag, this whole event. It... definitely happened, did it?'

'Course, man!' said Waffle, recoiling in offence. 'Clear as day, the bag fell to my feet!'

'I see. And you hadn't been... smoking any of your own weed at any point in the preceding hour or so? Or drinking heavily? Or just sleeping heavily?'

'No, man! It was 8:30 in the morning and I was sober as a judge. I was on my way to get a new job.'

'Ah yes, this job. How's that going?'

'Let's come back to that,' said Waffle dismissively, with a wave of his hand.

'OK. So where's this bag now then?'

Waffle looked around him once more and lowered his head and his voice conspiratorially. 'It's at my flat.'

'I see. And Clairmont Avenue – is it still disgorging bags of weed from the sky?'

'I haven't checked.'

Harj nodded, seemingly satisfied.

'But you have no idea where it came from, and you don't know who it belonged to?'

'No clue.'

'And nobody's come after you for it, then?'

'Nobody. To be honest, I was a bit nervous to start with. That's why I didn't tell you before. I thought it might lead to some trouble or something, but everything's been quiet. I don't think anybody knows I have it, or is looking for it. I think it was just discarded for some reason and it's all been forgotten about.'

'Well, that's good.'

'I know, right?'

'I mean, you could've had all kinds after you. Police, drug dealers, all kinds.'

'Yeah, I know. I mean, maybe it wasn't the brightest thing to take it home, but nothing bad has happened, so it was all pretty sweet in the end.'

'So what are you going to do with it?'

Waffle picked up his second, fresh pint and took a few good gulps.

'Well, that's the thing. I don't want it. Or, at least, I didn't. I'd knocked the whole thing on the head for Nat's sake, and I was happy about it, too. Plus, it's strong... like too strong. It's mental stuff and I don't think it's that good for you.'

'Do you not think?' asked Harj with a smirk.

'Yeah, but proper strong. It's not like a nice, calming smoke. I think it's beyond what people should be doing to themselves.'

'You could sell it?'

Waffle nodded. 'I could. And I did sell a bit to Learner Joe, but I don't really wanna be a drug dealer either. Especially given its strength. But then...'

'Go on...'

Waffle shifted uncomfortably in his chair. 'Well, I met this geezer at the yoga place. He's a nice bloke and everything, and he wanted to buy some. I think he's got money, I think he'd take a chunk of it. Plus, Joe might want some more soon.'

'But you're not keen?'

Waffle took another large sip. 'I didn't think I was, no. That's what the mission was about. But then this whole thing with Nat coming back. I mean, what's the point? I could chuck it all in the Thames but what would be the point? I've lost her forever and that weed could seriously sort me out. I could use it to pay rent for years, maybe even get a deposit on me own place. Maybe buy a car even.'

The two fell silent for a moment, each nursing their drinks.

'Maybe Nat will come back again?'

Waffle looked down sadly at his pint and shook his head. 'No, man. She's not coming back. I know what she's like, she sticks to her guns. And that conversation earlier was very final. No, she's got her TV remote now and she's left for good this time, no doubt about it. I just need to accept that I'm one of life's losers, and the world seems to enjoy watching me fail. I can't seem to manage anything properly: girlfriends, jobs, paying the bills. I mean, yoga's supposed to be the most chilled thing in the world, and mainly involves sitting down on the floor, and I even got kicked out of that after one day!'

He shook his head and picked up his pint once more, before letting out a long, though bitter-sounding 'Aaaaah!'

'I mean, here I am, early afternoon on a Thursday, and I'm nearly three pints down already. No job, no prospects, and half pissed. I even dragged you away from your honest labour to join me, just so you can watch me make a mess of my life. I bet half the pub are just enjoying watching me fail right now!'

He looked around the pub and the few sparse tables of drinkers, and for a moment fancied that a group of five young men at the back were indeed watching him closely, but when he turned back to check with a frown, they were deep in conversation or concentrating intently on their phones.

He shook his head sadly and let out a low 'pff' to himself. Harj gave Waffle a sympathetic smile. 'So, what's next, then?'

Waffle slammed his empty glass down onto the table. 'Next, my friend, is another pint or three. I intend to fully erase this sorry day from my memory! Maybe I'll even smoke some of that evil pink shit when I get home, there's nothing stopping me any more. The mission is over, and Waffle Mark 2 is dead!'

He raised his empty glass triumphantly. 'Long live Waffle Mark 1!'

Chapter 28

'Is that such a bad thing?' Mike asked, taking his first sip of beer for some time.

'Falling in love? Depends how you look at it. I mean, in normal life no, of course not.'

'But working undercover not so good?'

'Well, that's the thing. It was tacitly accepted, encouraged almost. Our job was to be as convincing as possible, and what better way of integrating than to start going out with someone.'

'But going out with someone isn't the same as falling in love, is it?'

Phil smiled. 'You're absolutely right there, it's a pretty crucial difference. Our bosses didn't particularly care what we thought or felt, as long as it looked good on the surface. Having a relationship was a great way of laying doubts to rest about how serious we were, but actually falling in love is a different kettle of fish entirely.'

'So what happened?'

'Well, nothing much to start with. I moved into her place and we were just a normal couple. As normal as a girl and her undercover cop boyfriend who's lying to her about who he is and reporting her actions back to his bosses could be, at any rate. Match made in heaven!'

He laughed sarcastically and let his smile fall away as his eyes darkened.

'We were together for eight months. And we were happy, Lily and me. She was beautiful, and I was smitten. We had dreams, made plans for the future, all the things two young people in love do. She'd dropped out of uni a few years before and travelled overland to India, before coming home and moving to London. And the plan was that we'd go back there together and spend months, maybe years there. She'd been around the north a fair bit on her previous trip but had never gone down south, so we decided we'd head to Goa and find somewhere to live, try to pick up some work.'

Mike was shaking his head and smiling until Phil looked up and noticed. 'What?' he asked tartly.

'You. I find it hard enough to imagine you young, let alone with long hair. And now I'm supposed to picture you sitting in some flat, burning joss sticks and planning to go backpacking in India. It's a bit too much.'

'Yeah, well. We were all young once, even me.' He looked around the pub theatrically and leant forward conspiratorially. 'I tell you what...' he said in a whisper as Mike moved in closer. 'I even used to play Leonard Cohen LPs from time to time.'

'Leonard Cohen, eh?' said Mike with an appreciative whistle.

'From time to time.'

Mike nodded his exaggerated approval and picked up his pint. He decided not to mention that he had no clue who Leonard Cohen was.

'And this India plan, this was a secret I suppose?'

'From the bosses? Oh yeah. Though it wouldn't have been hard to tell them it was just a lie I was spinning to get her on side.'

'But it wasn't?'

Phil looked at Mike levelly through his featureless, grey eyes. 'No. I was deadly serious. I wanted to go, desperately. I wanted *us* to go, to take Lily away. Away from London, away from the group, and away from the job. I wanted nothing more than to come clean, to tell her everything and to start a new life, just Lily and me as real, normal people. And the further away we could go, the better it would be.'

Mike held his gaze. 'Right. I see. And so you'd, what? Turned? Become one of them?'

Phil scoffed and looked away. 'Yes, no, doesn't matter. I didn't give a shit about either side by then. I mean, I was pretty sympathetic to the group's philosophy, sure. I still thought they were a little naive, but they were just honest kids, doing what they believed in. I mean, ending war? It's a bit much to hope for, but it's not such a bad thing to want, is it? Though frankly, a few marches and a few leaflets stuffed through letter boxes weren't ever going to achieve much. We may well have convinced Mr and Mrs Smith at number 23, maybe even a whole street or block of flats, but to my knowledge, nobody with nuclear codes was living in SE17 at the time.'

'But you would've left?'

'The force? At the drop of a hat. Lily and I were making our plans together, but I had a whole other set of plans to work on in here.' He tapped the side of his head. 'What I would say to the senior officers, how I'd arrange it. Would I just run away and try to leave the country without saying anything, or resign and leave it a few months before sneaking off with Lily? It was a difficult time, I was under an enormous amount of pressure, and most of it in secret. I was living a lie both ways, in the end.'

'So... why didn't you go? What stopped you?'

Phil rested both hands on the table in front of him and, once again, deflated. He closed his eyes slowly as his head began to tilt forward, his hands seemingly the only things stopping him from melting completely into the table. He breathed in and out a few times, and it was a considerable while before he spoke. When he did, it was so quietly that Mike could barely hear him.

'Lily became pregnant.'

Mike's mouth fell open and then shut again. 'Oh shit. Really?'

Phil opened his eyes and turned a little, giving Mike a withering glance in place of a reply.

'That was it. My superiors found out, and they decided to bring me out and end it all. It was all set up anyway, we all had escape plans laid that could be put into action if ever needed. Stories we'd tell over the years about relatives abroad who were always asking us to come over and join them, parents that would need caring for in distant cities at some point, that kind of thing. Excuses for a sudden disappearing act that could be dusted off at a moment's notice so we could be brought out quickly without blowing our cover.'

'But what about Lily?'

Phil began nodding very slowly as his eyes became heavy and

distant, the images in his mind apparently taking precedence over anything he was looking at.

'Well, she was delighted to start with. She was over the moon. This cemented everything, our whole relationship. We were going to head off on our big adventure sooner rather than later, get to Goa before the baby was born. But she could tell something was wrong. I knew before I'd even reported back what this would mean for me, and she sensed it. I knew it would be over, and not just the job. There was every chance I'd get sacked. I mean, standards were pretty low, given what we were doing for a job, but even then it was pretty frowned on to start having families with witnesses.'

'So what happened? Did you confess all to her?'

'I told her we had to have a talk, a serious one. God, I'd spent all day with it whirring around my head, trying to work out what to say and how to break it to her. I think she thought we were going to talk about our trip, about how we had to leave soon, she actually looked excited when I started off. And then yeah, I told her – I told her everything. I tried to explain how I was in love with her and how that was all that mattered. Nothing else was real, it was all just bollocks, roles we played, a uniform, and that nothing mattered except us and how we felt about each other.'

He went quiet and stared towards the table, as if hypnotised by the rising bubbles in his beer, his head shaking in slow motion.

'So, how did she take it?' Mike asked hopefully, but got no immediate reply. 'Um... not well?' he added, awkwardly, to fill the silence.

Phil grunted. 'You could say that. She told me I'd done nothing but lie to her from the very beginning. That I'd used her. That not only was I a pig, but the very worst kind: a deceitful, dishonest, lying pig.'

Phil's eyes closed slowly at the memory, and he grimaced to himself. 'And you know what the worst thing was?' he said, opening his eyes wide and turning to stare at Mike. Mike said nothing, but just shook his head imperceptibly.

'She was right. She was 100 percent right.' He tried to laugh, but it came out as more of a sneer. 'What did I really expect? Seriously? That she was going to say none of it mattered and throw herself into my arms? God, I was so naive.'

They sat in silence for a moment, Mike unwilling to offer another question that might seem insensitive. He was desperate to take a swig of beer, but this also seemed inappropriate for the moment, so instead he just kept his eyes low and waited for Phil to continue.

'She was screaming at this point, and who could blame her? Screaming and crying. I'd just torn her world apart, destroyed everything she believed in, and all in about two minutes flat from start to finish.'

He took a deep breath and slumped back into his chair. 'She told me to leave. Well, told me to fuck off actually, and that wasn't her way normally. So I did, simple as that. I could've stayed, I could've tried to calm her down, but I didn't; I left. In the movies, they just give their women a tight hug, don't they? They keep hugging them until they just stop crying magically after a bit. Well, I don't think that's how it works in real life. I decided I'd come back in the morning and try again when she'd had time to cool off, but I couldn't see any way of talking her round then, so off I went.

'But next day, I got my orders. I was told I'd been pulled out, the escape plan had been put into place and I was never to return to the group. A story had been put out that I'd had to move to Cornwall to look after my dying mum, and that I wouldn't be back. They'd make me write a few postcards over the next few months, that kind of thing, but otherwise, my days of being undercover were finished and I was back at a desk, effective immediately.'

'Jeez,' said Mike, a little unsure of how to respond. 'So you didn't go back and see her the next morning, then?'

Phil turned to meet his gaze and gave him a contemptuous sneer. 'I didn't have any choice! I was shut up in the safe house for debriefing for a week and had no way of getting back to her!'

'Ah, right. Yep,' said Mike, reddening.

'I'd have gone back that next day, though, if I'd had the chance. I'd have been over there like a shot to talk to her. I didn't sleep for the first few nights in that bloody house, running it all over in my mind. Pretty much just paced back and forth, I barely even sat down, let alone slept. I worked out all the options and, in the end, I realised there was only one thing to do. I'd jack in the job, propose to Lily and, hopefully, make her see that I was genuine.'

'But what about the repercussions? Weren't you afraid that they'd charge you, send you down even?'

Phil was shaking his head. 'Nope. Didn't care. I mean, I *did* care, and I didn't want to go to prison at the point that me and Lily finally made an honest go of things, and the thought of missing the birth put the fear of God into me. Hence all the pacing and whatnot. But it was the only way of doing the right thing by her and I was content to take whatever punishment was heading my way in order to be with her. Sometimes you just have to admit that you fucked up and take what's coming to you, however bad you think it'll be because it's the right thing to do. You need to show the world, and yourself, that you're not scared of paying the price for your actions.'

Mike found himself nodding along, and was aware that he was now fully invested in this story – it suddenly felt extremely important to him that Phil and Lily lived happily ever after, and screw the pigs!

'So you went back after the week in the safe house?'

'You bet I did, the first second I could. I was like a dog let out of a cage. I'd been told to go home and get my uniform together, to get ready for my new posting, but I drove straight around to our flat to talk to her.'

'And had she calmed down by then?' Mike asked.

Phil looked at him again, but his expression was soft. He looked almost confused, as if he hadn't heard or understood the question properly, and held Mike's gaze for several seconds, his brow furrowed and a look of infinite sadness in his eyes.

'I don't know, I never found out. She'd gone. Left.'

'Where to?' Mike asked, suddenly feeling alarmed.

'I didn't know. There wasn't a scrap of her stuff left, and there were no clues at all. Some of the others were around, they'd clearly helped her get away, but they weren't in the mood to help me, they made that absolutely clear.'

'Do you think she told them who you were?'

Phil shook his head. 'Nope, no way. They'd have said, and they would've acted a lot worse to me. I mean, they basically pushed me out and told me to piss off, but it would've been very different if they'd thought I was a copper.'

He closed his eyes for a moment as the memories washed over him.

'No, she just told them I'd dumped her over the baby, or something like that. Made me out to look like a bastard, which was enough to get them to push me around. But she hadn't told them what an *utter* bastard I'd been.'

Mike took in a deep breath and thought it through. 'I take it you didn't resign then?'

'No. Didn't seem to be any reason to resign over something I didn't have any more. They cut my hair off, stuck me back in a uniform and pointed me to a beat in North London. The pregnancy was never mentioned again and was swept under the carpet. I doubt it was even written up. And that, as they say, was that.'

Mike frowned as a thought came to him. 'But I don't understand. What about Bob Cole? What's he got to do with all this?'

Phil nodded once with his eyes closed, as if remembering something forgotten. 'Ah yes. Well, the thing is that he was around at that time too. He wasn't exactly one of us, but he was a regular fixture on the scene and sold weed to a fair few of the group. Me too, in fact, I'd buy from him occasionally, just for appearances' sake, of course.'

'But you didn't inhale, right?' Mike asked with a snort and a wry grin, as if he'd just caught him in some devilish checkmate.

Phil looked at him flatly. 'Of course I inhaled, you idiot. The choice between being found out as a grass and, well, smoking a bit of some isn't a difficult one. He had decent stuff too, that Bob.'

Mike wiped the smirk off his face and coughed lightly. 'So, he was smalltime then I guess? Just the local dope dealer?'

'Exactly. But devious and cunning, even then. I didn't trust him as far as I could throw him.' Phil looked upwards as he did a quick mental calculation. 'Less than that, even, come to think of it. He'd hang around with us a bit, but nobody really liked him, he just provided a service. He was very ambitious, but cocky with it, a bit smarmy, you know?'

Mike nodded that he did.

'He had this Jag he used to drive around in, for example, metallic gold. It wasn't worth a great deal, it was a good twenty years old and pretty beaten up, but he made a big show of it constantly. He'd bring it into conversation all the time and would always refer to it as "The Jag", never just "my car." Like, someone would agree to buy some of his weed and he'd never have any on him, I think deliberately so. He'd always have to go back outside to his car to get it. "Sure," he'd say, "I'll just pop out to The Jag and get that for you".'

Phil shook his head at the memory. 'I mean, it's not like he was going to impress anyone who made of point of living in a squat and going to anti-war marches, was it? Nobody else even had a car as a point of principle, they only accepted my van because it was necessary to transport us all around in. They all thought he was a flash little twerp.'

'But with good weed,' said Mike, the hint of a sarcastic smile playing on his lips.

'But with good weed,' Phil repeated.

'So what's the connection, then?' Phil asked, frowning. 'I still don't get it.'

'Well, I bumped into him as I was leaving our flat, having failed to find Lily. He was in his car, *The Jag*, and he saw me walking past and shouted hello. I stopped and we got talking a little bit. I disliked the guy and never had much time for him, but he was the least unfriendly face I'd seen that morning and I was upset. He'd obviously heard all about it from the others, and he was trying to sound sympathetic, but I didn't really believe it.

'Anyway, he was talking about her leaving and then casually dropped in about her going to Spain, as if I already knew. I was knocked for six, I had no idea she'd left the country. He must've seen the look on my face. "Oh, didn't you know?" he asked, all innocently, and I couldn't speak, I just shook my head. "Well, she wanted to get as far away as possible," he carries on, as if this is going to make me feel any better. "She's got a group of friends out there from her India days and wanted the emotional support. What with the abortion and everything."

'Shit,' said Mike, looking down at the space between his feet.

The pub continued its lunchtime rituals around them, everyone deep in their own conversations, or tucking into their lunches. Somewhere near the bar, someone laughed uproariously, and a fruit machine blared a cheesy tune. Nothing was said for nearly a minute, both men sitting alone with their thoughts. Mike had no idea what to say and was grateful when Phil started talking again, though when he did, it was in a hoarse whisper that Mike had to strain to hear.

'So that was it. I never went back and didn't see any of them again, Bob included. Not until 2008, about 15 years later.'

Mike looked up, his curiosity piqued. 'Why, what happened?'

'I nicked him. I didn't even make the connection straight away, but we busted a gambling den behind a car workshop under the arches in Bermondsey and rounded up everyone there. It was only when we got outside and were sticking everyone in the van that he caught my eye. He didn't say anything, but I saw him do a quick double-take, then smile at me. Then he turned away and carried on as normal, never looked at me again. He realised that not only was I a copper, but that he potentially had some dirt on me. Very useful to a man in his position, I suppose.'

Mike was now fully alert and with eyes wide. 'So he blackmailed you?'

'Yep. Well, no, not for a few years. But eventually, yes. It wasn't much, just a small favour, I suppose, and was brought up quite delicately. No huge threat, not at first. Just a kind of "you scratch my back and I'll keep your secret safe" kind of thing. But it's the classic way, isn't it? Each time I did something, I was more and more at risk of him shopping me in and the more I had to lose. I was an idiot, a complete idiot. I should've told him to get stuffed the first time, but by then I had a career to lose and the favour seemed small. I thought maybe I'd get him off my back. Idiot!'

Phil was shaking his head, his mouth set in a sneer, and as he shuffled in his chair he winced, and held his right side.

'So what did they do to you then?'

Phil waved the enquiry away nonchalantly. 'Nothing worth writing home about. Just a bit of a warning, that's all. Toe the line or face consequences, that kind of thing.' He put an arm out to pick up his pint and flinched again, though carried on regardless and refused to catch Mike's eye.

'Shouldn't you have that looked–'

'I'm fine, Mike, I'm fine. He's not going to do anything that'll stop me getting that weed back for him. Not yet. It's nothing a few whiskies at home tonight can't fix.'

Mike pondered for a moment. 'So, how did he find you anyway? He seemed to be waiting for us on the way back from that yoga place.'

'He *was* waiting for us. He's got one of the radio blokes down at the nick on his payroll, or so he says. All he has to do is ask discreetly and he can find our where we last radioed in and where we're heading.'

Mike looked shocked, and Phil gave him a weary smile. 'It's a dirty world, Mike. And like I told you, he's a sneaky little bastard.'

'So, um, what kind of things did you do for him?' Mike asked cautiously, unsure if he wanted to know the answer or not. 'You know, over the years?'

Phil could sense Mike's trepidation and gave a hollow half-chuckle. 'Oh, nothing too bad, not really. Finding people, handing over personal information, losing the odd piece of evidence. I didn't shoot anyone, if that's what you're thinking. Nothing like that at all. But it was all wrong, all very wrong. And it builds up inside you: the guilt, the self-loathing. The feeling of... dirtiness.'

He turned suddenly to face Mike with a desperate look in his eyes. 'I'm not bent, Mike, I'm not a bad copper, you have to believe me. I've spent 33 years in the force, and I've done everything I can to put away the bad guys. I've got principles, I honestly have. And maybe this sounds stupid, but of all the things I've done for Bob, at least none have involved getting anyone innocent into trouble. It's been trading one bad guy for a different one, that's all, it's just that it's been him making those decisions for me, and him always getting away with it.

'But I screwed up, and I screwed up massively. And that snowballed until I've ended up here, chasing around London after a bag of his precious weed when we should be doing something more useful.'

He started to pound the base of his fist gently but rhythmically on the table. 'And all because I didn't stay and try to comfort my Lily, but just walked away. I took the coward's way out and I've suffered ever since.'

Chapter 29

Harj held open the door of the pub and put a hand behind Waffle to steady him as he tried to exit, each arm stretched out to his sides to support himself against the door jambs. Despite it now being early evening, the brightness of the summer sky was still enough to make him blink and then squint. As his eyes adjusted, he settled on keeping just the one open for the time being.

They got out onto the pavement and Harj held Waffle upright with both arms around his waist.

'Look, Woff, I really need to go, alright? I was hoping to get a couple more hours done on the wall, but it's too late now. If I don't get back for my dinner, though, Michelle will make me sleep in the spare room.'

'Yeah, yeah, no problem at all, brother. Hoo-hoo!'

Harj released his grip cautiously and doubtfully, as when trying to build a house of cards, but Waffle managed to keep himself standing after a few exploratory calibration wobbles.

'You sure you're alright to get home? Shall I call you a cab?'

'A cab! Pfft! It's, like two minutes away, man! And yes, I am most serpently capable of driving myself home on my feet. Don't you worry about me!'

Harj appraised him closely and concluded with a quick shrug that he'd known Waffle get himself home on many occasions in a worse state than this.

'OK, then. If you're sure.'

'Sure as sure is eggs,' said Waffle, before smiling through a burp.

'Alright. Well, take care Woff, and if you need anything then just give me a call, yeah?'

Waffle nodded deeply and then attempted to make the waggling phone call gesture with his right hand, the thumb and little finger extended, but he only achieved a wildly shaking fist in mid-air that looked more like a spasm.

Harj paused, looking unsure, but then took a deep breath and patted his pockets to check for his essential possessions. 'Have a good night, Woff. Take it easy, yeah?' He gave Waffle one last slap on the shoulder, heavy enough to be manly, but not too hard that it might unbalance him.

Waffle watched him as he walked away, then called after him. 'Easy like Sunday morning, brother! You know it! Hoo-hoo!'

He took in his surroundings once again to get his bearings and then struck off towards home just as the pub door opened behind to disgorge five young men. They stayed near the door watching carefully as the man in the green hat staggered off down the road in a zig-zag.

* * *

'WHAT NOW?' said Lenny.

'We follow,' said Tommo, his eyes not leaving the tall man for a moment. 'We follow, discreetly. I don't think he's gonna be hard to keep up with, y'know?'

The others chuckled.

'We need to find out where he lives, so there's no point stopping him now. We follow at a nice safe distance, and then when we get to his place we wait until he's inside and then we'll pay him a visit. Yeah?'

They all nodded.

'So, stick with me, and take it nice and cool. Try not to look too suspicious, we're just ambling our way casually back from the pub, yeah? OK. Let's go.'

* * *

WAFFLE DECIDED to take the walk home without any urgency. He wasn't especially hungry with his belly full of lager, and the thought of being back in his empty flat with its missing TV, missing clock, and missing girlfriend didn't fill him with any particular desire to rush back. Plus, he couldn't coordinate any speed above the slowest walking pace with any real sense of confidence, and he felt a lot like a car trying to negotiate a bumpy road with loose wheels hanging on by a thread and broken suspension. And with a pissed-up driver.

After a couple of minutes of lurching along the pavement, he decided he might take a break. The concentration needed to walk straight while keeping upright was taking its toll on the one eye he trusted to stay open, so he veered off the pavement and let his legs fold beneath him until his bottom landed clumsily – and slightly painfully – on the edge of the kerb. He knew it hadn't been a dignified piece of sitting, but he felt the gratitude of a pilot who'd brought a damaged plane down heavily though with no casualties.

In the corner of his one good eye, he saw what he thought was a group of men scrabbling out of sight behind the corner of a wall, like a gang of kids playing Blind Man's Bluff with great enthusiasm. He shook the image out of his mind and took in his new surroundings at ground level.

There were parked cars about ten yards away on either side of his sitting spot, so he felt perfectly safe from passing traffic where he was. He leaned back on outstretched arms, feeling the warmth and roughness of the concrete under his palms, and raised his chin to the setting sun to bask in its orange glow.

What's that line, he thought to himself, *that one from Oscar Wilde or someone like that? Something to do with being in the gutter and looking at the stars?* He kept his eyes closed but his eyelids glowed red from within. *Ah well,* he thought, *maybe this isn't quite as poetic as that. But I'm definitely sat pissed on a pavement looking up at the sun. That'll do.*

When he brought his head back to the level and opened his eyes, he was surprised to see a pigeon no more than three feet away, eyeing him beadily. He made no more movement for fear of scaring him off, but instead just flicked his eyebrows up in greeting. 'Alright, pigeon dude?' he said, as softly as possible.

The pigeon said nothing, but merely shuffled its wings for a moment and then sank its body to the ground to sit also, watching Waffle closely the whole time.

'Yeah, man,' said Waffle, 'take the weight off. It's good down here.'

* * *

'WHAT'S GOING ON?' whispered Lenny. Tommo was at the front of their unnecessarily crouched group, and the only one with a privileged enough position to be able to peek around the wall.

'Man's having a sit down,' said Tommo, without feeling.

'What for?'

Tommo turned back to them. 'I couldn't possibly say, but I imagine it's related to those 8 or 9 pints we just watched him sink in a few hours.

'Is he alright?'

'I'm sure he's fine. Just let him be for a bit, he's not going anywhere fast. Unless you have somewhere more important to be, we sit tight and when he gets going again, we follow.'

'Yeah, ok.' Lenny waited patiently for a moment but then had visions of the man having left briskly while they'd been talking. 'Is he still there?'

Tommo chewed the inside of his cheek in exasperation but turned to take another careful look anyway.

'Yeah, he's fine. He's just talking to a pigeon.'

* * *

'So, what you been up to? Busy day?'

The pigeon remained almost motionless, its head just moving a little from side to side. Waffle nodded in understanding.

'Bit of flying around, finding some food and shitting on stuff, yeah? Gotcha.'

He recalled that the Seated Pigeon Pose had been one of the things he'd learnt in that first yoga session. It'd been a bit of a stretch in his inflexible jeans but hadn't been too taxing. It was funny how it seemed so long ago that he'd been at the Yoga Lawn, but he'd only arrived yesterday and had left this morning. The yawning chasm of a lager canyon seemed to delineate the two halves of today into very separate experiences. But if he hadn't agreed to leave after his talk with Fran then he'd still be there now, probably just finishing the last session of the day. Maybe even doing the Seated Pigeon Pose at this very moment before looking forward to some vegetarian dinner.

Hmmm, dinner. Perhaps he could eat now, after all. Perhaps one of the Taj Mahal's chicken bhunas would do a very nice job indeed of soaking up the booze. He could pop into Mr K's on the way back and pick up some more lagers too, perhaps. If there's one thing that 8 pints of lager love best, it's the company of more lagers.

Decision made, he nodded his farewell to the pigeon and stood up quickly, stretching his arms out to his sides as if warming up for a marathon. A moment later, he felt the blood drain from his head and appreciated that perhaps he'd stood up a little too dramatically for someone in his present condition. He moved a foot to address his balance, but caught it on the edge of the kerb, unbalancing him still further, and as he tried in vain to keep himself upright, the last thing he saw was the pigeon flapping its wings to ensure a hasty retreat as he fell back onto the pavement with the sickly cracking noise of his head hitting the concrete.

* * *

'SHIT!' hissed Tommo as he once again took a quick peek.

'What's happening now?'

'I think he's dead.'

'What?!'

They all pushed past each other to come into the open around the corner, and the five stood in a line surveying the scene from across the road. The tall, thin man was splayed out on his back on the pavement, his body laid out in an almost-perfect 'T' shape. A man on a food delivery moped had parked up and was bent over the prone body, his helmet pushed up to his forehead as he examined the fallen man with his hands on his knees.

'Jesus!' said Soapy with low gravitas. 'What did that pigeon actually say to him?'

The others turned to look at him silently as a jogger and a lady with a young child joined the concerned onlookers on the far pavement. The jogger appeared to be the first to do more than just stand and stare, and he knelt next to Waffle's head and was making a gentle examination of the injuries. From where Tommo and the others still watched and waited, it appeared as if the man was still unconscious, but after a few minutes there were too many people in the huddle and blocking their view to say for sure.

'Should we go and have a look then?' asked Playboy.

Tommo thought for a moment. 'Nah. We shouldn't get involved. Let's just hang back and see how it plays out. If he gets better, then we continue with the plan.'

'And if he's dead?'

'Yeah, that'd be a problem,' said Tommo, gruffly. 'That'd be a real problem.'

A while passed and not much seemed to change. People left or joined the group around the body at various intervals, but it maintained a core size of around seven or eight. From where they were standing, catching glimpses of the man through the legs of the bystanders, it seemed as if he may have moved a little, but was still lying flat on his back and hadn't sat up at any point. His head was now resting on a scrunched-up piece of clothing, though, and it was possibly just this addition that had led to his moving.

Eventually, a siren could be heard in the distance, growing steadily closer, and Tommo and the others resisted their natural urge to flee. It switched off as it approached the scene, but the arrival of the ambulance was announced instead by splashes of blue light washing over the nearby buildings in the dusk.

Once parked up, both occupants got out, and the small crowd dispersed to clear the way.

'OK,' said Tommo, 'we need to get over there. We need to be able to hear what's going on. If they take him away and we don't know where to, then we're back to where we started.'

The group started to move forward as one, but Tommo held them back with an outstretched arm.

'Woah, hang on. Let's not go over all mob-handed. Plus, we might need my car if they're gonna move him in that thing.' He reached into his pocket and handed his keys to Lenny. 'Take Soapy and D with you and bring my car round so it's handy. Playboy can come with me.'

The two of them sauntered over casually where a tight circle had now formed around the two paramedics at work.

The driver, a surprisingly short woman with a pink streak dyed into her long, blonde ponytail, was silently examining the man with practised speed and precision, while her colleague, a large man with a shaved head but an impressive gingery beard was asking simple questions to try and get a response. The circle tightened gradually as everyone edged forward to hear more clearly.

'Can you move back, please,' said the paramedic in a soft Welsh accent, 'give him some space. Thank you.'

It seemed that the man was now conscious, but groggy and slurring. He managed to tell the paramedic his name, age and today's date, but it was difficult to understand him too well. After more questions and the conclusion of the examination, the two medical staff had a quick conference.

'No sign of concussion, just a slight cut to the back of the head. Anything else?'

'Nothing,' said the woman, 'bit of a graze to the elbows where he broke his fall, but nothing that a plaster won't sort out.'

'OK. Well, I think inebriation is the main problem, the cut is superficial. I think he's good to go home.'

'Agreed,' said the woman, and she stood up to grab some paperwork from the cab.

'OK, Darren,' said the paramedic in a clear, slow voice, 'can you tell us your address? And is there anyone at home who can look after you tonight?'

Tommo craned his head forward to listen to the answer, but the man slurred a response that was difficult to understand. Clearly, the paramedic also failed to understand, as he tried asking a couple more times before changing tack.

'OK, Darren. I'm just going to check your wallet and phone to see if I can find some contact details, is that OK? Promise I won't take any cash… unless you have twenties or fifties.'

'Yeah, OK,' came the woozy response, and the paramedic fished out a mobile and wallet, which he then flicked through.

'Dead.' he said to his colleague as she returned.

'What?' she almost shouted. 'It was just a slight knock to the head!'

'No, no. The phone. Out of battery.'

'Jesus, Mark,' she replied, clutching her chest with her hand. 'You need to stop doing that, seriously.'

He grinned. 'Yeah. Nothing with an address on in here, either,' he said, rifling through the two tenners and a bank card. 'Ah, there's this, though...'

He picked out a business card and flicked it front and back a couple of times to read it. 'Some yoga place. But there's a mobile number on here with next Wednesday's date on it. They might have an address for him at least?'

The woman nodded. 'Sure, yeah. Worth a try.'

A moment later and someone had apparently picked up. 'Oh yes, hello there, this is Mark Davies, I'm a paramedic with the London Ambulance Service, who am I talking to please? OK, thank you, Miss MacRae, do you mind if I call you Fran? Thank you, Fran. Look, we're here with a Darren Jones, he has a card of yours in his wallet... no, no, he's fine, he's just had a little too much to drink and taken a bit of a tumble, that's all... what do you mean by "again"?... Oh, I see. Well anyway, we were wondering if you had an address for him at all?... You do, oh that's excellent, thank you. Hang on, let me get my pen... '

Tommo edged forward as far as he could and concentrated hard to prepare a mental note of whatever was coming next.

'OK, shoot... yes... yes... yes, got it, thanks.'

Tommo swore quietly under his breath.

'And do you know if there's anyone at home who can look after him?... OK, well we do need to be sure. He's fine but not in a condition to be left alone for a few hours at least, you see.... Well yes, we will if we need to, but it's a valuable bed taken up for the night and we'd far rather he stayed at home if at all possible... No, I'm afraid we have no other contact details for him at all... No, we checked that too, it's out of battery... OK, well if there's nobody home, would you be able to come and check on him do you think? Yes of course, I appreciate that, but it's important he has someone with him as I say.... Yes of course, we'll try at his home first... Yes of course we will... Yes, I promise we will.... Yes, cub's honour, we'll only call you again if there's nobody else there, but you'd be able to come then, if needed? OK, well that's very kind of… Oh. She's hung up.'

Tommo slapped Playboy gently on the arm and they walked back to where Lenny had parked the BMW just up the road. Lenny got out of the driver's seat as they approached, and with a slam of three doors, they were all inside and eager for news from Tommo.

'Right then,' he said after a dramatic pause. 'Follow that ambulance.'

Chapter 30

Fran pulled up alongside the parked ambulance and cut the engine. She sat for a moment in the dark parking area that ran along the back of the row of shops, doubting once again whether she should've come. She'd doubted this several times already since getting the phone call from the paramedic and had paused at each of the key stages that her journey had comprised. She'd even got out of the car and walked back towards the Mad Parrot after having driven so little distance that she was still in the same parking space, merely further to one end of it.

She looked out of each side window and then at the rear-view mirror, but all aspects gave much the same impression of a slightly grubby parking-cum-bin area behind some pretty grotty shops with some pretty grotty flats above them. It was everything she expected and less from Waffle. It occurred to her that she wasn't in much of a position to gloat, seeing as she lived above a grotty pub herself, so she reprimanded herself mentally and tried to think more positively. One good thing was that Wolfgang, her car, had got here without breaking down, which was always a bonus. She was inordinately proud of the pale yellow Beetle, and although she'd sometimes have to explain that it was one of the 'new shape ones' if conversation ever turned to her car, she was very aware that, even so, he was now 23 years old and with 130,000 miles under his wheels was no spring chicken.

She patted the steering wheel as she'd started doing with every breakdown-free journey since the big one and took a quick sniff of the Plumeria cutting that she religiously replaced every week in the little built-in flower holder attached to the dashboard. This feature of the car she considered a little naff, but she also knew deep down that it was one of the reasons she'd chosen it in the first place.

With ambling thoughts of her car shaken from her mind, she once again came back to the main question: what was she doing here? On what level could she be the best-placed person to look after someone whose only connection to her was that they'd met a day and a half ago? And the most prominent features of their shared experience so far was that she'd taken a moderate dislike to him and had subsequently given him a bollocking for his behaviour. The irony now was that the bollocking (and, to some extent, the dislike) was related to his drunkenness, the sole reason it seemed that she was now being forced to look after him. What must she have done so wrong in a previous life to deserve this?

And yet, here she was. Her sense of right and wrong, altruism, and perhaps even loyalty to her customers meant that she'd driven across town to help this stupid, lost soul when she had far better things to be doing with her time, and a business to run. She had paying yoga students staying in her rooms at that very moment! She was too nice for her own good sometimes, that much was obvious. Still, she was indeed here and it would be childish to go back home again now. The ambulance crew were clearly waiting for her and they, presumably, had even more important things to be doing than yoga.

She filled her cheeks with air and then blew it out slowly. *Right. Fine. Fuck's sake. May as well get on with it.* She figured she only had to stay with him until it was completely clear that he wasn't going to vomit or die, or any other stupid thing he felt like doing. She could be back home by 11, hopefully, midnight at the absolute latest. She needed to be up at 5, after all. Oh god.

She grabbed at the door handle, stepped out, and forced herself to walk towards the concrete stairwell that ran up to the flats above the shops. As she walked, she caught a glimpse of some movement in the corner of her eye, and glancing towards a car parked at the far end of the yard, she fancied she saw a collection of heads all shrink from view as if startled. Probably a load of youths up to no good, she thought. She had no urge to find out more, though, and increased her pace a little as she refocused on her destination, which was the flat with the front door left ajar and lights on inside. Sure enough, as she reached the door and peered inside with a gentle knock and a speculative 'Hellooo?', she saw the day-glo jacket of the short, blonde woman from the ambulance, so she stood up straight and walked inside.

'Ah, Miss MacRae! Thank you so much for coming.' It was the voice of the bearded paramedic, who was shaking the water from a mug he'd just rinsed out before placing it on the draining board. He walked towards her, drying his hands on his trousers, and shook her hand. 'The patient's here and all ready for you,' he said cheerily. 'I don't think he should be any trouble, but he's still a little dizzy. He knows where he is and everything, but I think the combination of the drink and the little knock to the head has made him a bit woozy and disorientated. Should be right as rain by the morning, I expect.'

The paramedics both moved to the side to leave a view of Waffle slumped on his sofa with a coffee mug in front of him on the little table. He was wearing a blanket over his shoulders and a sheepish, lopsided grin that appeared to contain a straight mix of embarrassment, impishness, and drunkenness.

'Great,' said Fran with as much enthusiasm as she could muster, which, objectively, was fuck all.

The paramedic looked at his watch, then raised his eyebrows to his partner, who immediately made a move towards the door. 'Right then, thanks again and we'll leave you to it. Any problems, just call 111. Or 999 if anything too weird happens, but that shouldn't be the case.'

He was now at the door and smiled at them both in turn as he pulled it shut with a jolly 'Good night!'

Fran turned back to face Waffle, who had picked up his mug and was trying to drink from it. It took him a couple of attempts to find his mouth, and once he did, it quickly became apparent – at least to Fran – that the cup was completely empty. He increased the angle of attack gradually until he was holding it fully upside down above his mouth, with nothing more than a single drop of cold coffee dribbling out of it. He leaned forward to place the mug back on the table, but left it on the edge so that it fell to the carpet with a soft thud as soon as he relinquished his grip.

'Oops,' he said, looking up at Fran through swimmy eyes. 'I think I'm drunker than I think I am,' he slurred thickly.

Fran swore under her breath, dropped her bag onto the floor and crouched to pick up the mug. Without saying anything, she took it to the sink and opened various cupboards and drawers until she had everything she needed to make two cups of coffee. She put the drinks down and perched herself on the far edge of the sofa. Waffle thanked her with a smile and they sat wordlessly for a while, each alone with their thoughts.

'So,' she said, after some time had passed, 'I've known you now for...' – she consulted her watch – '32 hours, and you've managed to get pissed twice in that period, both times at great inconvenience to me. That's actually pretty good going, in a sort of dickish way, isn't it?'

Waffle fixed his face into a pained and awkward rictus. Various elaborate and explanatory apologies wheeled and danced across his mind, but he didn't feel confident that he could pull any of them off without embarrassing himself. 'I'm sorry,' he said eventually, settling on a safe bet.

Fran realised that she'd perhaps been spoiling for a fight and had tried to antagonise him with her question, but his vaguely pathetic demeanour and sad eyes took the wind out of her sails. She nodded a silent acceptance of his apology and decided to calm herself down with a few deep breaths. She picked up her coffee and blew across the top of it a few times as she gazed around the room. From what she could make out, the flat was mainly this one room, containing as it did a sofa, small dining table behind it, and kitchen area off to the side. Two doors led off it, presumably to a bedroom and bathroom, and a third half-size door that she assumed was for storage.

Small and basic though it was, she had to concede that it was surprisingly clean and tidy. The main feature appeared to be the enormous collection of records arranged along the wall in front of her, and the shelves above that held the hi-fi, books, some drinks bottles, and a few ornaments and trinkets. She was surprised by the lack of any TV at all and gave Waffle a little credit for that in her mind.

She was also surprised to see bowls for cat food and water in the kitchen. She looked around but couldn't see anything that might utilise these, though they were both topped up, so she figured there must be a live cat around the place somewhere. The thought of Waffle being responsible for another life in addition to his own made her feel a little concerned initially, but on the assumption that he managed it successfully, she decided that it was actually quite impressive. After a moment's further reflection, she decided that being impressed by someone's ability to keep a cat alive was rather telling, and she went back to just being concerned.

'So,' she said, for lack of any better way of filling the void, 'this is Chez Waffle is it?'

Waffle nodded solemnly and waved a proprietorial hand around him. 'All mine, as far as the eye can see.'

'And how far's that?'

He screwed his face up theatrically and held one eye shut as he took another sweep of the room. 'About 6 feet currently, but I'm planning on phasing in the dining table within the next two hours. The far wall should be back online by morning.'

'Have you ever thought that you could be a little kinder to your body? I mean, sobriety's not so bad, y'know.'

'Sobriety's OK in moderation,' he said with a waggle of his head. 'But yes, I have been thinking that a lot lately, as it happens. That's what the yoga was for, it was meant to be a new direction. But I just had a couple of... blips.'

Fran raised an eyebrow. 'Blips?'

'Yeah. Blips. I thought I wanted something and was trying hard to get it. But it turned out that maybe I didn't need it, anyway. Plus, I was useless at trying, it seems. Stuff in life can be harder than you think it's going to be sometimes.'

She watched him for a moment, chewing her lip. 'I'm afraid I have no idea what you're talking about. That's just word salad.'

He smiled. 'Yeah. Sorry. I was waffling, as usual. Ignore me. I'm just having a kind of mini existential crisis, but it's not something you can help with, I don't think.'

'I don't have much to offer except yoga, I'm afraid.'

'And you're brilliant at it!' said Waffle with a sudden burst of enthusiasm. 'Seriously. What you've done, building a business like that, it's really impressive.'

Fran felt the warmth of her cheeks as she waved him away. 'Oh, stop it. That's just the yoga talking.'

'Nah, honestly. You've done something with your life, something you love. You should be very proud.'

She shook her head, but couldn't resist a small smile at the same time.

'It's hardly too late for you. All this existential crisis stuff, I mean, you're not exactly on your deathbed, are you? You're what, thirtyish? You've got plenty of time to do whatever you want in your life.'

'Yeah, I s'pose,' Waffle said, without much conviction.

'I mean, sure, it's probably a bit late for you to become an astronaut, or play for England, or get that gold medal in the 110-metre hurdles, but there's plenty of other stuff to achieve in life.'

Waffle was nodding in silent contemplation. 'Do you know,' he said, suddenly remembering something, 'that Olympic gold medals are mainly silver?'

'I did not know that.'

'It's true. They actually have the same silver content as the silver medals, with just a tiny coating of gold. They're like, 98.5 percent silver I think. Or is it 95.8? No wait, that's Capital FM. Either way, it's a lot of silver.'

'That's an excellent piece of general knowledge, thank you.'

'The gold medals are worth loads more though, cos even the little amount they have is so valuable. So they're worth, like, 800 quid each, instead of half that for the silver ones.'

'Very interesting. And what about the bronze medals, then?'

'They're just bronze,' he scoffed dismissively, 'worth fuck all.'

'Ah. I see.'

They settled back into their own thoughts, the thrill of sports-based trivia gradually fading away. They both picked up their coffees and took small, nibbling sips of the hot liquid. Fran was still perched on the edge of the sofa, and with two hands clasped around the mug and her mouth hovering over the steam, felt a little too hot in the July evening, and unable to relax. Her eyes ranged over the enormous record collection in front of her, and it occurred to her that she'd never actually listened to one before. She'd listened to plenty of music of course, but even CDs seemed a little quaint, and although she was fully aware that vinyl was making a solid comeback, she doubted Waffle's had all been bought recently in an attempt at keeping up with the latest fashionable trends. She glanced at him out of the corner of her eye, her gaze taking in the same purple trousers he'd been wearing at the Yoga Lawn, his dirty flip-flops, and that bizarre green hat, sat askance on his head. No, she thought, it definitely wasn't an attempt at looking hip.

'You've got a lot of records,' she said matter-of-factly.

'Certainly have. They're like my children!'

'That's a lot of kids.'

'Yeah, well, you know how it is. You start off by agreeing you'll stop at two, then before you know it you've got twelve hundred and sixty-three.'

Fran let out a small laugh, despite herself. 'They certainly take over the living room, too.'

'They do. Plus you're always cleaning them, they don't always play nicely and... er... they scratch easily?'

She laughed, more freely this time. 'You do know the world's moved on, though? I mean, you've heard of Spotify, right?' She waved her hand across his collection. 'All this and more, accessible from your phone.'

'I'm aware of its work,' he said, with an exaggerated sniffiness. 'But that's just computer files, ones and zeros. You don't get to hold the music in your hand, place it lovingly on the turntable, and then sit back with a 12x12 piece of artwork to pore over, or liner notes to read.'

'Yes, but think of all the money you'd save! A tenner a month for all the music in the world!'

Waffle shook his head. 'Nah, man. It's not for me. For a start, my phone's usually dead and I'm not even sure it'll run Spotify. Plus...' he nodded to his records, 'half this stuff's not on there, anyway. You might be able to get the latest Ed Sheeran single the moment it comes out, but dig a little deeper and there's some serious gaps.'

Fran was genuinely surprised. 'Really? I thought they had everything ever recorded, or something?'

'Pfft! It's seriously lacking in 1960s all-female garage rock, it's like the Japanese psych movement never even happened, and I could list any number of live Tito Puente albums that have just like... vanished into thin air.' He made a flicking gesture with the fingers of both hands and swivelled his eyes from side to side.

'I had no idea,' said Fran, nodding seriously, but failing to suppress a smile. 'Not even Tito Puente, eh?'

Waffle narrowed his eyes and looked at her sideways. 'I know, right? To be honest, the Afro-Cuban jazz genre as a whole is woefully underrepresented. I mean, I'm sure you'd struggle as much as me to get through the week without Puente's 1963 *Live in Puerto Rico*.'

'Ach, maybe,' she said, a mischievous look in her eyes, 'though frankly I preferred him before he went commercial.'

Waffle wriggled out off the blanket that was still around his shoulders and indicated a move towards the records. 'Shall I put some music on then?'

'Aye, if you like.'

'What do you fancy? Your choice.'

She looked at the records with trepidation; despite being begrudgingly impressed by the scale of the collection, she felt mildly intimidated by the idea of having to flick through them all to make a selection, and wasn't even sure she'd find anything she knew. She suspected there'd be relatively few Take That albums.

'Do you have...' she made a show of thinking hard, screwing up her face while she looked to the ceiling, hand clutching her chin. '... do you have any early 60s live Tito Puente?'

'Hmm, interesting choice,' said Waffle as he stood up unsteadily and then cautiously knelt in front of his collection, putting both hands on the floor to his sides to keep him upright. 'I mean, it's a challenge, but I'll see what I can do.' He flicked through the record sleeves, muttering artist names and album titles under his breath as he went. Eventually, he pulled out one with a swooshing sound and swung around to display it flamboyantly in both hands. 'I have *Live in Puerto Rico* from 1963, if that'll suit madame at all?'

'That'll do perfectly,' she said, nodding regally with eyes closed.

Waffle set the record to play, and they sat in silence for a while, feet tapping gently to the mambo rhythm. Fran found herself gazing vaguely at the wall in front of her, and her eyes settled on the dark circle where the clock had been. 'Someone's stolen your clock,' she said, pointing up at the mark. 'Or was it one of those commemorative plates they advertise in the back of the Sunday supplements? Don't tell me... William and Kate's wedding?'

Waffle let out a short laugh, but didn't catch her eye. 'Nah, it was a clock. My ex took it with her when she left.'

'Oh. Right,' Fran said, her smile dropping. She tapped her nails on her coffee mug, unsure whether she should try and change the subject or just stay quiet.

Waffle looked over and noticed her unease. 'It's not a problem, all in the past,' he said cheerfully. He looked up at the dark circle on the wall. 'Bit grubby though, innit? I should probably get a new clock to cover that up. Or a commemorative plate. Though I'm more of a coronation kind of guy, weddings just deserve mugs or tea towels in my book.'

'How long's it been, then? The, um, lack of clock?'

Waffle thought for a moment, and looked at his wrist where a watch would've been if he'd had one on. 'Er... six days.'

'Oh! Shit!' she said with some alarm. 'I thought you were going to say six months or something. Um... sorry, I didn't mean to...' she trailed off awkwardly.

'Nah, it's alright. I'm good. It's been a bit difficult, but I'm OK about it now, I think. And I've got a clock on my phone anyway.' He smiled sheepishly and brought his phone out of his pocket to wave it at her, seemingly unaware that it was out of battery and displaying nothing but a cracked black screen.

Fran thought for a moment. 'Is this all connected to the yoga then? Is that why you came, to clear your head or focus on something else?'

'Kind of. Yeah. That and some other things. I felt like a change of scene and to get out of here for a while.'

'Right, yeah. No, I understand that.' She took a sip of her coffee and put the mug down on the table. Her eyes suddenly widened. 'Oh, shit! You were there to try and get over it all, and I kicked you out! Were you drowning your sorrows in the pub with Arlo? Oh no, that was really insensitive of me. I mean, if I'd known...'

'No, no,' said Waffle, putting down his own mug and raising his palms to slow her down. 'Firstly, you didn't kick me out, we both agreed I should go. And secondly, I was being a dick. I wasn't moping or anything, not then. We just went to the pub and got pissed, and that was stupid. No, you were right to ki... agree with me that I should leave.'

Fran eyed him carefully. 'OK. Well. Let's not go through all that again, but I do feel a bit bad about it now.' She sat back, relaxing a little. A thought occurred to her, and she looked at him with a wry smile. 'You weren't there to try and check out the hot yoga babes were you?'

'God no!' he said with a snort. 'No, not at all. Seriously. I didn't even realise it would mainly be birds, I hadn't given it any thought at all. It was just a random idea to get away.' He laughed. 'I mean, I'm not Arlo!'

'Arlo?!' Fran almost shrieked it. 'But I thought he was...'

'Rich?' said Waffle with a raised eyebrow.

'What? Oh. No, doesn't matter.'

A new track started on the album and Fran made an effort to appreciate it, drifting off into her own thoughts. She wasn't sure it was exactly the kind of thing she'd ever listen to for pleasure, and if anything, it reminded her of the kind of music that might be played in a novelty-themed restaurant. Still, Waffle seemed to be enjoying it and was absent-mindedly flicking one of his flip-flops to the beat.

She watched him for a while, his head bobbing gently in time, with his eyes closed. He looked extremely peaceful, though for a second Fran wondered if he'd maybe fallen asleep. She felt a slight wave of pity for him, left by his girlfriend and living alone in his tiny flat with nothing but hundreds of weird records for company. No wonder he drank so much.

'So, are you going to try and find a new Mrs Jones, then? Get back out there and all that?'

He started from his half-doze, and looked around him in a quick movement before turning to Fran and squinting his eyes to focus.

'Huh? Wha? Oh. Oh, nah. I'm good.' He closed his eyes again and continued nodding away to the music.

Fran decided she should keep him talking. She figured she only had to stay another hour or so, now that he seemed to be slowly sobering up and in no danger of coming to any harm, and the thought of staring at the walls while he nodded himself to a snoring sleep was too much to bare.

'You should. Would be good for you. Ooh, a friend of mine has just joined a new dating site, she says it's great and that there's loads of people on it already. Plus, it's not tacky at all like some of the others.'

'Nah,' he said, opening his eyes again and reaching for his mug. 'Not for me. I don't like all that stuff, it's too techy. It's like the Spotify of meeting someone, it's too... digital. I'm all analogue, me!'

'You're such an old fogey,' she said teasingly. 'Have you ever tried it? A dating site?'

'Nope. I'm happy as I am, thanks. I think I'd rather be single than have to go through all that malarkey.'

She considered this for a moment. 'Would you say you're risk averse?'

'I don't like any board games,' he said, stretching his arms above him and yawning.

'Very funny. But seriously though... I mean, not even Monopoly?'

'That's the worst! Take all the most depressing aspects of life: rent, tax, debt, prison, and then see if you can start an argument with all your family and friends by bankrupting them. The only reason for buying a station is so you can jump in front of your own train.'

'I don't think that bit's in the rules.'

'Who knows? Nobody's ever read them! Still, would make the game a lot shorter, wouldn't it?'

When the Tito Puente record eventually reached the end of the side, the room was filled with a repetitive fizzing noise as the needle bounced back into the groove repeatedly. Waffle went to turn it over, but held it out towards Fran like an offering, with eyebrows raised questioningly. 'Side two, or something else?'

'Um. Perhaps something else.'

Waffle looked a tiny bit disappointed for a fleeting moment, but smiled and nodded, then began searching for another record. She hadn't wanted to appear rude, but she'd decided that Tito Puente was perhaps a little busy for her tastes, especially at this late hour, and its primary effect was to make her want to order tapas.

'Have you got anything to eat?' she blurted out suddenly, her peckishness seemingly asking the question for her.

Waffle placed the needle onto the new record, and turned to face her. 'Er, yeah, sure. Do you want me to make something, like a salad maybe?' He couldn't think of much else that he had in the fridge that was vegetarian, though was a bit unsure of how safe he'd be cutting anything with a knife seeing as he still couldn't see straight. Al Green began to emanate softly from the speakers, a buttery smooth voice over a gentle soul groove.

'Nice choice!' said Fran, hugely grateful for the replacement of the frantic mamba rhythms. 'But no, don't go to any trouble. Just maybe if you had anything snacky to hand. I'm not usually up this late, just got the fancies a bit!'

Waffle nodded and checked the kitchen cupboards. He had some chocolate digestives but also a variety of nuts and mixed seeds that he'd bought to sprinkle over salads, so he decanted these into a couple of bowls and brought them over. Fran was quite impressed, though said nothing, and grabbed a few nuts.

Chapter 31

In the parking area behind the shops, five young men sat patiently in an old, red BMW 3 Series. They'd followed the ambulance at a distance and then parked up a few spaces away from it when it had pulled in, wedged into the darkest corner and away from the one security light that mainly lit up the large, commercial wheelie bins. Half an hour later, a pale yellow VW Beetle had arrived, and a lone young woman had stepped out. She'd seemed a little hesitant initially, but had eventually headed up to the flats with a determined stride. On her way, she'd turned to look right at their car, but the group in the BMW had all shuffled down in their seats to stay out of sight as quick as a flash. Their reactions were finely honed from their years working the streets, they'd been far too quick for her to see them, they were sure of that.

'Who's that then?' Soapy asked, when they deemed it safe to sit back up again, 'D'yer reckon it's his missus?'

'Nope, doubt it,' said Tommo, flicking a glance up at Soapy in the rear-view mirror, wedged in between Playboy and D as usual. 'Me and Playboy heard that ambulance bloke talking to her on the phone. Sounded like she didn't even know him that well, and sort of gave the impression that he lives alone. No idea who she is, but I don't think she's his bird or anything. Maybe someone he works with, something like that.'

'Well, she looked pretty fit,' said Soapy with a lascivious snigger, 'I definitely would!'

Tommo rested his elbow on the top of his seat and twisted to face him. 'You'd what, Soapy? Make a tit of yourself in front of her? Giggle? Drool?'

Soapy's grin dropped, and he looked down at his feet, which were balanced on top of each other on the transmission tunnel. 'I was just saying,' he said quietly to himself, as Tommo finished staring at him and turned back.

'What d'yer reckon then, Tommo?' asked Lenny from the passenger seat. 'Should we go in or what?'

Tommo scratched his nose as he shook his head. 'Nah. It could get messy with two of 'em in there, I want him alone.'

'So how long do we wait?'

Lenny received a reproachful look. 'Don't tell me. You've not had any dinner and you're hungry.'

'That wasn't what I was gonna say!'

Tommo said nothing but continued to study him.

'I mean, I was just asking for information, that's all. Like, are we gonna stake the place out all night or what? What's the plan?'

Tommo continued his silent stare until Lenny finally cracked. 'But yes, since you ask, I am a bit peckish. I only had a few snacks earlier and we never even had any lun–'

A raised palm from the driver's seat silenced him. 'Look. We'll sit here for another hour, yeah? See if Little Miss Beetle leaves him to it. And if so, then we watch her leave and then get up there. If she doesn't go, then we may as well head home, she might be there all night for all we know. It's not as if we don't know where he lives now, but we're so close, I'm not letting him get away from us.

'We don't know what he's planning, he might be shifting that weed first thing for all we know, we don't have the luxury of time. So... we sit tight for an hour, and if nobody's moved, then we go home and I'll pick you all up at 8:00 in the morning, right? Then we carry on as we were.'

'Another hour, then. OK,' said Lenny, nominally agreeing but with the sad eyes and voice of a little boy who's been told he can't have any more sweets until his braces come off in two years' time.

'Fuck's sake! Look, get out and go round the front to that shop and see if it's still open. Fill yer boots with whatever crap you can find in there, but I want you back here in two minutes flat, yeah? I don't want anything to kick off here while you're choosing between the Cornish pasty and the chicken and mushroom slice!'

Lenny nodded curtly and reached for the door handle, a smile creeping across his face as he turned away.

'Actually, stop! Get back in!'

Lenny's face crumpled as he took a deep breath and fell back into his seat, trying hard to arrange his expression into one that didn't convey petulant anger.

'I've got a better idea,' said Tommo, squirming in his seat to pull his mobile from his jeans pocket. 'You're right. None of us have eaten. There's an Indian takeaway a few shops along, should still be open an' all. Let's get a quick order in and you can go and pick it up and bring it back.'

Lenny's face cracked into a wide grin. 'Nice one!'

Half an hour later, the BMW was parked as before in the corner, lurking in the shadows. Now, though, its windows were all heavily steamed up, despite them all being half opened. Through these gaps wafted the laid-back grooves of Chill Rap music, set so low it could only be heard from within a few feet of the car, along with the rising steam from a selection of curries and side dishes, the tang of garam masala hanging heavy in the air.

Another half an hour after that, with no other comings or goings from the flats, and the yellow Beetle still where it had been parked, the BMW fired up and slowly edged out onto the main road, all four windows disgorging empty takeaway dishes as it went.

Chapter 32

'So, what about you?,' asked Waffle, sitting down after replacing the last Al Green record with another. 'Is there a Mr Yoga?'

Fran wrinkled her nose. 'There is not, no. I think I work better in life on my own, to be honest.'

'Fair enough. Is that just a euphemism for "I can't keep a boyfriend" though?'

She scowled at him for a moment, unsure if he was being rude or not, but his cheeky grin and twinkling eyes signalled his teasing.

'Maybe,' she said with a small laugh. 'I've had three in the time I've lived in London and they've all been disasters. The first one slept with my best friend, the second one just stopped answering the phone and was never heard from again, and the third one pawned a bracelet my mother gave me.'

Waffle whistled with respect. 'Well, you know what they say about London… you're never more than six feet away from a twat.'

'I thought it was "rat"?' Fran said with a frown.

'Either or.'

'Ah!'

Waffle leant back on the sofa and knuckled his eyes. He was looking tired, Fran thought, she'd be able to head home soon.

'What did he pawn the bracelet for? That's really low!'

'It is. Simon was an arsehole, and he used my bracelet to get cash for cocaine. I didn't even know he used it, he had this secret addiction. Not one he could afford, apparently. Turns out he'd snatched the odd tenner from me in the past and I hadn't noticed. I just thought I was being ditzy, or spending more than I realised. Then a ring went missing, and I started thinking I was losing my mind. He even helped me spend an hour searching for it, both of us on hands and knees scouring the floor of the bedroom. Scheming bastard!'

'Eww, that's so bad.'

'Yeah. Anyway, nothing else went missing for a bit, but then I wanted to wear my mother's bracelet for a posh party we were going to. It wasn't the most valuable thing, but totally priceless to me. I went berserk and turned the place upside down for it. But I knew for a fact I hadn't touched it for months and it was always shut away in my jewellery box, so I couldn't understand it at all. I didn't suspect Simon at first, but I knew it must've been taken, so I said we should call the police. He got really defensive and funny about it and we had a big row. I knew then that something was going on and challenged him. Eventually, he confessed. He broke down in tears, begged forgiveness, promised he'd never do it again, the whole shebang. Like an idiot, I gave him a second chance, and less than a fortnight later he'd taken a twenty from my purse. I knew for a fact it was missing as I'd just taken it out on the way home that day.'

'And that was that?'

Fran mimicked a waving hand as she mouthed *bye bye*. 'Yep. Learned a valuable lesson there I think. Or escaped a close call. One of those kinds of phrases, anyway.'

'Yeah, big time. He sounds like a massive bellend. Though, three out of three, that's quite a record you've got there. You sound like a bit of a twat magnet, no offence!'

'Some taken,' she said, nodding her thanks with a smile. 'I haven't quite reached the stage of shaving off my hair, wearing dungarees and steering every conversation around to how all men are cheating bastards, but I'm not far off. Like I say, I think perhaps I'm better off on my own.'

'Yeah, well, that's not something anyone can tell you, is it? That's entirely up to you.'

She picked up her coffee and took a sip, but winced at the now-cold drink and put it back, instead opting for a few more nuts from the bowl.

'So what happened with your girlfriend, then? You said she left?'

He gave her a quizzical look.

'If it's not a personal question, of course,' she added quickly.

'Ha. No, not personal at all. We can move on to my relationship with my dad and my irrational fear of spiders afterwards, if you like.'

Fran sat upright with a start. 'Oh, I'm sorry, I didn't mean–'

Waffle smiled. 'I'm joking, it's fine.'

Fran raised an eyebrow and grimaced with embarrassment. 'Sure? We can go back to Tito Puente if you like?'

Waffle rocked his head from side to side, weighing it up. 'Afro-Cuban music or dissecting failed relationships... Hmm, it's like the world's darkest quiz show. I'll take dissecting failed relationships for ten points please!'

'I was just going to ask what happened, that's all. Like, did it just come to a natural end or did you... I don't know, did you do something wrong?'

Waffle thought for a moment. 'Oh, it was me. I suppose I didn't put enough into the relationship. And wasted what money I made on takeaways, and drank far too much lager.'

'Oh? You amaze me,' Fran said with a sly grin.

'Some taken,' said Waffle with a wink.

'So you didn't cheat on her, or steal any jewellery, or have a drug problem then? That's something, at least.'

Waffle smiled awkwardly and began to scratch the back of his neck. 'Well, certainly not the first two.'

'Oh?' said Fran, looking at him sideways. 'But drugs?'

Waffle continued to avoid her gaze and was now examining the backs of his hands. 'Sort of, yeah. Not coke or anything though, nah. Just weed.'

'I see.' Fran was watching him closely. 'And was it a problem, would you say?'

'It was for her!' he said, with a forced laugh, but immediately coughed, frowned and shook his head, as if to strike the comment from the record. 'That's in the past though, anyway. I don't do it any more, that was the old me.'

Fran nodded. She was tempted to dig further but was aware that she'd moved the conversation from being a friendly chat to a borderline interrogation, so decided to reduce the pressure. 'And was getting pissed up and collapsing in the street also the old you?' she asked, unable to resist one last little jab.

Waffle smiled weakly. 'What can I say, I'm a work in progress! But there's no more weed and I haven't had a single takeaway since she left.'

'Ah well, two out of three ain't bad, eh?'

'Exactly. It's what Meatloaf would've wanted.'

'Except maybe the bit about cutting out the curries,' Fran said with a giggle.

'Yeah, he looked like he used to enjoy a good takeaway.'

'He'd do anything for love, but he wouldn't dopiaza,' said Fran, laughing freely at her own joke.

Waffle chuckled and threw a peanut at her. 'No, but his favourite was a bhat out of hell.'

'Enough!' shouted Fran, now laughing hysterically, 'No more!'

'Why stop now?' asked Waffle, now laughing too.

'Because I don't know any more Meatloaf songs!' she squealed between heaving sobs. 'Or curries, for that matter!'

Waffle pushed her playfully, and she fell onto her side, still laughing.

'That's a lucky escape actually,' grinned Waffle, 'I had one about a dead ringer that I'd have probably regretted.'

Fran sat up straight again and threw a cashew nut at him. 'Eww, close escape then!'

Waffle flinched and let out a stifled cry as he cupped one eye with his hand.

Fran stopped laughing and looked at him with sudden concern. 'Are you OK?'

'Yeah. You nutted me in the eye, though!' Waffle's face was scrunched up, and as he moved his hand away from his face and cautiously blinked a few times, Fran could see that his eye was red and filling with tears.

'Oh shit! God, I'm so sorry!' she said, as she shifted across the sofa towards him. 'Let me have a look!'

Waffle cautiously moved his hands away and offered the injured eye towards her, though struggled to keep it open. 'I assume you're a qualified optomo... optommy... eye doctor?'

'Mmmmyeah... I did a first aid course once,' she said as she moved closer and tried to get a good look, moving his head by the chin to get the eye into the light.

'Oh OK. Presumably you covered nut/eye impacts?'

'Not so much. Though I did get to do CPR on a dummy. And I bandaged someone's finger. So I'm basically a GP now.'

Waffle tried blinking a few more times, and a steady trickle of tears ran down his face. 'How's it looking then, doc? Will I still be able to look at the piano?'

She brushed away a tear from his cheek with the edge of her thumb. 'No. I'm afraid it's going to have to come out. I just need a spoon and some TCP, it'll be over in a jiffy...'

'Nooo!' Waffle exclaimed in mock horror, grabbing both her wrists and holding them away from his face. 'I have a phobia of anything to the left of me! I need to check it at all times!'

'Oh really? Can't you just move your head?'

'Not quick enough. There are some seriously fast attack spiders in this flat and they favour striking from the west!'

Fran started laughing again, and Waffle watched her through one eye, the other scrunched up so tightly that it looked like he was doing a poor pirate impression.

'At least you can focus properly with just one eye open.'

He was still holding her wrists loosely, and she pulled them away just enough that he was instead holding onto her hands.

'I can,' he said softly.

She was watching him intently and found herself edging closer along the sofa, barely aware of making the movement herself. She'd never noticed the colour of his eyes before and was surprised to see such a deep, inky blue, with little flecks of yellow around the edges. She assumed the other one was the same.

Waffle began to fall backwards, so slowly that it was barely perceptible, and Fran matched his movement perfectly. Their eyes closed in sync as she made the last movement forward, her lips parting slowly as she moved her leg behind her for balance.

There was a sharp knock and then a sound like a small maraca being shaken once. They opened their eyes and pulled their heads back as if the other had pointed out the proximity in alarm.

'Shit!' said Fran, looking down at the floor. She'd knocked the bowl of seeds onto the floor where it had upended its contents onto the carpet.

'Don't worry,' said Waffle, sitting up to mirror Fran and releasing her hands, 'it's nothing. Leave it for now.'

Fran seemed distracted and was now looking around the room, awkwardly. 'No, no, I should clean that up, they'll get trampled into the carpet, you'll never get them out. Have you got a hoover or something?' She stood up and continued to avoid eye contact.

'Honestly, don't worry about it, Fran,' Waffle said, smiling, 'pretty sure there are worse things in that carpet!'

'Ha, I can imagine! Let me just clean it up now though, I can't leave it like that.' She righted the bowl and was trying to pick up the seeds between her fingers, with little success. 'Hoover?' she asked, looking at him for the first time since she'd got up.

Waffle nodded towards the back of the room. 'In that cupboard,' he said, shaking his head but smiling warmly at her.

'Yeah, yeah,' she said, her hands on her hips. 'Just humour me, OK? I've got certain standards.'

They held each other's gaze for a moment, both smiling, and then she broke away with a work-like, 'Right then!'

Waffle lay back onto the arm of the sofa, beaming contentedly to himself, his hands behind his head and his eyes closed.

He was dimly aware of the flick of the latch and the soft sweeping sound as the door dragged against the carpet, his mind on other things. After a pause, there was the sound of a zip being dragged open.

He opened his eyes in a panic and pushed himself bolt upright. 'No! Leave it, I'll clear it up tomorrow!'

He stood up quickly, too quickly, and leaned against the sofa edge to avoid a repeat of the incident from earlier. Fran was standing by the cupboard, the holdall at her feet and a bag of the weed in both hands. She was staring at it as if she'd found a bomb wash up on a beach, a mixture of shock and fear on her face. She slowly lifted her face to look at Waffle, and he could see the glint of a tear as it ran down the side of her nose.

'No, look...' he said, faltering, 'it's not what you... I mean...'

She shook her head sadly before letting the bag drop back into the holdall, then stood for a moment staring into the distance, her hands still out in front of her as if holding an invisible object. Waffle leapt around the sofa and headed towards her, but she suddenly snapped out of her trance and looked around her, as if she'd been teleported into the flat for the first time. She marched across the room, wiping her tear as she went and ignoring Waffle as he jumped out of her way.

'What the fuck,' she muttered under her breath, 'what the fuck am I doing here?' She picked up her bag from the floor and rifled through it roughly before zipping it shut with a violent yank.

'Fran, I–'

'What am I doing? Fuck's sake!' She was almost shouting now, though still to nobody in particular, and especially not Waffle, who was standing at a safe distance and watching on with pain etched across his face.

'I've got a business to run, I've got clients to manage. It's nearly one in the FUCKING MORNING!'

She flung her bag over her shoulder and strode towards the door.

'Fran, please! Just stay a minute and I'll explain everything. Sit down, I'll make a coffee.'

She twisted the latch, but then stopped and turned. She looked at Waffle, then swept her gaze across the flat. 'I'm a fucking idiot,' she spat, then yanked open the door and slammed it behind her.

Chapter 33

Waffle woke to the sound of the letterbox snapping shut. It wasn't the kind of sound to trigger any particular excitement in him; the post these days was split almost equally into junk and bills, so he tended to put off seeing what had been delivered until he needed to use the front door and was forced to either step over it or pick it up. For a moment he wondered why he was not usually woken by the sound of the post being delivered, but on opening his eyes fully he realised that he'd been sleeping on the sofa.

There hadn't been any specific physical reason why he hadn't made it to bed the previous night. Sure, he'd still been a bit pissed and a little woozy even from the pub session with Harj and the subsequent fall, but after chatting to Fran for a few hours he'd perked up remarkably. Ah yes. Fran. A mental image of her discovering the weed and storming out coalesced in his mind's eye, and he winced at the memory. He'd done it again. He'd screwed up royally just as things were starting to come together. And now she too had left. Added to the list.

He looked up at the clock on the wall to see what time it was, but it only informed him, once again, that it was time to get a new clock. He stretched out a leg to get his phone out of his pocket, but that only informed him it was time to start charging it more regularly. With a sigh, he swung himself upright and plodded off to put the kettle on and plug his mobile in at the wall. As he made himself a cup of tea, his phone flickered into life, and a moment or two later it pinged to let him know he had a text from Harj asking him if he'd got home safely, sent the previous evening to his dead phone.

Waffle leant against the kitchen counter and composed a reply as he sipped his tea: 'Yeah. Eventually. Bit of a long story.'

'How can it be a long story?' asked Harj, as Waffle picked up his call a minute later. 'You live about half a mile from the pub. Don't tell me you went for a curry on the way home?'

'Ha! No, man, nothing like that. To be honest, I got a lift home most of the way anyway, didn't get chance to stop for any food.'

'A lift? For half a mile? Who from?'

'Er... some nice ambulance people.'

'What?!' Harj's shriek distorted in the little phone speaker. 'What did you do, Woff?', he said with an air of resignation.

Waffle thought for a moment. 'You know, I'm not a hundred percent sure, now I think about it. I remember falling, seeing stars, chatting to a pigeon, a Welshman with pink hair, a girl with a big beard, and then Fran from the yoga place came to look after me.'

'Err... chatting to a pigeon? A Welshman with pink hair? Did this definitely all happen?'

Waffle paused. 'I mean, I think so. The gist at least. I might've got some of the details mixed up.'

There was a muffled noise from the other end of the line and a sound of a revving engine in the background. 'Look, Woff, I'm just driving to work, are you at home? I'm not far away, I could pop in if you like?'

Twenty minutes later and the two of them were on the sofa, Waffle having brought Harj up to speed with the previous evening's events.

'Well,' said Harj, digesting the update, 'I think you're absolutely right.'

'About what?'

'That was a long story.'

Waffle nodded. 'Yeah. Would've made for a pretty lengthy text.'

They sat in silence for a few moments.

'And so that was it then? She actually stormed out like that? You've not heard anything from her?'

Waffle shook his head sadly. 'Nope. And I'm not expecting to. I mean, look at it from her point of view. She tells me she doesn't like drugs, I tell her I basically agree, and then she finds ten kilos of weed hidden in a cupboard, some of it bagged up and ready to sell. God knows what she thinks of me.'

'I think we both know what she thinks of you, Woff.'

Waffle looked up at Harj and frowned. 'I was being rhetorical, man.'

'Yes, sorry mate,' said Harj, nodding, 'sorry.' He sipped some tea and then cleared his throat. 'But, Woff... um, is it important?'

'What do you mean?'

Harj turned away from Waffle's gaze and took a moment to build up to his next question. 'I mean, does it really matter if the girl from the yoga place thinks you're a drug dealer, or an arsehole, or whatever else?'

Waffle continued to watch him through narrowing eyes.

'Like, it's all a bit awkward and embarrassing, of course, but it's not like you were gonna see her again, is it? The whole yoga thing didn't work out too well, did it, so I assume you weren't planning on going back?' Harj now tried to catch Waffle's eye, but he'd turned away. 'You were going through your whole mission thing to get Nat back and, OK, that's not gone well so far, so I understand you being a bit depressed and everything. But isn't last night just something you should try and forget about and let go? Maybe you should try and get a message through to Nat, see if she'll meet up perhaps, give it another go at showing her how you've changed?'

Waffle had begun shaking his head as Harj spoke, and he continued to for a while afterwards.

'No,' he said eventually with some force. 'That's the thing, man.'

'What is?'

'Yesterday at the pub I was in a mess. I see that now... and I'm sorry about that. I shouldn't have dragged you out of work just so I could get wasted in your company. That was pretty selfish.'

Harj put a hand on Waffle's shoulder. 'No, mate, don't be silly. That's what friends are for, isn't it?'

Waffle nodded his thanks but thought he noticed Harj glancing at his watch on his outstretched wrist.

'I've had time to think now, though. I was in a bit of a state last night but I reckon my brain was processing everything all night anyway, while I wasn't watching it. And I think Nat was right.'

'About what?'

'About us. About us being a couple. She said that we'd gone through life while just being nearby each other and that we'd never really been close. That hurt me when she said it because I thought she was everything and that we were perfect for each other, but I think I know what she means now. I think she might've been right.'

Harj was shaking his head, trying to keep up. 'So, the mission thing?'

Waffle shrugged a shoulder. 'Maybe I didn't need to bother. Or maybe I was doing it for the wrong reason.'

'I'm not following...'

Waffle turned to face Harj, his expression serious but his eyes moving around as if still trying to make sense of his own thoughts.

'I thought Nat leaving was the worst thing that's ever happened to me. She was everything to me and I needed her. I wasn't capable of living by myself because I was such an idiot, and couldn't manage to even look after myself properly.'

'She was the ying to your yang,' said Harj, his expression earnest.

'Shut up, man,' said Waffle, frowning but smiling.

'Sorry, sorry. Carry on.'

'So when she left, I knew I needed to change. I thought I needed to change for her, to get her back. So we could carry on like before.'

Harj raised an eyebrow. 'But...?'

'But maybe I was wrong. Maybe I didn't need to change for her at all. Maybe I was wasting my time.'

Harj was frowning again. 'Okaaaay. I'm not sure if this is a beautiful moment or not, to be honest.'

Waffle jumped up, his face suddenly animated. 'Gimme a moment! I just need to get a few things together!'

He bounded across the room to the cupboard, swung open the door and dragged out the holdall of weed into the centre of the room. He then rushed into his bedroom, and Harj could hear his heavy footsteps, interspersed with various cupboards and drawers opening and slamming shut. Waffle reappeared a few moments later, his expression now alive and almost wild as a grin stretched across his face.

'I know what I need to do!' he exclaimed loudly as he grabbed his phone from where it was charging on the kitchen work surface. 'Can you drive me to the Yoga Lawn?'

Harj looked confused. 'Err... drive you? Now? Um... well, I'm supposed to be working on the wall but the van's full of paint crap, mate. I mean, there's only the passenger seat and that's got paints and stuff on it. I could probably clear it out though if it's important... might take a little bit of time, but if I can bring stuff up here then I can sort it...'

'Excellent!' sang Waffle with enthusiasm as he continued to busy himself at speed around the flat. His train of thought was punctuated by a knock at the door, but with no let up in his speedy pacing, Waffle changed direction. 'Mr K, I expect! Probably wants some rent money,' he said, winking at Harj as he passed him. He flung open the door with a smile and was punched so hard in the face that he was knocked backwards several steps before falling.

Chapter 34

'Get that guy!' Tommo shouted to Playboy while striding forwards to subdue Waffle, who was lying on his back and touching his fingers to his nose. Harj was still seated and had pushed himself as far back into the cushions of the sofa as possible, both his hands in the air and a look of panic on his face as Playboy marched towards him with his fist pulled back.

'No, no, don't hit me, I won't move!' Harj shouted, half turning his head and closing his eyes in preparation for the impending strike.

Playboy paused, and seeing there was no threat he stood back a little, ensuring the man had no means of escape while he watched Tommo bundle the tall guy with the hat onto the sofa alongside his friend.

'Where d'you come from?' Tommo barked at Harj angrily, 'I thought he was alone!'

'I... I got here earlier, just popped in on the way to work,' Harj replied, only half looking at Tommo from behind his hands.

'Fucking Soapy!' Tommo said under his breath, 'I told him. Be ready at 8, I said. I told them all, didn't I?' he said, swinging around to face Playboy.

'Yeah, he's never ready. He's terrible.' Playboy tutted and shook his head like a clucking mother at a coffee morning. 'Should I get the others up from the car?'

Tommo surveyed the scene. It was two-on-two, but the men on the sofa were pretty weedy-looking, plus sat low down on a squidgy sofa. He and Playboy held the high ground and were both considerably more gym-honed. He felt nothing other than dominance and superiority. And anyway, they weren't planning on staying long.

'Nah, we're nearly done here.' He scanned the room and found what he was looking for immediately. 'Huh,' he said with a satisfied grunt, 'you've even got it out and ready for us!'

He walked over to the holdall that was alone in the middle of the room, pulled the zip open and nodded his satisfaction. 'Looks like there's a bit missing,' he called over to Playboy, 'but that'll do.' He zipped it closed, picked it up by the handles, and resumed his position alongside Playboy. 'You can have that on us,' he said to Waffle with a sly grin, 'unless it's still here somewhere?' He looked down at the coffee table and then the kitchen work surface, searching out any clues for the missing bag's presence.

'No, man,' said Waffle flatly while staring at him intently with cold eyes, 'it's long gone. Sold, dealt, smoked.' He had a trickle of blood running from his nose but he left it alone and had both his hands on his lap.

'So be it. But you've caused me a lot of aggro, chasing around trying to find this bag.' He was pointing at Waffle now, his expression darkening and his voice rising. 'This is mine, you understand, and you took it from me. You had no right, no right at all!'

'I just found it on the pavement, man. I didn't see a forwarding address or nothing.'

'Don't get smart, understand?' Tommo had moved towards Waffle with his fist now bunched, but he stopped short and checked himself. 'You better steer clear of us, that's all I'm saying. We've got our rightful property back, but this ain't over. If I see you around, you better cross over to the other side of the street, do you hear what I'm saying?'

Waffle held his gaze but said nothing. With no reply forthcoming, Tommo readjusted his hold on the bag straps and nodded to Playboy, and the pair of them backed away slowly towards the door, keeping both men in sight the whole time. Tommo opened the door behind him and pointed out his finger again, this time alternating between Waffle and Harj.

'Right, we'll be saying goodbye then. You two stay where you are, yeah? No funny business, we've got backup downstairs so just sit tight and wait until we've... ungh!'

He dropped to the ground with a thud, and as Playboy lurched round to see what had happened, he was cracked across the face with a wide swing, and he too fell like a dead weight as his legs gave way beneath him.

Waffle and Playboy stared with open mouths and wide eyes at the huge silhouetted figure in the doorway holding a heavy glass jar in both hands. 'Lads,' said Learner Joe casually, acknowledging them both with a nod. 'Is this a bad time?'

* * *

IT TOOK a few seconds for Waffle to speak. He tried a couple of times but although he could make his mouth move, no sounds came out. He shook his head and rubbed his forehead, to clear his thoughts, looked once again at the two crumpled bodies by the door, and then at Learner Joe who was still standing over them, with a grin on his face and the glass jar in his hands.

'What's in there?' Waffle asked at last.

'Hmm?' said Joe, looking confused for a moment. He looked down at his hands. 'Oh! These, yes. Well, these are special. They're a present for you. Hash cookies made from the last of that weed you sold me. Turned out pretty well, if you don't mind me saying, though they're a bit potent! Did a big old batch for you though, got a bit carried away. Here...'

He stepped over Tommo's prone body and walked towards the sofa, offering the jar out to Waffle. 'Sorry, little bit of blood on there, but it'll wipe off.'

'Oh. Er, thanks,' said Waffle, his face a picture of confusion. He looked down at the large Kilner jar, which had a long crack running up from the base and a smear of blood streaked across it. Inside it was a goodly number of very thick cookies in a dark chocolate colour. 'I think I'll pass, if you don't mind.'

'Oh, no problem. Now, later, keep it for guests, regift them, whatever you like. But please, do take them as a peace offering.'

Waffle accepted the proffered jar and gave his thanks. 'Peace offering? How do you mean?'

Joe's smile faltered, and he looked down at the floor. 'Ah. Well, I owe you an apology, as it happens. I came over to have a chat actually, wanted to tell you a few things.' He moved as if to sit on the arm of the sofa, but Waffle stood and stopped him with a raised hand.

'Um… could we do this in just a minute?' He waved at the two prostrate figures on the ground. 'I think we need to sort this out sharpish before they come round, and we need to get going. Plus, they said they've got backup down in a car, they could be along any minute.'

'Quite right! Let's tidy up here first,' said Joe, clapping his hands together. 'Where are you off to, anyway?'

Waffle picked up the holdall and moved it away from Tommo, and then checked himself for his keys, wallet and phone. 'Um, a yoga place up the East End. I need to get over there now to sort a few things out.'

'Need a lift?' asked Joe with enthusiasm. 'I don't have to give my next driving lesson until…' he checked his watch… 'Tuesday!'

'You sure? Well, if you don't mind, that'd be great.'

'Happy to help. Now… should I have a look outside and see what's happening down there? See if any more visitors are on their way? Any idea what we're looking for?'

Waffle shook his head. 'No idea at all. First time I've seen these geezers.'

Joe left the flat on tiptoes, surprisingly deftly for such a big man, and took a peek around the corner of the wall down to the cars parked below. He then retraced his steps, shrinking back from his vantage position and sliding back into the flat.

'Three blokes in a red Beemer, looking dodgy as all fuck. I imagine they're your men.'

Waffle nodded. 'OK, cool. What are they doing?'

'Not much.' He frowned. 'Though I've gotta say, it looked a bit like they were playing one potato, two potato. Right, what's the plan?'

Waffle looked around the flat. 'Let's get these two outside. We can leave them against the wall so they're out of sight, but their mates will find them when they come up. They must've thought you were going to a different flat so you go back down on your own, act casual and then drive your car round to the front by the shops. Me and Harj can sneak out the other way and drop down off the walkway, there's some kind of telecoms box next to the wall on the other side, it's not a big drop. We'll meet you out front in 30 seconds.'

'Right you are! I'll see you in a sec.'

Learner Joe left the flat again and casually wandered off along the walkway, the sound of his whistling growing fainter before echoing back up to them as he descended the staircase. Waffle and Harj picked up the two men in turn, and half carried, half dragged their dead weights out of the door and to one side, keeping close to the wall at all times. They propped them both up into sitting positions so that it looked as though they'd both fallen asleep while chatting on the floor.

Waffle went back inside to grab the holdall, took a last look around and then, with a nod of satisfaction, pulled the door closed behind him.

'Ready?' he said to Harj.

Harj nodded, his face alive with excitement and a little fear. 'Ready!'

'Come on then,' said Waffle as he moved away, 'follow me.'

Harj bunched his fist and shook it purposefully as he took off after Waffle, like a member of the Scooby Do gang. 'To the Yoga Lawn!'

They passed the last two flats and rounded the corner at the end to pass away out of sight. The two men slumped against the wall didn't move, but a moment later Tommo's eyes opened gradually before he squeezed them open and shut a few times to clear his head. He moved his hand to his shoulder, which was throbbing horribly, and tried to move his neck a little, which was stiff and painful. He wiped his mouth with the back of his hand.

'The Yoga Lawn...' he said, thickly.

* * *

WITH THE BAG tossed into the boot and everyone inside, Learner Joe selected first gear with a slight crunch and set the Micra lurching into traffic with as much speed as it could muster. After a few twists and turns, they settled into the stop-start rhythm of the Old Kent Road, heading vaguely north to aim for Tower Bridge.

'So,' said Waffle from the passenger seat, what's all this surprise visit and present stuff then? What did you mean by "peace offering"?'

Joe changed lanes to go for a gap, but was forced to swing back again on the receipt of a long blast of horn from a double-decker bus. 'Well, the thing is,' he said awkwardly, clearing his throat with a cough, 'I had a little visitation a few days ago, at my office.'

'Oh yeah?' said Waffle, unsure what direction this conversation was going in.

'Yes. A couple of men wanted to know where you lived. They knew about the weed, you see, and had somehow traced it to me. Unreliable customer, I assume.'

Waffle looked down at the jar of cookies in his hands. 'And you gave them my address?'

'I'm so sorry, Waffle.' He flashed a glance at Waffle, and his expression was pained and earnest. 'I had no choice. I tried to put them off but they threatened me. They knew all about my business and my lack of licence and the dealing... said they'd expose me and I'd maybe go down for it.' He made brief eye contact again and Waffle could see tears beginning to pool in his eyes. 'I really am sorry, and I should've told you as soon as it happened, but I felt so bad about it, I was ashamed.'

Waffle put a hand on his shoulder and gave him a couple of taps. 'It's OK, man. If you had no choice, then you had no choice. It's all good.'

Joe forced a smile and tried to wipe his eye quickly while nobody was looking.

'Well,' said Waffle, gazing out of the side window, 'I guess that explains what just happened then. I'm not surprised you gave in, those two boys were pretty hench! And I've gotta say, I was wondering if it was all a bit quiet since I found that weed. I mean, I heard nothing from nobody. I was half-expecting either the cops or some drug dealers to come and find me, but nothing happened. I guess it's the drug dealers who found me in the end then!'

As Joe pulled up in stationary traffic, he scratched his chin and turned his head away, as if seeing something very interesting off to the side somewhere.

'Err... well, it's funny you say that. You see, it was the police who came to see me. I've no idea who those blokes earlier were.'

Waffle's mouth opened and shut again. 'Ah. So I have everyone after me then?'

Joe turned back to face him and forced an awkward smile. 'Looks like it.'

Waffle thought for a moment, tapping his fingers on his knee, then turned to look at the traffic through the rear window.

'Well, it's no problem. We've escaped, and nobody knows where we are or where we're going. There's no hurry, it's all good.' He beamed a smile to Joe and Harj in turn, then suddenly pointed through the windscreen to somewhere up the road. 'Yes, I thought it was around here! Joe, man, you need to pull into that turning past the next lights, that big retail park thing.'

'Ah, OK, whatever you say. Are we going shopping then?'

'We sure are, brother, we sure are, hoo-hoo! Got a few things I need to pick up.'

Waffle pulled his phone out of his pocket and began to write a text. 'Yo! Arlo man! You still at the Lawn? I'm on my way up, I need to see Fran urgently. I have something for you as well… I think you're gonna like it!'

Chapter 35

Learner Joe pulled into the car park next to the Mad Parrot and the three of them got out. They stood for a moment in a line, looking up at the building, a monolithic black slab against the pale blue sky.

'So,' said Harj, 'this is it, then? The famed Yoga Lawn?'

Joe was shaking his head slowly as he wiped an imaginary tear from his eye. 'It's beautiful,' he sobbed.

'Oi!' said Waffle as he swiped him playfully across the top of his head. 'You know what they say, you can't judge a yoga retreat from its pub.' He stabbed gently at Joe's chest. 'It's what's inside that counts.'

'Beautiful,' Joe repeated with a sniff, and the three of them started walking to the front door.

When they reached the reception desk on the first floor, Waffle dropped the holdall at his feet and carefully lowered the cookie jar onto the counter from the crook of his arm. He waited for a few moments, but nobody appeared, and he assumed from the itinerary of his previous visit that everyone would be in their rooms for some quiet time before the day's checking-in ceremony. He tapped the bell on the counter, hard enough to raise a satisfying pinging sound, but not too loudly as to fracture the peace too much. Harj and Joe hung back near the stairs to give Waffle some space.

A short while later, the door to Fran's room opened and she stepped out softly, pulling the door shut again with great care. She took a few steps and lifted her head to greet the visitor with a smile, but this fell like a dropped scone as soon as she saw who it was.

'Surprise!' said Waffle with outstretched jazz hands and a wide but hopeful grin. 'I know it seems like only yesterday you saw me last.'

Fran appraised him with contempt and she chewed her lip as her dark eyes turned almost black. 'Yes, Waffle, it is a surprise. But not in the *birthday party* sense, more in the *blood in your stools* sense.'

Waffle winced.

'And no,' she continued, with a slight wobble to her voice, 'it doesn't even seem like only yesterday, it feels like it was a few hours ago, just before I squeezed in about 90 minutes of fitful sleep.'

She noticed the jar on the counter and nodded to it. 'I hope those aren't some kind of present for me,' she said dismissively, craning her neck forward with a look of confused alarm on her face. 'Is that bloo–'

'No, no!' said Waffle, springing forward and scooping the jar up in his arms. 'Ignore these,' he said, as he handed it to Joe.

'Look. Fran.' He scratched the back of his neck as he searched the walls and ceiling for inspiration. 'Thing is… I've been thinking. I know last night you said–'

'Woah, hang on, Waffle!' Fran shrieked at a volume far from befitting her usually serene surroundings. She had walked around from behind the counter and was now pointing wild-eyed towards the holdall at Waffle's feet.

'You've brought that? Here? What the fuck do you think you're doing?'

Waffle had both his hands up defensively in front of him. 'No, no,' he said, his eyes imploring, 'it's not that simple. Look, I just need to talk to you about all this.'

A clunk from further down the corridor announced a door shutting, and Arlo padded barefoot towards them. 'Fran, what's going on?' he said with a concerned frown before recognising Waffle and breaking into a grin. 'Hey, mi amigo!' he almost shouted, throwing his arms wide as he joined the group. 'So! What have you got for me then, old bean, I've been waiting patiently since you texted!'

Fran swung her eyes between the two of them, and then down at the bag. 'Oh no. Oh no, no, no. Waffle, absolutely not, this is my place of business and I will not stand for this! It's bad enough you take my clients out to get drunk, but now you want to *deal drugs* to them? Here?!'

A staccato clumping sound from the staircase behind them made the whole group turn, and two men rose steadily into view with each step. Harj and Joe moved to the side to allow the men room, and they walked the few yards necessary to approach Fran.

'Thank you for calling earlier, Miss McRae, we do appreciate it when people get back in contact. We came over as soon as we could.' Phil cast his gaze around the silent group before addressing Fran again with a generic smile. 'Everything alright? Thought we heard some shouting…'

Fran took a deep breath and kept her eyes on Phil's, now unable to look at Waffle. 'Oh. Yes, thank you, Inspector.' She coughed. 'I, umm, had a bit more information regarding what you came to see me about the other day.'

'Oh, excellent,' he said, reaching into his jacket for his notebook and pen. He paused with them out in front of him, pen poised, and again looked to the faces of everyone circling him. 'Is now a good time? I can wait if you're busy?'

Fran looked down at the floor and then up at Waffle. She stared intently at him, her eyes hard and accusing, but her brow crumpled by a tumult of conflicting thoughts.

'Well…' she said, still not taking her eyes from Waffle.

For what seemed like an age, the seven of them stood in frozen silence, a knot of people around the reception desk. Phil's eyebrows were raised questioningly at Fran, but when she didn't meet his eyes, he turned instead to Mike, who simply shrugged.

'Is there somewhere we could talk, perhaps?' Phil asked, looking around him at the tense faces. 'Is there a quiet room, somewhere we could sit down?'

Fran started and looked suddenly at him, then flicked back to Waffle, chewing her lip.

'Yes. Of course,' she said. 'Follow me, please.'

'Mike, nobody's to leave, alright? Start getting some details from everyone here, I want to know what's going on.'

Mike nodded. 'Guv.'

Fran took the seat at her desk and gestured to the spare chair as Phil closed the door behind him with a forceful yank.

'Thanks,' he said, putting his notebook and pen on the desk.

'Lovely flowers,' he said a little awkwardly, nodding to the vase on the desk containing several long stems blooming with bright orange petals.

She looked at the cutting, admiring it with affection. 'Thank you. They're *plumeria rubra*... frangipani,' she said softly, running her fingers gently against one of the petals.

'Ah, I see. Very nice,' said Phil, tapping his fingers on the edge of the counter. 'I'm a rose man myself.'

Fran smiled politely. 'I have a big plant in the studio room, but I always have cuttings here and in my car. It's my namesake, I love having them around.'

Phil frowned. 'Your namesake? How do you mean?'

She looked up at him and smiled patiently. This clearly wasn't the first time she'd had to explain, but she didn't appear to mind. 'Frangipani. That's my full name.'

Phil raised his eyebrows. 'Oh, I see. Fran. Right. I just assumed it was Francesca.' He picked up his notebook and scribbled something quickly.

'Everybody does. It's kind of cool like that, it's like a secret in a way.'

'Unusual name, though. I bet you had no problem getting a good Gmail address.' He was anxious to get back to the job in hand, but he was a big believer in keeping people talking and making them feel comfortable, whoever they were. You never knew where good information was going to come from in a case.

'Yeah, I think I'm the only Frangipani MacRae around,' she said, laughing. 'My parents were kind of hippies, you see. They had some big plan to go to Goa in India, and the frangipani is the state flower of Goa or something.'

Phil rocked back a little in his chair, and the blood drained from his face, leaving his skin white and clammy. His eyes were wide and unblinking and he grabbed at the edge of Fran's desk for support. She wondered if he was having a heart attack. She remembered seeing an advert for this not so long ago, about what you were supposed to do.

Wasn't there an acronym or something for the steps you should take? Or was that for strokes...

'Are you alrigh–'

'What. Did. You. Say?' Phil spoke quietly, but each word was enunciated with force. His eyes appeared to be swimming and the knuckles of the hand holding onto the desk were white.

Fran's face was now contorted with worry, she had no understanding of what was happening.

'Which bit?' she asked in a small voice.

'You said your parents had a plan to go to Goa...'

'Well, my mum told me that. I never knew my dad, he left before I was born, Mum said.'

Phil let out a sharp breath as if I'd he'd been punched.

'Fran... MacRae,' he said. He closed his eyes. 'Tell me your mother's name. I know what it is, but I need to hear you say it.'

'I don't understand what's–'

'Please, Fran. Please. Just say her name, so I know for definite.'

She paused, unsure what she was supposed to have said wrong, or was supposed to be doing. But she could see no reason not to do as he was asking. She took a deep breath and looked at her frangipani with a frown, confused.

'Lily,' she said after another pause. 'Her name was Lily MacRae.'

She looked back at Phil, and saw that his eyes were full of tears.

* * *

OUTSIDE THE OFFICE, Mike had found a pen on the counter and the group was patiently waiting for him to take each name and address down, one by one.

'So, it's Arlo... A, R, L, O... and how do you spell Windsor-Beauchamp? Windsor like the place I assume, but...'

At this moment, the relative quiet was broken by the sound of more footsteps on the staircase, but unlike the rhythmic, steady beat of two pairs of feet slowly ascending, this new noise was a cacophony of thuds, a blur of hurried stamping from an uncountable number of rushing bodies, and it was loud enough for the office door to fling open as Phil and Fran rushed out. Five young men appeared in single file, a light film of sweat on their tense faces, and as they reached the landing, they fanned out into a line, the two groups now facing each other like flanks of infantry.

Mike threw a glance at Phil, who was looking incredibly pale and a decade older since he'd last seen him five minutes previously.

'You OK, Guv? he asked quietly, 'you look like you've seen a ghost.'

Phil turned his grey eyes towards him and gave a single, sharp nod. 'I have,' he said.

Tommo took a step forward and took in the scene slowly with a humourless sneer before settling on Waffle's face. His eyes were like polished flint, shining brightly but cold as ice.

He raised a sardonic smile with a grunt. 'Looks like we're last in this time, yeah?' He turned slowly to make a big show of looking behind him, then shook his head. 'Don't think anybody's gonna be surprising us from the rear. No more dirty sucker punches.'

He tilted his head to the side and ran his hand down his neck and shoulder with a wince.

'So,' he said, as he scanned their faces briefly one more time, 'nice to meet you all and everything, but we must be going.'

He took another couple of steps forward and bent to pick up the holdall.

'Woah, hold it there!' Mike thrust a hand out towards Tommo while his other went for his warrant card in his back pocket, 'I'm not sure what's going on here, but we're the police!'

Tommo paused and looked at Mike with a kindly but patronising smirk, as if a small child had just told him to make sure his teddy bear got an equal share of ice cream.

'I don't give a fuck who you are,' Tommo spat, his face hardening again, 'but there's five of us and we're taking that bag. So unless you're some kind of Miami Vice types packing Glocks, then I suggest you stand aside.'

He eyed Mike up and down, appraising him quickly for his physical risk, then moved to the man standing next to him wearing a jacket and tie and holding a notebook, settling on his middle-aged spread protruding from above his belt. He laughed.

'I don't think he's gonna be much help to you, no offence old man! That biro looks well lethal. Now, if you'll excuse me…'

He bent forward again, this time keeping his eyes firmly glued to Mike's. As he lifted the bag off the ground, Mike made a move to rush forward, but Phil thrust his arm out to act as a barrier. 'Leave it, Mike. Let him take it.'

Mike flashed a glance at Phil, a look of anger in his eyes, but Phil did a quick shake of his head. 'Not now,' he said quietly, and Mike relaxed his stance again as he let out a deep breath.

Tommo half smiled and began nodding slowly. 'That's right, easy now,' he said, as he started walking backwards with the holdall in his grip. Soapy and D moved onto the stairs first, then Tommo followed, only turning at the last second to take them head-on. Lenny followed with Playboy bringing up the rear, watching the remaining group closely to ensure nobody was making any movements before he too turned and joined the others in thumping down the stairs at speed.

As soon as they were out of sight, Mike spun round to face Phil with a look of pleading etched onto his face.'

'Guv, I could've taken—'

'Doesn't matter, Mike. You need to prioritise. Some things aren't worth it, you know. Now come on, nothing stopping us getting after them, is there?'

There was a moment's pause, and then all seven of them ran to the staircase as one.

Chapter 36

Mike threw open the door into the Mad Parrot's lounge bar and ran for the main entrance, quickly followed by six other people, like a hyperactive conga line. The patrons of the pub, both of them, lifted their heads to see what the commotion was, their expressions betraying the annoyance they felt at having to respond to a second interesting event within 30 seconds of a first.

They burst onto the pavement to see a red BMW reversing out of the car park at speed, its rear wheels spinning violently on the patchy gravel of the rough and broken surface, throwing up loose stones and a cloud of dust as it went. It crossed the pavement with a squeal of tyres and was just pulling into the road when there was an almighty crunching sound as a black Range Rover careened into it, lifting the rear of the BMW into the air before coming down a few feet away with a crash. Glass from the rear window and lights scattered everywhere, and the BMW's bumper skidded down the road in a shower of sparks for several yards.

The Range Rover had definitely won this particular fight and looked fine apart from a stoved-in front grille and lights, but then the repair cost would probably be significantly more than the entire value of the 3 Series. Big Bob and his minder opened their doors at the same moment, and both stepped down into the road, with Bob moving to the front of his car to inspect the damage while his minder ambled casually towards the BMW. Bob poked his nose briefly around the point of impact and then turned to face the watching group in front of the pub with his arms held wide and his face a picture of an innocent wronged.

'What the fuck?' he asked the assembled group, 'I literally just got it back from its first service! Literally!' He turned to inspect the damage further, prodding a crumpled piece of metal in the Range Rover's bumper with an outstretched finger. 'Six hundred quid it was,' he muttered to himself, 'AND they valeted it. Fucker was gleaming just this morning!'

The BMW had engaged first gear with a crunch and was now trying to move forward, but its rear wheel had been snapped half off its axle and was hanging at a jaunty angle, only just touching the ground. It was spinning wildly, a wraith of bluish smoke building up around the tyre and starting to rise into the air. Despite the scream of the engine and the screeching from the tortured tyre, the car was only managing to creep forward at a snail's pace, and everyone watched as it merely pulled a little further back into the car park, snaking towards the wall of Ali's Kebabs until the front half of the car was wedged against it. Finally admitting defeat, the engine was cut and the rear tyre fell silent. The passenger door opened first, and Lenny stepped out, pulling the holdall with him, soon followed by Tommo, who had to shimmy across from the driver's seat to drag himself out of the opposite door.

The two of them stood and glanced at each other, a nervous energy apparent in them, but Bob's enormous minder had been waiting for them to extricate themselves from the BMW and was now facing them and making the *slow down* gesture with his outstretched palms. Their eyes swivelled to take in the scene, but neither moved, although Lenny's grip on the bag's handles tightened. The nearside rear door opened, and Playboy emerged slowly, shaking his head and holding onto one elbow. His top was ripped down one arm, exposing a bleeding cut which, added to his existing black eye and bloody cheek, made his apparent unhappiness appear justified. He stood next to his companions as D appeared from behind him. The far door opened too, and Soapy jumped out and then ran up the road as fast as he could, not even turning to look behind him once. The remaining four of the gang all watched him disappear into the distance, jaws slack with disbelief.

The minder stepped forward and made a move towards the holdall. Lenny initially pulled it away with a jerk, but the enormous man merely raised his eyebrows questioningly and held out his palm. Lenny relaxed his grip and handed it over with a reluctant drop of his shoulders. Tommo seethed silently next to him.

'Well, well, well,' said Bob finally, moving forward to command the scene. 'What do we have here, then?' He pulled a cigar from his inside jacket pocket and made a show of slowly removing its packaging piece by piece, discarding the loose bits of plastic wrapping into the breeze. He looked up to scan the small crowd to ensure he still had everyone's attention, then ducked his head into his cupped hand towards a lighter. Once lit, he replaced his lighter into his jacket pocket and took several shallow puffs with his head held high, but watching down his nose the whole time at the audience.

'So,' he said at last, turning to Tommo and Lenny and pointing to the bag. 'I recognise that. That's mine, that is. You must be the little scrotes who stole it from my boys last weekend.' He let out a hollow laugh. 'I don't know who you think you are, or whether you know who I am. But I can tell you this, you young lads... you don't know who you've been dealing with.' He paused and frowned. 'Unless you *do* know who I am, of course, and then...' He trailed off. 'I'm not a fucking amateur, you know! I'm not to be messed with!'

He took a drag of his cigar and blew out a long stream of smoke into the sky. 'I'll come back to you lot in a minute. I'm very much not finished with you yet.

'Obviously, I know who you are,' he said, addressing Phil. 'And your little assistant. And maybe you've led me to the right place after all, by the looks of things. Against all odds. Eh? Against all odds, Phil?' He chuckled gently to himself and looked around for some moral support, though none came. 'But it took you too long, Phil, you were supposed to have this sorted days ago. And now you've made me come out here to...' He pivoted on his heel, surveying the surroundings with a grimace that hinted he'd caught a whiff of something silent but violent. '... this absolute shithole of a place. And I'm a busy man, Phil, I'm supposed to be at a very important meeting in about half an hour regarding my new office. So we'll keep this brief if you don't mind.

'I've no idea who any of you lot are,' he said, addressing Waffle, Fran and the others with a dismissive flick of his hand. 'And frankly, I don't give a shit. Though, what's in that jar?'

He was eyeing Joe's glass jar with narrow-eyed curiosity and stepped forward to examine it a little more closely.

'Is that blood?' he said, frowning deeply as he squinted even further at the jar.

'Err, they're cookies,' said Joe, choosing to answer the first question and ignore the second.

'Are they? I see. Chocolate are they?'

Joe nodded. Bob watched him for a moment, clearly waiting for something to happen, but Joe simply returned his gaze in silence.

'Well, give us one then! Fuck's sake.'

'Oh. Right,' said Joe, springing into action. He unlatched the lid and proffered the jar to Bob, who took a quick puff of his cigar and then pulled out a cookie.

'Not bad,' he said, through a noisy mouthful, 'not bad at all. Nice and chocolatey. Very… chocolatey.'

He turned to look at the minder, who was still watching Tommo and the others like a hawk, and gestured to him with the remains of his cookie. 'I think Mr Perkins might enjoy one of these, too. Why don't you go and offer him one?'

Joe looked at Bob, then at the giant bodyguard, shrugged, and wandered over to hand out another cookie.

'Right!' said Bob, swallowing his last bite, replacing the cigar in his mouth, and dusting his hands together. 'DI Phil Collins. Go and take that bag from Mr Perkins and put it in the back of my car, please. You've been a complete waste of space in this task, the very least you can do is load my belongings for me. Chop chop.'

All eyes turned to Phil, but he didn't move. Instead, he pulled his cigarettes out and, without hurrying, placed one between his lips and lit it.

'No,' he said simply after blowing out his first lungful.

'I beg your pardon?' Bob sputtered. He cupped an ear and turned it towards Phil. 'Come again?'

Again, Phil took his time. 'No,' he said eventually.

'I don't think you're really getting the hang of this. I'm not asking you, Phil, I'm telling you. Now, last chance. Go. And. Get. That. Bag.'

'I'm not doing it, Bob. I'm not doing anything else for you, ever. I've made some pretty terrible decisions in my life, but I've just been given an opportunity to try and make amends for a couple of them, at least, which is exactly what I intend to do. And the very first part of that process is to stop doing anything for you. That starts here and now.'

Bob was shaking his head slowly, and his lips had parted into a humourless grin. 'You want to think very carefully about that, Phil. You know what I know about you, and you know that I might have to start telling people that information. This will not end well for you.'

'Not interested,' said Phil. 'You can tell anybody you like whatever you like.' He looked at Fran beside him, and his expression immediately softened into a gentle smile. 'None of that matters any more. Not to me. Do your worst, I honestly couldn't care less. I've walked away from things before simply because it was easier to do so, and I've paid the price for that. But one thing I can tell you here and now is that I won't be doing that again. I'm staying put and there's nothing whatsoever you can do about it.'

'I see.' Bob reached into his jacket and pulled out a gun, matt black and large in his small hands. He pointed it directly at Phil's head, who swallowed but didn't move. 'Maybe this will persuade you?'

'Jesus!' said Mike, taking a step back and tensing. Fran grabbed at Phil's arm with both hands and let out a loud gasp.

Phil and Bob were now locked into an unblinking stare, neither appearing to do so much as breathe. Bob cocked his head and raised a single eyebrow, and Phil responded by glancing over to the bag and back again. Bob licked his lips.

'I thought you were all gonna come with me!' said a meek voice, and everyone turned to see Soapy reappear from behind the BMW. He was out of breath but walking slowly, and he slotted into place between Playboy and D like a naughty child.

Seeing that Bob was momentarily distracted, Mike lurched forward towards him, arms outstretched as if to make a rugby tackle, but Bob saw the movement in time, and taking a defensive step back, he fired the gun. The crack of the pistol reverberated off the pub and the other buildings as everyone made an involuntary flinch, flexing at the knees to drop into almost a squat. Mike stopped dead and grabbed his left forearm with his other hand. He slowly angled the palm upwards, sneaking a sideways glance before snapping it shut again with a small cry of alarm.

'You shot me!' he shouted at Bob, his face a picture of surprise and panic.

'Well, of course I shot you, you stupid pillock! You ran at me while I was pointing a gun. What else do you expect me to do, dock your pocket money? I'm not a fucking amateur, y'know.'

Mike stood still for a few moments, holding his arm and looking awkward, then he walked back to stand beside Phil again. Phil gave him a look that comprised a frown, a quick shake of the head and then a flash of a smile that Mike read, quite correctly, as something like 'Well, that was fucking stupid. But thanks.' Mike nodded his receipt of this, and their silent conversation came to an end.

'I hold you responsible for that, actually Phil,' said Bob, 'if you'd just done as you'd been told, then we could've avoided all this nastiness.' He paused for a moment and looked confused, then swung his head up to the sky and jerked his head in all directions, as if looking for an escaping bird or insect. Then he looked down at his feet and massaged his temples before looking up, frowning deeply and swivelling his eyes left and right.

'Hmm,' he said, 'bit odd.' He shook his head swiftly to clear his thoughts. 'Anyway, where were we? Ah yes! Mr Perkins, seeing as Phil here won't oblige, would you be so kind as to pop that bag in the car for me, please?'

The big minder moved to the car and threw the holdall onto the back seat, slamming the door shut behind it.

'Admittedly, that was simple,' said Bob, 'but it just lacked all the significance and drama for me. Still, we've all learned a lesson there I, think. Now, what we…'

Once again, Bob started to look in all directions, then he closed his eyes tightly, then flicked them open wide again. He let out a small moan and sank slowly onto his haunches, where he began to examine both his pistol and cigar in turn with great attention. Learner Joe nudged Waffle gently and nodded down at the jar in his hands with a wry smile and a wink. Waffle frowned at first, then he too let a smile widen on his face. He looked over to Bob's henchman, who was slumped heavily against the Range Rover and staring vacantly into the far distance with immense concentration. 'Hoo-hoo!' Waffle said under his breath with enormous glee.

Bob stood again, replaced his cigar into his mouth and then walked purposefully towards Tommo's car. As he neared it, he raised his gun, and the gang moved out of the way with significant speed. A loud cracking sound filled the air and a small puff of smoke emanated from the front tyre, which quickly deflated, lowering the bonnet of the car a few inches towards the ground.

'Basic common sense really,' said Bob, 'need to make sure none of you lot try and follow us.' He looked over the BMW, studying the smashed up rear and hanging wheel for a moment. 'I mean, obviously it's fucked anyway, but can't take any chances.'

Happy with his work, he strode over to where the other cars were parked. His legs almost gave way at one point, and he stumbled, but he maintained his balance and gave the evil eye to the flat piece of road behind him as he continued.

'I believe this study in undercover mediocrity is yours, Phil,' he said as he approached the silver Vauxhall Corsa, and again he lifted his gun and fired off a shot at the front tyre. This missed, so he fired again, this time successfully smashing the front indicator. He held the gun up and examined it with a frown, turning it over in his hand a few times, then taking aim again and finally hitting the tyre.

'Not sure ish working properly,' he said with a slur, as he moved unsteadily to Joe's Micra.

'This anybody's?' he asked, gesticulating towards the car, and Joe looked around him as if expecting somebody else to volunteer first before begrudgingly raising a tentative finger in the air.

'Still dunno who you are,' said Bob thickly, 'but doesn't matter, I'm gonna shootfucker enway.' He turned back to the car and tottered dizzily, clenching his eyes shut several times. A film of sweat was now visible across his forehead, glistening in the bright sun. He stared at the ground and remained transfixed for a few moments, then suddenly started to stamp violently onto some unseen object on the ground. 'Ha!' he declared triumphantly, before turning his attention back to the car. This time he let off a volley of shots into it and around it, managing to shatter the rear side window and puncturing the bodywork several times before successfully hitting a tyre, and even this was only achieved by walking several feet closer and using both hands to steady the pistol.

He turned back to the watching crowd and wiped his brow with the arm of his jacket. 'Phew!' he said and walked a little further away groggily. From behind him, a steady trickle of liquid could be seen dribbling out of the perforated Nissan, running a little way in a thin stream and pooling gently in a shallow pothole.

Bob was now staring at the sky with apparent concern, and aimed his gun upwards to some point in it for a moment, before bringing it down again with a shake of his head. 'Not worth it,' he said vaguely to himself.

Waffle followed his eye-line, but couldn't be sure for certain whether it was a passing plane or the sun which had offended Bob. He looked over to the minder, who had now slid down the door of the Range Rover and appeared to be sleeping deeply on the floor. He exchanged a smile with Joe.

'Right then!' shouted Bob with a flourish, 'S'all over, gottago. Big meeting.' He took a last drag of his cigar, took the butt out of his mouth, and examined it closely in his hands. He edged his face closer and closer to it as if noticing something startling about it, before he let out a sudden shriek and threw it away from him in a panic. He laughed nervously. 'Thatwas close!'

Behind him, a small flame sprang up from the ground as the cigar ignited the leaking trail of petrol, and it flickered and danced its way back to Joe's car, then increased in intensity as it found its way to the source.

Joe let out a stifled shout of 'Woah! No!' and made a move in the car's direction, but Waffle held out his arm to stop him. 'Leave it,' he said with a shake of his head.

Bob, who'd missed the initial drama, now turned and saw a large flame licking up the bodywork and taking hold on the rear tyre. He looked captivated. 'Ooh!' he exclaimed with a childish delight, 'look at that!' He watched for a while before electing to move a little further away, and it seemed as if everyone was now watching the blaze slowly take hold of the beleaguered Micra.

A sudden commotion from the other direction made everyone turn, however, and they watched as Tommo, Lenny and the others had formed a sudden and coordinated charge towards the Range Rover. Tommo yanked open the rear door, grabbed the bag and the five of them sprinted off away from the pub. The bodyguard woke briefly to point wordlessly at them, broke into a big smile as he waved goodbye, then fell back asleep again.

Bob started to scream, and he raised the gun towards their disappearing outlines and began firing wildly. After a few shots, there was silence, save for the furious clicking of the empty gun. 'Noooooo!' Bob wailed, 'My weeeeeeed!' He brought the gun up again and tried firing in vain for several more pointless seconds, now sobbing audibly.

Mike looked at Phil. 'Should I go after them?'

Phil smiled and shook his head. 'No, leave it. I don't care about any of that. I just want Bob.'

He stepped forward towards Big Bob. 'Robert Cole,' he said, in a loud, clear voice, 'I hereby place you under arrest for... well, a whole load of stuff, actually. A lot of drug things for a start though, possibly blackmail and definitely shooting my constable, but we'll sort out the details later. You have the right to, y'know, blah blah blah.'

Bob's eyes widened and his whole face became etched with fear. 'No!' he shouted, 'you can't!'

He pointed the gun at Phil before belatedly remembering it was empty, then tossed it away.

'Look... Phil, lissentome... I was on my way to the estate agent meeting about my new offish. Remember?'

He was nodding his head vigorously, as if he could force Phil to recall something with enough persuasion, and the effort to focus his mind was taking an evident toll on him, the sweat under his arms beginning to show through his jacket.

'I needed to... sweeten the deal f'you r'call.'

Phil looked uninterested. 'So?'

Bob was blinking continuously, and every now and again he tried to grasp something in the air around him, as if he was catching invisible mosquitoes in his hands.

'Itsin the car, Phil. The...the... sweetener.' He looked at the others suspiciously, then leaned forward towards Phil as he continued in a low voice. 'S'fifty grand, Phil. For the estate agents. But... but... you can have it, Phil. Take it! All of it! S'all there!'

With apparent effort, he relaxed his features and tried to force a smile. 'S'money for nothing, Phil! Eh? Money for nothing!'

Phil was shaking his head. 'Dear oh dear,' he said, tutting noisily. 'Are you trying to bribe a police officer?'

'Wha? No! I just… ' He frowned and shook his head violently while staring at the ground. 'Yes! Yes, I am! Take it Phil, I'm begging you!'

Phil took a drag on his cigarette and blew out the smoke towards Bob, who started coughing and waving his arms around his head to clear the air.

'Oh, and Money for Nothing, Bob? That's not Phil Collins, that's Dire Straits – you fucking amateur.'

Bob's eyes goggled in his reddening face, and he spluttered something incomprehensible.

'Cuff him, Mike.'

Bob turned unsteadily and settled himself for a moment before trying to move again.

'You'll haveto cash me furse!' he shouted over his shoulder, and he set off towards his car, one leg useless and dragging behind him, and occasionally dropping to his knees before picking himself back up again. Phil nodded to Mike, who started trudging slowly after him, still holding onto his injured arm. Bob was now moving at a snail's pace and muttering quietly to himself, and Mike turned to gurn at Phil with a shake of his head and roll of his eyes.

'Worst police chase ever,' said Phil to himself, as Mike took his time in wandering up to the staggering drug dealer, grabbing him by the arm and dragging him back again.

'So…' Fran turned to face Waffle, chewing her lip. 'What did you want to tell me, then?' She looked over to Phil. 'I mean, I've already heard the most shocking piece of news of my entire lifetime, but what did you have to add to that?'

'Huh?' Waffle looked bemused, and glancing between Phil and Fran just confused him more. 'Er, well. I wanted to apologise. I've given a lot of thought to what I want out of life, and the answers surprised me a bit. But, if it's at all possible, I'd like you to give me another chance. I just wanted another opportunity to show that maybe I'm not the bad things you think I am, not anymore. And, well, maybe I'm being a bit too hopeful, but I just think we have something and I think it'd be a waste to throw that all away before we've had a proper chance to see if I'm right or not.'

'Wow,' said Fran, clearly taken aback. 'That's quite a lot to take in.'

'Yeah, I know, and I don't want to put too much onto you at once, but I've got some things I want to do here, and if you'll just let me try to do those, then maybe we see how it goes.'

Fran narrowed her eyes and wrinkled her nose. 'Things? What things?'

'Well,' said Waffle, looking down at his feet. 'For a start, I wanted to come back and try the yoga again. And seriously, this time, give it a proper good go. Not in jeans either!'

Fran gave a very formal nod. 'OK. That is approved. What else?'

'Well, I don't want to be rude. But, erm... I did notice a few things need repairing around the place. There's the odd thing that could do with a bit of TLC, shall we say. Your office door needs sanding down for starters!'

Fran started to smile. 'Hmmm, OK. And you can do that, can you?'

'I can. I'm pretty handy, as it goes.'

'I see. Well, in that case, maybe you should stick around for a bit.'

'Yes! Hoo-hoo!'

'But...' She looked him up and down with a frown. '... do you have some yoga gear then? And tools?'

'Ah! There's actually a slight problem there...'

Chapter 37

Half a mile away, Tommo and his gang stopped to catch their breath. They'd been running flat out for minutes, and although Playboy looked like he could carry on further with no problems, the others were at the point of exhaustion, especially Tommo, who'd had to carry the heavy bag.

They peeled off the road and found a gap in a hedge that they could squeeze through. This led to a steep, grassy embankment, and slipping in turn down this led them to a narrow road that wound around the back of some old industrial units and warehouses. All the walls up to head height were thick with brightly coloured graffiti and the large, low windows that faced the street were either covered in black iron grilles or permanently boarded over.

Turning down a side street, they found a wide, tunnelled entrance that led through to some kind of open yard, and they turned into this and leant against its cool walls to allow their lungs and legs to recover.

'Man, that was intense!' said Lenny, blowing out his cheeks, 'I mean, cops, baddies, shooters! That was something else!'

Tommo didn't look so happy. 'My car, though. The rear's all stoved in, it's scratched down the driver's side, AND that crazy short dude shot it!'

'D'yer reckon you can claim on his insurance?' asked D.

Tommo had started to sneer at the stupidity of the question, but checked himself and pondered it seriously. 'I dunno. Maybe. Do drug lords have motor insurance? I guess they probably do. I mean, he probably gets someone to do the actual paperwork, but his motor must be worth 100k, surely he's got it covered.'

'In fairness, that damage down the side was from you trying to get away, so not sure you could claim for that,' said D earnestly.

'Emotional distress,' said Tommo, 'I'll stick it all in together, he can't prove nothing! I wonder if there's an option on the form for being shot at, though?'

They all considered this for a moment, alone with their thoughts and still breathing in deep lungfuls of air.

'Still,' said Tommo, nudging the bag with the end of his foot, 'we've got this back, and that's definitely something.'

'Er, Tommo,' said Lenny, looking concerned. 'Why did it chink like that?'

'What do you mean?'

'You kicked it and it sort of made a chinking sound. Why would it do that?'

All eyes turned to the bag, and Tommo lowered himself to a squat and reached for the zip. He pulled it fully open in one smooth motion, and they all gasped.

'What the...'

Tommo started flinging out items of clothing in handfuls onto the road. A couple of pairs of soft, baggy trousers in a patchwork quilted pattern, a few light t-shirts, some new flip-flops.

'No, no, no!' He started grabbing with both hands wildly, then came to two heavy carrier bags from B&Q, wrapped up in a towel. He yanked them out of the holdall and heaved them upside down so that they disgorged a power drill, screwdriver set, a hammer, a plane, a set of chisels, and various other small tools and fittings. Once he'd done this, he picked up the holdall itself and upended it so that the last few loose clothes and a couple of receipts dropped out. He then threw it as hard as he could into the road with a wild and lengthy scream.

* * *

'So, what you're saying is, you bought a load of tools and yoga gear on the way here, but it was all in that bag those men ran off with?' said Fran with an expression of extreme bemusement.

Waffle beamed. 'What can I say? I don't think we'll be seeing that again, but it's all just stuff that can be bought again, isn't it?'

'Hang on,' said Arlo, frowning. 'What did you mean when you said you had something for me? I thought you meant you'd brought me some...' he looked at Fran cautiously, and then continued speaking behind his hand in a whisper. '...weed.'

'Yeah, well. In a way, I did.' Waffle called Joe over and took the jar from him. 'Here,' he said, handing the jar to Arlo. 'Chocolate hash cookies. I don't want any of this stuff any more, but I figured you might. Though from what we've just seen, I'd take it pretty easy with them!'

'Oh, cool! Thanks,' Arlo said, turning to Fran with the hopeful expression a small boy gives his mum when receiving a penknife from a wayward and irresponsible uncle.

'Hey, your life,' she said, throwing her arms up. 'But not in my retreat you don't!'

'I'll take it home with me,' Arlo mouthed to Waffle with a wink.

'Woah!' said Bob, still just about standing thanks to Mike's support, but his eyes wild and spinning. He spoke with considerable effort. 'So... the drugs... weren't in that... bag?'

'No, man,' said Waffle. 'I bought all that stuff and needed something to put it all in. Nice holdall that, good solid straps.'

'So...' Bob was trying to think hard despite the circumstances; his eyes were darting around in all directions and he kept licking his lips. '... the drugs aren't... aren't... lost, then?' He began to smile, though combined with his wild eyes, this made him look extremely deranged and dangerous.

'Not at all,' said Waffle with a lopsided grin, 'they're still here.'

Bob broke into a manic laugh and began hopping from foot to foot, though he had to be held up at one point when he lost his balance and began to fall.

'Where?' he shrieked, now visibly shaking with excitement.

Waffle nodded his head over Bob's shoulder. 'The back of Joe's car.'

Bob spun round just as the Micra, which was now fully alight across its whole length, gave a sharp 'WOOF!' sound with a small explosion that was enough to blow out the front windscreen.

Bob sank to his knees and started to cry. It wasn't even the cry of a desperate and tragic adult, but that of a baby, wailing for its milk. He fell forward onto the dusty road and began pounding his fists against the road.

Just then, one of the Micra's tyres gave way with a loud 'pfffft!' sound, and the little Nissan sank another couple of inches into its fiery grave.

'Well,' announced Phil with a certain amount of finality. 'That's it. I'm retiring. As of now.'

Chapter 38

Fran closed her eyes against the surprising warmth of the early October sun and lay her head back in the wicker chair. Her hands lay still on the laptop's keyboard, and she smiled to herself, a deep and peaceful smile that stayed on her lips for a long time. She could just about make out the distant drone of an airliner, high above her, and she focussed her mind on this, trying to detect its direction from the faint sound alone.

A voice broke through her meditation and brought her back to reality, but although she opened her eyes and shielded them against the sun, her smile remained.

'Want a top-up?'

She let her hand fall and turned to her side to check on the glass, next to a notebook and pen on the painted wrought iron table. It was still half full.

'No thanks,' she said, smiling up at the standing figure, 'I think I forgot I had it, to be honest. How's it going?'

Phil was pulling off his heavy, yellow gardening gloves, and he placed them on the table with his secateurs.

'Yeah, I think I'm finished there for now. All coming together, though. There'll be an explosion of colour next May, you mark my words!'

Fran looked over to the side of the studio building behind him and admired the neat row of rose bushes, all neatly trimmed and tied in with two lengths of metal wire that ran along the full length of the newly painted black shiplap. The soil in the border was now covered in bark chippings too and was looking very smart indeed.

'That looks great,' she said, sitting up. 'You're a clever old stick, aren't you?'

He pulled up the other chair and dropped into it, brushing down the stray bits of cut leaf from his work trousers as he sat.

'I have my moments,' he said. He nodded to the laptop. 'How are you getting on?'

The screen had gone black, so she tapped the spacebar to bring it back to life and twisted the laptop towards him. 'What do you think?'

He nodded in appreciation. 'Impressive,' he said, 'I think you have to have been born after a certain year to make those things work. I mean, I can turn them on and bring up a recipe or some gardening tips, but I can't make stuff like that. I wouldn't know where to begin.'

Fran wrinkled her nose. 'Ach, it's not so hard. There's nothing YouTube can't show you how to do. And I used a template anyway, I didn't do it from scratch or anything.'

'Ah. Well, don't go telling me all your secrets, I'm still labouring under the impression that you're perfect and infinitely talented.'

She reeled in mock offence. 'Oh, I didn't say I wasn't.'

Phil smiled and let his gaze wander down the garden and along the horizon.

'Let's go for a little walk,' he said suddenly. If you're not too engrossed in your design work, of course.'

'Hey, I was working!' she said, noting his mischievous grin, 'I was just resting my eyes for a moment. You know what they say about computer screens and eyestrain... very important to take regular breaks.'

Phil sprang out of his seat. 'Yeah, yeah, whatever, up you get.'

She watched him for a moment without moving. 'I know what you want to do! Have you not had your quality time today with her today?'

'Don't know what you're talking about,' he said, already walking away and fishing for his cigarette packet, 'Come on.'

She jumped up with a grin, and put her arm in his as they gently ambled down the sloping lawn, chattering nonsense and laughing together. The garden was wide and ran almost the whole way around the property, but in this direction only went for about 20 or 30 metres until it met a wooden fence that ran in a straight line off into the distance to their right. Beyond the fence were a series of sub-divided pastures which ended at the treeline further down the hill.

They both took their usual positions leaning against the fence, the gentle breeze heading towards them up the hill and blowing their hair away behind them, along with Phil's menthol smoke.

'Here she is,' said Phil with a childish glee, as he reached into his pocket and pulled out a carrot, 'here's our hairy next-door neighbour.' The deep chestnut mare strolled over to him, its pace quickening a little as it spied the orange treat being waved in front of her. She pulled back her lips to expose huge, stained yellow teeth which she used to grip the carrot just short of Phil's fingers, pulling it away from him and shimmying it into her mouth in one.

'Absolutely disgusting,' said Phil with relish, 'her table manners are quite atrocious.'

The horse eyed him dispassionately as it crunched noisily and repeatedly, then nuzzled her nose into the crook of his arm to look for more.

'You love it!' Fran said, reaching out a hand to stroke her mane.

Phil offered a flat palm to show he had nothing more to eat, and the horse licked it anyway. He looked down across the trees, and over to the side, where the view opened up across the hills.

'Sometimes it feels like we're a thousand miles from London, doesn't it?'

Fran picked a loose strand of hair that was being blown across her eyes, and tied it over her ear. She too was gazing out towards the green expanse.

'Do you miss it?'

'London?' he replied, with curiosity.

'Well, yes. And the job.'

He thought for a while as he smoked.

'Do you know, I don't think I do. I mean, I absolutely loved some of it some of the time, but I don't miss it. It was what I did for over 30 years, but I feel like it's something I once did a long time ago, perhaps in a different life even, and not anything I need to do any more.'

She nodded. 'Heard from Mike recently?'

'Yeah, he sends me the odd email. He's still having physio for his arm, but his medal came through, which I think he was pretty proud of, even though he keeps saying he wasn't bothered. Plus, he's a sergeant now, so he's stopped getting stick from the other twerps who got there first. He's quite the hero, it seems.'

'Ah, that's good. He seems nice,' she said vacantly. She stopped idly stroking the horse and turned to face Phil. 'You didn't have to do all of this, you know. I mean, all the money for a start, and moving down here and everything. I didn't expect that.'

He looked down at her and smiled, then smoothed away the furrows in her forehead with his thumb.

'Yes, I did. But it's not about *having* to do anything, not at all. It's what I wanted. It's what I want.'

He looked up and once again scanned the horizon. 'I can't tell you how happy it makes me to be here, with you. We have an awful lot of lost time to make up for, and I intend to spend as much of my remaining years as possible doing just that.'

'Remaining years! Jesus, you're 54!'

He laughed. 'It's a turn of phrase. And anyway, it's not like it's just me that's helped out, especially financially. Certain other people have too, whether they intended to or not!'

'Well, I just want to say thank you.'

'You have hundreds of times already, Fran. Just accept the reality! You're here, and I'll be here for as long as you want me around.'

She put her arms around him and snuggled into his warm hug. 'Thanks, Dad,' she said into the arm of his woolly jumper, drawing in the smell of roses and menthol as she held her eyes tight.

'Yo! You two!'

They both turned and watched as Waffle strode towards them with a wave, his gangly, loping gait immediately recognisable at any distance.

'Roses look great, hoo-hoo!' he said, clapping Phil on the arm. 'Very smart indeed!'

Phil took a shallow bow with eyes closed. 'You're too kind.'

'And how are you?' he said to Fran, kissing her briefly but gently. 'How are the invites coming along?'

'Nearly there, I think. And I spoke to a printer in town earlier. They can have them all done any time over the next week once I get the files to them.'

'Excellent! Now, I want to show you both something!' he said, rubbing his hands. 'Got a minute?'

Fran and Phil looked at each other and nodded. 'Let's do it,' said Fran, and they both turned to give the horse one last ruffle of its mane.

'Bye, Lily,' Phil said softly, tickling its nose, 'see you again soon.' The horse gave a soft snort in response and padded at the ground.

Fran looked up at him and swore she saw him wipe something quickly from his eye. He gave her a quick glance. 'Bit of dust in the wind,' he said and winked. She rested her head on his shoulder for a moment, and then the three of them headed back up towards the house together.

Waffle led them to the front of the studio where there was a ladder and various tools on a workbench. He pointed upwards, grinning. 'What d'yer reckon?'

Fran looked up and held her hand over her mouth as she gasped. 'Oh!' she said, 'it's beautiful!'

Running over the doorway were the words 'Rose Garden Yoga Retreat' in carved wooden letters, painted a soft pink. She threw herself at Waffle and hugged him tightly. 'Thank you, thank you!'

'My absolute pleasure!' he said, smothering her forehead in kisses. 'There's still quite a lot to do inside, but it's all on schedule. And Harj is coming over first thing to do some more painting. He reckons two more full days and it's all done. Learner Joe's coming with him, actually. Says he can help out and he wants to drive Harj, seeing as he finally got his licence.'

Fran beamed up at him, her eyes filling. 'I don't know what to say, really,' she said at last, 'to both of you.' She pulled Phil by the arm and hugged them both.

As they all stood back again to admire the new sign, they heard a meow from just inside the doorway, and a cat appeared shyly, just poking its head into view.

'Hey, Tito!' said Waffle, bending to scoop him up. 'Glad you could join us!'

'How do you think he's enjoying the countryside?' said Fran, tickling him under the chin.

'Oh, he loves it, don't you Tito? I mean, I think he misses the leftovers of the Taj Mahal curries if we're both being completely honest, but it's no substitute for the fresh air and open spaces, is it Tito?'

Tito mewed his agreement as Waffle and Fran both fussed over him. Phil too was looking at him, but with an expression of consternation.

'You know, every time I see your cat I think I recognise him from somewhere.' He shook his head and frowned. 'Ah well,' he said, putting his hand out to stroke the fat, one-eared ginger moggy with a white face, 'maybe not.'

Thank you

Thank you ever so much for reading this book. It might sound a bit trite, but it's entirely genuine! I thought it might be quite hard to write a novel, and take a bit of time, but it turns out it's way harder than I thought, and took a lot longer. So to have it in people's hands and to know that they took the time to read it means a lot. I sincerely hope you enjoyed it.

If you did, please do consider giving it a rating, or even a brief review, on Amazon, or Goodreads, or share a brief note on social media. It's very, very hard for new authors to get any kind of exposure, and for readers to take a chance on someone they don't know, so good reviews and ratings make an awful lot of difference. And they make me feel nice inside.

* * *

I'd like to thank my mate Spam for being a sounding board for the entire process of writing this book, and offering endless advice and suggestions. If I told you exactly how many times I phoned him at inconvenient times with a 'What if…' or, 'Is this bit actually funny?', or 'OK, I think I've finally cracked it…', you'd think I was exaggerating.

Huge thanks also to Steve Edwards for the fantastic cover. I said I wanted 'classic comic crime caper,' and he nailed it.

I'd also like to thank all the followers of my Skint Dressage Daddy blog, whose encouragement led to the two books it spawned and gave me the confidence to attempt a novel. I hope you liked the bit about the horse.

Lastly, I'd like to thank my other half, Hopskotch, because if I don't she'll be annoyed.

Other books by Daniel Skinner

From Nags to Numbnuts, **2018**

Stable Condition, **2021**

If you have any interest in horses, you might enjoy my two previous books which chronicle the years attempting to cope with having a dressage-crazed daughter.

Both were Amazon bestsellers in both the UK and Australia.

* * *

"Made me laugh out loud on most pages"

– *Horse & Hound*

"Hilariously explains everything you need to know about the world of horses"

– *Absolute Horse*

"A delight… A must for all horse addicts, confused parents, and other halves"

– *Haynet*

"Hilarious! Actually wee'd myself laughing! Both books are brilliant – you, Mr Skinner are a comedy genius!"

– *Amazon review*

"If you are thinking of buying this book may I suggest that you also purchase from the health and beauty department a big box of tissues, some bloody good and very expensive anti-wrinkle cream and waterproof mascara ….!!! Because you are going to need it!! You will find crows feet and laughter lines deepen with every page you turn!!!"

– *Amazon review*